ALL-DAY BREAKFAST

ADAM LEWIS SCHROEDER

ALL-DAY BREAKFAST

Douglas & McIntyre

Douglas and McIntyre (2013) Ltd.
P.O. Box 219, Madeira Park, BC, VON 2HO
www.douglas-mcintyre.com

Edited by Barbara Berson and Derek Fairbridge
Text and cover design by Carleton Wilson
Printed and bound in Canada

Canada Council   Conseil des Arts
for the Arts   du Canada

BRITISH COLUMBIA
ARTS COUNCIL
An agency of the Province of British Columbia

Douglas and McIntyre acknowledges the support of the Canada Council for the Arts, which last year invested $157 million to bring the arts to Canadians throughout the country. We also gratefully acknowledge financial support from the Government of Canada through the Canada Book Fund and from the Province of British Columbia through the BC Arts Council and the Book Publishing Tax Credit.

Cataloguing data available from Library and Archives Canada
ISBN 978-1-77162-064-2 (paper)
ISBN 978-1-77162-065-9 (ebook)

For Griffin & James.

Friday, October 21.

MY MOTHER-IN-LAW, DEB, was built like a hummingbird with long veiny hands instead of wings, and in her wafting green muumuu she looked like the ghosts my kids made out of Kleenex.

"You know what?" she said as she floated into the kitchen. "You still haven't put out the one I had framed."

"It's still in a box." I clattered through the cutlery drawer. "I'll find it."

"Have you put *any* pictures of her out?"

Of course not—we all remembered what she'd looked like.

"Couple on my bedside table," I said.

"You add salt?"

"I did." I cut Ray and Josie's havarti sandwiches diagonally and slid them into ziplock bags. "Tastes like garbage without salt."

"I only wondered because you're, you know, so health-conscious."

I got a hand on the Cream of Wheat spoon before she did, then draped my unknotted black-and-gold tie over my shoulder so it wouldn't dip into the pot while I stirred. Substitutes have to maintain a decorum that I've seen plenty of permanent-position teachers neglect—namely, we can't show up to work spattered with goop.

"Oh, you made coffee," said Deb. "Thank God."

She poured into a kitten-covered *Lydia* mug that I hadn't had the balls to leave back in Wahoo.

"Now, what can I do for their lunches?" she asked.

This was a Friday. The night before, she'd driven her Corolla the two hours from MacArthur, because once a month she came to hang out with the kids and, apparently, to help out around the house.

"All taken care of," I said, screwing the tops onto their aluminium water bottles.

"A-ha, I see an opening!" In her fuzzy slippers she quick-shuffled toward the kitchen table, heaped with clean towels. "I'm going to fold this or I'll smack you in the mouth!"

She set her mug on the corner of the table and black coffee sloshed across one of the lacy white pillowcases—wedding present from my college roommate Hank, who'd died the year after, car crash driving home to Kansas. Our pilly pillowcases in college had smelled like unwashed feet, and I remembered Lydia shaking her head in bald amazement as we'd ripped away Hank's wrapping paper—there was such a thing as *new* pillowcases?

"Oh, no." Deb gazed up at me with her face as long as a deflated balloon, the defiled object clutched to her chest. "I'm sorry, Peter!"

I breathed slowly and deeply up my nose, then gave my left earlobe a reassuring pinch—a trick I'd developed in recent years to keep myself from screaming in oncologists' offices. Deb wasn't dissuading me from my belief that it's better to just get things done yourself.

"No, no, it's cool." I released the earlobe and threw a dishcloth down over the spill. "Pop it in the wash, put your feet up and you can decide what's for supper tonight."

"Oh, burgers, definitely!" She tugged open the closet door that hid our washing machine. "The whole drive, I was salivating for a burger—there's so many Fuddruckers billboards!"

"No, no meat." I folded the last towel and dropped it into the basket. Pinched my earlobe a half-dozen more times. "I'm pretty sure you know that."

"I can get the tofu-and-mushroom ones for you and the kids, Walgreens has those, and you won't mind if I actually cook beef on your barbecue?"

Carcinogens! Jesus Christ! I wanted to yell.

"I won't mind," I grinned, treating the Cream of Wheat to a stirring it wouldn't soon forget.

She pushed the buttons and shut the closet door then looked around with a forced little smile that put dimples in her cheeks. She'd really wrinkled up in the years I'd known her, but the lines were so uniform around her eyes and mouth that in the right light they weren't even there. She took Ray's orange jacket off its hook, shook a pine needle off the sleeve, hung it up again. She sat down beside her coffee and dangled a slipper from her toe while I set the maple syrup and spoons beside her.

"What's your hurry this morning?" she asked.

"Every morning's like this. Get all the stuff done, then once they sit down I can hang out with them."

"You could get them to set the table and that—Josie's old enough, certainly."

"I get it done myself, no problem."

"You know." She wiped coffee off her chin with the back of a freckled hand. "I can't say how you could possibly be doing anything differently right now, but I really get the feeling that you're hanging by the skin of your teeth."

Hey, I thought, *thanks for noticing!*

"That's not the case," I said.

"Where's *your* lunch?"

"I've got that field trip to Velouria. They're feeding us."

"Next weekend, you know what you should do? Go over and see your mother."

"I'm not taking the kids all the way to Pawnee just for a weekend, no way. The last—"

"I know that," she said. "I mean I'll stay ten days, you go over there by yourself and I'll take the kids to the movies, put them to bed, all of that. Tell her I said hello."

"Well, I'll see how the week goes." Down the hall I shouted, "Kids? Hey?" Then I told her, "I haven't been over there in a while."

"I had that impression," said my mother-in-law.

Is she still your mother-in-law if her daughter's been dead six months?

"Okay, the pictures," I said. "It's the three of us now, right? I'm striving for normal. So reminding them every time they walk through the living room that there's supposed to be four, that isn't normal. There's three of us."

"So you've got one crappy picture on the fridge. That isn't healthy, really not."

"Well, it's normal."

She grunted and threw back the last of her coffee like it was a shot of tequila. Seriously, what could contribute less to the planet than a mug covered with kittens? My cup said PITTSBURGH STEELERS, sure, but the Steelers are the greatest franchise in football history, with a longer half-life than plutonium.

"My god," she said, "the radio last night was just one Congo talk show after another, and it was all moms and grandmas talking about their sons coming back with their lips cut off. The LRA grab them in the dark and hack away with machetes, can you imagine anything worse?"

I could remember Lydia's belly, big and square like she'd been pregnant for a third time, but all she'd been carrying was tumours. The night we'd sat in front of baseball on the TV and finally agreed that the treatments had all been a waste of time, how we could've spent the previous weeks watching the kids climb Mayan pyramids and wade through green Yucatan surf. Too late for any of that, as we'd watched the Kansas City Royals flail silently at one pitch after another.

"'Cut off from their unit,'" Deb went on, "that was all any of them said, like all of our soldiers are out there with blindfolds on or something!"

"I guess the jungle's like that at night."

"And I kept picturing—oh my god—little Ray with *his* lips cut off, waiting to sit on Santa's knee, trying to eat a sandwich, all with his lips cut off, and I had to pull over! Had to pull the car over!"

She put her wet face in her hands. Shifted her slippers slightly.

"Congo's ten thousand miles from here," I said. I stood beside her and rested my hand on her bony shoulder—she felt like a hot washcloth. "And at least those guys aren't getting killed, right? They're back with their families."

"But their families can't *look* at them! A person's in one piece then they're not in one piece, we can't *imagine* that, they say they don't even feel like human people! How can they say, 'Hey, life without lips isn't really that bad,' when they can't even pronounce half the syllables in the alphabet?"

Was she on meth? Hadn't she lost Lydia just as completely as I had? I rinsed the sandwich knife under the tap.

"At least they are alive and with their families," I said.

She wiped her eyes on the muumuu's shoulder then grimaced at me, blinking gummy lashes.

"Okay, please don't make this about her," she said. "Let's just agree that there's plenty of kinds of horror in the world, does that suit you okay? It's not a competition. I know, I have to stop myself in the grocery store every time someone starts telling a supposedly sad story. 'It is not a competition,' I tell myself."

I scrubbed down the sides of the sink.

"And after," I said, "you sit in the car feeling sick."

"Yes," she nodded.

"The reason they don't kill them is that they think no one else here will volunteer after they see a veteran walking by with half a face. Leave one guy alive now, just mangle him, and that's ten guys they won't have to fight later. We've got a half-million troops in Africa, and the LRA is already worrying about the guys coming after that."

"No, the radio said the LRA's trying to outdo the M23 so the stupid UN will negotiate with them first. It's just dollars and cents, that's the most horrible part."

"The M-who?" I asked.

Josie stumbled down the hallway, the back of her wrist thrown dramatically across her eyes, blond Ray hopping after her with the belt of his bathrobe tied around his ankles. Before their mother died they'd both sworn by Rice Krispies because of the noises, of course, and had said Cream of Wheat—not with brown sugar but maple syrup, Lydia's preference—was slimy. Now Cream of Wheat with maple syrup was all they'd eat before ten.

"Way to hop," I told the kids.

"It's not my school day," Ray announced.

"Look," I said, "this isn't preschool anymore. Fridays you go to school like the rest of us."

"Every *day* you say you don't have school!" Josie grinned, because today she evidently found him hilarious rather than brain-damaged.

"More syrup," he said, sluicing off my initial outlay with his spoon. Spilled milk had already soaked across the chest of his *Bakugan* T-shirt.

"Isn't this field trip going to put your afternoon behind?" Deb stared at her raisin bread in the toaster. "Want me to pick the yahoos up from school?"

"Man, when I planned out this week I'd forgotten you'd be here," I said as the end of my tie flew dutifully past my face. "I'll get them from the sitter, it's okay."

"Oh, no, no." Now she had the freezer door open, tapping the edge of the counter with her butter knife. "I'll get them."

"You really don't mind? I'm happy to get them."

"Not even a breakfast sausage in here, hey?"

"There's string cheese in the meat drawer!" Ray offered, diffused sunshine from the sliding-glass door highlighting his three dozen freckles.

"Oh," Deb said. "No thanks."

"They're awesome!" said Ray.

"*So* awesome." Josie pushed up the sleeves of her *Wahoo Warriors* hoodie—I'd have to buy her a *Hoover Hooves*. "But they come wrapped in too much goddamn plastic."

"Hey now!" said Deb.

"She's right," I said, checking my tie in the hall mirror. The bottom inch overlapped my belt precisely. "That crap gets into everything— albatrosses in the South Pacific. And you know which carcinogen is the easiest to avoid?"

"Okay. Burnt meat," Deb admitted.

Removing the stink-eye from Josie, she inspected the bubble-jet version of our wedding photo on the fridge door, making like we hadn't been arguing in the first place.

But now my kids and I were also looking, from our various angles, at Lydia with the foot-long veil clipped to her brown hair, her ivory dress reduced to featureless space by the glare of the camera's flash. But our eyes didn't see that whiteness. All any of us saw was a mass of char-coal-tinged carcinogens eating their way up from her colon, roiling like an electrical storm, the fridge motor's hum providing a soundtrack.

"Today is Mom's birthday," Ray whispered over it.

This had been their shtick since we left Wahoo—apparently every day in the year was now Lydia's birthday. Weird, but I figured it was better than them throwing things out windows.

"Today *was* Mom's birthday," said Josie.

"Here's teamwork for you," I told Deb. "The Giller Think Tank."

She gave her head a shake like she'd been doused with seawater.

"Her birthday's right after Christmas! If *anybody* would know that, I—"

"Exactly," I said. "This house overflows with brains."

The kids put their bowls in the sink, then Josie ran to get her silent-reading book from the back of the toilet, Deb went to pull sweatpants out of her suitcase and Ray ambled into the privacy of the living room to pick his nose, leaving me alone to stare down Lydia's picture. The dimples on either side of her mouth, the dance of infinitesimal eyebrows—it didn't look to me like a dead person's smile.

Nine drips of Deb's coffee still glistened under the table, so I stomped across to the broom closet. Like always I'd been left behind to mop up.

I KEPT THE passenger seat heaped with yellowing handouts from my school back in Wahoo just to disguise the passenger seat's sheer pas-sengerlessness, and Josie wouldn't be allowed to leave the back seat until she topped eighty pounds. That was Nebraska law.

During our first semester at UC Denver, Lydia had had passport photos taken, a block of four, the way they always come, and one had ended up in my wallet. In the picture, the relationship between her upper lip and teeth looked particularly earnest, and her hair was straight and parted down the middle in some kind of retro-sixties thing. That had been a new look, and with each of us away from home for the first time, I'd hoped the hairstyle might somehow symbolize a new-found sexual liberation. For that one rare instance I'd been entirely right, and had found myself between her legs more often than most people have to pee.

Before I started the car's engine I slid the passport photo out of my scrubbed-clean ashtray and pressed that tattered little rectangle between my eyes.

The first doctor, an emaciated guy with liver spots on his temples, had told us the blood in her stool was from harmless polyps. Harmless. Then he'd decided months later to send us to the specialist, who'd said, "If only we'd seen you sooner." That's teamwork.

I held the picture to my face; it had the slightest smell of apricot lip balm. The car's suspension creaked around me.

IN THE HOOVER High parking lot, I pulled in beside Ken Beckman's white Mustang, some early seventies model. My mom's boss at Alliance Ready-Mix had driven the same car, combing his sideburns in the rearview mirror, though if she'd ever ratted out some of the financial crap he pulled he would've been crying in jail instead of tooling around Knudsen, Nebraska, with his elbow out the window. I would happily put my federal tax dollars toward a roaming arbitrator who travels the country, cracking guys like that across the throat—but whoever'd have the balls to actually do it?

Anyhow, Ken Beckman wore a red satin Cleveland Indians jacket, taught shop and carried a wad of keys that looked like a medieval mace.

"Your exhaust's looking a little blue." Ken prodded his nostril with a knuckle as he locked the Mustang, tried the handle, locked it again. "Leave your key and I'll get my auto-shop kids to at least change the oil."

"No, thanks, Ken. I did notice that. I got it."

"Yeah, when? It's been running blue since the first time you pulled in here, and when you going to get around to it, with little kids at home and all? Japanese cars don't run on optimism."

"I prefer to look after it myself." My hand snaked up to my earlobe, but only for one reassuring pinch. "Thank you anyway."

"Well, I'm not going to change the oil behind your back, so don't worry about that." He circled around the Mustang to try his passenger handle too. "Just don't come crying to Mr. Beckman when parts start dropping off."

OUTSIDE MY CLASSROOM, Franny Halliday sat beside her locker, changing out of sneakers into a pair of cowboy boots while a swaying rope of red licorice dangled from her teeth. She was on my list for the field trip.

"I don't want to spoil your breakfast," I said, "but highly processed foods kill you faster than a handgun. They just plain make war on your body's cells."

She wore a denim skirt, a clunky bead necklace and a big white sweater with a panda down one side—my Josie would've called it a dorky outfit, and Josie was eight.

Franny smirked. "What's going on, honky?" she asked through her licorice.

"Why do you call me that?"

Boots tugged on, she sat up straight, smoothing her skirt down her shins.

"Sorry!" Her brown hair was so staticky that it floated above her shoulders. "I'm just excited about Velouria—there'll be time to stop at Ye Olde Candy Shoppe on the way in, right? They sell Curly Wurly bars."

"Why'd you call me honky?" I asked.

More kids dragged themselves around the hallway, so I wanted the conversation to be over—what kind of autocrat did I look like, looming over her like that?—but I also didn't want to spend my day beside a girl whose tongue was not connected to her brain.

"I don't know," she said. "I just thought that compared to Mr. Reid you're kind of a honky."

His bearded face looked down at us from a photo on the wall. Some award he'd won.

"Mr. Reid isn't African-American," I said.

"Nah, German, I think. He fought in the Gulf War!"

"Really? For Germany?" I'd been eleven during the Gulf War, but as a substitute, you can't let them imagine you ignorant on any subject at all. "I don't remember Germany sending—"

"No, man, the Americans!"

She picked up her sneakers in one hand and banged them into the bottom of her locker—green Converse, with trailing yellow laces patterned with JESUS in red letters. There was a ton of religious families in Hoover so I didn't see the need for her to change her footwear just on account of that.

"I don't know if we'll have time to stop the bus," I said.

"Haw-haw!" A bony shoulder bumped into mine—Clint Denham. All in tight denim, the huge red scarf his mother'd knitted him bundled around his neck. "You still around, Mr. G? Taking us over to Velouria after all, hey?"

"I've been telling you for two months that I'm here until Christmas, but every morning you act like seeing me is some big surprise."

"I'll tell you why that is!" He took a step back in his big leather shoes, nodding solemnly. Brown hair fell in his eyes, and three or four wiry ones poked hopefully from his chin. "It's because every Saturday night I'm sitting at home with my folks, right? TV trays and all that, and right at the second when my brother goes down in the basement to play his drums—the exact *second*—I think, I bet Mr. Giller's in Hollywood by now. They scooped him up in the Walgreens parking lot." He looked down at Franny and smacked his lips, then suddenly displayed the same stony grimace as when he'd heard noon-hour improv had been canceled. "Gone to California."

"See you out at the bus."

I navigated around a couple of freshmen as I moved to my classroom door.

"We ought to hook up at lunch," Clint was saying behind me. "With tongue and everything."

Franny had her legs stretched in front of her, and he tapped his pointy shoe against the sole of her boot. She rolled her eyes.

"We're at the plastic factory at lunch," she said.

"That's cool. We can do it there. You can't spend the rest of your life wondering what's it like to make out with hot guys, that's pathetic to the point of crisis."

Franny eyed him like he'd taken a dump between her legs.

"Keep talking like a bitch," she said, "you'll get noogies 'til your nose bleeds."

"That's cool anyway. I like short girls with big sunglasses."

I'D MET MY Lydia when *we* were sixteen, working as counselors at Camp Lake Picu in Dundy County. Deb knew the camp's owners, so Lydia was the canoeing instructor while I ran a special cabin for bed-wetters.

"I don't do anything in particular." I tried to sound adult as we sat on the porch of her boat-shed, overlooking the water. "The idea is maybe they'll feel less self-conscious sleeping amid their own kind, so with reduced anxiety maybe they'll quit peeing."

"How often do you change their sheets?" she asked as she un-braided her hair.

"Every morning whether they need it or not."

I'd heard it was possible to unhook a bra using only one hand, and she was being very patient with me. She shook her head as two senior campers stood up in their canoe to cannonball into the emerald water.

I THREW MY raincoat over the back of the desk chair and took my corduroy sport coat off the hook—Lydia's dad had given it to me the Christmas before he died, and it had been my lucky teaching jacket ever since. For all the luck it had brought.

Here was a new arrival: on my desk a one-sheet fax sat propped against the framed photo of George Reid on a canoe trip in the Tetons. Thankfully I love a good list, otherwise it might've occurred to me that George should sit home with his resectioned bowel and let me teach the goddamn class like I was paid to. And seriously, faxing? In 1987 he must've figured it was the future and stuck with it despite history siding against him, like drivers of electric cars after 1908.

Peter, most of this should be unchanged from previous years (seven and counting) so I thought I'd send it along after (obviously) changing what needed changing.

FIELD TRIP: *Chemistry 11, Dockside Synthetics, Friday October 21*
1. TRIP/PURPOSE: *Dockside plastics factory in Velouria to see how science is applied to industry and the manufacture of a variety of products*
2. TRANSPORTATION: *Bus booked for 8:45, tour 10-1, return 2:15, lunch provided (even veggie dogs!)*
3. PERMISSION FORMS: *see checklist on clipboard, attendance there too*

4. PARENT VOLUNTEERS: *Colleen Avery (Megan), Doug Melloy (Shawn)*
5. CONTACT PERSON AT SITE: *Rob Aiken, 402-466-9807 (cell)*
6. INSTRUCTIONS IF RETURNING AFTER DISMISSAL: *n/a*
7. HOMEWORK: *write summaries, details that struck them particularly*
8. SPECIAL CONDITIONS, ALLERGIES: *lunch will be nut and dairy free*

Good luck!

If we were back at 2:15 that'd be perfect for me to get the kids at four. Otherwise I'd just call ahead to the sitter's house, but what kind of weirdness could possibly befall us between Hoover and Velouria?

"Uh, Mr. Giller?"

Eye-linered Grace Bradford, in her skull-bedecked hoodie, stood between the nearest tables. Her skin was slightly tawny so there might've been Asian blood in her lineage, or Mexican or Pawnee or Arapaho. If I'd ever managed to become a geneticist I probably would've known at a glance. She held out a sheet of white paper.

"I signed a form about your vacation homework," I said. "For surf camp or whatever it was."

"This is to put on a school event." She stared at me down the length of the paper like she was sighting a gun. Her hair had recently become more blue than black. "Mr. Vincent didn't want to, but he said if I could get three teachers to sign maybe he'd change his mind. You're a real teacher, right?"

I unfolded the page. NBZAMBI MARCH, it read. *Any lunch hour, bowling gift certificates for best costumes, signs encouraged to attract media attention. Students have a voice to protest.* Then three empty lines for signatures.

"This looks great for Halloween, why'd Mr. Vincent have a problem?" I felt across my desk for a pen. "How do you say it, 'nub-zambi'? What is that?"

"*Nbzambi*'s the original Congolese word for a zombie, like the walking dead, and that's how everybody has to dress up." She hoisted her bum onto a table. Her short nails picked at the crumbly particleboard edge. "And my mom's gone to Taiwan so the surfing's postponed."

"Hold on, I didn't think about what exactly you're protesting—are you saying we should be *out* of the Congo? Because I don't know if I agree with that." I clicked the pen a couple of times like it'd help me think. "I'm not a war nut by any stretch, but for the average Congolese it'd be a huge mistake if we pulled out right now—our men and women are precious, yes, but defending women and children is also their *job*. And you want students to, what, dress up with their arms falling off and stuff?"

If she'd rolled her eyes with more vehemence she'd have damaged herself.

"Not at *all*!" she spat. "I just want, like, Day of the Dead costumes, like with faces painted white or skeletons and stuff. Everybody says, 'Oh, let's have our arms fall off and blood pour out of our mouths,' but I'm not into that stuff. I've already got the T-shirts made."

"I can definitely see the value in raising awareness of the human cost without necessarily saying we should pull out, but if you want attention you might as well go gory and *get* attention."

"Nobody should stay in the Congo. Even the people who live there should just get out." She pulled her legs up to sit cross-legged, and picked at a hole in her jeans. "Just no blood and guts, no bones sticking out—tons of people with painted white faces, walking around not saying anything? They'll be freaky!"

Entirely true. But I handed the paper back unsigned.

"It sounds like you want signs to say 'Empty the Congo Entirely,' but that's obviously not practical and I have to watch my step here, right? I've got kids of my own, and for the time being I'm not exactly picking and choosing the work I get."

She slid down to the floor with a thump. "So put your kids over the rest of the world," she said to the blackboard. "Nice priorities."

With that in mind I put extra pens in my jacket's inside pocket, got my clipboard and headed out toward the staff room, because at 8:15 the second pot of coffee was usually pretty fresh, or if it wasn't I'd have time to make a new one.

The white-tiled staff room smelled like dishwasher soap. A dozen women sat with their legs crossed on the couches while the loveable Grey and Dreaper, a couple of oversized math teachers with beards, sat playing canasta with Mahinda, a twig-necked divorcé from Sri Lanka.

"Stay after dismissal today, Peter," said Mahinda, "and I will teach you to play once and for all. Against two colonials they will never win."

"Tell me again how I'm a colonial?" I asked.

Cam Vincent, our principal, circled the table to peer down at their hands, sporting a jet-black crewcut like he'd walked straight off an old baseball card.

"Giller, listen." Cam stretched hairy arms way over his head like he'd been up early digging coal. "Turns out Nella's having her back surgery right around Christmas, George should be back by then, and her blocks are mostly eleventh grade, so—"

"Oh, yeah, believe me, I want any classes I can get. All these kids are great," I mostly bullshitted. "Really engaged with the material."

"Young and motivated," sneered Dreaper. "Kids'll be the perfect age when we bring back the draft."

"No, no, if they already had *Doctor* Reid," said Grey, "then Mensa's got to have helicopters circling overhead. This is Genius School!"

Back in September they'd giggled until they'd spilled their peppermint tea, telling me how Reid had his Ph.D. in Biology but instead of lecturing at Harvard he'd parked his ass back in his hometown to teach high school like a sucker. I could've told them that, similarly, I'd started my master's in biochem—planning to delve into stem cell research on, not surprisingly, Parkinson's disease—but switched to education in order to earn an imminent-baby-supporting income somewhat sooner. But then Grey and Dreaper would've pointed out that if I'd only stayed in medical research I could've bought and sold Hoover ten times over. I massaged my irate earlobe.

"Help, Doctor Reid!" Dreaper waggled his hands. "I swallowed a roofing nail!"

"I don't feel this Congo mess will carry on much longer." Mahinda licked a fingertip and commenced rearranging his canasta hand. "You see it with the Tamil Tigers at home, or the IRA, the PLO in those other places, if these rebel movements cannot renounce violence they eventually go down in flames."

"Bullshit," said Dreaper, setting his cards down to reposition his belt under his gut. "These M23 guys we're fighting now, they were the Congo Army, then they quit for better money from the Rwandan guy! They've got a million guns, a million guys with nothing else to do, and we're scrambling around trying to keep them from raping their own women! And that's a noble cause, I'm not going to complain about that, but that's not a job for a human being! We're getting torn to pieces by these M23 guys circling around at night, we—"

"Infrared goggles," offered Cam. "See anything in the dark."

"Tried that, remember?" Grey cupped his hands behind his head, displaying damp armpits. "That infantry platoon killed those endangered goddamn anteaters."

"Isn't it the LRA we're fighting?" I asked.

"That's the trouble over there," Cam said earnestly, dragging the back of his hand beneath his chin. "Can't say who exactly we're engaging. Boys just keep coming home with their lips cut off."

We all went quiet, the soles of our shoes squeaking absently on the tile. The women on the couches were laughing at yet another story about that kid with Asperger's.

"So the ball hits the *bottom* of the rim," gasped Melissa Jordan, ponytail swaying, "knocks his glasses *clean* off, and then he's *so* mad, he makes these fists and—"

"What we need in Africa," Dreaper said, "is cyborgs. Enhanced humans."

"With jetpacks on," Cam intoned.

"Robots." Dreaper frowned at his cards again. "Just program them, 'Kill bad guys.' Our men and women can come home, go back to farming, selling cars."

"My point exactly." Mahinda winked. "The criminals will lay down their arms in the face of superior technology."

"What time's the assembly?" called Ange Helms, our clunky-heeled-shoe home ec teacher. But passable ankles, Mahinda had once muttered.

"Not 'til 11:15," said Cam. "But I might bring him through some classes if he's here early. Coming over from McCook."

"What assembly?" I asked.

"It's not on your watch, don't worry about it." Cam raised his prodigious eyebrows. "But, say, Giller, want to swing by Sunday and watch some Steelers? Jacksonville, right? What a joke."

"Sorry, I'll have to pass," I said. "But thanks."

"Ah! Already spoken for. I'll have to be quicker next time!"

I shuffled over to the empty coffee machine and dumped the soggy filter in the trash. We didn't have a single plan for Sunday, but I didn't want to be burdened with a lot of friends if and when we moved to another town. And I liked to send the kids downstairs to play Wii on Sundays while I watched the games, so I could jot the stats down on my own. All last season, stretched on the bed beside me, scarf around her head, Lydia had rooted for Cincinnati just to be obstreperous, and, boy, their receivers had had hands like feet, right from Week One. They really had looked sick.

AT 8:45 WE stood outside the cafeteria exit, the eleventh-grade boys in long shorts and girls in crop tops even though it was cold for October, possible snow smelling raw in my nostrils. Jordie, Devon and Todd had called in absent so that left me with fifteen for the field trip, and no sign of my parent volunteers.

I did another head count but the skater kids were playing leapfrog or something so I got twenty the first time, then twelve. Couldn't blame the skater kids if they kept warm. I watched through the shrubs for anything yellow that might swing into the parking lot. This would be *my* first visit to a plastics factory too, and I was holding onto the thinnest hope that I might be able to teach something. *Well, we all thought the chemicals pouring into those moulds smelled evil and must slowly be killing the world, sure, so you can all quit going to the dollar store to buy Frisbees and sunglasses, all right? We won't know for a thousand years exactly how that crap will pervert nature at the most fundamental level.* Kids will happily scrawl "pervert" in their notebooks regardless of context.

"Hey, hey, Megan." Clint, all in denim, leaned past my elbow. "What up, girl?"

"Come *onnnnn*, make it come!" moaned Megan Avery in her sequinned-butterfly cardigan. "Did you know we're missing appliqué in home ec today?"

"Teachers don't run the buses," I said, then noticed the kids wandering across the parking lot toward the swaying magnolias—they enjoyed many noon-hour cigarettes in there at their campfire ring overlooking a trickling culvert—so I squared my shoulders for the day's first authoritarian holler.

"So I'm *not* ridiculously late!" called a svelte woman in a black tracksuit, skipping across from a green Taurus wagon. "Oh, Megan! Which teacher is this?"

"It's Mr. Giller," said Megan. "Dr. Reid's off sick."

"Bowel resection. I'm Pete Giller, his substitute." Jesus, had she thought Kirsten McAvoy would be the sub? "Glad you're joining us today, Mrs. Avery."

I put my hand out to shake, all hearty and businesslike, but she just grasped my fingertips while performing a disturbing little curtsey.

"I heard that he wasn't having surgery *at all*," she whispered, "but that the poor dear was spending his stress leave in California!"

"That's where the best ones go," said Clint.

"I don't think that's the case, ma'am," I said. "I heard from him this morning."

"Are you really wearing that jacket to Velouria?" asked Franny.

I instinctively checked the top button. "Why?"

"It's just, you know, you've got a clipboard and a corduroy sport jacket. You look *exactly* like a teacher on a field trip."

"But that's—"

"But didn't you ever want to be something more?"

"Okay, all right. I like the panda sweater, by the way."

"It's worth fifty bucks on eBay!" She smoothed it down over her belly. "And the best coaches are in the stands, my dad says. His raunchy ideas are culinary. Be that as it may, Gillbrick, you could use a little shaking up."

"It's not really Mr. Gillbrick, is it?" Mrs. Avery asked Megan.

"I say Gill-*brick*," Franny announced, "because the guy is *solid*."

"Sorry to interrupt. It's like almost nine." This was blond Harv Saunders, an up-and-comer on the varsity basketball team. "Is the trip definitely *today*?"

Wide-eyed Mrs. Avery tilted her head like she was deciding which puppy she wanted, though she was only reading her watch. Then like Zeus's cloud mercifully descending in some old Greek play—I'd read half a dozen at UC Denver, after all—a long yellow rectangle flashed past on the other side of the shrubs.

"Okey-dokey." Mrs. Avery nimbly clapped her hands. "Let's get a line started right here, everybody!"

With a hiss of pneumatics the bus's door flopped open and the driver scowled down—a skinny guy in blue coveralls, his red beard trimmed into a gigantic rectangle. I let the kids climb on, putting yet another pencil mark beside each name as its owner hunched by. Skater kids at the back of the line crushed cigarette butts under their sneakers. I waved a hand in front of my nose at the nicotine stink, and Harv, headphones around his neck, must've thought I'd meant it for him.

"Oh, I just smell like that," he said, putting his nose to the shoulder of his blue hoodie. "Our whole house smells 'cause of my dad."

"Climb aboard, Harv," I said. "My dad was the same."

Amber and Grace flashed me slick fake smiles as they filed by. They wore the same skull-patterned hoodies but blond Amber had scooped on more eyeliner. The Avery women hung back by the trash can—they formed an interesting contrast, scientifically speaking, in that the mom possessed a wizened sort of Disney cuteness while Megan was homely as a shelving unit.

"My dad's running late but he said he'd be here for sure," said Shawn, pushing long bangs out of his eyes as he climbed up.

"It would've been great to have him," I said, "but we can't wait."

"His dad's got problems." Eric arched his brows and ran fingers through his prodigious mullet. "Gets stuck taking these *huge* dumps."

"Shut up, man," said Shawn.

"Okay, *now* go ahead," Mrs. Avery said, nudging Megan forward.

"You go first! I don't want you to look at my bum."

"You'd rather look at *mine*?"

Megan nodded earnestly. "It's nice!"

Her mother kissed her cheek before sashaying up the steps. Moms of the world are universally adored while the dads sit home on the toilet.

The inside of the bus smelled like bubble gum and feet. The Averys had taken the first bench on the left so I swung in behind the driver.

"What time's your tour?" he rasped over his shoulder.

"Ten o'clock," I said. "It's an hour to Velouria?"

"I'll vaporize some fuel," he said, slamming the door shut even as the bus lurched over the first speed bump.

"It'll be *so* nice if we get there on time," said Mrs. Avery. "It is so *tough* to schedule around two jobs, but it's so worth it when you have a child, sir, you'll see."

"Why would you think I don't have kids?"

"Did you sub here last year? I don't remember."

We took the last speed bump before squealing onto Casement toward Highway 33. I twisted in my seat and took yet another head count. Three seats back Grace reached around the cloud of staticky hair to tug out Franny's earbuds, trying to be funny, but one of the cords snapped in two—Franny's face went red, her bracelets clanking.

"Well, Mrs. Avery," I muttered, "last year I was teaching in Wahoo."

"Please. Colleen." A hand to her heart. "And my nieces are in Wahoo! Oh, but the youngest graduated the year before last. You would've remembered her, she's *big*."

"That's so sweet!" called one of the girls, with an enthusiasm so rare for an eleventh-grader that I had to turn and see who it'd been: Franny blinked back a grateful mistiness while she clamped blue headphones to either side of her head. Their owner, Harv, slid back into his seat behind the Averys.

An asymmetrical grin cut across Mama Colleen's cheek. "Mind if I ask why you left Wahoo?"

"Well, the sub lists aren't too extensive in either place, but here there's an extra dollar an hour."

Which was bullshit—Hoover actually paid worse. But we'd needed the change, and there'd been a cop named Holt in Wahoo who liked to walk down North Chestnut with his fists on his hips, and his ten-year-old son liked to knock kids onto the schoolyard gravel and say, "Aw, sorry," and I said the son ought to be suspended but the administrators just stared from behind their potted spider plants. I'd been covering the tail end of a mat leave. I caught the tough kid passing a note that said JASON IS A FAGGIT and told him to stay after school, then once he was alone in the classroom I deadbolted him in and went to the staff room to pour myself a coffee. By the time the custodian let him out the tough kid had peed himself for dramatic effect, but it turned out the administrators must've been on my side all along because they said they wouldn't even phone the district provided I took my name off the sub list. I got things *done* by myself, see that? My Lydia had been dead a month so my thinking at the time had been crystal clear, forever sliding coins into the wrong parking meter.

"Oh, I see," Colleen said. "I'm only picking your brain because my sister always complains how Wahoo smells like a sewage plant. Their house is right next to the sewage plant."

Anyone who says *pick your brain* can't really be visualizing it.

"No, smell never bothered us, though I have to wonder with any of those operations what the discharge is going to do in the long run."

"Oh, my," she said, massaging her temples. "*I* worry what it's doing *right now*."

"Harv, hey!" Eric yelled from the back. "Isn't that your dad?"

Where Casement joined the highway, a blond man in a dress shirt was stapling a sheet of magenta paper to a telephone pole. The bus blew by him, ruffling his hair.

"Yeah," said Harv, "he, uh—"

"Is he, like, looking for work?" Eric asked.

"Shut it, Eric!" Franny yelled, holding a blue headphone out from her ear.

Harv looked across at me and smiled sheepishly.

FIVE YEARS BEFORE I was born, Pvt. William R. Giller waded through the gray mud of the Mekong Delta—8,500 miles, the atlas says, from Nebraska—trying to flush Communist insurgents in cone-shaped hats and indigo pyjamas out from villages of supposedly democratically inclined farmers who also wore cone-shaped hats and indigo pyjamas. Discharged back to Knudsen, NE, Dad pushed a broom in the flour mill until I came along, when Aggregate Grains of Pawnee County burnt to the ground in ten minutes and he subsisted on the disability payments he received for his smoke-damaged lungs.

The Knudsen Lutheran church proposed building swank baseball diamonds so we could host county-wide tournaments—simple, right? But Dad, in his sweated-through golf shirt, stapled fliers to telephone poles, declaring OUT-OF-TOWNERS BRING IN UNWANTED ELEMENTS. This might've been a hard-won lesson from the swampy Mekong, but every kid just thought he was a jackass. Out-of-towners, like from Lewiston and Pawnee City? Knudsen couldn't join the little league without diamonds, so we couldn't even pretend there was such a thing as a baseball scholarship unless we had a parent who'd drive us up to Burchard—and who had a parent like that?

"We could make our own league," we said. "The Shit-hole League."

The Lutherans got too busy arguing about Dad to get the diamonds built.

"You could look right at them," he told me, teetering on the edge of my bed, "and never know what they really were."

Keister the dog had been backed over by then. As I got older I was able to fight back more effectively on the living room floor, and Dad seemed to like that even better. His expanding gut stayed hard as a rock.

In twelfth grade, Mom started taking me into Lincoln on Saturdays, showing me art galleries and even a play. She hadn't turned chubby like other guy's moms, and her legs got looks.

"I don't care if you even get *married*," she said in the middle of the sunken gardens, solid hands on my shoulders, "but I want to teach grandkids to canter. I see buck-toothed girls on palominos. Leave 'em with me, then go to Europe if you want."

"But I don't want a buck-toothed wife," I said.

"There are worse things," she whispered, retying her chiffon scarf over her head.

I told Dad I was making hunting knives at Buck's apartment but instead pimply Buck and I were studying like maniacs for scholarship exams. "Giller," he'd whisper whenever I dozed off. "Your mom's totally Alanis Morissette."

And after midnight I was calling modestly toothed Lydia in MacArthur while we simultaneously filled out applications to the same dozen schools.

Then from my eventual dorm at UC Denver I'd call Mom when I knew Dad would still be asleep—not to worry, I won't be talking about the guy much longer—and one morning she told me that after fifteen years his lungs had somehow *recovered* so the doctor had said he was no longer eligible for disability. They went to Pawnee City where Dad started as an apprentice millwright. So, yeah, once I was long gone they actually moved away from Knudsen.

The *Pawnee Republican* of November 18, 1996:

> *A 41-year-old Pawnee City man, formerly of Knudsen, was killed when he was ejected from a 1991 Buick Skylark that flipped multiple times before colliding with the Sit-Stay Dog Food warehouse on the northeast corner of Broadway and Sheridan.*
>
> *State police reported William R. Giller was pronounced dead at the scene by Pawnee County coroner following the 10:45 p.m. crash. One witness reports the Skylark traveling in excess of 90 miles an hour as it turned south off Western. Giller, the sole occupant of the car, was not wearing a seatbelt.*
>
> *Pawnee City fire and ambulance personnel assisted at the scene. An investigation into the crash is continuing.*

Even at four sentences it seemed long-winded. The investigation found cocaine in his system. The symptoms of Mom's disease were still in our future and every morning she was bicycling to the accident site to look for more windshield glass to keep in her purse—I couldn't understand her grief at the passing of an asshole, so we weren't talking much. And what did I insist to the minister, beside the cooler at the after-service potluck?

"Families are shit, Your Worship," I said, waving the wasp away from my beer, "and I'm not going to have no part of 'em."

Yet years later, I'd set Josie up on the change table, unbutton her sleeper and put my nose under her drool-slick chin—that sour scent of pure baby.

"*Hey*," I'd say in a goofy voice. "Dat smells pretty *good*!"

And she'd give a deep-throated chuckle before gazing across the room at her mother, who'd be on the couch asleep, or folding laundry, or embroidering daisies onto a curtain. Her auburn braids curled down onto her T-shirt, her sinewy shoulders creaking with strength.

So while we were in Hoover my kids' Grandma Jackie sat waiting in Pawnee City, with doctors, acupuncturists, massage therapists and her rattle-brained son all unable to end her latest ordeal. Their grandpa was in heaven, apparently, stapling flyers to the Pearly Gates and eyed nervously by St Peter.

"JUST THINK ABOUT *Charlie and the Chocolate Factory* and all the wonderful happenings at *that* factory!" Rob Aiken shouted over the machines' roar. "When people hear there are tours at *our* factory, they all jump!"

We stood in the loading dock between a parked forklift and towers of cardboard boxes stacked on pallets. The kids shuffled their sneakers on the pebbly concrete and blinked up at the black rafters, as though the wonderment might put them to sleep. Rob had a yellow collared shirt tucked into his jeans and close-cropped white hair. He laced his fingers in front of his crotch like he was about to hoist someone over a fence.

"Is there really going to be lunch?" asked Colleen. "I brought a little burrito just in case!"

"Yeah, oh, hot dogs!" Rob said. "Now, just through here, let's get started. We're going to see the pumps we use to load the res—uh, the additive with."

A loose-limbed guy in orange coveralls rolled up a handcart and stacked it with boxes, wagging his elbows like he had a Run-DMC song playing in his head. Rob skipped over to him, put a wide hand on his shoulder.

"Ah, no, pal!" Rob hollered. "Latches for the bins won't go on until next week! If it's ball bearings just take a box at a time, things weigh a hundred pounds!"

The guy unloaded his boxes without a break in rhythm, and Rob turned back to us with a watery smile.

"Lot of guys off sick this week but we've got good people filling in!"

We ambled after him through a pair of tall steel gates into the main room of the factory, smelling of machine oil and garden hoses. It was the dimensions of a football stadium. I'd done construction work during summers in college, and I wondered how many guys it had taken to build the operation in the first place, much less to keep it running. Brown and green machines filled the floor, each with white dials, blinking red numbers and ten or fifteen greased and whirring axles winding up spools of plastic two and three feet wide. If they'd replaced the banks of fluourescents and the guys in orange with gas lamps and half-starved ten-year-olds, Dockside Synthetics could've been an Industrial Revolution cotton mill. A few eleventh-graders looked up but mostly they just kicked their toes against the concrete or tried to give each other wedgies. Pierced-lip Willow, in jean shorts, held hands with black-clad Craig, an inch shorter than herself. Rob turned to us, chin raised amicably, hands still a hammock in front of his crotch.

"So to start, here's a machine that measures the amount of additive that's going into the plastic for garbage bags."

A mile of light-green plastic film, stretched taut between one set of rollers and another, climbed the wall next to us in four-foot incre-ments, then over and under the rafters fifty feet above our heads. There were too many machines cluttering the place to see where the film came down exactly. It was cold and my shirt chafed my nipples.

"Now, through here," Rob yelled, "the guys are running extrusion moulds!"

Brace-faced Lydia performed ballet turns. Her orthodonture was so severe that confusing her with my Lydia was not possible.

"Which chemicals exactly are going into the garbage bags?" asked Megan.

"Well!" Rob raised his hands to his chest as if to catch a basketball. "For *these* bags we're using polyethylene terephthalate, and we're tak-ing a chance on that because it's a lot sturdier than you'll usually find for a domestic trash bag."

"It's a wonderland!" said Colleen. "Your father would love this, wouldn't he?"

"Any of this could be on a quiz," I announced.

"And what's its molecular breakdown?" Megan asked.

I stood taller in my shoes at that. Harv clicked a ballpoint and prepared to write on his hand—he could *not* miss this.

"Terephthalate is $C_{10}H_8O_4$." Rob thrust a hand out for each element, like he was pat-a-caking the periodic table.

"H_8O_4," Megan echoed. "That's a lot of gas for a plastic bag."

"No, dude," Amber hissed out the side of her mouth, "don't ask that!"

"Do the bags contain coltan?" asked Grace.

"Coltan? I don't know it," said Rob.

"They dig for it in the Congo. It's in lots of things, people don't even know."

"Now, not to get off on the wrong foot, Rob," I called, "but is there anything really *beneficial* to the environment that your operation might be putting out?"

Colleen looked back to show me her lopsided smile and oversized Bambi eyes.

"Oh, good question, you'd be surprised! For sure there is." Rob intertwined his fingers again, bounced them against his groin. "Our new Split-Proof line is fifty percent less likely to lose its integrity at curbside, and *that* keeps waste out of our groundwater."

"Sorry," said Harv, half-raising his hand, "but fifty percent less likely than what?"

"Well." Rob nodded earnestly. "Than our popular line."

He led us around for another forty-five minutes, explaining what various read-outs meant and introducing us to a dozen different guys who grimaced at us from behind their safety goggles while brandishing aerosol cans of lubricant.

"Oh!" Rob clapped his big hands. "I called you Walt 'cause you're wearing Walt's coveralls!"

The substitute valve-tightener rubbed the freckles on his nose and tried to look cheerful. I didn't have to wear George Reid's coveralls, true enough, but his name was on my classroom door and his framed photo, for some research citation he'd won, watched me from across the hall—he wore a blue-and-pink checked shirt in the picture, in front of a blue and pink backdrop, so it looked like his bodiless head was just floating there, all forehead and beard. I imagined him hovering behind us like the Great Gazoo on *The Flintstones*.

"Dockside's travel bin is the only one in the industry that's TSA approved," Rob announced. "Hundreds of companies manufacturing travel bins across the country, but ours is the only one that has that, uh, approval, so we think that's pretty neat."

Behind us a set of double doors yawned open to reveal a loading bay and a gleaming white semi-trailer with a tangle of tubes emerging from a hub in its roof. Stenciled on its side:

DO NOT USE STEAM

BOILING WATER OR SHARP OBJECTS TO CLEAN

ENTER ONLY IN SOFT-SOLED SHOES

"What's all this go into?" I asked Rob.

"That stuff? Can't say for sure! We always get, uh, approached by businesses that need specific equipment for a stage in their manufacturing, whether that's, oh, custom moulds, extreme high temperatures or additive introduction, we always say, 'Hey, if we can make plastic, we can make anything!'"

"How about plastic explosives?" grinned Eric.

Shawn frowned from behind his bangs. "Dude, no."

"No weapons," said Rob. "Now if you'll just follow me around here, we're nearly, nearly at the end!"

"You sure love your job," Colleen told him. "That's so nice to see!"

Harv lobbed an imaginary three-point shot into a bin of translucent beads.

"You see," said Rob, "what we have here is plastic turning from a solid to a liquid—sorry, liquid to a solid. See, it goes up forty-five feet there..."

It sounded like monsoon rain but there were too many criss-crossing pipes for us to see exactly what was happening up near the ceiling, though down where we were, the clear plastic was perpetually forming the shape of a hot-air balloon thanks to a constant gust of wind from below. The plastic bubble looked like a cross between a twenty-foot goblet and an upside-down tornado. Light shimmered across it.

"Cool," said Amber, snapping her gum.

Harv, a few feet in front of me, nodded whole-heartedly as he stared straight up, his head craned back into his hood. Little Craig started licking Willow's neck.

"I want a tent like that." Colleen trailed fingertips across her teeth. "All our camping trips."

"That *is* cool," said Grace. "Whoa."

Rob stepped away, hands clasped behind himself—his work was done. It could have been *my* moment if I'd chosen to embrace it, but how to make it teachable without aggrandizing the plastics industry?

"Moments of beauty," I improvised, "when you least expect them."

I thought they'd look back at me and roll their eyes, but they kept their pierced and mascara'd and acne-blighted faces trained on that flickering balloon.

I noticed a pink glob, the size of a quarter, on the back of Harv's head. Had it been there all along?

"How long does it stay suspended like that?" Megan asked.

"Oh, all day, three eight-hour shifts!" Rob smiled, rocking forward. "It looks like a solid piece, I know, but there's twenty gallons of the stuff coming down every minute!"

Harv ran a hand over his head and brushed across the pink glob. Most of it stuck to his fingers so he brought it down in front of his face and sniffed it. Strands stretched between his fingers. With his other hand he felt his head again.

"We'll head upstairs from here and look over some pamphlets," Rob said, "so if anybody's in the mood for a hot dog, we've even got veggie…"

Another pink glob appeared on Harv's shoulder, and he smeared that away with his hand, too, then glanced back at me, brows furrowed, showing his front teeth as if to say, *What the hell?* I pursed my lips and shrugged, then I looked up too but didn't see anything in particular. I counted seven pipes of various widths passing directly over us.

"Is *that* what it's called?" Colleen was asking. "*Gossamer?*"

"Say, Rob!" I called. "I've got a student over here who's—"

"No, man, it's okay," said Harv, gingerly dabbing the glob on his head. "It's—"

Then a blanket of goop dropped over all of us, plastering our hair and our faces, filling eyes and mouths—warm as bathwater, salty as homemade Play-Doh. The kids let out half-gargled yowls. While the stuff kept falling on us I wiped at my face with my sodden shirt sleeve and tugged at kids' wrists and hoods until we'd slid away from the machines. We weren't getting smothered anymore, though dropping goo kept spreading in wide puddles across the concrete.

"Nolan!" Rob shouted hoarsely, clearing his face with gummy hands. "Shut down number nine!"

Eric had fallen down like a turtle but Harv sloshed across to pull him up.

"What's that?" some guy yelled from above us, as though he hadn't heard a thing before. "Say something?"

"For fuck's sake shut off number nine!" hollered Rob.

THE DOCKSIDE LUNCHROOM was upstairs from the offices and bathrooms, and at the end of the row of white tables a big picture window looked out over the factory floor. We worked our jaws through buns and wieners as we gazed down at orange-coverall guys, working their mops and buckets across the concrete beneath Pipe #9. The stuff had been warm and sticky, sure, but it'd washed away with soap and water.

"A defect in the join," Rob was saying in my ear. "Too much pressure and the thing just opened up like it had a zipper down the length of it, you understand?"

"Uh-huh," I said, and lifted my veggie dog from the paper plate.

The kids, all dressed in orange, had pulled their chairs up to the window too. We smelled acridly of citrus soft-soap after scrubbing ourselves in the company showers, and Dockside had even cracked open a fresh carton of coveralls while our clothes tumbled through the company washers and dryers.

"At least the new guys know how to mop a floor," Rob sighed.

"What's happened to your regular guys?" I asked. "Flu?"

He nodded—he had bags under his eyes like he hadn't slept in eight days.

"Too many guys sharing Mr. Daniels at the company picnic."

"We should've walked through school with that pink crap all over us." Grace sat on the carpet while Amber braided her damp hair. "That would've been a parade."

"If you want to freak people out we could just wear these crap outfits," said Amber.

"Your go next, Franny," said cold-sore'd Jacob as he slid back onto his chair. "There any more grape soda?"

"Why, yes, there is," said Rob, reaching for a two-litre.

Behind Megan's plastic chair, Colleen in her tracksuit shifted her weight and sighed—she'd been far enough to the right that just a single drop had landed on her neck. She gave me an exhausted half-smile and absently fluffed her hair up on one side. The clock said two o'clock but it felt like we'd been in Velouria since the day before.

I followed Franny to the other end of the room. The coveralls didn't flatter her figure—she looked like a Weebles toy from the seventies. The first-aid attendant, Clayton, was a curly-headed guy with a handlebar moustache.

"Any news?" I asked, as Ryan Farnsworth straddled the examination chair.

"Everything clear so far," Clayton said in his gravelly voice. "All the eyes and ears check out. I'll trust you guys to say if you noticed any—Jeez! What the shit?"

He held Ryan's face steady to peer at the underside of his jaw.

"What's this scab, it's all down your—how come nobody *else* has this?"

I felt the pinch on my earlobe before I realized I was doing it.

"Might be mustard?" suggested Ryan.

"Oh, hey, yeah. And this shit on your neck is presumably relish."

"WHAT KIND OF factory is it?" Red Beard asked, as I stood taking another head count in the aisle of the bus—yes, one parent volunteer, fifteen kids.

"Garbage bags," I said.

"Thought it must be a planer mill," Red Beard rasped. "You smell like sawdust!"

And what tremendous teachable moment did I deliver during the ride back?

"Accidents will happen," I told them as the October sun ambled over the ragged cornfields. I said it fourteen times, which was as often as Megan Avery complained that her butterfly-sequinned cardigan should *not* have gone through the industrial dryer.

"There's the place, G!" Franny called from the back. "Ye Olde Candy Shoppe. Okay, not cool, now it's behind us."

"You have been very good about this little crisis, Peter," Colleen said, leaning across the aisle and shaking my knee. "Especially since you're not the real teacher. But you need to make him stop at the next gas station, understand?"

"What for?"

"I need a Slim Jim!" Megan yelled. "I need some meat!"

Man, when she said that, I realized how much I could've gone for a Slim Jim myself, all spicy and wet inside its plastic wrapper—heck, was that some post-traumatic symptom, were we all protein-deprived? I looked around to see if everybody was salivating but ninety percent of the kids were already dozing with their earbuds jammed in, Little Craig with his head on Willow's shoulder.

"Can't stop, I already filled 'er up while I was waiting around," Red Beard rasped over his shoulder. "I got to hurry and get it swept out for the Shriners tonight!"

"Shriners'll kick you out for no reason," Harv announced behind us. "That's what happened to my dad."

ONCE WE GOT back into Hoover, the school secretary and first-aid attendant, red-headed Kathleen, decided she had to look a few of the kids over before we could send them all home. She sat Eric in a rolling chair behind the office counter and held his hand in her skirted lap while she found his pulse.

"Oh, nurse," he sighed. "Everything's going woozy."

Kathleen leapt up, her chair spinning away.

"He's fine!" she announced. "They're all fine!"

Which was okay with me—I had to pick up Josie and Ray, after all, get Chick'n strips into the oven and ball clean socks into pairs.

"You got through all right?" Cam winked at me. "I spent the whole afternoon leaving messages on the parents' machines, and the ones I actually talked to thought I was telling them their kids were radio-active or something."

"Accidents'll happen." I rattled my car keys. It was only 3:40 so I had plenty of time to be at the kids' sitter by four o'clock.

"So I can leave it to you to call those parents back!" Cam clubbed me on the shoulder. "Nah, I'll take care of it."

"What's the sawdust smell?" Kathleen asked no one in particular.

Now I smelled it too—something we must've stepped in back in Velouria.

AS I CURVED up Clemons Avenue the sun was settling behind the trees, throwing yellow light and black branch-shadows in long bars across the street. One more turn and another two blocks to the sitter's, but then I spotted Harv Saunders standing on the sidewalk, hands in his hoodie pockets, staring up a driveway at a green split-level rancher.

The door of the house stood open.

I wasn't desperate for friends, no, but it'd be an understatement to say that Harv reminded me of myself at an earlier time. I stopped at the curb, leaned across my pile of obsolete handouts and rolled down the passenger window. He glanced at me over his shoulder, his white face longer than should've been possible—maybe the pink goo *had* affected him physically.

"What's up, Harv? Everything all right?"

He shrugged. I could hear voices from the house: a gruff male and shrill female, and from their teetering rhythm it sounded like alcohol had a voice too. A badly primered pickup sat in the driveway. I stepped out of my car and looked across its roof at him.

"My dad's girlfriend," he said. "He sent me out here a minute ago."

"You got somebody's house you can go to for a while?"

"Won't be all night." He looked from me back to the open door. "I'll hang out."

The dregs of the summer's marigolds huddled along the edge of the driveway, and a wooden deer silhouette stood under a birch tree, making the place look a hundred percent homier than my own house did.

"Your dad *hit* you?" I asked, heat rising into my scalp.

"Just sent me out here."

I trudged around the car, past Harv and up the driveway. Evening was coming on and the backs of my hands felt cold.

"It's fucking *cheese*!" the woman yelled from inside.

The man roared an inarticulate response. I went up three steps and rapped my knuckles against the grapes carved into the front door. Inside, carpeted steps went up to what must've been bedrooms, while in the living room to my right, a woman with her back to me lifted a rubber tree back into its pot. A brown La-Z-Boy recliner relaxed on its side, surrounded by potting soil and three barrel-shaped lights on tripods like I'd walked onto a movie set. There wasn't a camera, but one of those white light-bouncing screens blocked the front window. The uriney musk of stale beer was so thick I could've bottled it. Barstools lay toppled under a counter that looked through into the kitchen— sounded like the guy was banging racks inside the oven.

"It *cannot* be the same every *time*!" he yelled.

"What're you going to do?" Harv asked behind me.

"What's your dad's name?" I whispered.

"*My* dad?"

"No, man, somebody else's."

"Dave."

I rapped the door again. The woman straightened up, flicking brown hair over her shoulder. Her lipstick had smeared so it looked like her mouth was on her cheek.

"Oh," she said. "Yeah?"

"The fuck's this?" Dave asked, stomping in from the kitchen, a plaid oven mitt on each hand. He was definitely the guy we'd seen stapling fliers—blond like Harv but with a moustache and black glasses. He marched to the woman and moved sideways between us, brandishing his mitts like they were serrated.

"I'm from the high school," I said. "There was an incident on the field trip to Velouria today, and—"

"I know." The human crab pushed his glasses up his nose with the thumb of his mitt. "Message on the machine. Thought they were complaining about Harv here sucking cock in back of the school."

Harv leaned against the doorway and folded his arms. He still had $C_{10}H_8O_4$ written on the back of his hand—couldn't have showered too thoroughly in Velouria.

"We could sit," the woman offered, picking something off the end of her tongue.

"I'm not talking about anything like that." My hands darted from one earlobe to the other, then I folded my hands together. "I wanted to say that Harv might need an early night, and to ask that if you have any, ah, health concerns that you contact the school first thing Monday morning."

"You must think I'm an awfully shitty parent if you gotta come in here and tell me all that." He dangled his mitts beside his knees and looked at the floor. "Maybe you can tell *Harv* here that if he wants to step up like the big man, he can—"

"Let's all sit down over here," the woman said. "I'll get this…"

"You going to all the parents with this?" the man asked.

"Yes, sir."

"And what do you *do* again, Mr. Buttfucker?"

"I teach high school."

"I ride with the State Troopers Auxiliary on Saturday nights."

My dad all over again. It was a mistake, sure, but for the sake of families everywhere I thought I'd have my say this one time.

"Most kids," I said, resting my elbow on the doorknob, "appreciate it if their mothers and fathers can act like human beings. It makes a real difference, long-term."

"I'm on the PTA, all right?" Still staring at me, Dave Saunders took his glasses off to clean them on his shirttail—his eyelids were yellow. "So you can kiss your little job goodbye. What's your name?"

"Like you said, the name's Buttfucker." I stepped back onto the front step. "Make sure Harv gets enough to eat tonight."

"It's lasagna!" the woman called.

I started down the steps, and the door closed behind me. I'd got Harv in from the cold—that had been the main thing, right? Ear in hand, I hurried to my car but then he was jogging out to the sidewalk. His house was quiet behind him. In the twilight everything looked brown.

"Uh, thanks, I guess," he said.

"Sure," I said. "Let me know if you have any problems, one way or the other. It, uh, happens some families just don't quite fit together."

He put his foot on my bumper.

"Or some people don't deserve to have children. My grandpa said that one time."

"Well, that's a fine line. Being a parent isn't the easiest. Different pressures on everybody." I opened my door. "Where's your mom, if you don't mind my asking?"

"We don't know."

A pickup truck stopped in the street and a girl in a black-and-red Pizza Hut uniform slid down from the passenger seat.

"What's going on?" she called to Harv. "Is Dad okay?"

Then I felt anxious as a mother bear about Josie and Ray—I wasn't late yet but every second was absolutely critical, like it might be faster if I ran behind the car and pushed it. As I flew up Clemons, they had to be thinking, *Even when Mom was so nauseous she could hardly hold the steering wheel, she was never late picking us up.* And from the look on Carla the sitter's face, when I finally stood smiling in her carport, she also believed some people didn't deserve to have children.

"Your mother-in-law called at ten this morning to say *she'd* be getting them from school." She glared at me through the screen, working a toothpick behind her bicuspid. "Sometimes I think if the Lord hadn't screwed your head on tight you'd—"

"I can survive without additional information," I said.

AT 4:30 I was home again, rubbing my feet—they *did* smell woody, like I'd been camping—and watching NFL-wide completion-percentage stats scroll across the bottom of the TV while Josie, Ray and Deb dug something up in the backyard. Smelled something yeasty in the oven. The phone rang.

"Peter Giller!" I answered, always anticipating the board office even if I was booked for a month already.

"Mr. Giller, this is Miss Federici? Ray's teacher?"

If he'd done something praiseworthy they'd have sent home a participation ribbon in the front of his daytimer, maybe a certificate slathered in *Toy Story* stickers, so this wasn't good. Acid reflux quivered up into my chest.

"Oh. What's up?"

"I thought I'd better call 'cause there was a bit of an incident today."

She described how at Colts Neck Elementary one of the long ceiling tiles was being replaced in the primary boys' washroom, leaving a black rectangular gap that showed the air ducts. At recess Ray had kicked his shoe up into the gap so that it landed on the next tile over, eight feet above the floor, and one of the boys had a brother in fifth grade, tallest kid in the school, so with this tall kid standing on a chair and Ray on this tall kid's shoulders, they'd tried to retrieve the shoe—I could picture it up in the dark and cobwebs, a little white Adidas I'd bought at the Target in Kearney. Ray had wrapped his hand around it then slipped and brought that tile down too—his fall thankfully cushioned by his rubbernecking friends. Colts Neck had it in the budget to pay for a second tile, of course, but they'd decided that to make up for it Ray would help the custodian at recess for all of next week.

"But more importantly, how's Ray?" she asked. "He didn't limp or anything when I looked at him, but you know how once they're at home they let their guard down the littlest bit?"

"I haven't noticed anything," I said. "Maybe that's my fault about the shoe. We'd been talking about parabolas."

Miss Federici hung up to go walk her dog, and I breathed slowly and deeply up my nose. What would my own father, the great Bill Giller, have done in my situation? A headlock, for starters, then a knee in the small of my back. I went onto the back step and called Ray inside—they'd found an old birdhouse under the porch and both kids were up the ladder, trying to balance it on a branch. I steered him into the living room.

"Your teacher just called. You know what for, right?"

"You know what they call roly-polies here?" He tucked a lock of brittle blond hair behind his ear. "Pill bugs. In Wahoo they're roly-polies, remember?"

"The right name is wood louse."

He opened his eyes wide but I can't say he raised his eyebrows because he was too fair to have any. There wasn't any blondness on my side or Lydia's so she and I always joked that he was really Owen Wilson's—the sarcastic actor with the broken nose—though Ray's usual expression was too solemn for him to be Owen Wilson's. And he'd told the preschool class in Wahoo, with all the gravity of a burning bush, that his dad's name was Pete, *exactly like Pete Townsend in The Who.*

"Oh!" he said now. "Did she say I'm going into the split one-two 'cause I'm such a better reader than anybody?"

"Listen, no, buddy, she…"

I studied his oblivious face and felt pressure build in my chest— someone had lit a burner to fill it like a hot-air balloon, and ever since I was a kid that'd meant *angry,* but sitting there on the coffee table with Ray perched on our big green chair, I couldn't have said who I was mad at—Miss Federici, the Dockside guys, they'd all done their jobs, and God knew Ray had been through enough to justify launching a shoe into a bathroom ceiling. Jeez, why'd his hair look so flimsy? I'd have to look up how to get more vitamin E into his diet, or maybe he just needed to move back to Wahoo and hug his mom. Ray's eyes went to my left ear seconds before my fingers settled on it.

"Soup's on, sweethearts!" called Deb.

She ceded a point to our radical lifestyle and served storebought veggie pizza for supper. It steamed there on the cutting board and I fantasized about the thousand diverse ground meats that might gladly call a pizza home, all that salt, oh, and the grease—

"There was a funny accident on the field trip today," I said as I flapped Ray's napkin across his lap. "We all got splashed with some kind of plastic."

I threw slices onto everybody's plates. I glanced over at Ray and saw his eyes stretched as big as quarters.

"What's up?" I managed to ask.

"What was the accident?"

"Oh, buddy, I'm fine. Please don't worry about the accident. It was dumb."

He dipped a crinkle-cut french fry in his ketchup and somehow that reminded me of a severed finger.

"Everyone's really all right." I said.

I showed the table the reassuring smile I'd been practicing for so long—because we were making headway on this normal life without their mother, right?

"Why'd you guys have the assembly this afternoon?" asked Deb. She tilted her head at me. "They were late coming out."

"Oh," murmured Josie, "this solider guy came and—"

Ray covered his mouth, clattering his fork against his plate. Sick?

"It was so *not funny*!" Josie's eyes sawed him in half. "You're so retarded!"

"Hey, keep cool," I said. "What *is* so funny, Ray?"

Both hands over his mouth now, he looked from me to Deb and back again with huge, joyous eyes. Deb put her fingertips together to form, perhaps, a temple of serenity.

"He *said*," Josie went on, "that people without arms or legs need more understanding. There was this girl who fought in the Congo and these kids at this mall in Omaha made fun of her."

"That was on the radio," said Deb.

"Sorry." Ray let out a deep breath and picked up his fork.

"Was the soldier at the assembly missing an arm or a leg?" I asked.

"One of each." Josie chewed thoughtfully. "It was freaky."

"*Hey*," I said, "that doesn't sound very unders—"

"But he said if he had arms and legs he'd go fight *again*, until the whole war was over, because nobody who lives there can stop running away long enough to grow food or go to the doctor, so most kids our age are all dead, and you know what from?"

"Jesus." Should I have been impressed or horrified that she knew how fucked up the world was? "Malnutrition?"

Ray's eyes got big again, and he set his fork down.

"Landmines?" Deb asked.

"Nope," Josie said, "it's—"

"Diarrhea!" shouted Ray.

Sunday, October 23.

JACKSONVILLE'S SAD ATTEMPT at an onside kick went out of bounds and that was the game, 27–6 for the good guys, so I staggered out of my stuffy bedroom with my veggie platter's untouched celery—the sight of it turned my stomach, which was weird. And watching football didn't usually leave my legs so stiff. It was nearly dark outside, and the kids were panting and sweaty from Unicorn Quest, a backyard invention of Josie's, so while Deb took a bath I read them Roald Dahl on the plaid loveseat, and once Mr. Hoppy had successfully tampered with nature to win Mrs. Silver's hand I put their heads in my armpits.

"Gah," said Ray.

"Da-ad!" said Josie.

"While I've got you where I want you," I told them, "you should know that I love you donkeys an awful lot. I'm going to buy you each a trough to sleep in."

Josie brushed her hair off her face. "Dad, didn't you even notice?"

"Grandma bought all the lights!" shouted Ray.

Sure enough, strings of red and white Christmas lights had been hung in a horseshoe between the living and dining rooms, casting an aura of holiday pinkness.

"Do you like them?" Deb yelled from the tub. "Kmart had a huge sale and I thought what the heck!"

"I told her," Ray said quietly. "Mom only liked them on the tree."

"You'd think she'd remember," said Josie.

They both pressed their heads against my ribs.

"I guess we could try something radically different," I said.

Deb was boiling a pot of water and warming up the frying pan, so I poured my after-Dahl glass of Lucky Bucket then wiped off the kitchen counter. From my bedroom the TV spouted power chords and overly chirpy voices of indeterminate gender, which meant Josie and Ray had found one of those crap Japanese cartoons that serve only to promote collectible holographic cards. Another father would've switched it to something wholesome like Elmer Fudd blasting Daffy Duck in the face with a shotgun, spinning his bill around to the back of his head. Deb peeled carrots into my mom's green Pyrex bowl that Lydia had coveted for so long—carrot strips dangled over the side.

"What does hairy Mr. Vincent have you doing nowadays?" asked Deb.

"Still science. Bits of everything, nine through twelve."

"How about Stephen Hawking?"

"Theoretical physics might scare off the nines," I said.

"Oh, I know, but that movie of his life was just on, and God—*so* sad. A brain like that, and looking down at this body that's just, I don't know, useless. A dead fish."

I pictured half-crumpled Lydia in her last weeks, staggering across the ward to the toilet so she could at least *crap* like a human being. Deb might've been picturing the same thing because she was moving her tongue across her teeth and staring at the wall.

"Careful," I said.

She looked in time to not peel her finger.

"Maybe Hawking would want to be the other way around," she said. "He'd have a super-terrific body and a brain that couldn't tell one way or the other."

She slid cut-glass bowls of carrot sticks and dill-flecked dip into the middle of the island—in her production of snacks she defied the space-time continuum. Deb lifted the bag of perogies out of the freezer and dropped them on the counter with a crack. I took down the Aspirin.

"You all right?" she asked.

"Beer's doing something weird. But not a headache. Like an armache."

"There's bacon for the perogies, that ought to cheer you up."

I finished my glass of water. "Good joke."

"Oh, just look through there—aren't they sweet like that?"

She opened her camera bag, twisted out the legs on her tripod, and I tiptoed after her to my bedroom doorway. On the TV a lot of spiky-haired characters in puffy jackets sat astride a winged horse. In the big viewfinder Deb framed Josie and Ray, unblinking, fingertips to their lips, the bluish TV light flickering across their foreheads.

"When I put it on the YouTube," she whispered, "I'll call it 'My Little Zombies.'"

DEB COOKED HALF of her pound of bacon and primly set the steaming platter in front of her own place. The kids and I smirked at each other like this woman and her meat were bumbling exchange students from another hemisphere. The perogies and steamed broccoli made their rounds—as the red and white lights made the cutlery twinkle pinkly. Deb offered her granddaughter the bacon tongs.

"No, thanks," Josie scowled.

"Ray? You want to try a piece?"

He shook his head, a green floret drooping from his lip like a damp cigarette.

"I just don't think it's good for people to be, well, *cemented* into any one thing," Deb told us. "You can't even have a bite?"

"You know why we don't," I said.

"So tell me what we'll do after dinner."

"On Sunday we play Uno before pee and teeth," said Ray.

"Well, then, should we do something different this time?"

"Uno's fine," said Josie, brows furrowed as she spooned out sour cream.

Deb shook her head at me down the tablecloth. But her eyes twinkled.

"I told your father," she announced, "that he should go to Pawnee next weekend."

"Oh!" Ray slid a flap of brittle hair behind his ear. "Do we have to go?"

"I'm not going either," I said.

"If you kids *want* to go, you should go too!" Deb said. "You have fun when you visit Grandma Jackie, right?"

Josie looked at her sideways, sour cream now on her cheek.

"Yes," she said flatly.

"And Evadare's so nice!" said Deb.

"She smells." Ray worried a perogie with the side of his fork. "A little."

"No, *Ray*," said his sister, "that's Grandma Jackie."

"It's just her tubes," I said. "It's not her fault. Pass that bacon down here, Jos. I want a good whiff for old time's sake."

Josie set the plate in front of me then surreptitiously licked grease off her thumb. The strips were arranged in intricate angles like a game of pick-up sticks.

"It looks like the little pig's house," Ray said with his mouth full.

"Like, after."

"I just thought the exact same thing."

"It'd suck to be the pig," Josie murmured. "No house."

"I want to ask you seriously," said Deb, "how well do you remember Pappy Art?"

"Before he died?" asked Ray.

Josie rolled her eyes.

"Black jujubes," her brother said.

"And the noisy trains, do you still have those?" Josie asked.

"Are you all right?" Deb asked me. "You look like you're going to throw up!"

"I felt weird all day. I'm fine."

"Did you ever meet Dad's dad?" Josie asked her.

My head swam like I'd been smoking weed. I took two strips of bacon and laid them beside my broccoli. The only thought in my head was *This'll help.*

"Oh, Billy Giller was a man who liked his helpings." Deb beamed at the kids. "Pork roast, marshmallow-rhubarb pie, always lots of helpings!"

I speared my fork through the bacon, dragged it through the sour cream then crammed the masterpiece into my mouth.

"Was he real fat?" asked Ray.

"And *I* can tell you," I said as I chewed, "what Grandma Jackie *used* to be like. She was tall as me, wouldn't know that to see her, and her feet were two different shapes from where a horse stepped on her! Man." I finally swallowed, wiped my mouth with the napkin. "And she'd sing John Denver for a hundred miles—cheesiest stuff!"

"Dad," murmured Josie.

I smiled at the three of them with teeth that felt generous and expansive. *Ah,* something was saying inside me, *thank you.* They gazed at me in the wash of pink, like they'd been caught in the Dockside deluge too.

"You ate *bacon!*" Josie said with a catch in her voice. "You just ate bacon!"

"It's not veggie, I told you that," said Deb.

"Well, my headache's gone," I said, "that's the main thing."

"But you took the Aspirin, you said it was a bad arm!"

"Anyway, I feel a hundred percent better. I've got to do my prep for tomorrow, excuse me from the table." I stood up and cleared my plate.

"It's not going to murder me overnight, you guys, eat that up, then we'll have Uno!"

Josie dropped her head on her wrists, shoulders shaking—sobbing! Ray went around the table and patted her back, and Deb squeezed the kid's hand and glared at me.

"Hey," I told her, "careful what you wish for."

Because hadn't Deb been bending over backwards for me to eat bacon? But then as I carried my plate into the kitchen I saw Lydia in her wedding dress and remembered that *Never eat charred meat* was our family's mantra.

"Jos?" I called, my voice echoing in the empty room. I didn't want to go back and have her look at me. "I'm sorry, baby!"

"THIS FAT OFF the bacon's all congealed now," Deb told me as I dried plates. She held up my greasy old mason jar. "Into the trash?"

"Uh, no, no thanks. Josie's collecting it for a science project," I lied. "Just pop it in the fridge."

In those tearaway track pants, Deb's narrow ass looked exactly like Lydia's—yes, I consciously had that thought. I was sure having an evening.

"Did you put the bacon away? I'll make myself sandwiches tomorrow."

"Um, no," I said. "Haven't seen it."

"You still smell like sawdust, why is that? Go shower."

Monday, October 24.

I WOKE UP woozy, the baby pictures on the dresser crawling in and out of focus, so in my pyjamas and untied housecoat I tugged the second half-pound of bacon out from its hiding place under the romaine lettuce. I fried it up crispy as potato chips, and after generous taste-testing my nausea evaporated.

Deb stood beside the fridge with the pint of cream in her hand, diaphanous muumuu in its glory. Lydia, in her wedding dress, peered over her mother's shoulder.

"I guess I should be happy we're eating the same things now, but I read that only when bacon is really overcooked do its nitrite levels become dangerously high."

Nitrites, that sounded delicious—maybe I was craving more than just fat and salt? I put the bacon on the table beside two bowls of Cream of Wheat and yelled to Josie and Ray, then the doorbell rang. Early in the day, even for Jehovah's Witnesses. Before I could slump toward the front door I crammed two more strips in my mouth.

Amber and Grace, from the field trip, stood hunched on my porch. I knew it was a school day, sure, but hadn't really pondered what state any of my elevens would be in when they shuffled into my classroom. The girls wore ball caps and their skull hoodies, old eyeliner clotted at the corners of their eyes, and Amber seemed to be having a problem with one arm—a sleeve dangled loose.

"Mr. Giller?" said Grace. "Hey, it seemed like something was going on with you too, so we—"

"You hurt your arm?" I asked Amber.

"Not too bad," she mumbled.

Her baby-blue car sat with one wheel up on the curb.

"Hey," I started to ask, "have you guys been eating—"

"Show him," said Grace.

Amber glared, then with her one hand tugged up the hem of her hoodie until her shoulder appeared, in the middle of her belly where no shoulder was meant to be. I saw the knob of bone. It wasn't attached to her. My new-found aversion to celery became inconsequential.

"Oh," I said. "Jeez."

A purplish lip showed at the edge of the broken skin. The detached shoulder somehow reminded me of that hollow feeling I'd been having in my arms and legs.

"See?" said Grace. "It's gross."

"I must've slept on it funny," said Amber.

I ran my tongue around my teeth, collecting the lovely black fragments of bacon, and tried to picture exactly how much pink goo had hit Amber—more than had hit me, right? She lowered the hem and cradled the detached arm beneath the fabric, like it was a puppy she was sneaking into school. They needed some kind of help, these two, but it was hard to think past the heap of bacon I'd just set on the table.

"Does it *hurt*?" I asked.

They both shook their heads. As recently as Friday I'd have brought them in for breakfast if they'd come to the door for any reason, much less this dismemberment, but the bedside manner I'd perfected with Lydia had gone up the range hood like steam.

"Take it to a hospital?" I suggested.

Amber twisted her lips and studied my welcome mat.

"She doesn't like needles," said Grace.

"Tell the doctor you want general anaesthetic, that'll be the mask."

Amber took a creaking step backward.

"She doesn't like gas either," explained Grace.

They'd stick a saline drip in her good arm anyway, and jab her for tetanus, but I wanted them gone before the *nitrites* ran off the bacon—man, the word rang in my head like a bell!

"Take her to the hospital anyway," I told Grace. "You're driving, right? Or you want a cab instead?"

They just looked at each other, so I went inside to the hallway phone and dialed for a taxi they didn't need. I stood by the framed baby pictures but didn't even glance up in case I saw my reflection in the glass, because I didn't want to know what this version of me looked like.

The dispatcher put me on hold. I glanced outside. The girls and car were gone.

I slammed the phone down and ran back to the kitchen, fast as Antonio Brown. I found my kids in their terry-cloth housecoats at the kitchen table, knees up on their chairs as Josie pushed the plastic maple syrup bottle across to Ray. No bacon platter in sight. My quadriceps and hamstrings suddenly quit working so I fell on the floor—maybe I tripped? But I kept crawling toward the table.

I twisted my face up at the kids. "Where—where is it?"

"Holy cow!" said Ray. "You okay?"

Josie didn't even look at me, just held her hair back as she ferried a spoonful of cereal toward her mouth.

"In the garbage," she said.

"Shit," I yelled, "don't you know I *need* that?"

I stumbled to my feet and lurched toward the trash. With a gasp Deb turned from the sink, still testing the water with a finger under the tap.

"I told her it was a waste," she hissed, "but, Peter, I can see where she—"

"I *need* it!"

Like little nerve-gas victims the bacon strips lay splayed in the bottom of the bin, amongst apple cores, Deb's gushy tissues and a Baker's Chocolate wrapper. I scooped the bacon out, still warm like little birds, and thrust the handful accusingly under Josie's nose. Both kids' eyes widened and their little throats swallowed hard.

"Now, Peter!" Deb called. "Just you—"

I swung toward her, slammed the bacon back into the grease-smeared pan and carried the whole works into the sunshine on the back steps, slamming the door behind me.

"Sorry!" I yelled into the reticent wood.

I sat with the pan in my lap, gnawing through the bacon before tackling the pan itself, sucking back bubbly grease by the thumbful, but my arms still felt stuffed with lit matches. I licked the pan so the grease got all in my hair, then I dove under the steps for my dad's shovel—yes, the one we'd buried Keister with—and knocked the kids' birdhouse out of its maple tree and smashed the little thing to smithereens, bringing the shovel's blade down again and again.

I picked a splinter out of the shovel's handle, and maybe the bacon had hit my system by then because I finally remembered to take a long breath in. Their birdhouse was pulp between my feet—was that normal? The situation was going to take figuring out.

I remembered that I had Rob Aiken's phone number.

INSIDE, I TOLD the kids I was sorry and Josie said she was sorry too. Deb leaned against the counter with her arms folded—she'd already changed into her jeans and hummingbird-patterned sweatshirt.

"I'm going to call that grief counselor in Wahoo today," she said. "Get him to recommend somebody here."

"Bring it on," I said, for no reason I could really pin down.

"Did Ms. Federici say I had to be there right away to scrape gum?" asked Ray.

"No, buddy, no. Recess."

"I've started making the lunches," announced Deb. "That's okay?"

I showered to get the pig fat out of my hair, then as I dressed for school the nail of my big toe cut through the end of my sock. That happens with socks, especially if you don't clip your nails, so what was my civilized reaction? I lifted the TV from my dresser and flung it through the window into the front yard. The TV screen imploded on the lawn and long daggers of window-glass embedded themselves in the dirt. Deb was already out putting the kids in her car, so they were standing at the curb when it happened.

"Dad?" Josie called, voice breaking again.

Deb grabbed her hand and helped her into the back seat. An Alice's Flowers van was parked across the street, and at first glance I thought the guy in the passenger seat was pointing a camera at our house. But then the van was squealing off down the street.

I taped a garbage bag over the smashed window and headed to work.

I DIDN'T SEE the lunchtime wiener massacre myself because I was back at home alone just then, standing at the kitchen counter to fry and eat a freshly bought pound of bacon, followed by an arduous session of flossing carcinogenic material out of my back teeth— drawing blood more than once—and that ate up time, so right before the second bell I was running, tie flapping, down the main hallway toward my classroom. Cam Vincent caught me by standing stock-still under the picture of Eisenhower, sporting the same rubber-lipped half-smile of our former president, arms folded with an identical stoicism, though with hairstyles from *diametrically opposed ends of the animal kingdom.*

I thought those very words because, thanks to all that bacon, my brain was operating at the peak of lubrication.

"Peter. So," said Cam, "we had a cafeteria incident just now."

"Involving who?" I asked, though I knew. I might've gone wobbly in the knees if the bacon hadn't propped me up.

"Um." He gave me a look. "These were all kids from your Chemistry 11. I've got them in my office while Mrs. Abel tries to get the cops to come back."

"Why, did somebody—?"

"And I want the district counselors in here tomorrow, yeah. Amber Morton strolled in after C block, you see her?"

"No."

"She's got one arm. Acts like it's nothing—told me she's *always* had one arm, and the way she walks around, no trauma, no tears, I believed it for a second. I can't even think straight about it, I mean, how—"

"I need to talk to those kids, can I?"

He squared his shoulders as we passed the half-empty trophy case.

"I'd appreciate it if you could tell me what to do with them."

We sidled into the office and Kathleen, in a yellow dress, paused in watering her fern to give me an apologetic smile. We stopped at Cam's blue door, six inches ajar.

"Who's your class right now?" Cam asked. "I'll go hang out with them."

"The nines. Genetics quiz, multicolored hamsters and that."

"They hear about that human ear somebody grew out of a mouse's back?"

"Probably not."

"Kids love that freaky stuff."

He strode out into the hallway, more of a spring in his step now that I was apparently on the case, though I still hadn't found out what had actually happened in the cafeteria. Kathleen turned the fan on beside her desk and started typing.

"Seriously!" Grace was saying in Cam's office. "You weren't in gym with him?"

"I was last year," said Shawn quietly, "but I never saw anything like that."

How many were in there?

"But the size, I mean, it doesn't really matter what size it is when it's, like, soft." Was that Megan Avery, seriously? "It can start out real small and get big, you know, after."

"Really, Megan, *really*?" asked Amber.

"This whole thing is making me so turned on right now," Clint said, stonily.

"Sure it's true," said Megan.

I slid into the gap in the doorway. Grace and Amber were perched on Cam's desk and the rest of them sat in a circle on the floor like a "Kumbaya" singalong. Amber wore a green T-shirt that showed a snarling bear. One short sleeve hung like a napkin, because apparently she still had no left arm.

"Know what, bitches?" Franny sat up on her knees, some godawful purple brooch on her shoulder. "If we want to know if it's *so* big he passes *out* when it's hard, all we've got to do is *get* him hard!"

"Or we could ask his dick about it when Harv's not in the room," suggested Eric.

"I would totally fuck him either way," said Amber, applying chapstick then slipping the lid back on with just the one hand. "Front of my car. Gravel pit."

"Man, I would so pay to see that!" said Grace, hunting for something in Cam's jar of pencils. "You guys would look so hot together!"

This was the sad-eyed war protester? We'd lost our inhibitions, that's all it was. And for years I'd wanted to throw a TV out a window?

"Shit yes! So can we all at least agree on *that*?" Amber asked.

Down on the floor, Franny, Shawn, Megan, Clint and Eric and his mullet all nodded grudgingly. This was enough of a lull for Franny to notice I'd come in.

"Oh, hey, Gillbrick! They tell you we made the caff too popular?"

"They haven't told me a thing. So the hospital couldn't get it back on?"

Flexing her skinny right arm, Amber grimaced up at me. Whitest possible teeth.

"We didn't go," said Grace.

"Hey-hey, G," said Franny, "you can totally take us to Walgreens! Independence, man, buy up some bacon, get us a load of frying pans—"

"Shawn, am I freaking out right now?" asked Clint. "Is that what I think it is on your shirt?"

Shawn pulled his bangs back to look at the shoulder of his plaid shirt.

"It *is*!" hollered Clint, and though cross-legged he somehow launched himself across the office, tackling Shawn around the middle to press his face to his lapel.

"Aw, damn!" Megan shuffled over to avoid getting squashed. "I was next to him all the time and never even smelled it!"

"Dude," Shawn grunted. "Off."

"All right, listen!" I said, and my hands produced an almighty clap. "Who else in here has bacon on their shirt?"

They inspected each other, sniffed their own cuffs.

"Shawn, sorry, man." Clint sat up in the middle of the circle and retied his scarf. "That was a sweet little nugget."

"Can't we go now?" asked Amber.

"No, I've got to figure this out." I sat down, squeezing between the mullet and Megan's turquoise cardigan. "What the hell did you do to get shut in here?"

"Oh, honky!" Franny snorted. "It was classic!"

To synthesize the seven simultaneous stories: at 12:05, as I was sprinting across the parking lot to my car, these gentle, well-meaning kids approached the cafeteria and read the daily special scrawled in yellow chalk, BACON DOGS. But they found a dozen kids already in line and, God forbid, a couple of ninth-grade freaks actually in the act of *finishing* their bacon dogs right there on the spot! Mrs. Abel had gone out for a smoke, leaving the Culinary Skills 12 students to man the chafing dishes. My seven grabbed slotted spoons and chased everybody out, barricading the doors by locking the wheels on the ketchup cart. Ninety seconds later the chafing dishes had been licked clean and my seven walked out as though nothing had happened. One of the freaks had already called the cops on his cell phone, unfortunately, but Mr. Vincent met the officers at the front doors and no one, it turned out, had wanted to press charges.

"So where in all that," I asked, glancing at Eric, "did you get the black eye?"

"I was in the wrong," he shrugged. "Took more than my share."

"Okay." I draped my elbows across my knees. "I need to figure this out."

The kids looked at me. All sarcasm had evaporated from the air.

"Tell you what," I said. "Yesterday morning I was a vegetarian. Last night my mother-in-law cooked bacon for the family and I ate it before I realized what I was doing, I ate more this morning, then another pound from Walgreens just now at home. That's—"

"What kind did you get?" asked Franny.

"Oscar Mayer Thick Cut. On sale, actually."

Clint leapt to his feet, straightening his jacket.

"Stay on task, we aren't going yet," I said. "In the last eighteen hours I've eaten enough to make someone who *really likes bacon* sick, and I wasn't even that crazy about it back when I ate meat. Now, is that roughly the same experience that everyone's had?"

"I kept saying last night I was only going to eat a couple of strips." Grace rubbed her eye with the back of her hand. "So I cooked those, ate 'em, then I just did it again and again and again. I was up until one-thirty."

They all shifted how they were sitting.

"I kept waiting to barf, the more I ate," Shawn said quietly. "And I never did."

"And nobody had habitually eaten that much bacon *prior* to eighteen hours ago?"

"I totally got into Rhinoceros last night!" said Amber. "Do I look twenty-one? No, but I'm, like, 'Screw that, I'm not waiting five more frickin' years, I'm going,' and the bouncer just waved me in! I bought the wristband for dollar shots!" She held up her bare arm proudly. "Oh, it was the other wrist. But there were guys with rodeo belt buckles, like the big ones! And I said to this chick there, I just said, 'Drool.'"

"What about bacon, how much did you have?"

Her shoulders slumped. "Half a package. Just what Grace hadn't eaten yet, the little pig, and she'd stayed home to write some stupid Congo speech but she never did!"

"You better not slag Congo, bitch," said Grace.

"I know why you're into that, but you couldn't come to Rhinoceros too?"

"I threw down with my brother," said Clint. "And I utterly kicked his ass, and *he's* on the college wrestling team. He was crying at the bottom of the stairs, and I was, like, 'I will eat your heart, man, I will totally eat your heart.'"

"Oh," I said. "What did you mean by that?"

"No idea."

"C'mon, you!" Franny rolled her eyes at him.

"Shut up," said Clint, "you're the one who ripped her bathroom door off!"

"What? I had to pee so bad!"

"What about any unusual cuts or bruises or...healing?" I asked. "I'm sorry I couldn't help you with the arm, Amber, but it's really a miracle you never bled to death."

"Oh, no problem," she said.

"Okay," said Eric, nervously stroking his mullet. "The neighbor brought his dog over, ugly dog that looked like a butt, and I guess it didn't like me because it jumped up and it…" His hand stopped over his ear. "It bit me a bit."

"Tore your ear off?" I asked.

"Only halfway. But funny thing was, it didn't even hurt. Whole bottom half was just flapping." He moved his hand away but the ear looked pristine—maybe it'd been the other one. "I didn't really say any-thing 'cause I didn't want to bug the neighbor, right? So I put staples in it and went to bed."

"This ear that's on your head?"

"Yup." He tugged at it. "Just needed a good night's sleep!"

"Staples!" Grace smiled at Amber. "*That's* what we should've done!"

"What about the people who aren't here? What about Jacob or Ryan or Lydia, anybody seen them? Scott Barnes?"

"Jacob's brother said he's sick."

"Okay, okay, wait," said Amber from the desk, lifting her hand above us like a Baptist. "I just thought up a haiku about the thing we were talking about before."

"Seriously, Harv's dick?" asked Shawn. "Is it cool to keep talking about that?"

"What about Harv?" I asked. "He hasn't been here at all?"

"Aw, you never heard that?" Franny wiped her mouth. "Harv total-ly hates his sister, right? So the kid on the bus said Harv stuffed her mouth with bacon, Beanie Babies, then *microwaved her head*."

"It's that pink stuff," said Grace. She thudded her sneakers against the front of Cam's desk. "Let's be real. It's not like this is complicated. It's cause and effect."

"What was the name of their superstar—Rob something?" asked Clint. "We should call that guy up, ask him what the hell."

"Yeah, maybe Rob'll say it'll all go back to normal after, like, a day," said Grace.

"Why go back to normal," asked Amber, "what's so bad about this?"

"I do have his number, that's something." I sprang to my feet—usually I got stiff sitting cross-legged, but I was spry as a fox. "My last class Thursday's just prep, I could drive back to Velouria and talk to them, but let's see how the next couple days go, maybe this'll all, I don't know, subside." Maybe if I hadn't been their teacher, diplomatic to a fault because that was the job, I would've admitted there was no chance of that happening. "Megan, hey, what's your mom been like since Friday? Plenty of bacon?"

"She's loud," she said, toying with her cardigan button. "Yells a bit more."

"I don't mind that my ear grew back on," said Eric. "Guy without an ear would look screwball."

"Hey, my dad can call them," said Franny. "He does that all the time."

"Absolutely not, but thank you. I'll look after this."

"So then can we all go to class, Beanie Babies?" She climbed to her feet and brushed down her jean skirt. "Or is Abel sending us to hot, hot lesbian prison?"

"I guess I could take a ninja down," Clint said to no one. "They aren't tough."

"So was the idea that Harv would *eat* the head?" Shawn asked Franny.

"I think you should all go home and get some sleep," I said. "Seriously, does anybody know where Harv is?"

My concern was that I'd have disemboweled Dave Saunders if I was in Harv's position and the committee might frown upon that when Harv applied for scholarships.

CHEMISTRY 11 WAS last period, in my stuffy classroom with its tattered entomology posters and faded globe—Czechoslovakia was apparently still one country—and Dr. Reid's informational fax still on the desk. The only kids perched at their benches, of course, were the three who'd missed Friday's field trip.

"Where the heck are they all?" asked Devon.

"They found the bale of pot that fell out of that airplane," said Jordie.

I told the three boys that if you sketch the atoms in an inorganic molecule they'll line up to look either left- or right-handed, but an organic molecule is *always* left-handed, and how did nature possibly come up with that? Not curriculum, but it was cool, and kept me from smashing my forehead through the cabinet of Bunsen burners. Then I gave them handouts to color and, because I had a bad feeling, trotted to the office to ask Kathleen if there'd been any calls from Harv Saunders' home to explain his absence.

"There was this morning," she said, red hair in a bun now. "His dad said flu."

AFTER THE DISMISSAL bell she called me back to the office over the PA—an update on Harv, I figured. But Kathleen slid a milky-yellow business card across the counter.

"This, ah, gentleman just left," she explained. "Wanted to know the names and addresses of the kids and teacher who were over in Velouria yesterday. Said he represented the parent company. I said that access to that information would be between him and the school district, my hands were completely tied as far as handing over that sort of information. So he left this."

JAMES JONES, the card read. PENZLER INDUSTRIES. And a fax number.

"Thought you'd want to know," Kathleen said.

"He didn't say why?"

Compensation! I was thinking. *Deep-breathing methods to calm us down!*

"No. Just looked at me and wrote in a little book, then said he had lots of appointments and out he went."

"What'd he look like? Maybe I'll spot him around."

"Gray suit," said Kathleen, shrugging. "Gray hair."

Or maybe he's come to explain what the hell's happened to us.

IN THE PIZZA Hut parking lot a woman with a baggie over her hand picked up her little dog's poop.

"In the future the dogs will pick up after *us*," Josie said from the back of the car.

"And dogs'll poop in the toilet!" said Ray.

"That stuff's science fiction," Deb told them.

We waited behind a guy in a wheelchair at the takeout counter, manned by a fuzzy-moustached senior from the high school. A plastic bin beside the till asked for SPARE CHANGE FOR THE CONGO REFUGEES. I made Deb walk all around the restaurant, hunting for a short girl with a brown ponytail, and if there was no sign of her then all we were going to get out of Pizza Hut was pizza. Then just as it was our turn, the guy at the counter went on break and Harv's sister pushed past him, her black visor square to her brow like she was a ninth-inning relief pitcher.

"Hey," I said, "I don't know if you remember me, I was at your house—"

"What?" she said.

"Come on, we're *starving*," someone hissed behind me.

"Well, I'm one of Harv's teachers and I was worried he might've been sick today, because…"

"Harv's fine," she said. "Ask him yourself, he's across the street."

I peered out the window. A half-dozen people ambled around in front of Walgreens—mostly seniors with piles of plastic grocery bags.

"Is that him with the hat?" I asked.

"That's our boy," she said. "Were you going to order? Because—"

"Hawaiian!" screamed Josie and Ray.

"A large Hawaiian with triple bacon."

"I don't know why I bought the veggie burgers," said Deb.

The pizza was going to be twenty-five minutes so I left her and the kids solving a word search on the back of a menu and jogged across the street to where Harv, arms folded, leaned against the pay phone outside the Walgreens entrance. The setting sun was in his eyes so he had to tilt his sky-blue Oklahoma City Thunder cap to look at me from under the brim.

"Sir, would you be able to buy me a pack of Camels?" he asked, rolling a crumpled five between his fingers.

"Harv, it's me," I said. "Mr. Giller, remember?"

"Oh, sure." The five disappeared. "I was just out today with the flu."

"What are you—you don't smoke, do you?"

"Ah, no, no. My dad just…"

He lifted off his ball cap to scratch his hairline and in the blaze of setting sun across his head I saw a thick scar stretching from his left eyebrow across to behind his right ear. Weird I'd never noticed it before, since he'd always had a buzz cut. Tiny bald patches ran up either side of the scar.

"Jesus, man," I said, "did something happen to your head?"

He muttered that he'd been pruning elms with his dad and there'd been an accident.

"What in hell were you pruning with?"

"Chainsaws," he said.

"Christ almighty, how long ago was that?"

"Yesterday morning," he grinned. "My dad looked after it. He said we're going out on the dirt bikes on Saturday!"

"Well, Jesus," I said. "Maybe wear a helmet."

He peered behind me, so I looked too. No prospective Camel-buyers.

"Want to hear my movie idea?" He twisted his hat back onto his head. "See, there's this town where nothing's going on, but the parents think the basketball team might win the state championship even though the guys on the team are all, 'No way.'"

"Sounds great," I said through my teeth. "Look, I wanted to ask—"

"But *then* they sign up for this science experiment with, like, a professor who gives them all this strength and agility and stuff, so then they win the championship and the whole town's going crazy, shooting off fireworks, but then, just as the soundtrack's going all high-pitched and violins, the guys all fall down dead."

"Because of the experiment?"

"Yeah! So in the audience you'd feel really happy one second and then the next super-sad. And the parents would be looking down at the dead kids, and they'd be, like, 'Man, jeez, was that really what we wanted?' Cool, right?"

"What made you think of that?" I asked.

"I don't know—I missed the game the other night because we were late from Velouria, so I had to help Dad staple his notices up, that's when I thought of it."

"Jeez. What do his notices say exactly?"

OUT-OF-TOWNERS BRING IN UNWANTED ELEMENTS?

"Oh, just ads. He goes to old people's houses and gives 'em massages. Lot of his clients have passed away but Kim, that's his girlfriend, she makes good money. She's a notary public."

"Dad!" Josie stood outside the restaurant, hands cupping her mouth. "Pizza!"

"That your kid?"

"One of them," I said.

So if babbling and unrestrained healing were any indication of good health, I had nothing to worry about regarding Harv. I handed him five more dollars for lack of anything better to do, then I jogged back across.

"See you at school!" he called. "Don't tell my idea!"

Harv's sister stood behind the counter, our cardboard box merrily steaming. The guy in the wheelchair still waited for his order, hands folded in his lap, reminding me uncomfortably of my mom.

"I rushed it through," she announced coolly, "so you could be on your way."

As we walked back to the car, each kid propping up a side of the box, I saw that Harv was already gone. Just the pay phone dangling by its cord.

Those tiny bald flecks had been left by the staples they'd used to put his head back together. And how badly could Harv use some of that James Jones money? And who could bring that to resolution but me? I hadn't done nearly enough for my students, that was clear as Sprite, and though there was a telephone at home I couldn't walk back through my orderly front door until I'd talked to someone from Dockside.

"Deb," I said, "please just drive them up the hill. I'll walk up in a minute."

"Do, do you want us to wait for you?"

"Dad?" Josie called from the back seat. "What's going on?"

"Climb in for pizza!" Ray yelled.

"Easy, easy, guys. I'll catch up."

Deb rolled down the driver-side window. "Is this really what they need right now? Whatever this is can't wait ten minutes?"

"Stephen Hawking," I told her, not knowing what the hell I was saying, "maybe didn't have ten minutes."

As the car drifted up the street I trotted across to the pay phone. The bus must've come because the people waiting had disappeared, or maybe Amber had pulled up in a convertible and invited Harv and the old people to a nitrite-dripping sex party.

Dr. Reid's fax came out of my pants pocket. His sender's number across the top read 805-504-9090, which seemed weird since that wasn't a Nebraska area code.

CONTACT PERSON AT SITE: *Rob Aiken, 402-466-9807 (cell.)*

I slid my Visa card through the slot and dialed. A breeze pushed an empty Lucky Strikes pack up the sidewalk toward me while I listened to one ring follow another.

"Yeah? Hello?"

Sounded like our tour guide had maybe had a few beer.

"Hi, yes, this Peter Giller, we met on Friday? The field trip from Hoover?"

Nine-second pause. Glasses clinking in the background?

"This isn't such a good time for me. What do you want exactly?"

"Well, after our visit and the, uh, the spill, the students and I have experienced some side effects."

Not loss of appetite, numbing of extremities, weight loss, hair loss or colorectal disasters—those were Lydia's side effects. I'd moved on to something new.

"Okay, yeah," Rob said blandly.

"I was wondering whether you might be able to give some insight into what we're, um, experiencing—whether we can expect it to get more intense or if it'll calm down before too long."

"You talking about the bacon, wanting bacon?" A long, ragged sigh. And wheels on gravel? "No, from what I've heard that doesn't quit. What about the temper, smashing things up, has that started?"

Ten feet away, an elderly woman crept up to the bus stop, her purse's strap clutched in her hands like it was a weight she could hardly bear.

"Nothing like that has happened," I lied, just to see how he'd predict the other stupid things I'd already done.

"All right." He yawned. "Maybe you ought to bring your people out to see my people."

"What, at the factory? Hey, did you talk to this James Jones?"

"Jones. *No sé.* And, no, not at Dockside—Old Man Penzler's seen the last of me. You know Lancaster County?"

"Way out east, sure, around Lincoln? I'm from Pawnee."

"Yeah, we've got sort of a new facility out there. I'm going that way now. Get out to where Route 77 meets the interstate, then call me again, all right?"

"And would this be for a meaningful conversation between the two of us, or should I haul these kids two hundred miles too?"

"Ah!" His chuckle sounded like a shot glass rattling inside another. "Another night or two, you won't need me to answer that."

"Hey, why be a jackass? All we want is some kind of answer if—"

"I don't have an answer but we've got a solution, how's that sound? All right, looks like I'm getting pulled over," said Rob. "Look forward to seeing you."

I looked down at the receiver as though it might say something of its own volition. *Get thee to Velouria, why wouldst thou be a breeder of sinners?*

The bus-stop woman shifted a patent-leather shoe on the concrete.

"Excuse me." I hung up the phone. "Do any buses head up toward Hawthorne?"

"This next." She wore a single dot of pink lipstick. "We can go together!"

DEB MUST'VE BELIEVED that if you can't say something nice you shouldn't say anything at all, because the instant I bounded onto the porch she hurried out for that evening's power walk. The kids and I played Hungry Hungry Hippos and when Ray put a marble up his nose I didn't even lose my cool. Good, right? Then I was sitting at the table mowing through cold pizza with that weekend's *Hoover Hunter-Gatherer* up in front of me—only thing suspicious out of Velouria was an attempted truck-jacking—when Ray apparently thought it'd be hilarious to knock the newspaper out of my hands with a hammer because the same thing had happened to the tipsy admiral in *The Little Wretch*. I saw his white-socked feet shuffle up, then the hammer tore through the sports page like a fork of lightning, bisecting the Orioles' catcher until the steel claw embedded itself in the base of the ring finger of my left hand.

It happened as fast as that. I stared down at that hammer's silver head, streaked with rust and now a single unit with my body, and did I scream? No. I thought, *Ah, yes. This makes sense, it's all been building up to this exact thing.*

"Oh," I told Ray. "Let's be careful here."

I yanked the claw out of the pale finger then dropped a burgundy placemat over my hand while Ray shrank against the wall. His hands were little white balls and it looked like his neck was trying to eat his chin.

"A hammer is for what?" I asked.

"It's for…"

"It's for driving a *nail*, Bugface, you do not use it on *people*. Josie?" I called, voice straining only slightly. "Take Ray down and turn on *SpongeBob*, okay?"

He forced a tight smile, pale even under that blond hair.

"Sorry, Dad," he said. "I didn't mean to—"

And once they'd thumped down the stairs I finally lifted the place-mat—I would deal with it on my own before Deb came home. Something yellow showed inside the cut and I figured that might be bone. But it still didn't hurt.

In the bathroom I wiped it with a Kleenex and put Neosporin in the cut.

"Pyjamas!" I called down the stairs.

Deb read them their stories while I sat in the kitchen with an ice pack on the hand, then she went to bed herself. I could still make a fist. While I was brushing my teeth I tugged at the poor finger to see if the bone would click out of place or go a little wobbly.

Instead the finger snapped off in my hand.

No spray of good red blood, just a few drops of purple. The thing just looked wrong, sitting there in the palm of my right hand, and my left hand with a gap where my ring finger had been looked even more wrong, but it still didn't even sting, and I thought of those lizards that lose their tails for self-preservation—that can't *hurt* the lizard, can it? The shock would kill them. The shock ought to have killed Amber on Monday morning, too, and if it *had* killed her I would've been standing there on my porch with my useless arms at my sides. Wasn't I capable of more than that? I needed the bacon, sure, but I couldn't allow bacon to cloud my brain anymore.

I glanced at myself in the mirror—my eyes looked enormous—then dropped the finger into the breast pocket of my pyjamas and spat my toothpaste into the sink.

I took my tool kit out of the broom closet, found the staple gun, and with four half-inch staples, two on each side, I reattached the finger—those webs of skin between the digits gave me some raw material. Eric had been right to recommend staples. I lived in the science-fiction future where dogs sat on the toilet.

"How'd that happen?" asked Josie.

She stood in her nightgown in the kitchen doorway, holding a glass of apple juice.

"Ray got a little rough," I said, stowing the tool kit.

"But no emergency room, right?"

I shook my head.

"Can we get, um, pizza again tomorrow?"

"Grandma probably still wants hamburgers." I let my left hand lay flat on my pyjama leg. "You know you'll need to brush your teeth again after you drink that."

She grinned like we were in an ad, showing a mouthful of teeth perfect as Chiclets. *Her* kids would have perfect teeth too. Things would come up roses for my kids even if they'd already lost a parent and a parental finger.

Thursday, October 27.

WITH A CONSTANT knot of bacon in my gut I'd gone on teaching for three more days, battling successfully to keep my cool when students handed in half-digested worksheets or Ray forgot to flush, tugging my ear so relentlessly that the lobe scabbed over. I'd only seen my Chemistry 11 kids out in the parking lot, driving doughnuts in their parents' cars until Cam waved them off-site.

But on the Thursday morning, I'd finished our bacon supply at four AM, and someone had eaten that jar of congealed grease too, so as the sun climbed up the horizon I drove to 7-Eleven in my burgundy UC Denver sweatpants, on a mission!

When the doctors had started keeping Lydia overnight, she'd sent me home each evening with nineteen-point to-do lists describing bedtime snacks, breakfasts, recess snacks, lunches, pyjamas, school clothes, dishes, garbage pickups, emptying the litter box when we'd still had the cat, relatives and friends I needed to keep in the loop, homework journals I needed to initial and shows I needed to confirm the TiVo had recorded even though it'd be too late to do anything if it hadn't—I'd loved those lists of things I was perpetually qualified to accomplish, because otherwise in those days I'd been useless as a dead battery, capable only of nodding hopefully at the parade of doctors, squeezing Lydia's fingers, swollen from chemo, and reassuringly ruffling the kids' hair so often it had gone thin at the back. My heart had enjoyed a half-beat thrill whenever she'd slipped a scrawled-on gift-shop receipt into my hand.

A tractor towing a load of hay rolled slowly across the intersection.

With enough bacon, I could teach through most of the day before I drove out to Velouria to hopefully receive a single pragmatic answer to our manifold problems. I'd tried phoning the Dockside number that information had given me but hadn't even heard an answering machine—it was the kind of business that didn't need much contact with the public.

"Truck from Fontaine should've been here yesterday morning," muttered the green-smocked 7-Eleven clerk, gnawing a fingernail. "But we got no word from 'em whatsoever."

"Wait. You're saying you're *sold out* of bacon?"

No grocery stores opened before nine so I drove home, stinging earlobe pressed between my fingertips, and ate the eggs and toast Deb put in front of me. I thanked her, kissed Josie and Ray on their clean little temples and walked out to the car while something yawned wide inside me.

Halfway to Hoover High, my lane of traffic was brought to a stop by a flagman in a hard hat. They were laying a new sidewalk along the far side of the road and their machines cluttered the pavement. In the rearview mirror I watched the driver behind me dig patiently in her nose. I wasn't running late, and after thirty seconds or a minute, tops, I knew they'd stop the oncoming traffic to give our lane its turn. But I got out of my car, in tie and pressed white shirt, and ran between the oncoming cars to get over to that new sidewalk.

"Sir?" the flagman yelled. "Hey!"

The sidewalk crew wore hard hats and fluorescent vests. The foreman stood with his back to me, hands on his hips, while the other five or six guys all kneeled, smoothing out the cement with their big flat trowels. With the heel of my shiny-black dress shoe I kicked the foreman in the small of his back. His head snapped back and his hard hat tumbled off as he squelched hands-first into the wet cement.

The guys on their knees squinted up at me. One of the cars behind me honked its horn—*Watch out, workers! Crazy guy!*—right as the foreman sprang to his feet like he extricated himself from wet cement a hundred times a day, a sinewy-armed little guy with a half-cemented moustache. I threw a punch but he ducked underneath then shoved me hard in the chest, as if to say *I don't even want to fight you, asshole, I just want you the hell off my site*. I stumbled backward, caught my feet in a coil of something and fell onto my back.

I tried to sit back up but couldn't somehow—felt like my right shoulder was stapled in place. I couldn't figure out why, my eyes roamed around for some explanation. All the sidewalk guys were on their feet by then, hot for my blood, but they only walked as far as their foreman and stopped dead.

"Aw, fuck," one of them said.

I finally looked at the shoulder itself. A six-inch hunk of rebar had been set into that particular piece of ground, and I'd fallen on it so that a good three inches of steel, streaked with that purple blood, protruded from my shirt front. I heard a lady in a car start hollering.

"Don't try to move," the foreman said. "Call an ambulance, Jim."

"I'm all right," I said.

The problem was that I'd fallen straight onto the rod, and of course when you try to sit up from lying down your shoulders aren't still parallel to the ground, it's more like 45 degrees, and the rebar wasn't going to pop out like that. So I wriggled my heels against my bum and I got my left shoulder under me, then pushed so my right shoulder went straight up. The muscle made a sucking noise as the rebar moved through it, but then I was finally unpinned and dropped onto my side in the dirt.

"Aw, fuck!" the workers said, and knelt beside me.

After a couple of deep breaths I didn't feel too bad. *Don't let a school bus drive by*, I thought, *or Cam will call goddamn Kirsten McAvoy*. I rolled over and climbed to my feet. I wasn't even woozy, though my stomach grumbled. I smoothed down my tie.

"I can't apologize enough," I told the men, then sucked back another long breath. "If I've put you out any expense, just let me know. My name's Peter Giller, I work up at the high school."

They kept looking up and down between me and my long-lost rebar. The flagman was staring with his sign down at his knees so traffic wasn't moving in either direction. I jogged across to my car. I'd left the engine running so I pulled straight out into the oncoming lane, mouthed a *Sorry!* to the twitching foreman and sped off toward school. Never even fastened my seatbelt!

I parked behind the metal shop so I could go in through the cafeteria entrance. Mrs. Abel was by the oven, dolloping out a sheet's worth of cookie dough, and I asked whether she might have a little bacon that I could come back and eat after homeroom—I didn't have to tell her I preferred it burnt because that was the only way she cooked it. I grinned at her, full of hope, but she just stared back at me. A poster beside the cash register read WE WILL BE WRITING LETTERS TO URGE CONGRESS TO SPONSOR D. R. CONGO'S WOMEN & CHILDREN AS REFUGEES, IN THE CAFETERIA AFTER SCHOOL THURSDAY, THE MORE THE MERRIER THIS WILL SAVE LIVES, QUESTIONS? GRACE – LOCKER #174.

"You can't teach like that," Mrs. Abel informed me.

I looked down and saw that my white dress shirt—my only new one since Lydia had first been diagnosed—sported two gray handprints across the chest, a livid purple streak down one side like I'd been painted with a roller, and a small hole in the shoulder.

"Sure I can." I wiped my hair off my forehead. "What do these kids know?"

So instead of cooking my bacon she had a hushed phone conversation until Mr. Vincent sauntered down the ramp from the office then walked me out toward my car.

"This is stupid," I said, centring my tie. "I can teach!"

"Let's just talk a minute."

"Let's talk about the season—Week 15 against the Jets, what's that going to be?"

"No, just sit down here," Cam growled.

I sat in the passenger seat, the door hanging open while he stood beside the car and kicked pebbles across the pavement.

"I've had phone calls from all of the parents," he said, riffling a hand through his crewcut. "Halliday, Melloy, all of them telling me, 'Ever since that trip to Velouria my kid's been walking around like a zombie, knocking down the cat, cutting their feet with razor blades, blah, blah.' All I can say is, 'Well, *medically* they were given a clean bill of health, Mrs. Tits. Is there anything going on at home that might be a factor here?' And you'd think they'd say 'Screw you,' but, no, they get off the phone toot sweet."

"Don't herd us in with them," I said. "Zombies haven't got mental function. They drag themselves around looking for brains to eat. Shit, I can still *think*." I tilted the seat back and put my feet on the dash. Clumps of concrete all over my shoes. "I just haven't been in a good mood."

"So tell me why Amber—"

"Poor old Amber's arm fell off, sure, might be you could get the district health guys in here to tell you why that happened, but she's still thinking, all right?"

"But just for argument's sake," said Cam, "how does a zombie *know* he's not thinking? If he goes from eating macaroni and cheese one day to *braaains* the next, sure, he might notice a change in himself in *that* instance, but if the transformation takes six months, a year, well, people do *change*, right? He's just picked up some new hobbies, that's all. Altered his diet. It might take, say, a high school principal to tell the guy there's a difference. This large-scale medical stuff is out of our sphere, nobody expects schools to address arms that go missing, but lapses in judgement do concern me. See my concern?"

"Give me back my car keys," I said.

Cam squatted beside the open door.

"Don't take this the wrong way, Giller, but do you have a whole lot of friends?"

"Thanks for noticing," I said.

"A-ha. Show off these higher mental functions and tell me why you're crusted in blood and cement."

"They're the lot of the common man, Mr. Vincent. One day you'll be in them up to your waist. Hey, did you hear from this James Jones in the last couple of days?"

He shook his head with furrowed brow, trying to look engaged.

"He works for Penzler Industries," I said, "that's the parent company of that outfit in Velouria, and he was around here asking—"

"I know them." Cam got up, twisted to the left and cracked his back. "Saul from the board office called yesterday afternoon, said the lawyers for Penzler wanted contact information for everybody caught in the accident so they could start getting the wheels rolling on compensation. I pictured you and Ray and Josie at Disneyland and I said, 'Hell, yes, Saul, don't drag your feet—tell 'em what they need to know!'"

I knew Cam was finally saying something important but I couldn't take my eyes off the turquoise hatchback that was parking over by the fence. Kirsten McAvoy. Fake pearls and all.

"Did you call Kirsten McAvoy to cover my classes?" I asked.

"Listen, it isn't your effed-up *shirt* that's the problem." Cam wiped his nose with a lily-white handkerchief. "It's the state of mind that would allow you to wear that shirt into my school that's the problem."

"Please just give me my car keys."

"Hold on. Kathleen's been calling around to get you a ride."

I set my feet down on the parking lot and got out of the car. I felt tall!

"You *listen.*" I jabbed Cam's sternum with two fingers. "You run and get me a plate of bacon in the next thirty seconds or—"

Meep-meep! Deb pulled up beside us in her red Corolla. Kirsten McAvoy clacked past on her turquoise pumps and thick ankles, scrapbooking binders clutched to her chest. She grinned at us, waving her car keys.

Deb lowered her window.

"Let's get you cleaned up," she said. "I turned on the tub, so we can't dawdle."

"Thanks for coming down so quick," said Cam. "Don't let him near your brain."

"Oh, you know me better than that," said Deb.

AT THE FIRST red light, Deb put her elbows on the steering wheel and looked sideways at me. She hadn't put on her makeup yet so her eyelashes were invisible.

"You know, I won't be upset if you find a girlfriend," she said. "I don't know what she'll think of me being underfoot, but the woman has to be out there somewhere."

"Are you crazy? Give it ten years."

"She's out there somewhere."

She worked the clutch pedal, ready to go.

"When you played football, Lyd always called you 'Captain America.'"

"Until my shoulder got torched," I said. "Could barely write finals."

"I just remembered it because I thought you could go on one of those dating websites and call yourself that. 'Captain America.'" The light changed and she turned left up our hill. "Are you still allowed to burn leaves? Somebody's got a real bonfire."

A column of smoke billowed from the hill above us.

Every time I'd seen a burning house, even on the news, I'd imagined the resident spotting the smoke from blocks away, driving closer and closer, the pit of his stomach knotting tighter, until he sees that, yes, it's his own damn house.

And when we pulled up to squint at flames licking the underside of my roof and smoke pouring out of the upstairs windows, my gut instinct was to blame Deb for leaving the bathtub running—because that can lead to significant property damage, right? Then I thought that the simple act of talking to Rob Aiken on the phone had made this happen. He'd made it sound like things were going to get worse. I already had my door open.

"You dropped the kids at school, right?"

"Of course they're not *in there!*" Her seatbelt shot back over her shoulder. "For God's sake!"

Then sirens behind us—the fire department storming up the street like an invading army. I was already up the steps and at the front door, wondering how not having my keys somehow prevented me from getting through a locked door, while Deb pulled her car ahead a couple of houses to give the trucks room.

A bearded guy with a bullhorn walked me off the porch as burning shingles started to drop onto the lawn. The firefighters hooked the pumper truck up to the hydrant across the street. I stood beside Deb on the sidewalk, feeling weak as foolscap from my teeth to my tailbone, while the column of black smoke rose so high that Cam and Kirsten and Mrs. Abel might've been watching it out the staff room window and shaking their heads at the horror of it all.

"Anybody inside?" one of the men asked Deb.

"I told them, the kids are at school. I—I only just stepped out five minutes ago."

"Any pets?" he asked.

The kids had plenty of things they would have wanted saved— Roald Dahl, a cardboard box full of Josie's flying horses, a Hot Wheels carrying case shaped like a wheel, the still-boxed pictures of their mom—all kept in rooms where flames had already consumed every molecule of oxygen. Credit cards melted down to bingo chips. At least Deb had pictures of Lydia on her mantel back in MacArthur.

But there was *one* thing I figured I could save! I ran through the next-door neighbors' yard all the way back into the alley, then in through our back gate and across our backyard. The siding bubbled beside my head but I reached underneath the stairs and pulled out that shovel my dad and I had used to bury Keister.

A dimpled cop with a notepad was talking to Deb when I got back to the car. I stood beside them and watched the fire. Load-bearing beams collapsed on themselves in explosions of smouldering ash, but everything felt more *right* with that shovel in my hands. I choked back my compulsion to smash every windshield.

"And this is Peter," she said, nodding at me. "We only just got back to the house. He was at the high school before that."

The cop eyeballed my shirt. Besides dimples he had surprisingly bushy sideburns.

"You need medical treatment, Mr. Giller?"

"I'm all right," I said.

"Any connection between your, uh, injuries and this situation at the house, sir?"

I shook my head. The cop frowned and scribbled in his notebook. The fire chief climbed out of his red station wagon and muttered to one of the firefighters, then he came over and muttered with the cop. I felt like biting their faces, but not in front of Deb.

The roof crumbled into what had been our living room. The muscles down my arms flexed involuntarily. Man, the stuff a guy could rip apart if he were a house fire!

"After school today I'm taking the kids back to MacArthur," Deb said. "With their mom gone too, I'm sorry, but—you want to come buy them a change of clothes?"

"Jesus! You don't have to take them all the way to—"

"You come pick them up whenever you're ready." She folded her arms and leaned her hip against the car. "You sure as hell aren't ready now."

"You—you think this *my* fault?"

"I don't know. That's just the thing, I don't know. And if those sweet kids are going to be in your care I have to be able to say, 'No, Peter *definitely* had nothing to do with it.' The extent of your parenting right now is—you need a little time, Peter, and I can give them a safe place for as long as that's necessary."

Behind my shoulder, someone said, "Arson?"

I twisted around.

"Again?" the cop said.

He and the fire chief glanced at me then went on talking in lower voices, but from the way his lips moved below his moustache, the chief was still saying *arson*.

"Take me back to get my car," I told Deb. "At least leave me with that."

I gave the cop my landlord's contact information, said I'd be staying down at the Brennan Motel, then Deb and I went shopping for underpants and pyjamas and six new *Choose Your Own Adventure* books, like Josie and Ray would really feel those were a fair exchange as they were driven away from their friends and home.

Lost everything you own? Choose from 23 different endings!

Deb bought me a green-striped tennis shirt that I wore out of the store, then she dropped me and the shovel off beside my car. Purple blood had dried on the driver's seat and even after I'd scrubbed it with a wet wipe there was a stain that looked like a pig balanced on its front legs. I found paper and a pen in the glove compartment and wrote:

> *Mr. James Jones—What the fuck do you want from me?*
> *Peter Giller.*

Saul at the board office had provided names and addresses, according to Cam, and the next day the fire chief was on my lawn saying, "Arson." At least I had the business card of the guy who'd burned my life down.

I stopped at 7-Eleven and had the red-headed clerk fax my message to that number I'd been keeping in my wallet. As he rang up two dollars on the register I noticed the rotating rack of wieners behind his shoulder, its plastic case emblazoned with WHY NOT MAKE IT A BACON DOG?

JOSIE AND RAY were surprised to see me, waiting between Deb and the jungle gym at 2:30. We led them over to her Corolla, away from other kids, and I squatted on the dead leaves. Ray stared at me with round gray eyes—his mother's. *What the hell now, Dad?*

"We don't know what's happened exactly," I said, smoothing his hair across the top of his head, "but there's been an accident up at the house. Grandma and I think it'd be better if you stayed with her in MacArthur for a little while. You've got your rooms there already."

Josie let her backpack slide to the ground.

"You're getting a job in MacArthur?" she asked.

"No, baby," said Deb, squeezing a shoulder. "Your dad is going to stay here to sort things out."

"What *things*?" asked Ray. His face turned red while his arms bunched up like chicken wings. He looked ready to throw a TV out a window.

I said, "Grandma and I just think it'd be better if—"

"No, no, no!" Josie said.

She dove for my arm and gripped my elbow like it was a rope dangled over a burning ship. Same thing she'd done on the morning I'd had to tell them that their mom had passed during the night: Josie had grabbed for my arm then pulled Ray against us. I'd thought at the time, through my own fog, that it meant *I can't bear to lose my mom and I have to hold onto something, anything.* But Lydia had been out of their day-to-day lives for a couple of weeks by then, and I realized, squatting in the elementary school parking lot, that her clutching meant *You are our whole lives*, and that it had meant the same thing six months before. I pulled Ray's face against my neck, felt his wet cheek there, and I leaned across to press my forehead against Josie's.

"I haven't been acting like myself," I whispered. "I've been too angry."

"Sorry," said Ray.

"That's *okay*, Dad," Josie said.

"I haven't been angry with you two. Even when you threw out the bacon, all right? You guys go to Grandma's and I'll come get you when I feel better."

"How long before you come?" asked Josie.

Deb's chin had crumpled and she was blinking hard. Rock-solid Deb.

"A month," I told them.

It was possible I'd wake up the next morning with all of the rage dissipated from behind my eyes, so that I could see my way to MacArthur—the kids and I would only be apart one day in that case—and equally possible that my car would explode or I'd feel compelled to throw myself into a blast furnace, in which case we'd never see each other again. A month seemed like a decent compromise. Telling yourself *anything is possible* might feel terrific when you're eighteen and hitchhiking across the country, but when you're an underemployed widower and father of two it is a fucking terrible feeling.

Deb nodded and shrugged her shoulders, wiping her nose.

"Just one month," she muttered.

She picked up Ray and put him in the car. Luckily he'd left a stuffed rabbit on the back seat that she could jam into his arms. Deb got behind the wheel. I carried Josie around to the other side, and her dangling legs were so long that the toes of her sneakers whacked my shins. I buckled her in. She was breathing through her teeth, trying to hold herself together for the umpteenth time.

"Will you meet us at the house?" she asked. "To get our stuff?"

"No, baby," I said. "Grandma has new stuff for you. Surprises."

I kissed her forehead and shut the door before she could say any-thing else, then I dragged myself around the car and twisted into Ray's side to give him a hug. He squeezed back hard, then abruptly let go.

"See you before long, Bugface," I said, and kissed his forehead too. His fist hit me in the ear.

I slid back and shut the door. Once he'd done the same thing when I'd forgotten to order curly fries and after thirty seconds that had blown over too.

"Grandma doesn't like that kind of behavior," I said through the window.

He thrashed against the seat and Josie put a freckled hand on his leg. Deb backed out of the parking spot and I barely got my toes out of the way, though even if she'd crushed them flat I probably could've reinflated them with a bicycle pump. A school bus pulled out behind the car as they drove away so then I couldn't even see the backs of their heads, just THIS BUS STOPS AT R.R. XINGS.

A life without Lydia, okay, I was starting to digest that. But not Josie and Ray.

I TURNED DOWN Clemons though it wasn't exactly on my way. A giant black Escalade was parked in Harv's driveway so I didn't slow down, much less go in. If the house had looked empty I would've broken in and eaten his dad's driver's license or crapped in his oven and set it on low, but Harv was probably in there and kids shouldn't pay for their parents' fuck-ups. Sins of the father and that, Ezekiel 18:20.

How'd I even remember that? Funny how the brain works.

At a red light at the bottom of our hill, I pulled up behind a little Acura. He wasn't signaling, so I stayed behind him in the left lane in-stead of sliding into the right. When the light turned green he didn't even inch forward until every last oncoming car had gone by us, and then he finally rolled ahead and turned left. Hadn't had the decency to turn his signal on.

Well, I signaled and went after him, and thirty seconds later I stopped behind him at another light. It'd started raining. I reached for my shovel in the back seat, climbed out, walked four steps and smashed in his tail lights. Drizzle on my face while I did it. I glanced up at the side mirror and saw the driver staring back at me, and just from his cheek and eye I could tell he was Chinese. And I admit that that freaked me out a little because I'd never seen a Chinese guy before, not in Hoover. I got back into my car, shut the door and waited for the signal to change. The modern world trains us to act like nothing's happened. The Acura guy never even opened his door. The light turned green, he rolled ahead, I crunched over the shards of his lights and after a couple of minutes I pulled up in front of our house again.

Only the foundation was left, the front steps, what might have been our blue couch, and a tangle of charred timbers like a campfire Boy Scouts had peed on. Two firemen in shirt sleeves and overalls were unrolling yellow DANGER KEEP OUT tape around the perimeter of the property. The facing wall of the houses on either side of us were toasted black. I peered up and down the block and didn't see a single Alice's Flowers van, so until I heard back from Jones or drove clear across the state to Lancaster County, maybe that meant I was out of clues. But why not drive straight to Velouria and ask what was in that SOFT-SOLED SHOES ONLY tank?

"Hey, aren't you the guy—are you Giller?" asked a bearded fireman.

"I lived here, yeah."

"Your landlord was just here to poke around. Not a happy camper!"

The other fireman laughed and they went back to what they were doing. A tall balding man sauntered up the sidewalk, leading a black miniature poodle on a leash. Even before my bacon problem I'd wanted to smash poodles into the pavement, and this little rat's mucousy eyes kept glaring up at me.

"Aren't you Mr. Giller from the high school?" asked the bald guy.

"I've done some subbing."

Didn't want to own up to too much—maybe he had a subpoena because my shirt had traumatized some kid in the cafeteria.

"I heard you had a fire up here, thought I'd better lend my condolences. I'm Doug Avery. Our daughter Megan went on that field trip to Velouria, you remember?"

If Avery was looking for trouble, I'd duck when he threw his first punch, even with the extra reach he had on me, though the poodle might be a problem. Unpredictable.

"Sure. Megan," I said. "Whiz at the periodic table."

"Yes, sir. Now, we had a fire at *our* place last night too. Gutted it. Haven't quite accepted it in my mind yet. We're staying at my brother's place now, just over the way."

"Really, you too? Megan all right?"

"Well, that's the thing. That's the thing, we haven't seen her since Monday. She came in late on Monday, then Tuesday not at all. That's two days ago. Cereal bowl sitting there untouched."

He blinked hard. His eyes looked rheumy as the dog's.

"That, uh—that doesn't sound like Megan," I said.

Too homely to have run off with a motorcycle gang.

"No, it doesn't. Colleen's still all smiles about it, says Megan's at a sleepover and she'll phone any minute, but…" Avery watched his dog sniff around the puddles left by the firehoses. "And we heard most of that Chemistry 11 class was acting strange even before. Some business in the cafeteria, with the boys threatening people!"

"Yeah," I said blandly, "I'd heard about that."

"Little Scott Barnes, he's an athletic kid, went down on his back during the soccer game last night—*compound fracture* of the leg, everybody could see it plain as day, but he hopped up and kept playing, said it didn't bother him. Rest of the kids were just about sick! They had to strap him down on one of those stretchers just to keep him from hopping out of the ambulance! Feisty bugger."

"I hadn't heard that one."

"Now, my wife sent me over here, Mr. Giller, to suss you out. She figured, hey, all these troubles with the eleventh-grade field trip, fire at *our* house, your house, the Sutherlands' and the Mooneys', then Scott Barnes's mother in that accident…Colleen and I've almost started believing that something really *terrible* happened with that accident in Velouria, and now we're being badgered out of town before we can put our heads together, hash it all out. Does that seem logical to you?"

"Well." I encouraged my brain to participate, this seemed important. "If it really has been *organized* by somebody, I couldn't say why they'd do that. Obviously *something* happened to everybody in Velouria."

"Not there, Jocko, that's the man's vehicle!" Avery tugged the leash. "Now when we rolled into my brother's place this noon hour, it happened a friend of his was over. This friend's name is Svendsen, cheerful as all heck, made me think of a cocker spaniel—you know the guy?"

"I've only been in town a couple of months, I—"

"Well, this Svendsen's ex-military, Air Force officer, I believe, saw action in the Persian Gulf and just retired very recently. And after we got to talking about Megan, he told us that plant in Velouria is owned by this Penzler Industries outfit, are you familiar with them?"

"I know the name, sure."

"You do! Well, Svendsen said this Penzler has expanded like crazy in recent years, and their venture capital came out of *military* contracts. You aware of that?"

The firemen had been ambling through the wreckage, hunting on the ground for something, but now they looked up at me and Avery.

"I wasn't aware," I said softly.

"Well." Taking the hint, Avery tugged the dog in closer and nearly whispered. "Can you recall exactly what they were *making* over in Velouria? Because my girls only said garbage bags."

It was unbelievable to me that Avery could even hold this conversation, *any* conversation, while his daughter and her sequinned cardigan were two days missing and presumed God-knows-what, but I was keeping my cool pretty well myself considering that I'd just watched Josie and Ray getting spirited away. I tugged absently at my reattached finger and recalled that I had a hole through my shoulder that would probably show daylight if I stood, heroically, against the setting sun.

"In Velouria," I whispered, "they told us they were manufacturing garbage bags, and flexible pipes for the plumbing in motorhomes. They walked us through the whole procedure. Bit of this chemical, bit of that one, *abracadabra*—plastic."

"But if they put in a bit *more* of that one and a bit *less* of this, it's another kind of plastic *entirely*," Avery said quietly. "Were you aware of that?"

"Sure," I said. "That's just science."

The bearded fireman ducked under the yellow tape, wiping his palms on his overalls.

"Hey, Giller?" he said. "I'm probably not the one supposed to tell you—"

Then *why* tell me? My ears flushed hot, and I glanced around for a two-by-four that I could use to knock him across the teeth.

"—but you have been *slightly* lucky here," he went on. "I mean, it could have been way worse. The arson guys from the police came across a device that had been set to go off in the middle of the night—you believe that? That's what our chief's paperwork said. But they figured it must've gone haywire and ignited this morning instead. The diagnostic told them that. Because you have young kids and that, right? Would have been way worse in the middle of the night."

"Okay," I said. "Thanks for telling me."

All the time Avery was making a big show of rubbing his dog's belly while it lay on its back, but he threw me this meaningful look— incendiary devices in the middle of the damn night? *Badgered out of town?*

"This Svendsen had had about six beer," he whispered, "so he was real talkative. He said the plastic Penzler made was *for the soldiers.*"

The clean-shaven fireman seemed to be talking into a CB radio up in their cab.

"That could mean anything," I muttered. "Body armor or—"

"Right, of course! Well, my sister-in-law was trying to escort the guy out but when he started hunting around for his shoes he told me something else. Put his arm around me and said that plastic was meant to go inside the soldiers. *Inside.* Then ran out to his car in his stocking feet and drove away! My sister-in-law shut the door and my jaw hit the floor with this whole thing. I mean, our house had *just burned down*!"

His eyes bugged out. The dog sat down on the sidewalk and stared at me too.

"Soldiers," I finally said. "Like they're sending to the Congo?"

"I guess! Puts Penzler on a tight effin' schedule, hey? What do *you* think?"

"I don't know what to think."

"All right. All right," he said. "I'll ask Svendsen about it again if I see him. I'd better roll back along to my brother's, tell my wife I sussed you out."

I watched him saunter away up the block between the hedges and the line of elms, like we'd only been talking about the Steelers' post-season chances, and wasn't Coach Tomlin a snappy dresser? Beside me the clean-shaven fireman leaned his elbow out the fire engine's window.

"Guy seems pretty excited," he called.

"His daughter's missing and his house burned down last night."

"Oh, yeah, down on Mitchell! Thought he looked familiar. Hey, you still staying down at the Brennan?"

"That's right," I said, though I hadn't ever checked in.

He nodded, patted the outside of the door agreeably. His head jerked up.

"Oh, man, holy shit!"

I looked too—a car must've been pulling into one of the driveways, and now Doug Avery lay sprawled on his face beneath its bumper, mo-tionless as a pork sausage. At that distance it looked like he'd put on a red skullcap. The car was some sporty model, yellow—I couldn't see the whole car, a tree was in the way—and I was going to punch my fist through the driver's chest whether old Doug was dead or not. I started running and the fireman jumped down from the engine and ran beside me.

The yellow car was backing out onto the street.

"Hey!" the fireman yelled, waving his dinner-plate hand. "Hold up!"

Its tires squealed and it roared fifty feet then squealed again around the hedges at the corner. Only then did we get to Avery. The leash was still around his wrist and Jocko licked his ear, tail wagging. Doug's left leg was twisted backwards under him, and something like raw egg dripped out of the back of his head. A half-gallon of blood showed where his head had hit the right-angle of the curb.

Before he'd even stopped running, the fireman was calling into his walkie-talkie, and I didn't stop at all—I had enough bacon dogs in me that I figured I could chase that yellow car clear across Colorado, straight down the interstate, so long as I could keep one eye on him. But I slingshotted around the hedge and of course it was long gone. Just a woman in pink, raking leaves beside the sidewalk.

"You see that car?" I yelled. "Get the license?"

She scratched her chin on her knobbly work glove.

THE FIREMAN STOOD six feet back from the body, the leash in his hand and Jocko straining like hell to try to sniff Doug. The bearded fireman was sprinting up the sidewalk from my house, some kind of plastic tool kit in one hand, pulling a latex glove onto the other with his teeth.

"Don't bust a gut. No vitals," the clean-shaven one called. "Hang around to give a statement to the cops," he said to me. "They're looking out for the car. We'll see."

I studied how the blades of grass bent beneath Doug's elbow.

"Hey, I'm not going anywhere," I said.

Ah, yes, I thought. *This makes sense. It's all been building up to this exact thing.* If only Doug had been washed in pink goop with us, he could've sat up and asked for breakfast.

As the firemen bent over the body I wandered back toward my burned-down house. A baby-blue convertible was parked between the fire truck and the neighbor's brown pickup. Grace sat on the hood, gnawing pepperoni and swinging her flip-flops, while Amber probed the ashes of my front porch with her sneaker.

"Hey, hey!" She waved her one arm. She wore a SQUIRREL WHISPERER T-shirt.

"Why're you guys hanging around here?" I asked. "Might not be the safest—"

"We can see *that*!" said Amber. "Figure you didn't *want* your house to—"

"Weren't you all writing letters to Congress?"

"Screw that," said Grace, "we're the refugees now. Didn't you call the factory guy—he say anything good?"

"Oh." Child was using her brain! "Guy said to meet him way out in Lancaster County, but I'm going to head to Velouria before that, see what anybody has to say."

"We're in. Hey, crazy chick," she called to Amber, "come get in the car."

"What's that thumping?" I asked.

"It's that asshole!" said Amber. "Pop the trunk, I want to munch his face!"

Demurely, Grace slid to the ground and circled the car. "What's going on down the block there?" she asked, flicking up a pierced eyebrow.

"Megan Avery's dad got run over by somebody."

"Megan's hilarious." Amber clacked her nails on the back windshield. "Come on, come *on*!"

Grace reached beside the driver's seat and the trunk opened with a metallic burp.

"Yeah, about time," a man's voice hollered from inside, "you fucking—"

Amber's fist came back to her shoulder and descended.

I peered in—a shirtless, black-bearded, three-hundred-pound man held his hands to his nose as blood seeped between his fingers. He had a snake's open mouth tattooed around his eyes, a fang threatening each eyeball, and NAPALM DEATH written across his bare chest. The trunk smelled of booze and vanilla air-freshener.

"Mr. Giller, I am *sorry*, but you would not *believe* how rude he was to us."

"You drive a yellow car, sir?" I shouted down at him. "Huh?"

"Getting oud," he said, grasping for the lip of the trunk. "Nod funny."

Grace stood at my hip, unwrapping another Slim Jim, while Amber waited with that right fist still cocked, eyes darting from me to our large victim.

"One missing arm," she hissed. "He calls me a *freak*—not like it's a harelip!"

His head came up, then he raised his massive legs and lowered them to the cement. He staggered across to the opposite sidewalk, hands to his face like he needed to keep pieces from falling off.

"Done and done," I said. "Let's carry ourselves with some dignity here, girls."

"We were grocery shopping," said Grace. "You want some raw wieners?"

I sure did.

"No, thank you." I glanced at the firemen standing on either side of the silver emergency blanket they'd spread over Avery, and suddenly I felt snipers peering at us from every window. "I want to ditch you two," I said, "and get to Velouria."

"Hey, no way!" Grace chewed hard, already unwrapping the next one. "Can they splatter us with the stuff again, you think? I am seriously so sick of eating these!"

Again I heard sirens from down the hill. I shut my eyes for a second so I could think. I didn't need these two, no, but Hoover was not safe for any of us.

I took Grace's Slim Jim and started to chew. She just smiled at me, nodding, as if to say *That's cool, man*, but my imagination was out on the highway to MacArthur, telekinetically pushing Deb's car away from Hoover—God willing, they were already out past the Fuddruckers billboard.

"Can you just leave town?" I asked. "Where do your folks think you are?"

"My mom's in Taiwan," said Grace, "so I'm at the chick's place, but her folks are at the hospital 'cause her dad got backed into by a sand truck, so he's got whiplash."

"Sand truck? There's no snow on the ground!"

Amber shrugged, her empty sleeve flapping in the breeze. "That's what *I* said."

Two police cars slid up the block, sirens off now, stopping beside the fire truck. I trotted over and leaned in a window—it was my guy with the sideburns and dimples.

"Not here," I said. "Seven or eight houses up."

He nodded and drove away, followed by the next cop, then an ambulance that had appeared. Another car was in line behind them, a green Taurus station wagon.

"Mr. Giller!" Colleen Avery leaned over her steering wheel. "*You* haven't seen Megan around, have you?" She smiled, like Megan was off playing hide-and-seek, giggling. "You know, since our field trip she's been—"

"I don't know where she is."

"No? Oh, hello, girls!" Colleen waved at the two on the sidewalk, her voice all ice cream. "My husband was coming to see you. Has he already gone home?"

I leaned in her open window. A puffy-maned My Little Pony, stinking of strawberries, dangled from the rearview mirror. I shut my eyes so I could think.

"What?" she asked.

Somewhere beneath my surface, the person I'd been before Pipe #9 burst felt the merest ripple of the real horror of everything, but that person was only able to contribute the word *enunciate*.

"You're going to want some time to think about this," I said, trying to take some kind of ridiculous long view, as though she already knew what I knew. "It's been a hard week, and it's only—what day's this, Thursday?"

"What's *happened*?"

I looked at her. She only had the fingertips of one hand on the steering wheel, and her eyes and mouth had stretched wide like something was trying to emerge from behind her face. I reached in and softly took her wrist.

"He told me all this stuff about the military," I said, "then he went on up the street and a car ran him down. That's what happened. He's dead up there, under that blanket. I know that's the worst shit you'll ever hear and all I can say, seriously, is that when I find the jackass I'll rip his head open."

I should've worked for Hallmark! Her lips stuck out from her teeth and her gaze stayed on my forehead. I realized that her car radio was on, had been on all along, playing "Take It on the Run," by REO Speedwagon.

"Now I think there's no reason why we shouldn't go up to these cops," I said, "and tell them everything, everything possible, and call

all this shit to a halt."

She coiled her fingers around the steering wheel as though she'd fly into space if she didn't. She was going to say, *Yes, God, let's get help through official channels.*

"We can't," she said, throat sticky. "The police told us last night it was an FBI file, they told us to call a number, then the FBI told us on the phone that this wasn't a case they were able to pursue." She swallowed. "So I don't think we should talk to these exact people about it."

"But if it's an FBI file, why in hell can't they pursue it?"

"Doug said it must've—must be *their doing* to begin with."

"But, Jesus, how can we get into worse trouble than we've got already?"

"This is all going to work itself out," she said sleepily.

Her watery eyes finally settled on mine, but I don't think she was really seeing anything anymore. She'd lost her husband, but did she at least have her child sitting reassuringly beside her to remind her of the halfway-rosy future? No.

"I'll stick with you," I said.

I still hadn't let go of her wrist. Her arm tensed.

"Tell me the car that did it," she said. "Right now, make and model."

"Jesus, Mrs. Avery, I...it was yellow, sporty, I guess. Low to the ground."

"How old?"

"Last ten years? Could've been brand new."

"Have a spoiler?"

"Yes, definitely."

I pictured its spoiler jeering at me as the car rounded the corner.

"Then probably not a Chevy, thought for sure it would be. Mustang, Charger maybe. That weird Trans Am. Was it a big long family car or little and sporty?"

"Something in between?"

"You're helpful as a bag of crap." She shook my hand away to grip the wheel. "I'm going to see Doug."

I got out of the way so she could park at the curb, then she climbed out and swayed away up the sidewalk. She wore a blue tracksuit and silver bracelets. The cops were already hurrying up to meet her. I'd just announced that I'd stick with her but instead I walked back to Grace and Amber because I was suddenly spooked that these same police had an APB out on me for attacking those sidewalk-pouring guys.

The girls sat in their car, each dipping their fingers into a wet package of Wimmer's Jumbo Deli Franks that they'd wedged against the emergency brake.

"Is that Megan's mom?" Grace asked, chewing.

"She looks sad!" Amber announced jauntily.

"We aren't getting to Velouria before five o'clock," I said.

"The tour-guide guy said they run the place all day and night!" said Amber. "And if he lied to us, shit, he will *regret* it."

Grace rattled the keys. "How about rubber hits the road?"

"We'd better wait for, uh, Mrs. Avery. She might want to come."

"This is so screwed up!" Grace grinned. "The other day when the chick's arm fell off, I was like, 'This is all about my dad, Congo, it's the same stuff,' and now it's just worse and worse and I can't stop smiling—so screwed! I was going to get the firemen to sign my stop-the-war thingy, but then I'm like, 'Who cares?' Climb in and we'll go, G."

"I'll go in my car. Good on my own."

I slid behind my steering wheel, clicked the seatbelt. What had she been saying about her dad? Down the block, Doug Avery's gurney was hoisted into the ambulance. I stared at my ashtray. Lydia's picture slept in there, of course, and I felt I'd better explain to her that our kids weren't with me in our car. That I'd lost hold of them.

"Bugface," I said.

So I took the picture out and slipped it into my wallet. That seemed like a reasonable compromise, leaving the report of my dad's crash alone in the ashtray. Then I noticed the photocopies on the passenger seat—mythological coloring pages so kids could draw hilarious dicks on centaurs—and heaved them onto the back seat as Colleen came swaying up the block, her frail chin pressed to her chest. I'd honestly thought Josie would be the next person to sit up front beside me; the refutation of that belief just cemented that this Dockside business had spiraled out of control.

"Okay." Colleen slid onto the passenger seat. She shut the door with utmost delicacy so the latch barely clicked, her bracelets tinkling. "The fireman says it was a two-door, but he doesn't know the model either. Two-door, no spoiler, probably not the Mustang. Where're you going?"

"Velouria. Maybe they've got a simple explanation. I tried phoning but—"

She climbed out unsteadily, trotted up to the Taurus, reached inside her passenger door for something, slammed the door shut after a couple of tries then padded back to my car and climbed in. Between her knees she held a black metal cylinder, the handle for a multi-head screwdriver or something.

"What's that for?"

"It's stupid. It's a telescoping baton thing. I never saw the point but Doug insisted I had it every time we went to Omaha. When I cave in the guy's skull," she said quietly, "I don't want to bugger up my hand. Let's go find Megan."

"Go where? Doug said she was at a sleepover."

"That was bullshit," she sighed.

She sat pinned by the belt across her chest. Considering that a person or persons unknown—who probably had eyes on us at that moment—were burning our houses down, separating us from our children and making our loved ones leak egg out of their heads, it seemed like seat belts were going to safeguard us about as well as a paper hat. I inched away from the curb, waving inconspicuously to the girls.

"Hey." Maybe I'd come over all sentimental at leaving the Giller family's wreckage. "Don't you want your dog?"

"He's tied to the fire truck." Colleen wiped her nose on her sleeve. "If, if I can live without anything…"

I started a U-turn so we wouldn't have to pass the cops. The sun hit the side of Colleen's face so her teeth looked translucent, lit from somewhere back in her throat.

"If I can live without anything, I can live without Jocko."

I TURNED INTO the 7-Eleven, and Grace parked beside us.

"Getting supplies?" she called through her window.

"I want a supplies party!" yelled Amber.

I went inside without them. The piped-in air smelled like burnt plastic.

"Uh," said the red-headed clerk. "Mr. Giller, right?"

"Did anything come?" I asked.

He pushed a white page across the counter: a typewritten fax from Jones. I felt my heart give a haphazard thump.

> Mr. Giller.
> Please desist. Our legal department does not look
> kindly on inflammatory personal harassment. I do appre-
> ciate your current difficulties and from one family man to

*another I urge you to pursue fresh opportunities outside
Burroughs County.*
    Yours sincerely,
    James Jones.

Hoover and Velouria were both in Burroughs County, as it happened. I crumpled the fax and left it on the counter.

Badgered out of town.

I walked around toward the cooler.

"It's a dollar to receive the reply," the clerk called after me.

"Oh, oh—I'll take your picture!"

Franny, in a multicolored serape, held her cell phone up in my face. She closed one eye and the phone went click. Then she swung her plastic bag.

"Clint got to my house and I was like, 'This feels like a really special time in our lives, we need to take some pictures!' We stopped for breakfast patties—they're frozen, but who cares?"

Honest to god, she filled all the space between me and the cooler.

"And he was so sweet, he thinks I might be retarded—did you see him out there? His is the Geo with the dragons. His brother painted those!"

"Why don't you go out and eat?" I asked, because for me it'd been a while.

"Brick, c'mon, we had three packages of bacon at my house. Is that Amber out there? What're you Beanie Babies doing?"

"Sir," the clerk called. "Dollar to receive the reply."

"We're going to Velouria," I said quietly.

"Oh, gosh!" She brushed her hair back and it clung to her hand. "*We're* going to do that too," she whispered. "Just give our names and say, 'What up?'"

Someone moved into my peripheral vision—a thick-necked soldier dressed in that baggy desert-camouflage they always seem to wear regardless of region or season, and his tight black boots shouted that he had jumped out of sixty-five airplanes. He still had his entire face, so maybe Congo was still waiting for him, whispering from across the ocean. He held a bag of Doritos in one hand and Tostitos in the other—both products of the Frito-Lay company—and seemed to be determining which was heavier though the weights were printed on the bags. Would his brain spin a cycle or two slower, I wondered, if the government had dumped plastic into his head? Then the back of my neck went hot. I realized that he was standing there to observe us, though his eyes never left the chip bags.

"Shush a minute." My voice barely left my teeth. "Did you have trouble at either of your places? They burn down?"

Franny was shuffling through pictures on her phone.

"When I was really little, yeah," she muttered. "They all said it wasn't my fault."

A dozen people milled around the store, filling giant Slurpee cups and reheating chimichangas filled with the meat of government-bred Hereford/rooster abominations.

"This picture doesn't look like you," said Franny.

The soldier sighed, crunched the bags of chips back onto the shelf and stalked out the door, head tilted forward like he was confronting a hurricane.

"Sir," the clerk called, hands spread wide on the glass counter.

I held a hand up so he might try to be patient, pushed past Franny and finally got my eyes inside the cooler. The wire bin for the bacon dogs was empty, and the rest of the food looked like kids' feet wrapped in foil.

"Hey," I called. "Got any bacon dogs?"

"No, sir. You cleaned us out at two o'clock."

"I'm taking the goodies out to Clint!" Franny called, and the bell on the door dingled behind her.

"You got *anything* with bacon?"

"No," said the clerk. "But there's ham subs."

I walked toward him and he backed up a step. That was a good reaction. I lifted a red case of Coke off a tower at the end of the aisle.

"Do I look like I want a fucking *ham sub*?"

I smashed the case through the glass counter, filling the air with silver scratch cards.

Some concerned citizen immediately grabbed me from behind, but I prised his fingers off my wrists and twisted out of his grip—it wasn't the furtive soldier but some heavyset bald guy in a snowflake sweater. Kept coming toward me, his big hands out like catcher's mitts.

He said, "What the hell, man?"

So I hopped up onto him, wrapped my arms around his meaty shoulders and took his whole ear in my mouth, ready to dig my incisors in and buck my head around like a dog with a rabbit until the ear sheered away from his head and blood jetted onto the stacks of *Wall Street Journal*. But that kind of thing was still in my future. I pulled my mouth off his ear, instead I contented myself with driving my knee into his diaphragm until he fell down on his ass.

I climbed off him, trying to look casual. The other customers had retreated down the aisles, so I picked a can of Coke from the broken case and walked out of the store.

I opened the door of my car, feeling very sensible for letting the guy keep his ear. I'd risen above my rural origins.

"Mr. G!" Grace called through her window. "Let's carry ourselves with some dignity!"

Amber hooted.

"Don't do what I do." My tongue felt thick. "Hey, and don't follow us for a while. They won't connect us."

Foresight on par with Thomas Jefferson. Inside, it looked like a crowd was square dancing around the big bald guy. A woman in a calico dress pressed her face against the door.

I jumped behind the wheel, backed out, past the wizened shrubs. Glanced at Colleen—she'd slumped sideways like she was trying to sleep, her neck as white as vinyl siding. I bumped onto Casement Road and turned right for the highway, and she sat up, staring through the windshield with enough intensity for us to pass as a blameless couple out shopping for concrete lawn furniture.

"'Friends, Romans, countrymen,'" she said, like she knew how close I'd come.

October 30 – 7pm
Burroughs County BARN DANCE, Y'all Come Join the Fun
+ 2 yr old Snaffle Bits

The Agridome went by out at the end of Casement, and just before the merge lane onto Route 33, Harv's dad's magenta flyer flapped by one staple on its telephone pole.

"I'm not going to cry until I see Megan," she said flatly, answering the question I hadn't asked yet. "I've been thinking about her."

"Sure."

"How the Megan I really miss is the kid who never made a fuss, our little M, and how she's turning into an adult, that's fine, she can have opinions, but," she said quietly, "it's no different than if the sweet little kid had gone off and died."

"You know, ever since Velouria," I said, "most of the kids have been kind of stupidly overjoyed."

"And I'm not? Well, different strokes."

A jeep passed us, its bumper sticker: I'M ONLY SPEEDING 'CAUSE I REALLY HAVE TO POOP.

"And none of those kids have husbands," she added. "What about that thing up there? It's yellow."

"That's a Hummer."

"Just checking."

"Okay. Our houses burned down. Right?"

She ran a fingernail across her window.

"Then Doug came and told me that'd happened to cover up some kind of secret bullshit, then a minute after that Doug wasn't there anymore. To cover up some kind of secret bullshit. And maybe they didn't gun for me because I wasn't on the hit list yet, they'd lost track of who I might've been talking to. Or maybe bullets have been whizzing past our heads and I just hadn't noticed."

"No." She slowly twisted to peer into the back seat.

"How well do you know this Svendsen guy?"

"He's known Doug's brother for a long time. He did high-altitude parachute jumps for the Air Force, wearing oxygen masks. All his own research, he said."

A black station wagon roared past us on the left—it had white-and-green Nebraska plates but tinted windows all around. A silver Western Dairy Transport truck was barreling down from the opposite direction, not tapping its brakes for anybody, so I had to stomp on mine to give the station wagon space to cut in front of us, four feet between our bumpers. I glanced over as the tanker roared past, rattling my mirrors, then glanced in front of me and saw the black wagon's brake lights. I swerved onto the shoulder, gravel spraying, half my arm holding down the horn, but then he lay on the gas again and beelined into the distance. I let go of the horn and puttered back into our lane. My breath came out hard, though I couldn't say my heart was beating faster.

"Shit," I panted. "Thought that was going to be awesome, didn't you?"

Colleen shook her head, her hands flat against the dash.

"Thought that guy had come to kill us!" I bipped the horn two times. "Too bad."

"Yeah," she said flatly.

Then we had ten quiet minutes.

WE LISTENED TO a radio call-in show about Andre Agassi, the bald tennis player who used performance-enhancing drugs to win Wimbledon while wearing a giant feathery wig.

"Going around like regular folks," a caller growled, "when at heart he's, he's a monster!"

Colleen reached across and shut it off. Then I could just hear the road under our tires. I wondered how many of the cars and trucks whizzing past from Velouria were headed to Hoover expressly to confirm whether or not we were dead.

I wasn't a zombie like Cam had said. They're known for traveling in packs of five or six, sure, and I *was* doing that—but I'd never seen a movie where a zombie drives a car, and I *was* driving a car. Zombies shamble across the countryside in search of human brains, whereas I was driving to Velouria for…answers. I'd had a hole put through me and a piece of my body had come clean off, true, and I seemed to have a decreased appreciation for human suffering, but those by themselves didn't make me a zombie. A real zombie has to start off dead before coming back to life, and I had *never* been dead though Deb might have argued that some or all of me had died with Lydia. A theologian could argue that one way or the other, but then *I* could interject that even if there *is* a movie where a zombie drives a car, at no time in any movie does a zombie drive a car and count on his reattached fingers the ways in which he is *not* a zombie.

"Doug and I decided to travel the country, looking for her," Colleen finally said. "When the police came up with nothing, we were going to buy a motor home."

Then she was quiet again. She seemed to have a great interest in the brown grass in the ditches.

"What was your job before this started?" I asked.

"I'm the office administrator at Farmers Mutual."

I delved through my mental tool box for any joke I could crack about my insurance premiums, but nothing came—we had renter's insurance but I couldn't imagine ever seeing the sort of calm afternoon where I might sit down and fill out a claim.

"They going to miss you at Farmers Mutual, if you're gone for a while?"

I must've been trying to enforce some kind of normalcy, because she couldn't have cared. Ear-biters are notorious for trying to enforce normalcy.

"Oh, no," she said. "I took this week off. I want to clean up the yard before the snow flies. Then we're going to…"

She pulled her feet onto the seat and curled into a lima bean. Still with dry eyes.

"Why don't you cry?" I asked. "Might feel better."

"I said I'll cry when I see Megan." She gulped in a breath. "The plate on the black car, was it Nebraska?"

I told her I hadn't noticed otherwise, then kept checking my mirrors every eight seconds. On the average stretch of highway there are no yellow cars.

"I understand why we're leaving Hoover," she pronounced in a monotone, "but why Velouria?"

"Well, on a field trip, when one of the kids gets lost, the rule is always to go back to the last place we'd seen each other."

Colleen screwed her lips up—must've done that a lot, from the wrinkles.

"But who did you lose?" she asked.

"Good one. Well, I guess Peter Giller," I said. "That's what my mother-in-law thinks, anyway. Also my principal. And the police, we can presume."

"Oh," she said. "I thought you were going to say you'd lost Harv Saunders. He's seemed a little lost from the start, so I can't entirely imagine how he's coping with this."

"I saw him this week." *Chainsaw scar across his head.* "He seemed just fine."

"His mom was my best friend all through high school. Then we lost her. Doug would say I'm exaggerating, but honest to god, David Saunders ought to be in the electric chair. Stomped on her like she was a tomato worm. Marlene was just the sweetest girl in the whole world. Miss Burroughs County. Looked like Penelope Cruz."

I watched the pairs of headlights flicker on in the mirror and wondered if they belonged to my poor goddamn students. Returning to the scene of the crime.

Then I heard a bang in my right ear and thought we'd blown a tire, which would have left us sitting ducks on the side of the highway, but then my optic nerves relayed the fact that Colleen had put her fist through the plastic crust of my old dashboard. After a second she pulled her hand to her chest and started picking plastic out of her knuckles.

"If you wanted to get these kids someplace safe," she said, "you should have done that for Harv back in fourth grade. Of course Doug would tell you I'm exaggerating."

A baby-blue sedan appeared in my mirror, hands waving madly from either side of its palm-tree air freshener. For some reason I flashed a peace sign, and in response Grace turned her wipers on.

IT WAS PRETTY well night by the time we got into rainy Velouria. Dockside was on the far side of town, out past the used-car lots and feed stores, half of them still open with their lights blazing out across the sidewalks. I guess that suited the farmers' hours. There wasn't a turn-off for the factory, just a road out of town that suddenly turned into employee parking lots. It'd quit raining by then. Not one parked car loomed in our headlights in any direction, even though Rob had exhaustively described the night shift's duties.

The girls stayed twenty feet behind us. At the eight-foot chain-link fence I pulled up to the entrance gate the workers were meant to file through, but it was chained and padlocked, displaying a handsome plywood sign:

CLOSED FOR RENOVATION UNTIL FURTHER NOTICE.
MAKING YOUR COMMUNITY BETTER!
DOCKSIDE SYNTHETICS (A PENZLER COMPANY).

"Maybe," Colleen murmured, "this is what the FBI was talking about."

I got out and walked through the headlight beams just to tug the fifty-pound chain and make sure it was solid. It held, but the *clang-clang* it produced was so *loud*, the two idling cars were so *loud*, and with the dark factory looming above us and miles of parking lots behind, I could feel the eyes of things staggering around in the dark. Things even worse than we were, but a hundred more, a thousand more, and angry at *me*, pouring out of that hollow factory to swarm the fence. It was easy to imagine. I tried to ignore my car's rattle while I listened for them, but all I heard was a vehicle gearing down from the direction of town.

I was being stupid. I wanted to still feel in charge, so I walked over to Amber's car. Grace rolled the driver's window down—Creedence Clearwater playing "I Put a Spell on You" drifted out, with a smell like sawdust that'd been sitting wet under a tarp. Grace extended her bare arm. By the parking lot lights I could see a tooth resting in her palm, blood-smeared roots and all.

"Mine!" With the new gap in her grin, Grace looked like an eight-year-old. "We had a big argument!"

"People have misunderstandings, all right?" Amber called. "Seriously, does that say 'Dickside'? 'Dickside Synthetics'?"

Now I could hear that distant vehicle actually approaching, so I moved in front of the two cars as though I could shield *them* from harm, my fingers tingling with anticipation for the new car to knock me flying across the pavement, but then I'd make them poop in their pants when I got up and punched through their windshield. But the hatchback was slowing down as it came closer, and I squinted to make out the fire-breathing dragon on the hood, cruder than if Ray had fingerpainted it.

"Gillbrick!" Franny's head emerged from the passenger window. "We gotta hit the Curly Wurly bars!"

But all I could think was to get my hands on any of those unemployed Dickside Synthetics guys. Or on a ham sub.

THE PEGASUS GAS station on the way back into town stocked wet sandwiches at the bottom of a beer fridge. I piled them beside the register. I flexed my calf muscles over and over, hoping that might calm me enough to not veer back into 7-Eleven behavior. The elderly proprietor stood under a cardboard sign that read ASK ME ABOUT NIGHTCRAWLERS! I'd made the rest of the crew wait outside, and the old guy kept peering out his little window at the three cars like he expected Colleen to dance in with a telescoping baton.

"I see you don't have it in the cooler," I said, "but do you by any chance carry—"

"Bacon?" he asked.

I must've turned gray. I stood there with my wallet half-open.

"Oh, don't get spooked over it," he said, licking his thumb to pull a plastic bag open. "You just have that look about you."

"Uh, you don't stock luncheon meat of any kind? Because I don't see it."

"No, son. You weren't laid off from Dockside too, were you? Never seen you around, have I? Unless you got a haircut or something."

"I don't know any Dockside." I angled my head so hopefully I'd look confused as hell, perhaps deserving of lengthy explanations. "No docks around here, are there?"

"We've just got the creek, but it's all underground in the culverts nowadays." He started ringing in my sandwiches and each one bent limply as he ferried it into the bag. "Dockside's our factory over yonder, employed a mess of people until they shut up shop day before yesterday, and it was this time last week—it was my wife that pointed out how close the one thing followed the other—this fad went around a lot of the guys who'd worked there to start eating real quantities of bacon. They came in here after their company picnic cookout or whatever they'd had down at Plotkin Park. Funny, isn't that? Because nowadays they say bacon's not too healthy."

"*Tastes* good," I muttered.

"Supermarket down the road's been sold out since Monday, guys bought them out, so they started coming out to us, a dozen of these Dockside fellows we've known since they were kids, still in their coveralls from the factory! Asked if we still carried bacon, so I telephoned the supplier and yesterday the meat truck stopped *here* first instead of the supermarket, you understand, because they come in from Fontaine. And before that driver was out of his cab, oh, six, seven, eight cars and trucks came roaring up the road and pulled in all around him—penned him in! 'Who's this, street gangs?' I said. Well, it was the Dockside fellows, come for bacon."

I took a ham sub out of the bag and started to unwrap it. My hands shook like jackhammers. I should've eaten before we'd gone out to the factory, I'd timed it all wrong—my wrists felt like drinking straws.

"Bet the driver was surprised," I managed to say.

"*Was* he!" The old guy squinted at the roast beef sub in his hand—the price tag looked too waterlogged to read. "Dockside boys kept his doors pinned shut, and some of them took an ax to the back of the truck—I used to stock axes up until then, hunting knives too, but I got rid of all that. People too unpredictable nowadays."

I finally bit into the sandwich. Whichever part of my body kept track of such things detected precious little ham and wanted to know why it had been given so much soggy goddamn bread.

"They get the bacon?" I asked, mouth full.

"Oh, yeah." He puttered under the register for something. "Hundreds of pounds. Ripped the plastic open with their teeth, started eating it raw. I saw it all from in here, with the door locked. A couple of them got the big idea to cook bacon on their engine blocks, I guess that was on a TV show one time, you see that one? They never did get to eat it, though."

"They—they didn't?" The bread caught in my throat at the thought of what the poor bastards must've been going through. A teardrop swam at the corner of my eye.

"No, no, couple of police cars came. Guess the driver radioed for them, I hadn't had the brains to do it myself."

"They got put in jail?"

"That's twenty-four thirty-nine for all that mess of sandwiches. No, most of the boys got away. Just three officers, they couldn't keep all of them from driving off."

I gave him three tens.

"But," I said, "could they have scraped the bacon off the engine once they, you know, got where they were driving to?"

"I wouldn't know." He handed me my change. "Half a dozen of the boys got caught in the back of the truck, throwing hot dogs around in there, and once they were in the squad cars with the cuffs on I saw they had that bacon fat smeared all over their faces. All greasy and white, you imagine? Like clowns." He peered out his window. "Your plate says 'MacArthur Motors,' that right? You from way over in MacArthur?"

He held a notebook and pencil. *Sure*, I could've told him, *I'm from way over in MacArthur*. But the kids were in MacArthur, and no one could ever know that.

"No," I said, "I bought it used over there. I'm from Hoover."

Maybe I should've pretended I was from somewhere else entirely but I'd stalled too long already and had a face unaccustomed to lying.

"Safe travels, then." He finished writing then tucked the pencil into the notebook's spiral binding. "Sorry, ever since the trouble, I try to keep track of every little thing." He shrugged. "Not too many ways to make sense of it."

He deposited the notebook back under the counter. I could have reached across and ripped his arm out of the socket, but were James Jones's cronies really going to swarm through Velouria, seizing every spiral-bound notebook in their statewide hunt for me?

"That's perfectly understandable," I said. "Those guys still in jail?"

"The bacon bandits? Oh, sure! Waiting for the circuit judge to come through."

"And they're doing okay in there? Sounds like they weren't right in the head."

"Well, I heard from Martha Lovett there's some kind of flu bug going through the jail, the families went in and the boys were pretty laid up. Stranger and stranger, if you ask me."

"Yes, sir." I grinned and picked up my plastic bag. "Whereabouts is this jail?"

He'd been all set to pick his teeth with the end of a match.

"Why you want to know that?"

"Uh. Asshole cousin got picked up for marijuana possession." I shook my head as though smoking dope was inconceivable for any decent citizen to imagine, even when he'd nearly had fragments of some guy's ear in his back teeth. "Figured I'd swing by in the AM for my aunt's sake."

"Stupid little bugger. What's his name?"

"Jesse Turnbull."

"Don't know the name." He reached down for his notebook.

"Whereabouts is this jail?" I asked again.

"Left onto the main drag here, right at the fire station. In behind there."

"Good enough," I said, and went out the door before he could ask why my teeth had started chattering, in which case I would've had to tear his guts apart and smear the fat all over *his* face. Jesse Turnbull, incidentally, had been Lydia's bridesmaid, who'd been in Costa Rica the day of her funeral. Funny how the brain works, to come up with stuff like that—to hell with Cam Vincent, I was getting sharper!

I walked out between the bug-lights—which had nothing to kill so late in the year—and threw a wary glance at the slack-jawed faces peering from behind the three windshields. I gave my head the slightest shake and hoped that'd keep the kids from hollering my name and address. But would they be more likely to follow my game plan if they had a little luncheon meat in them, or if I kept them dangling?

I sidled up to each car and passed a couple of damp sandwiches to the passenger.

"Okay, all right, we got it," Franny whispered. "Radio silence. But Ye Olde Candy Shoppe is exactly six blocks *that way*." She pointed to my left with a green-nailed finger close to her chest. "I mean, C here broke his brother's leg this morning, and even he says he's down for an ice cream sundae."

"Shut…up," Clint mouthed, wolfing down so-called pastrami.

It had sounded, of course, like the bacon bandits had our symptoms, and maybe they possessed valuable insights, though if they'd solved our mutual problem to anybody's satisfaction they probably wouldn't have hijacked a meat truck. I did not glance across the roof of the car at the gas station window.

"What ice cream?" I said through my teeth.

"Didn't you see the sign, G? Big sign, bright colors, 'Velouria, Nebraska, Famous for Ice Cream Sundaes'?"

"Just follow me a couple of blocks first." I nodded down to Clint, the driver, who now had mayonnaise dripping down his red scarf. "Place we got to be."

I got into my own car, and as I slid the key into the ignition I felt the old temptation to pull the picture out of the ashtray. In the yellow wash of gas-station light, an unwrapped sandwich across her knees, Colleen sat with arms around her middle, like I might hit her with a rolled-up newspaper.

"I want to ask him if he's seen Megan," she said.

Her eyes looked like dark puddles with weeds around them. I hadn't thought of Megan. I turned off the car and Colleen climbed out, walking nimbly across the rainy concrete.

I focused on the sandwiches still in the bag. I tore through plastic wrappings, peeled out meat slices and jammed them in my mouth, barely chewing before I hurried on to the next. They used nitrites to process the meat and I could feel the blessed chemicals flood through my chest and out into my extremities like good-hearted lines of falling dominoes. Three sandwiches dissolved like that in a minute and a half, and I relaxed back into the seat, chewing a mouthful of what might have been roast beef. My suddenly steady hands said, *You may keep us another day.* Arms still wrapping her middle, Colleen walked out of the office, past the row of white propane tanks, back to the car. She got in and slammed her door, then sat looking at her knees. From the movement of her jaw she seemed to be chewing the inside of her mouth.

After each fresh diagnosis my Lydia had done the same thing, hunched in that very same seat.

AS I DROVE the quarter-mile into town Colleen constantly leaned forward and back, trying to get a look at every driveway and rain-slicked parking lot. A Ford truck up on blocks seemed to be Velouria's vehicle of choice.

"If we spot a sporty yellow car," I said quietly, "it won't necessarily be our guy."

"No, but he has to be somewhere on planet Earth. Wouldn't have stayed in Hoover, and his bosses are most likely here. My gut says Dodge Charger."

"There's more than one yellow Dodge Charger on planet Earth."

"I'll know it when I *see* it, okay?" She whirled in her seat as we passed a poorly lit cluster of cars in front of a bar. "Shut up two seconds!"

I smiled at her companionably—*my* little quest might've seemed just as nebulous, after all, and in the meantime I at least knew where my children were. I parked in the alley behind the red-walled, clearly demarcated Velouria Fire Station. The other two cars pulled in beside us. People's silhouettes walked by on the main street, maybe couples out for their anniversaries.

"That is so *not* the punchline!" a woman told somebody.

A guy strolled beside her in a ball cap and jean jacket. For normal people, every night is a good night.

"There's the ice cream shop Franny's so crazy about." Colleen bundled her purse onto her lap. "I can buy everybody something."

"Appreciate it. I'm going up to the police station, there's a bunch of Dockside guys in there—maybe they know as much about it as Rob Aiken does. If I'm not back here in an hour, you all drive away, okay? Just go where no one would think to look."

"I have a friend in North Platte."

I set a foot out on the pavement. "North Platte's good."

"You're going one place and we're going another," she said blandly.

"Just like at the gas station, yes. We survived. I will see you *here* in one hour." I got out, and leaned in to look at her. "Maybe take the kids in the store now so we don't look like freaks in an alley."

She sat propped against her door—all the fight in her seemed to have collected and dispersed like intestinal gas.

"I don't have lipstick," she said.

"You're fine. Honestly."

The four kids looked out at me from their cars, wide-eyed, hopping in their seats. They were good at waiting for instructions. Every year the seniors did a countywide scavenger hunt and this lucky bunch got to do it a year early.

"He said no spoiler on the car," Colleen told them behind me, "but I don't buy it."

The post office clock tower said it was ten after seven as I went up the police station steps. I held the door open as a middle-aged woman in a bulky sweater shuffled out, then she left me holding the door while she fished in her purse for cigarettes. Her mouth frowned like it didn't know any other shape.

"Gad," she said. "If you're going to see a detain-ee, you better take a Bible in there, and a priest too."

Everybody in Velouria was looking for a friendly ear.

"Who've you been in to see?" I asked.

"Oh, my *kid*," she said, lighting a Marlboro and exhaling hard out her nose. "Donny Brown. You must know him, right?"

"Sure," I lied.

"You wouldn't recognize him. He says some of them in those back cells need the doctor, so just now I asked the sergeant about it and he says the doctor comes in the morning. Full stop. Which of 'em in there is yours?"

"Jesse Turnbull," I said. "Got picked up with marijuana."

She gave me a weird look and went down the steps. Clint jogged up then, his jacket open to show off his NINJAS MAKE BETTER BOY-FRIENDS shirt.

"You don't need to be here," I said. "I'll run this alone. Go back and—"

"And eat *ice cream*?" His bunched fists looked like sock puppets. "I don't want to sit knitting, man! You know I broke my brother's *leg* when he was buttering toast, you know how messed up that is? You don't get to be king of everything, man."

"If I get in trouble here, there's no reason why we should both be in trouble."

"Dude." He shook his bottom teeth at me. "Way too late."

I was still holding the door, and I waved him through.

"There's no emperor but the emperor of ice cream," I said.

Two of the foyer's walls were covered with bulletin boards, as though the police station were the most obvious place for a second-hand leaf blower to find a buyer. Masseurs and notary publics. The third wall had a steel reception counter with a Plexiglas window, its speaking-hole the size of a quarter. Beyond the window a blond, crew-cutted cop eyed me from behind a crisp copy of *Rod & Gun*—he was such a ringer for Cam Vincent that it looked like the manufacturer had just reissued the design with a new outfit and hair color. SGT. DORFS-MAN, his breast pocket read.

"Help you fellas?" he asked.

I leaned in toward the speaking-hole, but not so close that I'd seem enthusiastic.

"I just want to see my cousin Donny Brown," I said. "Is there a room we go in to see the prisoners?"

"Visiting stops at six." He drummed on the magazine with a pen. "We're on the evening shift now, so that's that. Come back tomorrow morning at eleven, happy to bring Donny up for you."

"Aw, man." I rubbed my brow theatrically but not too theatrically. "We drove in from Fontaine to see Donny *tonight*—I have to be at *work* tomorrow morning!"

"Jay!" a man called from somewhere back in the station. "You gone on coffee?"

"No!" Sgt. Dorfsman kept his eyes me. "Been waiting half an hour!"

"Wait one sec!" called the voice.

"Didn't you just let his mother go back and see him?" I asked.

"Yeah, well, she's Doris and you guys aren't. What's your relation to *her* exactly?"

"Her sister's stepson," I said.

Clint, at my shoulder, just studied his scuffed pointy shoes, which was perfect.

"Okay! I'm here, I'm here!" A tall teenaged girl, her hair in a braid, slid in beside the sergeant on a rolling chair. "I had to TA the class, I'm so sorry, Jay!"

"Christ, Tina, half an *hour* ago!"

Dorfsman leapt up and stomped out of sight, shaking his head like a buffalo.

"I'm the intern," said the girl, smiling up at me. "Gets a little crazy around here! What can we do for you?"

"Well, we were about to go back and see—"

The station doors crashed open behind us and two scruffy guys hustled in, looking vaguely like little-league coaches in their ball caps and sweatpants. One carried, miraculously, a stack of fifteen pizza boxes, and the other a deflated basketball.

"This the recycling?" It was hard to tell which one was yelling. "Hell, I told you it wasn't!"

"Oh my God!" Tina shouted at them. "Get out of—this is the *last* time! You think your bullshit is funny?"

They looked baffled by that but went on yelling about the pulp and paper industry. I refused to lose my Donny Brown momentum. I stretched my arms apart and shepherded both of them toward the doors. *Go*, I thought, *before I feed you your legs.*

"Okay," Clint encouraged them, "there you go."

They tumbled out and down the steps, boxes and all, and I turned back to see Tina watching us with abject disgust.

"Can you *believe* that?" she asked. "My first *minute* here, and those losers come out of the woodwork! Sorry, who did you want to see?"

I stood up very straight, like a reliable citizen might, while I wondered how hard I'd have to hit the Plexiglas to bring the window down and put Tina through that wall behind her. I was strong enough. Grab Clint by the ankles and swing him like a bat.

"Donny Brown," I said. "Please."

Clint waited beside me—eyes down, hands clasped behind him.

"I'll buzz you in," she said. "Okay. Go ahead now."

She tilted her head meaningfully and I realized a doorknob to our right was buzzing. We stepped through into a particleboard hallway, then I closed the door behind us but not so the latch clicked shut.

"This," Clint whispered, "is fully like *The Matrix*."

We walked through to a little room furnished with what looked like a high school study carrel but with the middle board taken out so that two people could sit in the provided plastic patio chairs and stare at each other. Or, if they preferred, they could move the chairs and stare at each other from anywhere in the room. A steel door with a window in it led out into the squad room, jammed with a half-dozen desks and computer monitors and tattered motivational posters showing dolphins. A dark-haired cop sat facing me, pecking at his keyboard with the end of a pencil, while Sgt. Dorfsman sat with his back to us, reading his magazine and eating Irish stew out of a can—stuff must've been pulsing with nitrites because I suddenly had to swallow drool.

Tina hurried between the desks, leading a kid in a jean jacket by the arm.

"Here's your boy!" She held the interview-room door open with her hip and steered the kid inside. "Come tell me at the front when you're done, guys, and make sure to sign out. Ten minutes? Hurry up and sit down, Donny, before you fall on your butt."

She hustled off behind the squad room filing cabinets, and I caught Donny Brown under the armpits before he did fall on his butt—didn't feel like he weighed more than Josie. The door banged shut and the sergeant only glanced over his shoulder at it—he'd probably raise hell once his break was over.

"Please get him a chair," I said.

"Awesome," said Clint.

Donny was a blond kid with freckles, and because the rest of his face had the pallor of drywall the freckles looked fiery as the ends of cigarettes. His eyes were inside black bags and he could barely look up at us, but the worst was how badly his lips were chapped. I didn't feel the least urge to throw him through a wall. He smelled like sawdust—maybe we all did. We got him balanced on the chair. He lifted his eyes as high as my belly.

"Did, did Mom send you in?" he whispered.

"No, man, no." I knelt in front of him. "You worked at the factory, am I right? I'm the science teacher from Hoover, we got caught under that burst pipe and now things aren't right with us either, you understand?"

He nodded, though his head wavered.

"Other guys, they aren't going to live through the night with no bacon," he muttered. "I remember you guys, the other day. Dancing around. We saw you."

"How, uh, how do you guys get better?" Clint asked.

He'd stolen my question.

"Ha," Donny exhaled. "You're a real stupid kid. I said bacon."

"But, I," said Clint. "Bacon just makes you want more bacon!"

Donny stuck his tongue out, then withdrew it.

"How many Dockside guys are back there now?" I asked.

"Ha. None!" Donny's jaw tilted over to his shoulder. "Set our bail this morning—twelve grand for each of us. I was talking to my mom, ten minutes ago, she said she could cash her retirement fund, get me out. Took me back in the cells? Other guys are gone, Ben, Lars, all of them. Collis told me somebody came and paid for all of them guys to get out, and I was sitting right here talking to my mom, and I, I got missed! They had a van or something waiting in the back. Boom. Collis thinks it was Dockside but Dockside would've known I was in here, right? Aw, shit, you guys got working legs, run get bacon!"

"In a minute," I said.

He dropped his eyes, reached his right hand up and scratched hard at his temple, but the index finger folded sideways against his hand, dangling like a Christmas ornament. The rest of the fingers went on scratching.

"Dude!" Clint whispered. His lips worked themselves over his teeth, struggling to get the next syllable out.

"Donny," I said, "listen, did, did that gunk get on you guys *before* it got on us?"

"No, no," he murmured. Drops of purple blood, viscous as Vaseline, beaded on the exposed knuckle. "We mopped up that compound *after* it went on those kids. We had the respirators, the gloves, the whole shift of guys down there mopping, and you know what?"

"Take it easy," I said. "We've got plenty of time."

"The stuff was leaking onto the backs of our necks all the time, and we never even knew it. Never felt it. They hadn't shut the feeder all the way off. Some guys say they left it dripping on fucking *purpose*. You got anything salty?"

He scratched his chin, scratching hard, and that index finger dropped into his lap. Balanced there on his thigh.

"Who runs that Penzler outfit?" I whispered. "Who can tell us what's happening?"

"Corporate headquarters is like nine hundred miles away. Look it up on the fucking internet, man. And the other day he was saying he remembered these hippie doctors coming in like a year ago, asking about processing different crap."

"Hippie doctors," repeated Clint.

"He said this might've been their shit."

"Who said?"

"Our main guy. What's-his-name."

"Rob Aiken?"

"Yeah, funny name *now*, right? Shit!" He snatched up the finger and cradled it in his hands like a porcelain baby. "It's *me* now! Look at this, it ain't natural, man!"

Sergeant Dorfsman barged through the door.

"Time's up, Donny. Enough blowjobs for one night."

"You ate *bacon*, I smell it!" Donny clambered to his feet. "Gimme some!"

The sergeant backed up a step, hand on his holster. "No, I didn't…"

"Look at the goddamn kid!" I said. "Get him a doctor!"

"Back the hell up, Donny!" Dorfsman stammered.

Donny's eyes looked half asleep, but he shuffled forward like he wanted to stick his tongue down the sergeant's throat. He wasn't a fraction as angry as I would've been.

"Fun's fun," said Sgt. Dorfsman. "You sit the hell down."

He rammed a shoulder into Donny that sent him sprawling back into the chair, then the kid's momentum flipped him off the chair and onto his back. Clint knelt beside him and we tried to lift him by the shoulders.

"I told you," I snarled, "he needs a doctor!"

"He—he was—"

We sat Donny up and he looked, wide-eyed, from me to Clint to the sergeant, smacking his lips like he'd eaten too much peanut butter. His nose was missing. His dry sinuses winked at me in unison.

"What happened?" he asked.

"You—you're all right, son," said the sergeant, drawing his gun from its holster.

"Doctor!" I shouted.

"It's your fault!" Clint jumped up, backing Dorfsman into the corner. "You want to hit everybody in the mouth, hey? Let's do this!"

A figure skater yelling at a bear. Sergeant Dorfsman waved his gun vaguely at all three of us, backing toward the door, then he tore through it and turned to lock us in. Clint punched the window, making a dartboard of cracks. I could see the dark-haired cop, Collis, staring at us while yelling into a phone. I helped Donny into the chair again.

"Get me pounds of it," he murmured. "And liquid smoke! How come one leg's so much longer?"

His bare right leg protruded six inches out of its pant-leg. His knee or his hip had given way. The chair Clint threw at the door bounced off, so he started stomping the steel legs into a tangle—he was exactly like Watson to my Sherlock Holmes. I gave Donny a hard look, though his gaze kept roving around the room.

"We'll get you out of here, hey?" Though we'd need a wheelbarrow. "I'll get a—I've got a tarp in my car, I'll run and get that, and then we'll feed you, all right?

Donny pawed his face. He'd lost the middle finger too—it lay under the chair—and the sawdust smell in the room was pungent as turpentine.

"Hold tight." I squeezed his shoulder, gingerly.

I got Clint by the elbow—it didn't come off in my hand!—and we ran down the particleboard hallway and let ourselves back into the foyer, where the pizza-box drunks quietly studied bouncy-castle advertisements. We banged out the front doors then down the steps and toward my car a hundred yards away. I already heard a siren.

"So we peel out after that van that took the other guys, am I right?" Clint retied his scarf as we ran. "Somebody took those guys to fix them up—I know, right? Easy."

"How would we possibly follow that van?"

"We just, uh, traffic cameras! Because I don't want any of that shit with the hands and feet to happen to us, that was *retarded*. And the nose? The girls will barf when they hear that!"

"We won't tell the girls that part," I said.

"That's cool. I get you. Know where it'd be cool if that van went? Miami."

"We aren't following anybody right now. We're going back in for Donny."

We'd come to Velouria to find an antidote or a magnetic wristband or a deep-breathing exercise that would put me on the path back to Ray and Josie, so what did one zombie in the back of a town lock-up have to do with it? That Penzler headquarters he'd mentioned obviously ought to have been my next stop, but if *you* belonged to a species of which only a couple of dozen individuals existed, and that entire species was about to crumble into slabs of chipped beef, wouldn't you attempt to keep every one of them alive? Even Donny's last breath might impart a lump of invaluable wisdom, *Snowflakes will melt holes in your skin*, maybe, or *French's mustard is all you'll ever need* or *Go back to your children, man, hold them tight, and this nightmare will dissipate like steam from a mirror.*

I opened my trunk. The folded blue tarp, my old dog-burying shovel, two empty cases of Lucky Bucket—no bikers with snakes tattooed to their faces.

"But," Clint panted, "you were all, 'My name is Chuck Norris, I run alone.'"

I turned my head to peer out of the alley at Ye Olde Candy Shoppe across the main street. And it must've served karaoke as well as ice cream, because Franny and Amber swayed in the front window, backs to us, each with an arm around the other's waist, singing over "You Really Got Me" by the Kinks or possibly Van Halen, and they were both really nailing the guttural bottom of the *Oh yeeeeeeah*—maybe that was another blessing from Pipe #9. As their voices staggered over each other the track suddenly ended, and Colleen leapt up from somewhere beside them, clapping with her hands over her head. Might be I watched for a long while.

"Is it nap time?" Clint asked.

I pulled out the tarp and shovel and started back toward the police station.

AN AMBULANCE STOOD at the curb in front of the station now, and I could see two people rolling a loaded gurney out across the sidewalk—could we possibly be more useful than paramedics? I knew more about Donny's physiology, but was there a time limit to how long a hunk of one of our bodies could sit unattached before it…spoiled? It'd been at least five minutes since his left leg had dropped off.

"Run up into the foyer," I told Clint, "and get us a handful of thumbtacks."

The people were all inside the ambulance by the time we crept up, and it rocked at the curb like the medics were leaping up and down inside, and they probably were. I tapped the back door with the shovel handle. *Kong, kong, kong.*

"What?" they yelled from inside. "Tina, we *still* can't—"

The door was thrown open by a young guy with a black moustache, and a stethoscope tangled around his neck. He looked sweaty and slightly blue—"shock" was my diagnosis. Behind him a middle-aged woman with short red hair was already labeling a big ziplock bag that contained one human foot. A lean, hairless arm lay in her lap. Donny was sprawled on his back with an oxygen mask over his face, but he pulled that off with his remaining hand to gaze down the gurney at me and grin. He'd lost both legs and his left arm, and though his face was just missing a nose and a strip of check, a plastic zip-cord had been fastened around his head, right across his pathetic sinuses. He was in his underwear and his stumps looked like charred driftwood.

"Hey, it's the guy!" he croaked. "He knows about it!"

"What do you know about this?" spat the man, stepping down

onto the pavement. "Is it crystal meth?"

If he'd spent any time in a high school he'd have known that, despite many other drawbacks, crystal meth did not make your legs fall off.

"No," I said. "You can stick him back together if you've got a staple gun."

"Told you so," said the woman.

"No, just—how come he hasn't bled to death?" The man sat down heavily on the bumper and found his pulse on the side of his neck. "Are you his dad or something?"

"Hurry this up!" I said, throwing the tarp down, climbing in next to the gurney. "For all we know his head'll drop off. Why's that zip-cord around his face?"

The woman slowly looked up at Donny, then across to me.

"We're trying to save the ears," she said.

A crack showed down the front of his ear where it was trying to come away. A shudder ran between my shoulder blades.

"One of you has bacon in here!" I glared at the paramedics. "Give it to him! You want to save his goddamn ears, give it to him!"

The blue-tinged guy lowered his head.

"I *asked* you for bacon!" croaked Donny.

"You shit," said the woman. "Why'd you lie about it?"

"It's my dinner!" yelled the guy.

He got up and stomped onto the sidewalk, then we could hear him thumping up in the cab until he reappeared at the back door and climbed into the seat behind Donny.

"Hey, here we go." Clint stood at the end of Donny's gurney, offering me a handful of tacks. "I got you a baker's dozen. Uh, he still alive?"

"This is too many people," said the redhead.

The moustached paramedic was making a flourishy show for our benefit—unwrapping the wax paper, pulling his white-bread sandwich apart to extricate four pieces of dark, mayonnaise-y bacon. Salivating, I leaned in beside the kid's head and jabbed a green thumbtack into the top of the crack in his ear. Donny didn't flinch, just threw his head back and opened his mouth like a baby bird, so the paramedic broke a piece in half and dropped it in.

"Oh. Been dreaming of this," Donny murmured.

He must've just meant the bacon, because no one dreams optimistically of having no legs. Then he opened his eyes and gave me a long look.

"You guys better have pieces too," he said.

"Okay," said Clint and I.

The paramedic handed me all of the bacon and I took exactly two pieces, in a feat of incredible willpower, and put one in my mouth.

"Oh, burnt." I let out a long breath. "Perfect."

"Hey, thanks a bunch, guy," said Clint. "How you feel, you feel all right?"

Donny grinned at us, his teeth full of black flecks, then before I could eat the rest myself I crumbled the strips and dropped the bits into his mouth—might've been an arousing situation if he'd been a woman I lusted after.

"I'm going to run up to Dylan's," the redhead said as she slid past Clint. "He'll have a staple gun."

"Good!" I said. "Now where's his legs?"

"In the cooler." The guy pointed at a blue hatch beside me. "Hey, what's that—what's that stuck in his ear?"

"Thumbtack," I said.

I took a yellow one and jabbed it in place below the first—I could've sworn the crack was closing up already! Donny just stared at the ceiling, still chewing. The paramedic scrambled past Clint then said *Hunh* and a second later we heard a generous splash. Funny what'll turn some people's stomachs. In fact the sound of his vomiting was making me a little queasy. Donny reached up and felt his ear.

"More bacon?" he said.

"Step the fuck out of that vehicle," said Sgt. Dorfsman.

He stood behind the ambulance with his pistol raised, immovable as Harry Callahan in *Magnum Force*. The dark-haired cop from the squad room, Collis, peered at us through the open window from the cab, his own gun somewhere in the foreground.

"I'm trying to save this kid," I told them.

"Uh-huh," said Dorfsman. "Came at me inside. You've got explanations to make."

"No, no!" the paramedic guy gasped from outside. "Don't point that in there!"

"If he dies, it's your neglect that killed him." I dropped my hand below the gurney to feel between my feet for the shovel. "All of these prisoners you've had have specific dietary needs. Clint," I called, "go stand on the sidewalk."

If we were in custody we'd melt down to nothing, and so would the girls while they waited for us, and so would everybody. I'd have to take steps. Poor Sgt. Dorfsman—imagine the shift the poor jerk had been having already.

"He put my ear on!" reassured Donny.

A number of things happened then, in less time than it takes to inhale.

"You step *out* of—"

I heaved the shovel handle-first, and it flew over the gun and caught Dorfsman in the Adam's apple. His firearm discharged, and simultaneously the oxygen tank beside Donny's shoulder became this blue light that engulfed everything.

The gurney rocketed out of the ambulance, and I kept a hold on its railing. After thirty feet the whole thing crashed onto its side and I tumbled across the wet pavement, scraping my back and elbows over and over again, but how come Donny wasn't rolling beside me?

Twenty yards away, I picked myself up. The inside of the ambulance was ablaze and Donny lay below the back bumper, and he was nothing but a black torso. We'd only come along to help the kid out, apparently, me and my good intentions, and now he looked like he'd been scraped out of a frying pan.

My arms were black too. My windbreaker had melted away to nothing, and that tennis shirt I'd owned for seven hours hung in charred shreds from my shoulder.

No sign of Clint from where I swayed. Dorfsman lay in the fetal position against the curb. Collis threaded his way between the ambulance and gurney, his gun trained on the ground, eyes fixed on me. Seemingly unfazed. I didn't see the paramedic anywhere. A couple of civilian cars rolled toward us but stopped completely when they saw the situation that was unfolding, drivers rolling their windows back up. Pedestrians wavered on the sidewalk—those couples out enjoying the fact of their existence.

"Hands behind your head!" Collis shouted.

I stared at what was left of Donny and thanked God that Deb had removed Josie and Ray from my good intentions. *And that man who held the door for me*, Donny's mother would say, huffing on her Marlboro, choking back sobs, *that was the same man who killed him.*

"Behind your head!" the cop yelled again.

In my peripheral another ambulance came screaming up from behind me. Maybe the driver was too focused on collecting bodies off the pavement to notice Collis waving them away, or maybe I looked more like a victim than a fugitive, but the driver squealed to a stop five feet to my right, the whirling lights almost blinding me.

"No, no!" Collis hurried forward, gun raised.

I took three steps and opened the ambulance driver's door, engine still running—he was too busy pulling on latex gloves. I grabbed him by the shirt and threw him out onto the pavement.

"Whoa!" said the girl medic in the passenger seat. "Whoa, whoa!"

"Get away from there!" the cop yelled.

I glanced over and saw him aiming. I knew he was going to shoot, he'd have been crazy not to. I noticed the blade-end of my shovel—I loved the damn thing—was two feet from my toe. The driver rolled onto his side on the pavement.

Bam.

The bullet must've gone through my left thigh. All I really felt was a *pulling* sensation, no pain, but I dropped onto my knee—I couldn't help it.

"Okay," said Collis, shuffling forward. Eight feet, now five. "You're real lucky there's an ambulance here already. Now get—"

Clint loped over the smoking gurney like a goddamn panther, and in one bound wrapped himself around the cop's shoulder—beautiful to see—but Collis must've had some Rashard Mendenhall in him, because he shook the tackle off while I tried to put weight on my perforated leg. Clint sprawled against the bumper.

"*Now*," Collis huffed, gun coming up again, "get your—"

I grabbed the blade of the shovel and whacked him across the knuckles with the handle. He dropped the gun. Lurching upright, I laid the wood across his right ear but he kept coming forward like an absolute zombie, reaching for his nightstick as blood ran down his neck, and since he was going to be *that* determined I threw my shovel over the driver's seat and jumped in behind the wheel. The girl medic had already jumped out, and Clint jumped six feet straight up and came down on *top* of the open passenger door, so I hit the gas, tires squealed, and in the mirror I saw Collis crouched beside the gurney, firing after us, and even while we skittered around the post office Clint climbed down using the door handle and the edge of the window, then shut his door and pulled his seatbelt across like this was how he got to school every morning.

"Holy shit," I said, "you were pretty great with that stuff."

But then I remembered what I'd done to Donny Brown and couldn't think what else to say.

"Serious? You got *shot*, G—that was the *best*!"

The green digital clock on the ceiling said 7:38. My leg gave a single, hesitant throb—that was all we had to show for the previous half-hour.

"But we learned." I came to a red light so I turned right without signaling—nobody was behind us yet, but they would be. "To be vigilant about our bacon."

"That dude was so *sad*!" Clint made big gestures. "Left *behind* like that?"

I'd told Colleen to leave town if I didn't order a banana split within an hour, so I still had thirty-two minutes—or twenty-five, plus driving time.

My fingers were leaving coal-black skin on the steering wheel.

WITH OUR HEADLIGHTS off we rolled back across the Dockside parking lots, then I gave the ambulance's V-8 so much gas that she roared like a bull elephant and three seconds later we crashed through that chain-link gate. *Closed For Renovation* fluttered up past the windshield and away into the night for the first of its solo adventures.

"Uruk-hai ambulance," Clint said.

Then because we weren't actively *looking* for trouble I sent him back to close the gate—maybe the factory only had one of those drive-by security teams. In the side mirror I saw that the vehicle didn't say VELOURIA, just AMBULANCE, so they must've ponyed up with some other towns to buy a bunch wholesale, which would be terrific for us remaining incognito over a wide radius. Already doing such a great job with that.

That was the extent of my deep thinking, except for recalling Cam's theory that a real zombie would never notice his mind going.

We drove on past the VIP parking lot, where our bus had waited so patiently for us six days before, and pulled around to a loading dock. I slid out but the wind bit into my half-naked self so sharply that I climbed into the back and hunted around for clothes. They had a ridiculous Papa Smurf figurine hanging up in one cupboard and because it reminded me of any kid anywhere, not even my own specifically, I had to climb onto the gurney and lay there for a minute.

I hadn't been apart from Josie and Ray for six months. Only six hours. The project was too hard. I'd only watched one person die in my entire life, one had been more than enough up until then—then in the space of ten seconds I'd seen two more, assuming Dorfsman wasn't going to get up. I crumpled the blue gurney sheet again my chest. I had no way of knowing where my science-project mind and body would take me next, or take Colleen, or any of these rabid kids I was supposedly looking after.

I sat up and found the bullet hole through my pants but there wasn't much to see in the leg itself, just a spot that looked like a cigarette burn. I'd have to get some bacon soon to balance accounts with my body. I opened a cabinet behind the driver's seat and found a crisp white VELOURIA MEDICAL dress shirt in a dry-cleaning bag, and a fluorescent yellow VELOURIA MEDICAL jacket and a pair of black pants hanging behind that. I retired that new tennis shirt to the biohazard bucket.

"Okay," Clint panted. "I circled the place." He did a jumping jack. "I scoped out where we can get in. What's the story, we torching the place?"

"No." I was wiping soot off my hands before I started buttoning the shirt.

"Is it nap time?"

"How'd you break your brother's leg?"

"Hammer."

"You have some idea why?"

He shrugged. "Guy was busting my balls."

"What about?"

"Said he liked my shirt."

"Your parents see it happen?"

He sketched a half-circle with the pointed toe of his shoe. He eventually nodded.

"What'd they do?" I slid off the gurney so I could do up my pants.

"Don't know. I went out to the car."

"You'll be all right to go home after this?"

"You mean tonight?"

"No, once we all get fixed up. A week, a month."

"Maybe if I bring them, like, a million dollars and seven children."

"But that's the place where you want to end up?"

"Sure."

Which meant, as far as I knew eleventh-grade boys, that he was dying to crawl into his mother's lap and get rocked to sleep.

"There's this ladder around the side up to the roof." Clint swung his arms nonchalantly. "A bunch of pallets over there we could light."

We climbed one story and hopped across onto an air-conditioning unit, then I used the shovel to smash a second-floor window.

"Watch for all this glass," I whispered.

Climbing through the window frame took us onto a catwalk overlooking the cavernous factory, silhouettes of chains and conveyor belts standing out a little blacker than the rest of the blackness. The place felt frigid as a walk-in fridge, but even so, managed to smell of sawdust and cotton candy.

"We looking for more of the goo?" whispered Clint.

"Maybe," I said. "For all I know they make four hundred kinds. Let's look for, I don't know, clues. Recipes. A phone number."

I found a penlight in the pocket of my new yellow jacket.

"Didn't you talk to that tour guide guy? Didn't he tell you any of that stuff?"

We tiptoed downstairs to the bathrooms and a row of locked offices. The doors still said SUPPLY MANAGER or HUMAN RESOURCES but the relevant employee names had been scraped off. Renovation to make our community better.

"I'll see if there's bacon in the fridge," Clint whispered.

"Don't turn any lights on."

The shovel pried the knob off the site manager's door and as it swung open I prepared myself for rifling filing cabinets and hacking launch codes or whatever a hero on TV would've done. The desk was bare and its drawers empty, as it turned out, but on the credenza I found a sheaf of letterhead emblazoned with Dockside's Velouria address on the top right corner, and Penzler HQ's on the top left:

> *1616 Highway 91a*
> *Preston, OH*
> *43215-6108*

Preston, Ohio: a city of gray-suited men, goo-filled syringes spilling from their pockets, while secretaries ran off red-toner photocopies of my kids' faces. My brain clattered as I imagined getting us there. Anywhere in Ohio was eight hundred–odd miles east via the interstate, though I'd have to get onto I-80 via Nebraska 33, which started back in Hoover. Then east on I-80, passing forty-seven short miles north of Pawnee.

But first I rifled filing cabinets just so I wouldn't regret *not* having rifled them, though all I found were team lineups for an August 2006 softball tournament.

Clint crept in empty-handed, so I set him to work in the other offices, but it was the same crap in all of them. Never saw the half-expected portraits in oils of these fabled hippie doctors. I'd been damn lucky that the letterhead had been left behind, but then as I scrutinized a bare whiteboard for microscopic clues it occurred to me that it would've been even luckier—at least faster—if I'd tried a reverse-411 on James Jones's fax number or called information from a pay phone, asking for Penzler. Things a person with an adequately functioning brain might've done.

Another thing it should've done: not left Hoover without Harv.

I crept across into the men's room and gazed for a full minute at the urinals, the last place I'd peed as a normal man. I shone the penlight on my face and spent a few minutes at the sink scrubbing the black layer with hand soap and paper towels, but then I figured out it wasn't grime but my own skin blackened by the exploding oxygen tank, so then I just had to find the edges and peel it away one strip at a time, trying to pull a bigger piece each time—Josie would've loved it—until only black pouches around my eyes were left. The new layer everywhere else looked pink as a piglet, and that image made my stomach rumble.

I found Clint in the hallway, holding a white page triumphantly over his head.

"What?"

"Muffin recipe."

We tiptoed through the factory until we found a workbench and the classic red toolbox, crammed with a staple-gun, hammer and drill, pouches of nails and screws and boxes of staples—and I made sure they were the right width for the staple gun, too, because I'd been fooled by that when I'd built our rabbit hutch.

"Couple of staples?" Clint whispered. "Your finger healed right up?"

"And a good night's sleep, and half a pig of bacon."

"Man, I'm going to staple my whole *neck*! Like for preventative medicine."

We collected ten thousand from the drawers, to really do our ambulance justice.

I looked at my watch—8:45! I'd botched the operation by pulling that skin off my face and now Colleen was watching for the North Platte exit from Amber's back seat.

I PARKED THE ambulance in the alley behind the ice cream shop. But the rear entrance was locked, so I left Clint behind the wheel with the motor running, and I walked calmly around the block and peered in the front window. The place was still open, a dreadlocked kid strumming a guitar on a couch, but none of my girls were in sight. In my imagined role as coffee-breaking paramedic I pursed my lips and wondered whether I really wanted that latté after all. Jerked my head to gaze casually across the street, like maybe there'd be a taco stand over there. A gray cat appeared to be reading a newspaper but none of our cars were in the alley anymore.

I took deep breaths under the Velouria streetlight like a character in *On the Road* achieving a moment of grand catharsis, though really I was up to my top lip in steaming wet shit. I fumbled for my wallet, pulled out the picture and held it to my forehead without daring to look at it—maybe the kids she'd given birth to were in a safe place, or maybe not. The photo felt cool as a flower petal. The feed store beside the ice cream shop was still open, the pallets in front stacked with green-and-white fifty-pound bags showing grapes and watermelons spilling from a cornucopia. CALCIUM NITRATE FERTILIZER. It didn't say RETAIN APPENDAGES LIKE NEVER BEFORE! or even BACON SUBSTITUTE, but even so, I wondered if we could make use of the stuff if things got bad enough.

A siren shrieked behind the ice cream shop, only for a second. Clint.

I rounded the corner into the alley in a spray of gravel on my Fast Willie Parker legs, and there was the good ol' ambulance creeping toward me, headlights off, but by the streetlight I could see silhouettes of two people in the front. Relief flooded up from my feet. The passenger window came down and Grace leaned out.

"They're all in back." She held a striped straw in the gap between her teeth. "I'm the human peashooter, see?"

COLLEEN SAT BESIDE me in the front, looking for bluegrass on the radio, and her hissing aversion to static somehow distracted me from the likelihood that we'd hit a roadblock as we turned, say, from Pine onto North Locust.

"One of the barista girls said, 'Hey, is that anybody's car getting towed?' And we just had to sit their with our cones. I barely looked outside in case they knew what we looked like, and at one point all four of us went to the bathroom. The barista girl told us her uncle had worked at Dockside and for some reason they'd towed *his* car away. I'd just as soon go back to Hoover."

"That son of a bitch from the gas station must've had something to do with it. Called in our plates or something."

"And the worst?" Franny called through the little window from the back. "They were out of Curly Wurly bars!"

"Hazel Dickens," Colleen said, still turning the dial. "I want to hear Hazel. Doug wanted Megan to be named Hazel after her, did you know that? I wouldn't let him."

She found a song that sounded like a drum machine playing over a weed-whacker and an eight-year-old singing about her skateboard.

"Turn that up!" they hollered from the back.

Even by my standards it would've been stupid to have driven right through downtown Velouria, so I cut back to the side road to Fontaine so I'd be able to drop into Hoover from the north. I told Colleen the nine hundred things we'd found out and that we were bound for Ohio now via the interstate and Route 33, which meant driving back through the old hometown.

"Any reason to stop?" Colleen asked dully. "Franny said she tried calling every kid she could and got no answer."

No matter what Colleen said, her voice wasn't entirely steady.

"Parents have them all at the hospital by now," I said.

"Even all their cells phones, no answer."

"That's weird. She try Harv Saunders?"

"Probably."

"I'll check on him anyway."

The moon was nearly full. Ten miles before Fontaine, the forest to my right fell away for a few acres of field, and something made me lift my foot off the gas: some guy staggering parallel to the road, twenty or thirty yards away, arms out in front of him, staggering. He fell down. I stopped the ambulance. He got a knee under him and lurched to his feet again, the greenish moonlight across his shoulders.

"Jesus Christ," said Colleen.

Now he shambled forward with his arms swaying at his sides.

"What?" the kids called. "We only got windows out the back!"

He disappeared into the blackness of the trees, and I pulled back onto the road before a cop could stop and kindly ask if I was having any trouble.

Unwanted elements skulking in shadows. A guy could look right at these people, to paraphrase Dad, and never know the staples and scars they kept under their T-shirts.

JUST NORTH OF Hoover I bought fuel with the Pegasus gas card in the ambulance's ashtray. Apparently none of the kids needed to go in to pee, which I found odd.

"Is this almost Hoover?" Amber called. "We should stop at 7-Eleven!"

I immediately felt the guy's ear against my tongue again and a chill went up my spine. How many cops had come? Would they still be peering inside every vehicle? Were we the subject of a countywide APB out of Velouria? Would I be able to resist chewing off the *next* ear that got between my teeth? Because I'd been close.

"Oh!" said Colleen.

I lifted my foot off the gas. "What?"

"I thought that was Megan."

We turned onto Clemons Street off Casement. I'd never been out in Hoover later than my kids' bedtime, but even so, I thought the streets and sidewalks looked *too* deserted. A heavy guy with a backpack seemed to watch us from under a streetlight.

"Seems to be a lot of lights on up the street," said Colleen.

"One thing it better not be is fire engines."

"Is there a fire?" they called from the back.

The Saunders' driveway was empty but every light in the house seemed to be burning, the birch tree's shadow stretching across the yard. I banged on the door. *Hello, Asshole*, I thought, *I'm here to kidnap your son.*

After ten seconds the door swung open and Harv's sister blinked up at me. She wore a bikini top and jeans.

"Sorry to bother you so late," I said. "Not an emergency or anything."

"So how come an ambulance's out there?"

"Is Harv here?"

She pursed her lips, a silver cell phone in her fist.

"He took the bus to Chicago. I told him forget it, but maybe, you know what Harv's like—you saw him, he was okay the other night, right? He just needs to stretch. High school can really stifle."

"Your dad let him go to Chicago? What is he, sixteen?"

"Good night," she said, and shut the door.

Which meant Jones had him, that the military had strapped him to a table somewhere. I stared at the brass knob. *I would've loved to have rescued you, Harv, but I was completely too late.*

I hurried back toward the street, propelled by the wings on my ankles. Instead of spending the afternoon chewing ears at 7-Eleven I should've been disemboweling Dave Saunders. The verb suited the guy. I frowned at Colleen through the ambulance window—no Harv—but she smiled back like the place was a car lot and I'd just bargained the sales manager down to nothing.

In the shadows around on the driver side, Harv stood leaning a foot from the gas cap, his sky-blue Thunder cap in his hands.

"Mrs. Avery," he said quietly, "told me I can come with you guys."

"Oh," I sighed, "shit. Mrs. Avery's right."

I wrapped my arms around the kid, felt his brush cut against my ear. Might've been a bit much from his chemistry teacher, but the pink goo had made me unruly.

I MADE HIM ride in the back, the three girls up on the gurney and the two boys on the jump seats alongside.

"Sure, Franny, yeah, plenty of room on here," said Amber. "I sure love that skirt." The veils had dropped from her sarcasm. "Are those turtles?"

"Is it Friday morning yet?" asked Franny. "I'm supposed to be selling chocolate almonds for church today! This is way better—I mean, c'mon, right?"

"Hold up, G," said Grace. "Where we going next?"

"Hell, yes," Clint hissed. "Good one!"

"You said that there's a clinic for us outside Lincoln or something, that was for real?" asked Grace.

"I don't know much about it." I folded my arms, couldn't help it. "I'll go and talk to them, but first I'm taking you guys where you'll actually be safe."

"Hey, we're going to Ohio, yes, the bad-guy headquarters? Lincoln's totally on the way!" Grace drove her cupped hand along her forearm, but it stopped at her elbow to hop up and down. "We just stop to check it out—take in our drills, our staple guns, say, 'What up, bitches?'"

"I'm not taking you to Ohio," I said.

"Why do you get to decide everything?" asked Clint, pulling latex gloves from the dispenser. "Why you treating us like dipshits?"

"Hey, you think I *want* to be hauling six other people around, like that's the most efficient way to do this? I didn't ask you guys to come with me!"

"Yeah, you did!"

Couldn't remember whether I had or not.

Clint waved a dismissive glove. "Let's just get somewhere."

"Okay, boys better not look up any skirts," Amber said, pulling her hair back with her one mighty hand.

"You're wearing pants," said Harv.

"I could change that."

I stepped back and swung the heavy doors shut.

"Lincoln!" shouted Grace. "Or I scream 'til—"

WE DROVE OUT of Burroughs County just as James Jones of Penzler Industries had kindly suggested. The gas tank was full, so we could've carried on escaping eastward for hours, but after ninety minutes out on 33, I steered into a truck stop, so low on nitrites that the feeling had left my feet. Must've been pretty funny to watch me stumble indoors and hunt around for a table, followed by one shivering-tired woman and some ugly kids with pointed heads.

The place was crowded even though it was after eleven. The waitress sauntered over with her coffee pot. She was an older woman with ample hips.

"What do you serve at this time of night with bacon in it?" I asked.

She said, "You can order nothing *but* bacon if you want," and gestured with her order pad to a banner over the cash register. ALL-DAY BREAKFAST.

Clint and his chair fell backward but he continued through a flawless somersault across the thin brown carpet and came up on his feet.

"I love you," I said.

"I do hear that from time to time." The waitress slowly blinked as she scratched her inner arm. "What'll it be?"

"Well." My mouth had filled with a pint of saliva. "We can each probably handle, what, twenty or thirty strips of bacon? I'll hold onto the menu in case."

"Well, how many *exactly*?"

"Oh, God." Like constellations, the kids' faces spun around me—I already held my knife and fork in either hand. "Seven of us. Let's say two hundred pieces. "

She wrote *side b × 100* before sliding the pen into her blouse pocket.

"I love you," I said again, and meant it.

"Ma'am?" Grace clasped her hands as though in prayer. "We all love you."

"Yes, dear, okay. I'll see this gets out as quick as possible."

A horrible possibility occurred to me as she started toward the kitchen.

"Miss, Miss!" I called.

She stopped in her tracks and turned back, rolling her eyes for the benefit of the tattooed truckers at the table across from ours, and if those guys had looked sideways I would've smashed their heads together so hard they'd have spat out each other's teeth. But they just stirred their coffee.

"What *is* it?" she asked me.

"We don't want the bacon *too* quickly, all right? Overdone is fine."

"Burnt?"

"Burnt is fine, sure."

She shook her head over the order pad.

"For *each* of the two hundred pieces?"

"Peter," Colleen muttered. "Don't."

"I get the feeling you're taking our goodwill for granted here!" I called.

"Oh!" The waitress swallowed. "No, sir."

She hurried through the swinging door into the kitchen, where she and a guy in a crumpled chef's hat looked out at us through the rectangular order window. I waved at them, half-heartedly, to show that I was a regular guy, really just as bored to death as anybody else. Clint finally got his chair back beside the table.

"Know what my dad would say?" Franny folded a napkin into a hat. "*Exactly*."

"You don't tell them what you want, how're they supposed to know?" said Clint.

Colleen rubbed her eyes then looked across at me. They were bloodshot as hell.

"I like this place!" Harv spread his arms. "This is…really great."

Then I realized I didn't have cash in my wallet. Credit cards were gone in the house fire. After the shit I'd just stirred up! I must've looked confused as hell because the kids started to get up out of their chairs—I felt in the VELOURIA MEDICAL jacket's pockets and found nothing but chapstick and some flimsy business cards, BURROUGHS COUNTY EMERGENCY MEDICAL SERVICES, without anybody's name on them.

"Don't you have money?" Colleen asked quietly.

Throat constricted, I nodded dumbly. I was only capable of over-reacting.

"I've got plenty now, and I'll get plenty more." She set her purse on the table and it clattered like it was full of cutlery, though maybe it was just her baton. "Doug wanted Megan not to have to worry, so he got us both the fattest policies Mutual offered, and, oh, he was so excited!"

She smiled at all of us around the table and the kids did their best to smile back.

"Megan's great," said Grace.

"She's hilarious!" said Amber.

"Insurance is excellent," I said. "Hope we're around long enough to collect it."

Then I was so relieved about the money that I had to push my chair back and sit with my head between my knees.

"Say, buddy?" One of the truckers smiled ingratiatingly.

I straightened up. "What?"

"Where'd you go to school?"

"Champlain State," I snapped.

Though I'd gone to UC Denver. Before Wahoo we'd lived in Champlain, where the upstairs neighbor's son had written his para-medic-qualification exam up at the university, though for all I knew he'd taken the actual courses on Planet Krypton.

"That a good school?"

I must've heard that as an accusation, because my ears went hot—I had sufficient circulation for that, apparently, though the pins and nee-dles had spread up to my knees so that walking the four steps to crack his skull might've been a chore.

"Why do you ask?" I gulped, all ho-hum and normal.

"Oh, 'cause my niece is down in Velouria, too, thought I'd pick your brain to see how far away she'd need to go to qualify, you know? Good program at Champlain?"

"Oh, sure." I dropped a sugar cube in my coffee. "The lectures weren't so hot but the field practicums were amazing. Every night on shift I thank God I went to that school, their practicums are killer."

"That right?" He raised his eyebrows.

"There's a bloodwork research program in the lab that's just awesome."

"Huh, okay." He turned back to his friends. "I'll tell her."

"Bathroom?" asked Amber.

All four females got up and went. Colleen took her purse. I sipped coffee that tasted like weak tea. I'd impressed the hell out of myself—as long as all I had to do was *talk*, I could pass for a paramedic any day of the week, and that could get me in the door at Penzler Industries, 1616 Highway 91a, Preston, OH. A concerned medical professional representing the equally concerned citizens of Velouria. Harv and Clint were tearing their napkins to shreds and eating them.

"Say, buddy," the trucker called, "you all right?"

I was sitting with my cheek against the placemat.

"Just hungry," I answered. "Thanks."

"Shit, Harv," Amber said as she slid into the chair across from him. "What's up with your arms?"

The other girls sat and we all stared at his bare arms—they were peppered with what looked like scabbed-over chicken pox. He folded them to his chest.

"Yeah," he said. "They're just old cigarette burns. Not healing too good."

"How exactly did you get them?" Colleen asked, her chin on the heel of her hand.

"Well." He gazed past my shoulder. "After the thing with how my head healed up, they wanted to make a movie of everything else. They wanted to break a world's record for all the bacon they got in me, so that was cool, they filmed that for like two days straight. Then he and Kim were arguing like crazy, and Dad came in with the tin-snips and told me to put out my fingers and I just thought, I am getting *out of here*."

He smirked at us. Clint and Franny had lost interest and played demolition derby with salt and pepper shakers.

"Hey, what'd the team do this week if you were home?" asked Amber.

She'd smeared on mascara for some reason, then I remembered the Harv conversation in Cam's office.

"Dunno. We weren't answering the phone." He chewed a fingernail—his lips seemed too heavy for his mouth, so he looked slightly stupid. "You know I hit eleven threes last Friday?"

"*I* knew that," said Grace.

The waitress set down two platters of bacon, heaped high as footballs. The kids began to rake it onto their side plates, but I did not pick up a single piece, though my arms shook.

"Excuse me, Miss," I said. "I'm sorry about before."

She smiled down at me, squinting too much for it to be genuine.

"Well, we've both come out the other side. Stressful job you've got there."

"You're very understanding." I felt a vein twitch in my neck. "We're going to want some to go too, yes?"

"You give me a number," the waitress said, "and I'll see what's in back."

"My brother never even *took* Chemistry 11," said Clint, "and he could eat all this!"

"Wouldn't he barf?" asked Grace.

"He'd just burp in my face."

"You think he's doing okay?" asked Franny.

He glanced at her, tucked his chin down but kept on chewing.

"Christ almighty," one of the truckers said. "I never saw so much bacon!"

"Oh, we do this now and then." I rolled up my sleeves. "Our night to howl."

COLLEEN HADN'T WANTED to go to the till so she'd handed me the cash and taken the kids outside, so now I had four strips crackling in my mouth, my jaws working like shears, and another forty side orders crammed into three Styrofoam takeout containers that sent angelic gusts of steam up my sleeve. Backing out the diner door in my fluorescent jacket, I nodded once more to the wide-eyed truckers—obviously I was trying to drum up resuscitation work for myself—and considered beatifically that before long I'd have my whole litter of kittens well-fed and hidden away while I went off to serve my still-higher calling of figuring out how to deplasticize us. And who'd be accomplishing that? Just me, alone again.

I trotted around a Freightliner semi just in time to see Clint's denim elbow arc back, then his fist flashed out to connect with Harv's nose, reproducing the pop of an ice cube dropped in lukewarm lemonade. Harv swayed back one step then fell down.

Franny stomped the pavement. "Yeah!"

"Woot, woot!"

Amber slapped her thigh and Grace clapped. The four women stood beside the ambulance like a boisterous police lineup under the lot's yellow lights.

"Fuck him up!" Colleen yelled, hands cupped to her mouth.

"Aw, bash me around all you want," Harv said, licking his upper lip, propping himself on an elbow. "You *are* a panty-wearing faggot."

"Shit, just get up, man," said Clint, holding his fists stiffly in front of him. "I got to hit something so bad."

"Fuck! Him! Up!" the women yelled.

"Why do I have to deal with this?" I asked. "You two need bums wiped, you wipe each other's bums. The rest of us need to be some-where."

The boys dropped their arms and stared at me like I was directing a *Raging Bull* remake and I'd told them their acting stunk.

"Don't listen!" Colleen yelled, slapping her thighs. "Fight!"

"Is that the bacon?" asked Clint.

Then all six shuffled toward me, guided by salivary glands, so I cir-cled to the driver's side where I threw a long shadow. Colleen stumbled ahead of the others, arms extended.

"I'll hold those," she said. "You'll be driving."

I carefully set the three tepid containers between her hands, and she turned and gave them to Grace. Then she spun back and clocked me across the jaw with her left—like me, she still had a wedding ring on, so of course that stung. I teetered around a step, trying to shake it off as the blaze from the floodlights wove between my eyelids, then she must've leapt right on me because my head was jammed in an armpit as I looked at the ground and a elbow, pointy as a chisel, tenderized the middle of my back. Then I was slammed backwards into the ambu-lance, and a pair of fists tried to break through my belly to my spine. I could barely get an eye open to see her tracksuit bobbing there but, snaking my hands in front of me, I managed to get hold of her wrist.

"Don't you goddamn!" she said, and head-butted my chest.

I brought my foot up hard into her crotch then my knee connected with her chin so her teeth clacked together. She straightened up and I rammed a shoulder into her chest so she stumbled backward, pinwheeling her arms until she spread-eagled across the hood of a silver car with reptilian headlights. The old guy inside woke up, hollered and leaned on the horn, then he was out beside the little car before Colleen was even on her feet. He sported a comb-over and a puffy down vest.

"Look at my fucking hood!" He actually stamped a foot. "Lady, you better, you better have a checkbook, because…"

He couldn't have noticed the half-dozen of us happily beating the shit out of each other fifteen feet away or he might not have gone on, screaming at the bum-shaped dent in his hood. She meekly stood beside him, one hand pressing the small of her back while she wiped her mouth on her sleeve. She gazed up at the guy, back at the car. Its paint looked distinctly yellow under those lights. She looked back at the guy

"You in Hoover yesterday?" I heard her ask.

Then she grabbed the back of his collar and slammed his face into the car's roof, jumping back onto the hood for leverage. Blood and drool ran down the edge of the windshield, but after four or five good crunches, he pulled himself out of the vest and reeled away backwards. By then I had my arms around her waist. Thrashing, she flailed the vest at me so the zipper caught me in the lip.

"The thing's gray or something!" I bawled at her. "Not yellow!"

She went limp, spread her hand on the roof while I still held her an inch or two in the air. Her breathing hammered against me.

"Right," she huffed. "Hand's yellow too." She frowned at me over her shoulder, her eyes barely open. "So this isn't the guy."

I set her down. One side of the hood had the texture of a corn flake.

"Not ready for recycling, but it's getting there. I should leave him a number. Doesn't even have a spoiler, Jesus. A Chevette coupe." She shook her head, defeated, then her fist snaked out to whack me in the chest. "But that was fun, right? And the next guy's going down *twice* as hard!"

Amber threw an almighty swing that Franny ducked beneath, one palm to the ground like a ninja, but as she came up Clint hit her with such an uppercut that she wound up with the back of her head on the pavement and her groin against a lamppost. In the meantime I carried the vest to where the old guy crouched against the wheel of a Coca-Cola trailer, a handkerchief pressed to his nose. His hair had flopped over his left ear so he looked like a harassed rooster, and his forehead was nothing but oozing lumps. The saturated handkerchief dripped onto his already-bloody shirt.

"Sir," I said, "I cannot apologize enough. She's between facilities and she got away from me." My throat felt rough from what Colleen had done to me—I tasted blood. "Call this number, they'll be eager to discuss your compensation." I held out a business card. "You'll find first-aid personnel inside the restaurant, patch you up in a jiffy, but me, I have to get my patient on the road before we get another incident, alrighty?"

He pulled the handkerchief away and blinked up at me, his swollen eyes streaming tears. One of his front teeth had been shattered into an isosceles triangle.

"I'm taking the car to my son," he sighed.

A bubble of blood burst on his lip. Even compared to me, Colleen had turned into a full-on nut.

"Okay," I said. "You call that number first chance you get."

I strode back to the ambulance. Franny had Amber backed against the front of it, that ugly serape bunched in one fist and the other thrown back, knuckles already bloody. Clint lay on his side on the pavement, Grace's boot buried in his middle. Harv stood half-asleep, arms around the takeout containers.

"All right, everybody," I called. "Let's go."

Like a Sunday School shepherd I beckoned to them, even Colleen as she rocked the Chevette up and down like its shocks needed testing. The kids all unclenched fists, helped Clint to his feet, hobbled around to the big back doors. I climbed up behind the steering wheel and put the key in the ignition. Colleen walked through the headlights as they flared on, then stopped and picked something up off the pavement. She came around to the passenger door.

"Got a thumb here—any takers? Doesn't have nail polish."

Silence from the back.

"Wait, yeah," said Clint. "That's mine."

"I call staple gun!" yelled Grace.

As we rolled onto the highway Colleen kept pressing a tissue to her lip then looking to see how much it was bleeding, which wasn't much. She threw me a smile.

"Know how fun that was, smashing his face? That really was just *a lot of fun!*"

Friday, October 28.

EVERY TIME I saw a police car coming I tried to let my face droop so that in his headlights I'd look like an authentically haggard paramedic, when really I was so buzzed with nitrites I felt like a sparkler on a birthday cake. Every cop gave me the single-finger-off-the-steering-wheel salute.

"But losing fingers must be a distinguished Nebraska tradition!" From the passenger seat Colleen addressed the window to the back. "Think about it, all those poor stupid pioneers, caught out in snow-storms *without mittens*, and farming accidents—my god, the early days of threshers!"

"My mom's dad lost three fingers in a mill," Harv said. "He never—"

"And we don't know the first thing about the Native Americans," said Colleen. "This whole road might be finger bones!"

The driver ahead of us, in a black F-350 pickup, threw a cigarette out his window and it sparked across the road.

"No more deep thinking," I said. "Grab every smoker and kill them."

The remnants of unpopulated cornfields flickered past in the dark. An early-hours call-in show called *Out There* came on the radio. With his *cleverest-person-living-but-God-I'm-tired* delivery, Tom Exegesis kept proclaiming, "The truth is…somewhere…in the middle." With my fingers looking green in the light of the gas gauge, that sounded extremely profound.

"The truth is up yours," said Clint.

"Turn it up some more," called Grace.

He took an enthusiastic call from Scott regarding the pre-Hallow-een ghost tours recently conducted in Asheville, North Carolina, and how more than one visited spirit had followed overjoyed tourists back to their hotel.

"Now," Tom concluded, "is this a case of fifteen apparitions genu-inely wanting to go home with these fifteen people, or is it a case of fif-teen people inexplicably organizing themselves to tell the same story?

The truth, *I* believe, is somewhere…in the middle."

A nervous-sounding guy named Vince came on—I pictured him huddled in his parents' basement, sweat trickling behind his glasses.

"Love the show, I'm a first-time caller…."

"First time for everything, glad to have you."

"I've looked it up in the dictionary, and it just says, 'A corpse said to be revived by witchcraft,' but, God, there's more to it than that, am I right?"

"All right, hold on, so you're talking about a *zombie*? You're asking what constitutes a zombie?"

"Yes, exactly!" said the caller. "What constitutes—"

"And that'd be *way* at the back of the dictionary—I wouldn't have the stamina to go back that many pages, so I salute you, Vince. Now, why don't you start us off, what makes a zombie a zombie in the *popular* imagination? Or if you're of a more critical stripe, what makes a zombie in the *academic* imagination?"

"Bacon!" we all announced.

"They ought to eat brains, that's for sure," said Vince.

"All right, brains," Tom said wearily. "And they've got to have limbs falling off, things like that?"

"Seen it happen," I agreed.

"Right here," Amber said behind my head. "Poster girl."

"That's a—that's a *sick* zombie," said Vince. "That's ill health that makes 'em fall apart. A well-nourished zombie can walk around like anybody else, no problem."

"Ah, unless," countered Tom, "the corpse had decomposed *prior* to reanimation to the point that, you know, it was structurally *unable* to walk around like everybody else. That's your *Night of the Living Dead* model, am I right? That's an entire graveyard revived indiscriminately."

I waited for Vince to somehow bring the citizens of Hoover, Nebraska, into the conversation, but whether it would be to prove or refute a given theory I couldn't decide.

"C'mon, babies, ask how well they take a punch!" said Franny.

"You there, Vince?" asked Tom.

"The real reason zombies in the movies *only* eat brains," the caller murmured, "is Hollywood screenwriters can't think of anything else for them to do."

"Now, hold on one second," Tom replied lethargically. "*You* were

the one who said they *had* to eat brains, right off the top of this conversation."

"Yeah, but I was only—"

"And if you go back to Bela Lugosi as the zombie-master in *White
Zombie* in the thirties, Lugosi was killing these Haitian field workers
and bringing them back the same night they were buried, just so he'd
have a more complacent workforce, wasn't that right? And not one—
and here's my point—not one brain consumed in the entire picture."

"Movies weren't good back then," said Vince.

"Bullshit. I beg your pardon," said Tom. "But my reading on Haitian zombies, which is by no means comprehensive, doesn't rule out
the *possibility* of brains, since apparently if you fed a zombie even a
speck of meat or—what was the other one?—*salt*, meat or salt, if they
tasted either one they'd be reminded they once were human and col-
lapse on the spot, never to be revived."

"Oh, ho!" the kids hollered in the back.

"Okay," I told the radio. "We're talking different species."

"But that whole scenario still begs a *couple* of questions," Tom said,
ignoring us entirely, "the first of which is whether it would have been
possible for Bela Lugosi to reanimate a sugarcane picker, say, five, ten
minutes after death, and for that zombie to maybe think that he'd only
taken a *nap*, you see what I mean? The cells in his brain wouldn't have
deteriorated, maybe the only reason that the zombie of the *popular*
imagination shambles and slurs the way he does is that his mind has
rotted down to that little lizard-brain at the top of his spinal cord, isn't
that possible? The medulla oblongata? But my initial thought—and I
appreciate your patience on this, Vince—is that there might be people
walking around right *now* who aren't aware that they're zombies because they weren't clued in that they had died in the first place, is that a
possibility? You see what I mean, is that an acceptable stretch?"

I couldn't help but grin. Someone was speaking frankly about our
lives. Donny had in the Velouria jail, true, but this was less disturbing
visually.

"Vince?" asked Tom.

"I'm here. You just cut a little close to the bone there."

"Fucktard!" Franny yelled in the back.

But *was* there any chance the stuff from Pipe #9 actually *had* killed
us dead and brought us back to life an instant later? Jesus, but the hippie doctors of Preston, Ohio, had a lot to answer for!

"Perfect. An intellectual battle. All right, the second question is whether the zombie you're defining is the *cinematic* zombie, in which case we should look no further than the oeuvre of George Romero, or if it's the *anthropological* zombie, in which case we look—where?—no further than rural Haiti? But does it have to be *one or the other*?"

I squeezed the steering wheel giddily as I waited for it.

"The truth," Tom drawled, "is some…where in…the middle. Thanks for that, Vince. Next caller is on the line from Alberta, Canada. How are you, Betty-Anne?"

She wanted to talk about the past summer's *astronomical* increase in UFO sightings in southern Alberta compared to any previous year on record, and Tom countered with alarming statistics concerning the number of F-18s airborne over the North American continent on any given night, then he wondered aloud whether extraterrestrials might not be more attracted to the tarsands projects in *northern* Alberta.

Then he played a Pan-American Rent-a-Car commercial.

"Clint, get on the cell," said Grace. "Tell 'em what went down in Velouria!"

I passed a pickup truck pulling a shiny aluminum horse trailer. I remembered Rob Aiken mentioning an Old Man Penzler, and I pictured him as Bela Lugosi, with the widow's peak and eyebrows. Hell, was there even such a person as Old Man Penzler?

"Next caller's from out in Nebraska. Go ahead, Lydia."

I drew breath in so hard I nearly coughed.

"Hi," she said, "thanks."

"Aw, yeah!" Amber whooped. "My homegirl Lydia Dershowitz!"

Of course, with the braces. I reached across to the passenger seat for bacon.

"I'm calling because of the guy a minute ago—Vince?"

"Yes, recollections of Vince bring a warm bloom to one's cheek. Zombies, yes."

"She wasn't at school Tuesday," Franny announced.

"I, um, I guess I want it to be made public that a lot of the people like you talked about are living together as a community, uh, a co-operative, I guess, and I think that means they have more intelligence than that caller was giving them credit for. They're *organized*, I mean."

I took my foot off the gas and let the ambulance coast along the shoulder.

"Where is she?" asked Amber. "What the hell's she talking about?"

"Oh," Colleen exhaled. "Megan."

"Okay," said Tom, "so by 'people you were describing,' you mean zombies?"

"Guess so."

"And these people are zombies because, what? They eat brains to survive?"

"No, not at all! They eat—"

"Their limbs drop off as they shamble around, is that it?"

"They *do*," intoned young Lydia. "Yes."

Which was exactly how older Lydia would've phrased such a critical point. Colleen had her fingertips over her lips.

"Could be leprosy," Tom suggested.

"What that other guy said about it depending on what they eat, he *was* right, and that's not leprosy."

"Okay, but if it's not asking too much, what's *your* connection to all this? They shamble through your yard, is that it? Ride your school bus?"

I straightened the wheel and steered back into our lane.

"I'm one of them," Lydia said finally. "My job's to drive the shuttle between the factory and where we're living."

"Good enough. Thought as much. Now, where exactly is this zombie refuge?"

Silence.

"Okay, when did you first know you were a zombie?"

"Oh, man, before I got here my arm was just hanging there, like by one tendon, and I hadn't been hurt or anything!"

"No?" asked Tom.

"Slid off by itself!" I called out.

"It just started sliding off," said Lydia. "Wasn't eating right."

"Represent!" Amber yelled.

"All right, so zombies are organized. Listeners can knock the arms off Rosie the Riveter and paint her lips green, zombies *can do it*! Lydia, did you have a question? What prompted the call?"

"Because nobody here is eating brains," she said.

Then a split second of dial tone before the program engineer cut it off. She'd excused herself, goddamn it, from wherever it is she was.

"That is one example," said Tom, "of why we're on the books as entertainment programming and not as an informational show, folks, though we can all appreciate that culturally the zombie continues to resonate because each is, essentially, their own *worst enemy*. Their ignoble self. Yes, apparently I've given it some thought. Before we break for commercial I'll advise listeners with Egyptology questions to hold their calls until tomorrow night, when our good friend Dr. Leonard Avril returns to—"

Colleen shut it off. Beamed at me.

"It's that guy's place," said Grace. "Rob. That's where it's at."

I passed a sign for a rest stop and was tempted to pull in and put my head between my knees, but instead I maintained my beeline east. Lincoln, Preston, Pawnee City—every holy grail lay to the east.

"How come Harv's the only one not hollering back there?" I asked.

"He's asleep," said Clint.

Lights flew up behind us, then, with an annoyed honk, swerved around us into the passing lane. I caught a glimpse of a white Alice's Flowers van.

"You see that?"

Colleen nodded. "Flowers is all I've been thinking about," she said slowly. "I couldn't even stay to give him a funeral. He always talked about one Tom Waits song he wanted for when the people got up to leave."

"There's always time for a funeral. They have them for soldiers, I don't know, fifty years later if they find a body out in the jungle."

"His body was *right there*! I kissed his hand!"

"We had to go to prevent needing more funerals."

On the trip back to MacArthur I'd have to buy a Nerf football, definitely, and a book about astronauts. *Souvenirs of those couple of days when Dad was away, you remember that, Ray? That seems so long ago now.* Something yellow moved into the left lane to pass us.

"Holy shit," I whispered. "Take a look at this!"

I glanced at the front bumper going by, then I had to look at the road.

"No," she murmured. "No spoiler."

And I'd have run it off the road if it had? That seemed reasonable. The silver CHEVROLET flashed on its square back end before the car fishtailed into the night.

"Front end looked like a shark," I said.

She'd already shut her eyes again. "That was a Corvette." The closer we got to Lancaster County the more the exit ramps seemed to laugh up their sleeves, because they knew what was coming and we didn't.

THE BACK OF the ambulance was quiet, though I couldn't imagine how more than two of them could lie down at one time. Or what their sleepless parents back in Burroughs County had to be thinking. Clint's brother lying wide awake in his hospital bed.

Eighteen inches to my right, thirteen hours after Doug had his brain spilled out, Colleen finally let out one brittle sob like she was choking on a cracker, her face against her knee. I squeezed her bony shoulder, and she sucked a mucousy breath up her nose.

"I can't be *hard*," she whispered. "I can't. I'm so tired."

I rubbed between her shoulder blades, steering with one hand down the highway, pin-straight as Josie's hair. I had rubbed Josie's back too, when their mom had died, and held little Ray in my lap, their faces wet and ribcages shuddering. Loss affects you structurally. My hand felt gigantic across Colleen's back.

THE MID-MORNING SKY above southeast Nebraska was charcoal gray, like a saturated sponge hovering over us. Colleen slept sitting up, suspended by her shoulder strap against her cheek, snoring through the roof of her mouth. As I steered the ambulance onto the driveway, gravel crunching beneath our wheels, her eyes snapped open and she slapped her hands against the dashboard. Kids thumped in the back, empty bacon containers sliding around my feet.

"Who's house is that?" Clint muttered, throat sticky from sleep. "That your house, Mr. G?"

I slowed down between the blue-jay whirligigs and the umbrella clothesline.

"Shit," Colleen said between her teeth. "Is this Hoover? Is this a genius, what do you call it, hiding-in-plain-sight thing? These people's lives in your *hands*, and—"

"This is Pawnee," I said, peering at the front window's white curtains before I shut off the ignition. "This is my mom's house."

Colleen wiped a kernel of sleep from her eye. "What does she grow out here?"

"Got a hundred acres that she rents out for hay. Not in shape to do it herself."

"What about your dad?"

The curtains shifted six inches and, sure enough, Evadare's horn-rims peered out. I put the thing in park and turned the engine off, and without its rumble the world suddenly seemed so quiet that a section of my brain wondered if I'd finally fallen asleep.

"She's a widow."

"Oh," Colleen sighed. She fell back in her seat, though her hands were working on the seatbelt latch. I knew from experience that Doug couldn't have been out of her mind for long, but maybe she hadn't specifically thought *widow* too much.

"This looks like kind of a boring place," said Grace. "Just saying."

"Does she have chickens, though?" Franny asked.

The seven of us stretched our military-secret arms and legs as we navigated around the puddles—evidently it'd been raining out here. The non-ambulance air smelled fresh as daisies. The kids let us walk ahead, as kids will. A quarter-mile to the east, Sit-Stay Dog Food reared its gray roof, but I didn't bother to point it out. Franny brought her camera out from somewhere and asked us to turn around.

"You *could* leave them here for a while," Colleen muttered. "We'd find Megan faster—nobody'd look here for them."

"Not just them," I said.

"Does she maybe keep rabbits?" asked Franny.

I went up the front step—most of the white paint Lydia had brushed on during her first pregnancy had been scuffed out of existence.

"Well, don't take it personally," Amber said to Harv. "Just go in the bathroom when we get in, okay? Look if they have hair gel."

The white door swung open, releasing the hybrid scent of split-pea soup and ammonia, a monstrous thing. Evadare, in sneakers and daisy-print vinyl apron, stood with the toilet brush in her hand—hadn't thought to put it down when she'd heard us drive up. She'd put on weight around the middle and trimmed her perm.

"Pete!" she said, twisting her legs in the doorway. "I never expect to see you!"

Evadare was some kind of Ozark name though she was Czech. This apparent contradiction was more than I could stomach at that moment, and the gentlemanly hand I'd put behind Colleen curled into a fist.

"This is Colleen Avery," I grinned, "and these all are the collective pride of Hoover High, out on the junior class field trip! Everything quiet? All right if we come in and say hi to Mom?"

"Oh, yes, of course, do your best. Oh, sorry about this." She flourished the brush like a tennis racket. "You know how a toilet gets!"

Though that would've been her doing alone, since Mom didn't use a toilet. One by one we slid past her.

"Oh, but I hear about Hoover on the radio—so many *fires*, isn't it terrible?"

"Yeah, maybe this isn't a bad time to be out of town." I kicked my shoes off, like always, under the rack of gilt-edged State Fair plates. "I need to talk to you about that."

"But don't the children worry about their parents, they want to be at home?"

"No, no, not at all." Colleen flashed a smile like burnished steel. "Everyone's families are just fine!"

"Anyway, let the children come in and eat a meal. I always want potatoes with breakfast, will they have potatoes?"

Evadare addressed this to the kids but they were too busy staring at the crocheted afghans and driftwood clocks. The eternal blue-and-white palm-tree wallpaper.

"Oh, but your arm?"

"I was born this way," explained Amber.

Clint dropped to the floor, pulled the *Life* magazines from under the coffee table. Sure, there was enough here to entertain them for a week, maybe two. Keep a low profile, but still do some work around the place—maybe repaint the step!

"Colleen, okay, then you can help me with the frying pans, it will be nice to have someone to talk to. They want toast too? Peter, you go to your mother—no, not down the hall, she is in the study now during the day."

"Sure," I said. "Then I'll need to talk to you. About a big favor."

She turned in the doorway of the paneled kitchen, cleaning her glasses on the hem of her chiffon shirt. Her naked eyes looked vulnerable as egg yolks.

"I will be here whenever you want."

The study was off the back of the living room, so I went through the bead curtain and straight to the love seat beside Mom's big recliner. She wore a plaid shirt and purple sweatpants that she filled as though she were made of bread dough. She'd been sleeping, and she flinched a fraction of an inch when she heard the curtain, but when she saw it was me she managed to flicker an eyebrow and make a sound in her throat.

That was the most she could do, because the year Ray was born she'd been diagnosed with a degenerative disease of the nervous system—it was hard to know exactly what to call it. Most times I came through the door Evadare announced that now it was something else.

The acrid smell of sick person went up into my sinuses, distinct from that of a dying person—whether or not she wanted to, the last doctor said she'd stabilized, so there was no reason she couldn't last forever. Her hair was white now and stuck up like straw, and the shunt for the feeding tube made an extra lump on the side of her big belly.

"And how are you, Mom?" I squeezed her hand, and though I could feel the elastic strength running the length of her fingers she didn't squeeze back. "Josie and Ray, they're good. Send their love. I'm here with my school from Hoover, so they couldn't come. It's too bad."

I spoke loud and slow, though there was no reason to think her ears weren't working. Her head twitched like maybe she was trying to get a clearer look at me, so I knelt beside her footrest and looked up at her.

"Maybe I don't look so good," I said. "Been a hard trip so far."

Her eyes were the same as they'd always been—boring into me, then a smile flashing across her green irises, then boring in again. The rest of her I could never have identified as the person she'd been in Knudsen.

"I guess I probably need a good wash. I'll ask Evadare for a towel, hey?"

But instead of showering I went on sitting, clutching those fingers. Her eyes darted over my face, seeking to comprehend something, and I wondered if maybe because of Pipe #9 I was as unrecognizable from my old self as she was, so I started talking about George Reid's classes at Hoover High and which kids were a pleasure and which gave me trouble. Her eyes settled on the side of my face. We sat quietly then, listening to the clatter from the kitchen and the kids' voices just beyond the curtain.

"Hey, *yeah*," Grace was saying. "They wallpapered the light switches!"

"It's a valid design choice," said Clint, "it's a free country."

"No, c'mon," said Franny, "if you've got to paper over *everything*, you're covering deep emotional crap. I mean, how far does it go—the toaster?"

A pause.

"You're right about the toaster," said Harv.

"Oh, I've got to see that!" A floorboard squeaking under Franny.

"If you really think about it, though," said Clint, probably tightening his scarf, "your whole life is one long design choice."

"Ooh," said Amber. "Deep like Jacques Cousteau."

"Like, do you break your bro's leg or don't you?" Clint went on. "Decide."

"That paper on the toaster's pretty singed around the edges," said Harv.

"The stuff is everywhere!" cooed Grace.

I couldn't help but smile. Mom's eyes stayed on me.

"I remember," I whispered.

When they'd moved into the Pawnee house she'd bought wallpaper that was five dollars a roll over their budget, with that seersucker pattern through it, and if there'd been three feet left over Dad would've locked her outside. So she'd even papered the shelf in the guest room closet.

Mom was falling asleep, her eyelids drooping like drawbridges— no, now they came up again, but slow as a sunrise. Meanwhile I was wondering what Evadare had been eating off that empty plate on the shelf—must've been plain toast, I'd have smelled it if it'd been bacon— then suddenly, inexplicably, I calculated how quickly I could get through the picture window once the house caught fire, and if it would even be physically possible to haul Mom out after me. Would any of those five kids be able to haul her if I wasn't there? Could Colleen? Because after a person got doused from Pipe #9, Old Man Penzler tracked them down, ran them over and set their house on fire, that was standard operating procedure. Maybe the odds were only one in a hundred that James Jones knew where we were, that he'd even narrowed it down to Pawnee County, but that still made it too risky to leave the kids with my mom and Evadare. That had been my plan, but as I held Mom's damp washcloth I could clearly see it wasn't a good one.

"If he won't let us find the Rob dude, we should frickin' *walk* there! Clint, sit the fuck down, man!" Grace's loudest stage whisper. "We can't wander all over, think how rude you're being!"

"Sorry, Ma." My free hand wiped her chin with the purple washcloth. "They've kind of got tempers, these kids."

English saddle, she'd always insisted as we'd strolled around Lincoln. *I don't want you raising cowboys.*

"Okay," Evadare announced behind me. "The breakfast is served. They asked for bacon, but I'll give you ham salad to take away. What did you want to ask about?"

I got up and put an arm around her shoulders. Her eyes widened.

"Changed my mind," I said. "Forget it. After we eat I'll make a phone call."

"ROB?" I TRIED to relax my voice, so it wouldn't sound like the whole project wasn't on his shoulders. "Peter Giller here. Calling you back."

"I'd been *wondering* about you—hey, three guesses what I'm doing right now!"

I stared at the side of the guest-room bureau, papered with blue palm trees. I couldn't feel my feet. Then I could feel them again.

"Playing golf," I guessed.

"No."

On top of the bureau, a cut-glass dish held fragments of bluish windshield glass.

"Eating bacon," I said.

"Dang, you're not playing games. What do you want?"

"I'll be in Lancaster County in one hour."

"How many are you?"

"Seven."

"Superlative. All with the same problem?"

"One girl's lost an arm, everybody else, not so extreme. Though to be honest, it's our brains that need to hole up for a while. Been rough."

"Oh, it's one and the same. Diet and attitude." I pictured him waving a big hand back at Dockside, glorying in some esoteric contraption. "Where you coming in from?"

"Pawnee."

"Tell your seven they'll need clothes, toiletries, but food's taken care of—oh, and as of now, we're confiscating cell phones. All right, you got a pen?"

"Hold on, before I forget, wait—have you got a girl named Megan Avery there? One of my students?"

"Avery."

At his end, cutlery dropped onto a plate and I could hear him call out a question.

"She's learning the injector," he finally said. "Megan. She's on shift until two. Eyeball trouble, if memory serves."

When I came out of the guest room I heard Evadare's voice at a higher pitch than usual, and hurried into the living room to see her steering Franny out through my mom's bead curtain. The other four filed behind them.

"Hey, life doesn't last, Beanie Babies." Franny grinned, her big bracelets clanking together, and tried to show Evadare her phone. "We got to document it, right?"

"Give her privacy," Evadare snapped. "Her dignity!"

I slipped through the curtain.

"Sorry about that, Mom," I said softly. "You all right in here?"

She seemed to be studying the set of orange *Childcraft* books on the bottom shelf. She wasn't capable of reacting to any situation. In the middle of the spectrum between mother and her freakish son was a single functioning person.

"Okay, we've been fed," Colleen said at my shoulder. "We have to get them out of here, you know where? Because we have to go right now."

"But I haven't made ham salad!" Evadare hollered from the front. "And the TV said snow, you should wait."

I turned and took Colleen's hands, rubbing their thin bones beneath my thumbs. She raised her eyebrows, unsure, and wrinkles went up into her hairline. When was the last time I'd shown my teeth to smile and not to bite somebody?

"I found your Megan."

"NEXT STOP, LINCOLN, Nebraska," I announced to the passengers, flinging open the back doors. The sky was sidewalk-gray and fat snowflakes flitted like moths. "If you're backtracking to North Platte, Denver or points between, you'll be switching to a new coach, and—"

"It'll be so fly!" Grace grinned with that gap in her teeth, her shoulder pressed against the sharps-disposal bin. "I call shotgun, hey—shotgun on the zombie shuttle!"

"Hell, yes! Zombie Disneyland!" Clint worked his skinny denim arms like locomotive coupling rods. "I'm a-stockin' the gift shop!"

We'd parked under a big tall sign—just as Rob Aiken had described—shaped like a red coffee pot that read SAPP BROS. FOOD & FUEL and also GREYHOUND.

"We're early," I said, "so we ought to avail ourselves of the restaurant."

The kids started sliding out. Colleen was already striding across the parking lot on her pencil legs, leaning sideways against the wind—for all we knew Megan was waiting inside.

"No, wait. One thing," I said. "Everybody has to call home, right now. You can't use your cell phones where we going. Franny's got a phone, who else?"

Amber and Grace held theirs up.

"Like a hundred messages from my mom," said Amber.

"You don't call her back?"

"She'd freak."

"Jesus, trust me, until she hears your voice she assumes you're dead, doesn't eat or sleep, and Mom doesn't deserve that, right? Tell them you'll be away from school for a while, that I'm responsible for everything, even say that Mr. Vincent knows about it." My neck went hot as they rolled their eyes at me. "Don't tell them we're in Lincoln but tell them you're not *dead*, all right? I'll borrow somebody's when you're done."

They nodded glumly. Harv sat on his hands on the gurney.

"You don't have to call home," I told him.

"My mom's in Taiwan," said Grace, with such a tight mouth I couldn't see her missing tooth.

"Leave a message. Account for yourself one way or another."

They sat on the jump seats, phones to their ears, except Amber, who walked around and sat in the driver's seat. Colleen came out of the restaurant, showing me a quick shake of her head—no Megan yet.

With white spray-paint someone had emblazoned *Steph Eggers you rock me socks off* onto the Greyhound bus at the curb, motor rumbling benevolently like Emperor Elephant in *The Little Wretch*. "Emblazoned" was such a great word; I wanted it emblazoned on my tombstone.

Amber opened the door of the cab and slipped back down, wandering away to kick a hole through an aluminum trash can chained to a telephone pole. She swayed back toward us, mouth bunched like a fist, then fell onto Grace's shoulder and sobbed like the rest of us weren't even there, her one poor arm tight around Grace's back.

Harv crouched beneath the big revolving drum of the cement truck beside us. I stood beside him but he carried on squinting toward the far end of the parking lot.

"Is that my dad down there?" he whispered. "You know my dad?"

Between the big rigs and Camaros, an older-model motor home sat with its side door banging in the wind. A guy in a ball cap climbed the two steps and disappeared inside—only saw him from the back, but blond hair stuck out from under the cap.

"He rides with state troopers," Harv said through square teeth.

Our mystery guy leaned out, shaking a yellow plastic tablecloth. He wore black-rimmed glasses, true, but he also sported a massive ZZ Top beard that nearly obscured his WASHINGTON HUSKIES sweatshirt. The wind flipped the beard up in his face as the tablecloth was torn out of his hands. He ran after it, toward the highway.

"Holy, maybe I'm getting retarded," said Harv. "What's it say on the side there?"

"Bigfoot."

"I can't even read! See, when Dad was filming me yesterday, he gave me my brother's old *Maxim*s to look at, and you know what's good about *Maxim*?"

"The pictures," I said into the wind.

"Yeah, because I couldn't even read what the girl's *name* was, like not at all! I know what the letters *are*, no problem, but when they're all pushed together?"

"You were right." Clint kneeled on the ambulance's back bumper. "They *are* actually glad I'm alive. She says Jerry's happy 'cause there's no ligament damage."

"Waterproof mascara." Amber finally raised her head, wiping an eye. "Thank God, hey?"

Franny sat next to Clint, eyes red, and he put an arm around her. She held her phone out to me.

I dialed and then leaned across the passenger seat up front, collecting our pop bottles and Styrofoam as though I was just killing time with the call and the focus of my entire being wasn't really on a phone ringing on a kitchen counter inside Deb's house in that hillside subdivision where everyone kept their dangly Christmas lights up all year—that I wasn't actually *willing* myself to fly to MacArthur inside the telephone line's carbon filaments just like the Atom in the old *Justice League* comic. And this was a cell phone, so even in a comic book it wouldn't have worked.

"Hey," I practiced saying, "how are ya?"

I stayed bent over the passenger seat, head out of the wind so that Josie and Ray would be able to hear me.

"How *are* ya?" I said again.

But it just rang and rang. Not even Deb's answering machine. I stared at the numbers I'd dialed but they weren't wrong.

I backed out into the wind and found Colleen leaning over the hood, head down, her sleeves smeared with our trans-Nebraskan dust.

"You all right?" I asked.

She straightened up like I'd goosed her, then smoothed her lank hair back from her face as she held out a little red phone.

"What?" I asked.

"Drop this fucking thing in the trash," she said through her teeth. "I called Doug to tell him where I was."

I reached for the phone but she spun and threw the thing—it sailed over a half-dozen rows of parked cars until it clanged against a milk truck. Then she strode across the parking lot, inspecting every vehicle, her arms folded tight against her. It wasn't tracksuit weather.

THE WIND UNSNAPPED my cuff buttons as I trotted after her. Amber and Grace skipped over the parking lines, freshly eyeliner'd. It'd only been three hours since we'd finished that truckstop bacon but as I walked my legs felt hollow, knees and ankles crinkling like Dickside garbage bags—nitrite-poor anxiety suddenly fizzled at the corners of my brain, we had to eat!

"Here, hey." I slipped Franny's phone into her hand. "Thanks."

"Aw, you!" she grinned, hair particulated with snow. "Thanks but no thanks!"

She presented the phone again—someone's *finger* sat pinched in the halves, its open end smeared purple.

I looked at my right hand and saw that it was my finger.

"Aw, goddamn." I slipped the still-warm thing into my breast pocket—it smelled of cough syrup, sawdust. "Let's get some of the good food in us, hey? Maybe run, okay? But nobody lose their head in here."

"Hey, G." Franny stumbled over the toe of her sneaker. "You might be the first guy to mean that literally."

Clint giggled. "And I got your *back*, girl."

"I'd give an arm and a leg for some bacon," said Grace.

"Don't lose your, um, footing," muttered Franny

"Keep a civil, um…tongue in your head," said Harv.

"I'll knee you in the face," I attempted. Good one!

Inside, a sign above the cash register said HOTBAR BUFFET – $6.99.

I was still good at reading signs. A woman in a black skirt walked up with a stack of menus.

"Breakfast?" she asked. "Just yourselves?"

"How can we get bacon?"

"Oh," she nodded. "Your party's just around here."

We hustled after her between the tables. Old couples sat with tea-pots and putty-faced guys sat alone behind gently collapsing stacks of pancakes. What would Deb and the kids emblazon on my tombstone, anyway?

—PETER KINGSTON GILLER—

WHERE DID YOU FUCK OFF TO, MAN?

AND WHY IN SO MANY PIECES?

The waitress brought her red heels together beside a round corner booth, where Colleen already sat, eyes darting, behind a cup of coffee.

"Here!" the waitress said. "And we'll have more bacon out in just a minute!"

Colleen kept gazing toward the door. "Where are Clint and the girls?" A rope of spit snapped between her teeth.

"What you mean? They're right—"

"Over at the smorgasbord." Harv pointed. "Got their plates and everything."

"You go ahead." She waved a bracelet. "I'll hold the table."

No sign of Rob Aiken strolling between the booths, so Harv and I powered our way toward the buffet like a pair of Ben Roethlisbergers. A chafing dish piled with grease-beaded bacon waited alongside hash browns, pale scrambled eggs, beans and junk. Harv heaped eggs beside his bacon. My eyebrows might've gone up.

"Trying to be polite," he shrugged. "Did you talk to your kids?"

"No answer." I prodded through the bacon until I had forty-five strips that I really liked. "They must be out bowling."

"I just called home too," he said.

"What the hell—what for?"

"Well, I thought maybe the finger-chopping thing had maybe been a joke."

"Jeez, man. Were they there?"

"Dad picked up but when I said hi he passed the phone to Kim— that's his girlfriend you met—and she said, for my own good, I shouldn't come home anytime soon." He clacked the bacon tongs like a pair of castanets. "I didn't plan on going home right away anyway, I totally didn't, so that was cool."

The others were circling from the drinks station back to the table.

"Plenty of beans, Beanie Babies!" Franny called.

Under those fluorescents the turtles on her skirt really glowed.

"Try the white toast," called Clint, bacon dangling like a cigarette. "Amazing."

"Gosh," said a woman behind us. "Look at that snow come down!"

"Mr. Giller." Harv gave his plate a liberal puddle of ketchup. "Something else I've been wanting to say."

I nodded, the bacon between my molars saturating my tongue in joy.

"It's just that a guy can only control so much," he said.

"So…"

"That's all."

Weird. Deb had told me the same when Lydia had first gone into hospice, the exact words.

"No, okay," he said. "It's just there's been ten million times I've said, 'Hey, Harv, man, this is out of your hands. Not your problem, not your fault.' I appreciate what you've done for us, for *me* especially, and you should know we all appreciate it a lot. You took us to Velouria, right, but you couldn't have known what'd happen to everybody."

"Jesus, of course I couldn't—"

"No," he agreed.

He lapsed into stoic chewing.

The white squares of lattice around the table must've been hypnotic because I couldn't remember eating any bacon though I was down to six pieces. The girls wiped their greasy fingers on Clint's scarf and he just sat chewing, eyes rolled back in his head.

"Oh." Amber set her hand flat on the table. "Feel that?"

"Ah, shit," said Grace. "That's a good high."

The nitrite euphoria had spread to every part of my body. I shut my eyes and could've sworn I was floating above the table.

"I'm at my limit," said Colleen.

After five minutes I started back to the buffet for thirds.

"Giller!"

From the far corner of the restaurant Rob beckoned me over, his white hair combed flat onto his forehead. He was sitting with two other guys. I balanced my behind on the edge of the seat and put down my empty plate. All three of them nodded at me, but none of them quit chewing—immediately across was Clayton the first-aid guy, with his big brown moustache and orange Dockside jumpsuit, and beside him was a bald guy with his unzipped jumpsuit over a bald eagle T-shirt, two unsubtle staples connecting his left eyebrow to his forehead.

Need zombies? I could've told Tom Exegesis. *Check an all-you-can-eat bacon restaurant.*

Each of the three had a pyramid of bacon in front of him that must've weighed three pounds, like in those bacon-eating contests that won the English Civil War for Cromwell. Rob slid the saucer from under his coffee cup and stacked it with bacon, then the two guys pitched in too until strips were tumbling onto the tablecloth.

"Help yourself, Mr. Giller," he said through a mouthful.

"They aren't going to let us back in here," Clayton muttered, his mouth full. "That girl talked to the manager."

"Let's see what happens if they don't," said Bald Eagle. His patch said GARTH.

Rob swallowed and wiped his hands on a paper napkin.

"If they say no," he said, "we'll get that "Baconalia" deal at Denny's. And we've got more than we could eat in a month at home anyway." He straightened, burped, then grinned out the side of his mouth. "This is the Mr. Giller who was the teacher when the accident happened. This is Garth, Clayton."

"Mr. Giller?" Harv loomed over the table, his plate stacked high again. "You want some help?" He held his shoulders forward so his neck looked thick. "Everything cool? These the guys we're supposed to meet?"

"It's cool, Harv. You're a good fella, keeping an eye out."

"I *thought* you looked familiar," bald Garth said to me. "Thought you might've been the pet store guy back in Velouria. Forget his name."

"You forget your own name," said Clayton.

"Look who's fuckin' talking," said Garth.

"So you all came out here from Velouria?" I asked.

"Yessir," said Rob, "day before yesterday some of the guys got word about this place starting up so I figured I'd check it out. Wife and kids weren't too sad to see me go after that last day or two, so…"

The two other men nodded at that, sitting with a hunk of bacon in each hand.

"So how did word get through to you?" Clayton asked.

"I told you already," Rob beamed. "Giller tracked our number down."

"And on the radio!" said Harv as he slid into the booth.

"Oh, yeah, *Out There!*" said bald Garth. "Little Lydia!"

"And *that* is why she was put on toilets," said Rob.

"Not that anybody uses 'em," Clayton said into his moustache.

"*Last* thing we wanted, security-wise. Just sloppy."

"Giller, hey," said Clayton, "that looks pretty fresh. Forget to pick it up off the ground or what?"

His fork pointed at my right hand—the sticky socket from my little finger.

"Shit!" I yelled.

I pawed at my shirt pocket but it was like the damn thing was sewn shut.

"What's the limit again?" Clayton asked.

"Five minutes," grimaced bald Garth.

"Jock says ten at the outside," Rob grinned, "but, yeah, five's more like it."

"Aw, don't mess with him," said Clayton. "The poor guy."

I finally fished out the dried husk of my pinkie finger. Looked like it had been snapped off a mummy.

"Leave it as a tip," suggested Garth.

"All right, we're on our way." Rob fed his arm into a leather bomber jacket. "I'll go up and pay—you'll bring your people up front, Giller? Maybe I'll drive your vehicle, if that's all right, so we all know where we're going."

"Absolutely, yes." I got up too, shoving strips haphazardly into my mouth. I looked like a bacon dispenser. "There's a, uh, woman with us, Megan Avery's mother."

"She's affected too?"

"She threw Mr. Giller into a car!" said Harv. "He was whaling on her, and—"

"No, no," I said. "Other way around."

"Well, if our research ever gets to that point, it might be interesting to compare their problems, with their common genetics. So far it's only been three days, and I think the operation's pretty—"

"Mr. Aiken!" Colleen ran up, cheeks flushed, even her eyes somehow younger. She held his leather sleeve. "You *do* have Megan?"

She led the kids and me out after the three men. Snow was every-where, filling the air like when they used to empty flour out of the new mill's high hopper back in Knudsen, though instead of making me cough it just settled over my shoulders.

"You call her 'The Fugitive' from now on, right?" Garth grinned, wiping a final slick of bacon grease across his eagle. "The *one-armed man*, am I right?"

Amber tapped bacon against her front teeth. "Hardy har har."

Harv bent to tie a sneaker, wisps of snow snaking around his feet. Grace set her hands on his back and leap-frogged over him.

"Don't let it worry you, darling," said Rob, throwing an arm around Amber. "Some guys were getting hit with it this time last week, the company's doctors told them all their symptoms were, what—"

"'A pre-existing medical condition,'" snorted Garth, jangling car keys.

Clint leapfrogged Franny, then she vaulted over him, serape flap-ping, then her cowboy boot went out from under her as she landed. Went down hard on her ass, and man did we all laugh.

"The GP was no better," Rob was saying, "so by Tuesday our old graveyard foreman, Jock, he was getting a hold of everybody—"

"He said, 'Let's get our heads together about this,'" Clayton grinned beneath his moustache. "'Let's look after what needs looking after.'"

Amber shoved Harv between the shoulders, and he stumbled forward with an almighty fart. She hooted so loud that I didn't even pay attention to how embarrassed he was. The Dockside guys talked about guys' parts falling off but thanks to the Glory of Bacon most of us weren't paying attention.

"Can we please just get there?" said Colleen.

"And anyway, after just a couple of days some of the fellas, well, they've taken a real turn for the worse." Rob wiped snow from his brow. "In fact, a couple of them—"

"Aw, yeah, old Maximilian!" whooped Garth.

"Christ Almighty!" Ron held his fists to his head. "Let me finish a sentence!"

"But, hey," said Colleen, stopped beside a blue sports car. "What kind of vehicle do you guys drive?"

"See for yourself," said Rob.

Clayton circled to the passenger side of a big yellow crew-cab pickup.

She shot me a look. "Well, you never know, do you?"

WE'D DRIVEN THROUGH miles of empty farmland, then before noon we turned into a snowbound driveway. Rob gunned the engine and ploughed through the drifts, sashaying right and left as the snow bullied the wheels.

"And there's our bacon factory!" he grinned.

The ambulance rounded a snowcapped fence and coasted to a stop beside oblong shapes that might've been other vehicles. Thanks to my breath steaming up the passenger window I could make out only a couple of darker rectangles under the fluttering gray sky. Clayton and Garth in their yellow pickup crunched to a halt next to us. Rob killed our engine.

"Welcome, sir, to Pork Belly Futures."

"Everybody out!" I called into the back.

As we hopped down from the cab I was kicked in the chest by a wind from the Arctic's armpit. Rob and Garth tramped toward the distant left-hand rectangle and Colleen pushed past me, high-stepping over the snow to keep up with them. The snow was higher than my knees but the two men had packed down a choppy path. Nebraska: The Lost In A Blizzard State. Clint charged past as I blinked away Froot Loop–sized snowflakes.

"He said bacon *factory*!"

"The promised land!" Franny sprinted by too, her wispy hair diffused like a sparkler. "Like the fridge magnet!"

Clayton tromped up behind Amber and Grace, his moustache coated so he looked like Burl Ives. "No shuttle across for another hour, children, so you better haul ass!"

I fell into line behind Harv. I ignored the snow blowing through the front of my shirt by studying the back of his white high-tops kicking through the drifts. It was Friday, so if I hadn't taken him on our field trip he could've planned on running down a court in Hoover that very evening, waiting for a bounce-pass and hoping no girls could spot the acne between his shoulders.

Ahead of us, Clayton disappeared through a dark door, then I fumbled with the latch too and we hustled out of the snow into the quiet gloom inside the rectangle, a long room—I didn't realize how the wind had been yowling in our ears until we thudded the door shut behind us. The place smelled of pig shit. My crew stood stomping snow onto a blue tarp, but Colleen was already sitting on the nearest bed, her arms wrapped tight around her daughter, both with their hair in their faces, a fleece blanket decorated with baseball players thrown over their shoulders. Appliqué aficionado Megan wore greasy gray coveralls.

"I wanted to talk to him about my eye!" She suddenly bawled, ropes of spit between her teeth. "I wanted to say something about it!"

Colleen wrapped her arms tighter around her daughter, peered up at me.

"Hello," she said meekly. Her eyes were red and wet.

My own eyes felt hot and damp at the sight of them—my own kids' crunchable bodies tugged at me from across the miles—but I blinked it away with the snow.

"C'mon, guys," I said. "Let's not all stand here."

"But do you even know it *was* Dad?" hissed Megan. "Maybe it wasn't!"

We were between two long rows of cots, each bed strewn with blankets and backpacks and inflatable camping pillows and the occasional stuffed animal. Curtains were still drawn over the big square windows, but reading lights had been nailed to the wall over each bed and the yellow hemisphere cast by each one made the place like a movie theater as the lights go down. I could taste acrid pig shit on the end of my tongue.

"He wasn't mangled, Megs, anyone could've recognized him." Her talk trembled with enforced calm. "And once we get a bead on that fucking driver I'll pull his guts out like an inch at a time, I mean he will *suffer*, all right? Peter, how long are the guts in the human body?"

"Fifty feet in both intestines."

"No word of a lie, Sweetheart, I am going to chew up his guts and spit them out, I don't care what he's been eating, that's all I've been thinking the whole way here."

"All right," said Clint. "Cozy place here."

"Mom, okay," Megan murmured, her face pressed to Colleen's flushed neck.

"Who puked?" asked Grace, waving a hand in front of her nose.

"Guess it's not too hard to figure out this was a pig barn!" called Rob. He marched up the aisle between the beds and, with a flourish, threw a blanket around Harv's shoulders. "Hang your coats above the heater there. Linoleum's still shiny, see that? Jock fixed it up this past weekend, we put that plastic over the windows yesterday when it *really* started getting cold—but it holds everybody! Come on down here."

He led us up the aisle.

"Few sleepers here, came off the graveyard shift after breakfast—I did too, but heck, nitrites keep you limber!"

He thumped his chest. Lights were off where figures lay curled in sleeping bags, but the far end of the long room was bright thanks to a bulb dangling from a rafter. Beneath it, a bunch of my eleventh-graders played Monopoly on a long plank table.

"All right, guys," Rob announced, "as promised, here are the new additions to the wonderful happenings at the factory!"

Ryan, Eric, Shawn, brace-faced Lydia Dershowitz and dumpy Ursula got up from their benches—they all looked a little pale but otherwise intact.

"Hey, Mr. Giller," said Shawn, hair down over one eye. "You, uh, want something to eat? They're fixing you something."

Rob's phone rang—"Takin' Care of Business"—and he hustled into a corner.

"I could eat again," I said. Eat all the pigs that ever lived in the place!

"But how come you guys are all *here*?" Harv murmured. He shuffled a step behind me. "Like a bus brought you."

"Didn't you see the big ad in the paper?" Lydia ran her tongue over her teeth. "Jock ran that big-ass big ad in the Hoover paper—"

"'Do you crave bacon an unnatural amount?'" the old-timers all blurted together.

"Really?" murmured Amber.

"Nice arm," Ryan said, and as he grinned at her the skin from his cheek folded down like a strip of old paint. He casually pressed a hand over it.

"And then it gave Jock's phone number!" said Ursula. "And everybody was at my house so we called it, and Eric, Eric was like—"

"I'm like, 'Shit, yeah, do you got bacon *pills* or something? Cause this is *brutal*, man,' so Arthur drove the shuttle out to get us 'cause he's out of his mind!"

"Main thing," I said, "is that everybody got the hell out of Hoover. Did he pick up those Dockside guys in Velouria—Lars, I think it was?"

Shawn cleared his throat, moved his hair from his eyes. "He just got us."

Lydia suddenly brought her hand back and slapped Clint hard across the face.

"Whoa," I said, "kids—"

He rocked back a step, and before he could take a swing Grace clubbed a sturdy fist into Lydia's middle, and as she doubled over, Amber brought her knee up into Lydia's face. She flew backward onto the plank table, sending their lines of plastic houses flying. *Awesome*, I thought. *Tear her head off!*

"Cut it out," I said, and slid in front of my girls.

I helped Lydia down to the floor, and saw that the combination of train-track braces and Amber's bony knee had sliced clean through her upper lip and a solid inch up toward her nose.

"It's just fun." She prodded it with her tongue, separating the sides.

"How long did Rob and Jock say you were going to be staying here?" I asked.

"Yeah," said Clint, "I mean, are you guys, uh, cured?"

"There's plenty to eat," said Eric.

"But they didn't say anything about going home after a while, or bringing your parents out here or anything?"

The old-timers shook their heads. Lydia fingered her wound.

"Well, what is the cure?" asked Amber.

"I get the feeling there isn't one," I murmured. "They never said there would be."

"But, hell," said Eric, "there's bacon, and I don't mind if we stay three years!"

He gave a Nerf football a delighted squeeze.

"Want to see where the bathrooms are?" asked Shawn.

Franny collected Community Chest cards from the floor. "If we've got three years we should totally start a 4-H!"

"I could use the ladies' room," Colleen told Shawn.

"Hey," Eric called, "Mister, uh—"

"*Giller*," hollered Megan.

"Mr. Giller, sorry, right—you can totally take that bed, it was Jacob's and he won't need it now, right? Dude sleeps standing up."

"Sure," I said. "Very funny."

From their benches the kids sat looking at me, orange money in their hands.

"Did anybody ever mention that a place in Ohio might have a cure for all this?"

"There's a place in Georgia called Bacon County," said Eric, rattling the dice.

My crew had collapsed on various beds, except for Colleen, who was in the bathroom, and Franny, who'd started playing as the pewter thimble. Now that we were a big pack, I could probably quit keeping tabs on them. By then the pig smell wasn't making my head snap back—it was more like an Acrid Animal Shit aromatherapy candle burning off in a corner. I stretched out on Jacob's snarling-wolves blanket.

"When you sleep with your own kind," I'd once said as a bedwetters' camp counselor, "you might not pee the bed so much."

A pot-bellied, wispy-haired little guy pushed past a plastic curtain at the end of the room and set plates and a handful of cutlery on the table. It wasn't cold in there but he wore yellow work gloves.

"I'm Arthur, gentlemen and ladies," he called, "and I'll be feeding you. Just letting it burn for a minute longer."

And my kids and I vaulted to our feet—our legs were *that* ready for us to eat. The smell filled my head so suddenly that the walls became strips of bacon, bubbling with grease, the beds were bacon, the rafters.

"Lydia, dear," Arthur said, "look what's happened to you! I'll fetch a staple gun."

"My mom's cool," Megan slid onto the bench beside Franny. "Except when they saw my eye hanging out that time, man." She wiped snot across her canvas sleeve. "They *completely* lost their shit."

Eric waved his hands, a panicked spinster.

"Like, 'Agh, zombie!'"

"Aaaaaagh!" the kids all sang.

Megan laid her pristine face on the hard table, swallowed hard. Neither of her parents had mentioned her eyeball ever hanging out.

"IT HAS TO have altered us at a *genetic* level," wispy-haired Arthur said across the crowded table, with an intensity like he'd been up all night thinking about it. He'd already explained that he'd subscribed to *Discover* "back when we were in Velouria"—as though that life were years distant, instead of a couple of days—and still listened to NPR out in his truck with his dog, so he sort of had a background in science too. He'd been six months from retirement before he worked on that clean-up crew with Donny Brown, *still* feeling hungover from the company cookout three days before.

"See, the DNA strains they introduced have to act in combination with the DNA we've got already." He moved his hands apart as though DNA chains were eighteen inches long. "And nobody has the exact same DNA as the person next to them, you see, so that's why we have the same problems but with variations, like, uh, none of the girls seem to get as angry as you or I do, or you say you don't mind the cold, or some of us are held together by the bacon for a very long time and others of us aren't. Or in my case, I've got a thing with my fingers that not many people know about."

He held up those yellow leather gloves, wet with grease.

"I *can so* fart," said Shawn. "Fart anytime I want to."

"So do it!" Eric crowed.

"Don't want to."

Lydia laughed and light from the bulb flashed off her braces.

"No, no," said Colleen, three diners to my left. "We need to *define* 'a zombie.'"

Kids had their elbows on the table, mouths agape like she was Santa Claus.

"A zombie's anything that's wounded, like left for dead, but keeps moving forward, against all odds, okay?" She smiled laboriously at her daughter—trying to make sense was such hard work that sweat beaded her brow. "Could be a mouse in a trap, a whacked-out substitute teacher or a real—what did they call it?—reanimated corpse, even—"

"Could be an impoverished African nation," suggested Arthur. "But young lady, you've barely touched your pork!"

"You said yourself we're all a little different," she replied. "I go my own speed."

"Eating meat and salt," Arthur smiled coldly, "reminds us that we're human."

He must've listened to *Out There*.

"Arthur," Colleen asked, "what do you drive?"

"The snow's nearly quit." He stood up, clearing his plate. "Get enough of us out there with shovels, we'll be able to take you on the annotated tour!"

JOCK HAD RED hair, a faceful of stubble and forearms like a couple of hams. God, they looked delicious. We stood on the floor of the fabled bacon factory operated by fourteen of Penzler's victims—now twenty-one—my brain already so filled with operating procedures that it felt ready for slicing. Across the longest wall they'd painted PORK BELLY FUTURES with a blue roller.

"Because what future would we have *without* the place, am I right? If it wasn't for that ol' economic downturn we'd have been *so* screwed!" he shouted. "If Schwarz had stayed in business, where the hell would we have gone, right? I mean, you got a lot of disused pork-processing plants sitting around *your* hometown?"

He had to yell because we were walking between the skin-removal saws—which shook and rattled like hell as they started the process—and the liquid-smoke-injector needles that finished the first stage and also rattled like hell. The conveyor belts carried the product in a big horseshoe so we could watch the untouched fatty pork bellies drop out of the tumbler to the left while ten feet to the right the perfectly rect-angular bacon sides, dripping yellow, slid onto the steel table to have metal combs shoved into them so they could be hung up inside the smoker. The combs were even sharper than Lydia's braces, so a first-aid staple gun dangled from a nail every ten feet or so.

"No, not in Hoover," I said, shoving a comb in a couple of inches from the top of the slab. "We'd have mobbed the place. There's really no phone in here, hey?"

"Nope, nope, sorry—the phone company is one outfit that won't barter!"

Apparently he'd been one of the guys who'd corraled the meat truck at the Pegasus station back in Velouria, but instead of getting arrested he'd driven home where his brother-in-law Gord had kidded him that if he still had a jones for bacon then Gord knew a pork-processing plant sitting empty outside Lincoln. That afternoon Jock had driven out from Velouria and just before dinnertime he'd seen the future wait-ing like Noah's ark here in the field. First thing he'd done was to patch all the shot-up windows with black garbage bags, because, truth be told, Gord had discovered the place when he'd been looking for things to shoot at.

"Listen," I hollered, "I'd love to call my kids one more time, so is Rob the only one with a phone?"

"Hey, Jock?" shouted Willow. "Should we still get ready for the truck out back?"

Pierced-lip Willow, her legs all goose-pimples in her jean shorts, stood holding hands with black-clad Little Craig. Even though most of the eleventh-graders' duties were in the dormitory, these two had been assigned to the factory, but there didn't seem to be anything specific for them to do so—according to Arthur, anyway—they just wandered around looking for corners in which to copulate. *They don't have any more birth control than God gave a jackrabbit, so if she doesn't miss her period we all learn something else about our true natures.*

And if it hadn't been for the pink goo coursing through our systems we might've bothered to put in earplugs, too.

"What?" said Jock. "Oh, yeah, propane day! I suppose we can get ready, no way to say how fast this'll melt. Give me a hand, Pete, you don't feel the cold, right?"

I followed him down the back hallway.

"I'm happy to pitch in," I said, "but I really need to talk about—"

"I'll shovel the stairs, you roll the skid out of the freezer—you remember, third door on your left just there," he called over his shoulder. "The county might do the main road any minute, then the guy I called'll plough the—"

The outside door clicked shut behind him. I took the third door on the left into the freezer, ready to roll out a whole skid of finished bacon—apparently that was how they paid off the propane guy and every other supplier. But I must've gone in the second door instead, which seemed to be the cooler. They were all standing there, *looking* at me if they still had eyes.

Except for poor legless Maximilian sitting propped in the corner, Jock had stood all of them up so they wouldn't look quite so dead, despite the lacy frost tracing patterns up their cheeks and necks. They'd all been in for a couple of days already—Lonny, Jacob from my class, Leopold, others whose names I'd immediately forgotten—and unless there was a cure on hand they were never coming out.

"Oh, guys," I murmured. "Hi."

Jacob had staggered off the shuttle from Hoover, forgetting both of his arms on the seat—and too late to nail them back on, so those cold sores were now his most attractive blemish. He still wore his HOO-VER HIGH hoodie but the sleeves hung empty as burst balloons. Jock had wondered whether the cold might stop any subsequent parts from falling off, and so long as the guys didn't mind being borderline-vegetative, with barely a pulse between them, the experiment was a roaring success.

And their eyes would *follow* a guy whenever he wheeled a rack of bacon in for the three hour rest between smoking and slicing. That might sound creepy, their sluggish eyes creaking back and forth on near-dead batteries, but it was mostly reassuring, considering that one day I might find myself standing there. Moving eyes were better than nothing. If I could get near a phone Ray and Josie might come in from MacArthur to tickle me under the armpits, then come back a day or so later for when I started to giggle.

Jacob's gaze crept sideways toward the open cooler door even though I stood in front of him. A door clacked open out in the hallway.

"Pete!" Jock hollered. "Get the lead out! Might be on his way, am I right?"

I trotted next door to the freezer, picked up the loaded skid with the dolly and steered it out into the hallway. Each shrink-wrapped pound of bacon carried a blue SCHWARZ MEAT PRODUCTS sticker because a couple of thousand had been left in the packaging machine. It was true the cold didn't bother my hands much, but it still felt weird to hold onto things when I didn't have a pinkie, I felt more like the four-fingered Thing from *Fantastic Four* comics than I did like Captain America, even though Captain America was also a super-soldier secretly created by the US military. But if *his* blood was plasticky goo they'd never mentioned it in any comic I'd ever read. I turned backward so as to push the door open with my behind.

"Nah, forget it!" Jock called. We were beside the big generator, so it was just as loud as the factory floor. "He'll be a while yet!"

He'd only cleared a couple of ribbons down the concrete ramp, and though melt-water was dripping twenty feet down from the corner of the roof, deep snow still surrounded the place like we were a boat out at sea.

"I need a smoke anyway," he said. "Let me show you the forms just in case."

I pushed the skid against the wall. Every minute at Pork Belly Futures, the sicker I felt at not being en route to MacArthur. Bodily and mentally I felt solid as a cinderblock, but I'd seen in myself and others how quickly that could dissolve, and I couldn't remember the names of Ray and Josie's teachers at Colts Neck, that blue cartoon dog from *Laff-A-Lympics* or our phone number back in Wahoo.

"You know, I'm not stopping long," I said.

He lit a Marlboro and patted the step beside him. I set my bottom on the damp concrete as he unfolded a sheaf of paper. Our dormitory, containing poor Harv and at least one telephone, sat like a long shoe-box across the fields.

"Even if you're only here for the afternoon," Jock said, "I still figure you're a rung or two up on some of these other meatheads."

Jock had spent years as managing supervisor at Dockside and had been coming in from a cigarette break when Arthur and the rest had started the cleanup. Garth said if he ever met any of those higher-ups from Dockside in the street he'd rip out their hearts—and speaking from my own experience that wasn't just an expression—but that Jock was all right because he couldn't have known what the pink goo was really about if he'd been willing to roll his sleeves up that day and dip a mop in a bucket.

Maybe he *ought* to have known, though, which was why he was breaking his back to make PBF a going concern—Boy Scout leader to your poor, your hungry, your limbless and staggering. Or maybe that was me. But Jock was the only zombie I knew who was in regular contact with his family, even planned on going home for the weekend.

"So is that real clear?" he asked. "Make sure they initial *there* before they roar off, or shit will hit the fan!"

I wasn't sure how he'd managed to find so many suppliers willing to barter but it had required hundreds of phone calls. He'd told his wife he'd suddenly found a better job outside Lincoln, so did that mean he'd cut himself a paycheck out if this too?

Outside the distant dormitory tiny figures ran back and forth—must've been eleventh-graders playing Frisbee in the snow—as the six guys for the afternoon shift came trudging across the white field. All that stuff about the chosen people and the promised land, was that out of Exodus too?

Over the hum of the generator I heard something like a moaning from inside the factory. Jock scrutinized numbers and wrote happy faces in the margins.

"Listen," I said, "we're kind of skirting the issue here. What I need to know is whether you've got a bead on a cure for this thing."

"I guess you got all this straight—taught school, isn't that what Megan told us?"

"Uh, yeah," I said, though that life sounded distant as a TV show. "Listen, you hear something funny?"

"Anytime you want to talk about your condition, Pete, what it's doing to your life, where you're at, you just come to me!"

He pulled the door open, but long-haired, noseless Lonny stood there blocking our way. The last time I'd seen him he'd been in the cooler.

"Aw, shit, Giller!" Jock yelled. "You forgot to shut the door!"

Lonny gurgled and tried to grin at us. He didn't have much left in the way of lips and there was something purple smeared around his mouth.

"All right, you're okay!" Jock put a palm on his bare chest. "Let's get in and sit down!"

Then I noticed Lonny was holding a man's foot with eight inches of leg still attached to it—a blond-haired leg. Behind him, dark shapes shuffled up the corridor.

"Fuck, Jock!" I said. "He's eating Little Craig!"

After three days at PBF there had to be as many nitrites in Little Craig as in any side of bacon—one of *my* students. Over Lonny's shoulder I could make out Jacob and more of the Dockside guys shambling up the hallway.

Jock folded his big ham arms. "Well, Lonny-boy, this is a big problem!"

Lonny looked from Jock to me and back again. Then his entire arm dropped off and lay there on the concrete, its hand still grasping Little Craig's foot. His teeth were already bared, of course, but he snarled at us like a dog then bent down with his good arm, picked up the detached one by the wrist and tried to wallop us with his gummy knob of shoulder!

I leaned back to let it swing by, then stepped in and punched lip-less Lonny in the face as hard as I could. He flew five or six feet back into the hallway, stopped when he hit the crowd collecting behind him, then fell forward onto his face. He lost his grip on his detached arm, and *that* hand lost its grip on Little Craig's ankle, so did I pick up the lost arm and club him to death with it?

"Now, hold on, Pete," Jock was saying, "he just needs—"

No, I ran in, pushed poor Jacob out of the way and stomped the back of Lonny's head in with the heel of my boot. I had to brace myself against the walls, and after the first couple of kicks his head made a wet sound like Jell-o salad.

"Hey, now, Pete!" Jock was shrieking. "Hey!"

"Stop it!" Jacob yelled sleepily, but it came out like maybe his tongue was falling out, and how screwed-up was that? So I pushed *him* down onto his back and started to strangle him. I could only stay calm for so long. His throat felt cold as a pickle. Jock grabbed my shoulders and tried to pull me off but I was too invincible. Jacob gazed up at me, forgetting how to blink, no arms to push me off, save himself. And in that state why should he have wanted to?

"Listen," Jock hissed in my ear, "know what your problem is?"

I pushed my thumbs deep into his throat but he wasn't strangling fast enough—I needed a weapon. I elbowed past the other clammy dipshits crowding the hallway and ran out onto the factory floor. The whole noisy line was still running—sawing and skinning, injecting and trimming—and on the floor beside my stainless-steel table old Leopold from the cooler was crouched over Little Craig, eating his cheek. Leopold only had one leg but he'd been stiff enough that they'd leaned him against the cooler wall without any problem. Willow was chopping into the old guy's back with one of the hooks on a pole they used for the pork-belly tumbler, but he was having too good a time gnawing through to Little Craig's teeth to even notice.

I picked up a piece of two-by-four and jogged over. This was going to be great!

But then Colleen, dressed in dingy striped coveralls, a black grease stain across her forehead, picked up two steel combs from the table and buried them in the back of Leopold's head, like forks into mashed potatoes. He dropped onto Little Craig without a quiver, lying mouth-to-mouth like they'd been boyfriends.

"Oh," I said, dropping my two-by-four, "that's great." Because I'd had a beautiful long fight in front of me, and she'd gone and ended it.

Willow stumbled over to the wall and killed the power for the line, so it clattered to a stop with a disappointed groan. Half a cup's worth of blood coagulated on the floor, on Colleen, in spatters across the salt bags—we were all too viscous for any more than that. And based on Leopold and Lonny, it seemed that penetrating the brain was key to shutting off a zombie—*Jock, we really learned something about ourselves!* Colleen stood over the mess she'd made, breath huffing, hands out at her sides like a gunfighter.

I didn't feel like going back to kill Jacob anymore. I took the pole from Willow so she could push Leopold off her little dog-food boyfriend.

"How, how long we staying here?" Colleen picked up my two-by-four, broke it against the poor liquid-smoke-injector. "This is pointless!"

Jock ambled along the factory floor, holding hands with a couple of earless guys out of the cooler.

"You know what the problem with you guys is?" Jock asked again. "You lack a moral compass. I think we *all* do, a little bit, but you two *really* lack a moral compass."

I swung the pole like a bat against the side of his head but the shaft only snapped in two. He and the cooler-zombies turned to watch the hook-end slide out of sight under the brine tank, then he turned back to me.

"My point exactly," he said.

"My problem is that I should get the hell back to my kids!" I yelled.

"Then I think you should do that," he nodded. "And stop leaving doors open."

I picked Leopold up by the straps of his overalls and dragged him over to the pork-belly wheelbarrow. Guys in Dockside jumpsuits were running in by then.

"Sweet angel." Willow kissed Craig's half-a-face then sat up with blood smeared across her chin. "He's alive, you guys!"

"Shnbe," Little Craig announced.

"Clayton, do me a favor, buddy," called Jock. "Run out back and find the kid's leg for him. Hey, Garth, you there? Run around to the shop, get some of the three-inch wood screws and a drill. Willow, honey?"

She massaged Little Craig's hand, sucking nervously on her lip-ring.

"C-can't I stay with—?"

"Take a peek inside Leo's mouth, hey? See how much cheek skin's in there."

"WELL, IF YOU do go away for good, you'll be the first," old Arthur said. He swept snow off the hood of his truck while his little terrier hopped down from the cab and piddled on our footprints. "I told *my* kids I was on my way through to Lucinda's in Wichita but that I'd be taking my time, you see, and I do want to get there *eventually*, but…um."

"It'll be hard to leave the bacon," I said.

I picked at three flaps of forearm skin that Lonny had lifted off during the scrap. They felt ropy as licorice. Watching the dog sniff around, its owner keeping a step behind it all the time as I tried to form another sentence, that really reminded me of something from my messed-up recent past.

"Now that's not Frisbee anymore—what *are* they doing?"

I followed his gaze. In front of the dormitory, a dozen students shuffled from side to side, with significant jerks of the elbows, as a faint tinny beat drifted over the snow. Grace stepped out from the center of the line, pushed Shawn and Eric closer together, then the whole gang resumed dragging themselves back and forth. A slithery bassline.

"They're dancing to 'Thriller,'" I explained.

The kids were better off here, sure, but in the meantime all our everything had ground to a halt.

"You can't just walk away from nitrites," Arthur went on. "I spent thirty-six hours in my own basement, without the basic strength to climb the stairs to the kitchen, and with bacon in my fridge!"

"How'd you get out of there?"

"Tinky kept barking until the next-door neighbors finally came home from Mexico. Am I likely to leave myself that vulnerable again? No." He kept caressing the corners of his mouth with his gloved hand, and I guessed that as soon as I was ten feet away he'd start gnawing. "Nor should *you*. Make peace with Jock. Stay a few months with us lotus-eaters, that's what we are."

"No, man, I told my kids I'd be back in a month. I meant it."

He took some dry bacon out of his coat pocket and handed me a strip.

"So you did, you just explained that. But why the shovel?"

"He told me to bury Lonny. I guess just by the fence there."

I spun the shovel in my hand like a majorette—my heart fluttered at the prospect of getting traveling, though it was only four hours since Rob had set the e-brake on the ambulance.

"But surely you were *right* to finish him?" Arthur asked. "His humanity had expired?"

"I guess, but who else should Jock get to dig, right? How about Tink, he much of a digger?"

The dog rolled on his back beside my shoe, his stupid little feet in the air.

"No, I'm afraid not," Arthur said.

"You think Stephen Hawking would trade his beautiful brain for a reliable body?"

"Well, obviously he *does* have his brain." Arthur studied a boot print in the snow. "And I've never read about him complaining."

I couldn't dig the hole wide enough in the half-frozen ground, but I folded Lonny into the bottom and kept my boot pressed between his shoulder blades while I scooped dirt over him. Here was the quiet dignity I'd demanded of the kids.

"Sorry, man," I said.

Jock hadn't given me any protocol for a funeral. No one at PBF had died before that particular Friday.

THE KIDS STOMPED toward me, each with a shovel over the shoulder—evidently from the start Jock had anticipated a lot of digging.

"We're going to clear the road!" Eric called. He wore lime-green earmuffs. "Mr. Jock says he wants you the fuck out of here!"

"Doesn't surprise me." I stepped into the snowdrift to let them by. "Thank you."

"Gillbrick, did you seriously kill the Lonny dude?" asked Franny. "Like that's not just an expression, you *terminated* him?"

"Somebody had to."

"Cool," they said in unison, letting out breaths of steam.

"Hardcore," Lydia Dershowitz said, her upper lip flashing with staples.

Harv trudged by with a half-smile.

"How did it feel?" he asked quietly.

"Felt good at the time, I guess."

"Yep." He pulled his cap down to block the glare. "Bet it would."

"You killed Leopold too, right?" Eric grinned. "That dude smelled like dumps!"

"No, that was, uh, Mrs. Avery, and he's back in the cooler. Combed his hair over the holes."

Their hands crept up to their own heads. No one knows better than a sixteen-year-old how a hairstyle can make or break you.

Only Amber was in the dorm, writing at the table—demand must've been strictly for two-armed shovelers.

"I was left-handed before," she grimaced, shuffling her hand across the page. "Writing to my folks so I don't bawl on the phone. Grace and I are starting a skate-shoe company, ask what it's called."

"What's—"

"*Legless*. It's, like, the opposite, and it means drunk, so that's cool."

"You guys all getting enough to eat so far? Everybody gone to the bathroom?"

"Yes, *Dad*."

I took cold bacon from the platter.

"Your dad wasn't killed by that gravel truck, was he? He's still around?"

She shrugged. "Concussion."

"What about Grace, she got a hold of her mom?"

"No."

"Her dad's not around?"

"He, uh." She looked past my shoulder and down the dorm. "He died the summer before ninth grade."

I turned on the bench to see Grace, zipped to her chin in a sleeping bag, sitting up from her bed, exactly like a horror-movie scene where a guy rises from his morgue slab, and I thought *zombie* despite myself.

"Didn't they all talk about it, like in the staff room?" Grace asked sleepily. "They said, like, 'If you don't like the Congo war shit, go complain to Grace'?"

"No..."

Amber tapped her chin with the pencil. "Her dad got killed."

Grace swung her feet and set them on the floor, the bag still up to her chin.

"My dad wanted to prospect for coltan because you need it to make cell phones and laptops, and he heard Congo had, like sixty-five percent of it in the world, and he was going to buy us a boat for the summers if everything went okay, maybe Butler Lake. And my mom kept saying, 'That's right by Rwanda,' but the State Department or whoever was like, 'No problem, that was like twenty years ago. Let's not demonize Africa.'"

"No," I said, like a substitute teacher. "We shouldn't."

"So he went out in the Blue Mountains with a bunch of guys, and the first thing the LRA ever did that got in the news—"

"'Cause it was like two years ago," murmured Amber.

"First thing they did was tie him up between two trees and chop down to his skeleton, but they left his head alone so we could recognize him in the picture." No pauses for breath. "Not a lot of Asian guys in that part of Africa anyway, I guess."

She stepped out of the sleeping bag, shuffled past the beds, sat down beside me, picked out a strip of bacon and snapped it in half. She emanated a sleepy warmth. I put an arm around her. Her mouth was a hard line and her eyes weren't even misty.

"Can't believe they showed you the picture," I said.

"Wasn't supposed to." She crunched bacon between her molars. "I guess his clients or whoever started screaming in Congress and stuff, and there you go."

"Plus there was that thing with the old women," said Amber. "And that was *way* back. All their hands and feet."

The curtain behind the table flapped open, revealing ham-armed Jock in flip-flops, a white towel around his waist.

"So, Giller, if your chores are done and you've had your chit-chat," he said, "we'll hit the sauna."

JOCK HELD THE outside door open to reveal Rob, hunched in check-ered bathing trunks across from Colleen in an enormous purple T-shirt. The hot cedar smell was a solid improvement over pig shit. The door thudded shut behind us and I settled in my underwear on the bench beside Rob. My Lydia's Minnesota cousins all had saunas so she'd wanted one in our Wahoo place, but of course events had con-spired so that never happened.

"Ah," Rob sighed, "good timing, gentlemen."

"Getting ugly with you two?" asked Jock.

"Might say," said Colleen.

"Why don't you turn on a light in here?" I asked.

I'd seen a switch as we slipped in, but the only light now was from a crack at the top of the door and the barbecue full of briquettes, wink-ing and steaming in the corner, and presumably poisoning the air.

"I can't take any kind of brightness as of a half-hour ago," Rob said quietly. "Guess it's the ol' pupils. Nothing I can't deal with"

"Aw, heck, we'll all look after you!" In the dark Jock chuckled like Santa. "Takes a village, right?"

"We each fall apart in our own time and in our own way," said Rob.

By then I could make out a vague outline of Jock and Colleen on the bench across, and Rob beside me, running fingertips down his forehead.

"Two months ago, I lost seven guys off the day shift," he said.

"Some so-called accident?" blurted Colleen. "You *know* who must've got to Doug, but you—"

"Shut up, will you?" asked Rob. "Chivalry aside, shut up. I had seven guys enlist to go to the Congo after that horrible shit at the Catholic girls' school."

"Anglican," Jock corrected.

"Yes."

That had been horrible shit. The photos that'd leaked out hadn't told the entire story but it'd sure looked like the younger the girls had been, the more depraved the LRA had been in disposing of them. And what you could see of their expressions, on the ones who'd still had faces—they'd just looked tired, tired, tired of it all.

"I'm just glad they're not around for this debacle," Rob finished. "Thank God."

"And if they're dead now, these seven guys, they're better off?" Colleen asked quietly. "You're telling me my husband's better off too, so I'll calm the fuck down?"

"Young lady, no," Jock said.

"Hippie scientists," said Rob.

"But we've got science of our own," blurted Jock, "and Arthur says we can increase our nitrites in the liquid smoke to the nth degree! He's writing to a chemist from his magazine, then we'll be able to survive on a half-pound, quarter-pound of bacon a day! What's more, we're limiting the amino acids more every day—I really, truly mean that."

"But is there a *cure*?" I asked. "Are you even aware of such a thing?"

"Giller, hey, this is my fifth *day* with this thing operating, if you think—"

"Is there?" I asked.

"No!" Jock threw ghostly hands in the air. "Go find Mr. Penzler himself out in Ohio, ask him if there's a goddamn cure, ask his monkeys with the beards who came out to our place of work and set the thing up, putting our lives and livelihoods at risk!"

"Good," I said. "That was my plan anyway. Gas up the ambulance, I'm gone."

"Me too." Colleen held her head high. "Clint told us what happened in the jail, Peter, and that's not going to happen to my girl, you understand?"

"Don't be pissed at me, I've got no problem if you come."

"What happened in what jail?" asked Rob.

Colleen wiped her brow on the hem of her shirt. "I'm telling Megan to stay here."

"I don't imagine she'll fight you too hard on that." Jock's belly glistening like snakeskin. "She likes that boy with the hair in his eyes." He lowered his head between his heavy shoulders, flashed a frat-house grin. "But don't expect me to chaperone. Hanging a picture or contemplating marriage, always *drill beforehand*, you get me?"

"You sit on your asses," said Colleen, "like that'll keep you alive even five minutes! If you know this hippie doctor is the problem, let's see some action, let's—"

"I've seen you two in action," said Jock. "And you're welcome for the bacon."

She started out the door in a burst of cold daylight, so I could see how the T-shirt clung to her. A widow of twenty-four hours. A black ring encircled her thigh.

"What's the tattoo?" I asked.

"The Van Halen logo." She squinted back at me through an inch of open door. She seemed to be all bottom teeth. "Doug's favorite."

She let it bang shut, and while our eyes readjusted the three of us sat there blind.

"Please, God, Giller," said Jock. "Take that fruitcake away from here."

Then she howled, right outside, and something hammered against the door.

THE DAYS WERE so short that it was already dark by the time I'd loaded in the cooler full of bacon, warmed up the ambulance's engine and checked that my shovel was still under the gurney. Silhouettes approached from the dormitory. I leaned against the grill, waiting for Colleen. I had nine hundred miles to plan what we were going to say to Penzler and his bearded hippies so we could roll back into PBF with a cure. Then back to our lives.

"Hey, Mr. Giller?" Amber called through the darkness, her unseen boots crunching snow. "I think, with my arm already, you know, I think I'd better stay here in case …" Ten feet away, her feet stopped crunching. "You're not pissed off, are you?"

I was a head-stomping Lonny killer, so even *I* didn't know what might set me off.

"It's better you don't come," I said.

Then I smelled foundation makeup and there were three arms around my middle.

"I guess I'd better stay here too," Grace said to my armpit. "There's a bunch of white paint in the shed, when you get back we can pour it all over ourselves for the *nbzambi* parade, it'll look creepy-awesome."

"Speak for yourself, Crazy," said Amber.

"And I didn't hand in my phone," Grace whispered. "We've got Franny's number, and we told her and Megan we'll text all the time."

"Those two are coming?" I asked. "What the hell for?"

"Turn on the headlights and you might see each other," Colleen suggested.

I flinched at her voice, because who knew who she'd hit next and with what?

"You'll be back next week, right?" said Amber, unfazed.

"Back with results, sure."

The two girls' shapes drifted away, then Colleen must've gone beside the steering wheel and flicked the knob—a headlight flared up on either side of me. Franny, Clint and Harv stood out in the snow, shielding their eyes like I was a divine manifestation.

"Tell me you're not all coming," I called.

"Are you really wearing that jacket to Ohio?" asked Franny. "'Cause you look *exactly* like a paramedic."

"No!" I held up discouraging playground-supervision hands. "Why the hell do you think I brought you out here? I'm not dragging you into the line of fire anymore, so you all go back in there and behave yourselves!"

The kids stood there with their arms at their sides—their eyes didn't flicker, their jaws were square. They looked years older than when they'd climbed on the yellow bus to Velouria, like they already had rents to pay.

"Dude," said Clint, "we're in a line of fire no matter where we are, could be an ankle, a shoulder—"

"My ass could slip off any second," said Franny. "And it's not like you're a Navy SEAL, man. We don't make you any more fucked-up than you already were."

And so the polite children trudged past me to the back doors, while Megan stood in the glare beside the cab with her arms around her mother. She'd put her sequinned cardigan back on as though it was already time to resume our pre-Velouria lives.

"Okay, I'm in no position to discourage anybody." Colleen's voice cracked again. "I want to hold onto all of them and not move a step."

"Naw, if you left us here we'd just be waiting for you to come back." Harv rubbed his chin like he was at the foul line, concentrating. "This is way better."

People only say *It's your funeral* when it's an obvious exaggeration, so I didn't, just gave a solemn nod like some hard-assed movie coach— hell, maybe Harv'd had me in mind all the time to lead his doomed basketball team.

"Plus those old guys are super-creepy!" called Clint and Franny.

"Seriously?" That mighty right arm swinging, Amber ran out of the dark toward Harv, her mouth crumpled like a washcloth. "You aren't staying here?"

"Aw," he said, starting to smile.

She thumped into him so he stepped backward into a puddle then dragged them both out of it, holding her up. He put his fingers through her hair.

"Back next week?" she said to his chest. "I'm sorry but I really have to stay here just in case!"

"Oh." His back was straighter than I'd ever seen, his chin on her head. "Sure."

Considering that she'd once aspired to hump him on the hood of her car in a gravel pit, she was playing it pretty cool. Harv pressed his big hand to her cheek, pressing her wet face against him.

Saturday, October 29.

IN THE EARLY-MORNING darkness a SO MUCH TO DISCOVER sign welcomed us to Ohio, and I hoped that it was right. And that the "so much" could be discovered easily. From the back I heard the distinct crunching din of vast quantities of bacon being masticated, which meant the four kids were awake.

"We should've made all those girls come with us." Colleen bit the corner of her thumbnail. "I can picture all the awful things that could be happening around that place."

"What's the worst that could happen?" I stupidly asked.

"Lonny!" Colleen blurted. "You know what that place is? A leper colony. The patients get a place to sleep, they get busywork so they don't go crazy, next thing they'll build a chapel and a cemetery the size of a golf course. Doug and I had our honeymoon in Hawaii, so I read all about lepers."

"It's the best place for them, even so."

"I don't even think of her as my grandma anymore," Franny was saying.

"Look out there," I told them. "We're moving out of tall-grass prairie into the broadleaf forest biome."

"We just saw the back of a billboard," said Megan. "That's all we can see."

"Bet it's for the Ohio National," added Franny.

"Headlights flicker like lost souls," Clint declaimed.

"Trash can," muttered Harv.

"Shit, I just remembered hen judging's on Saturday!" yelled Franny. "I bought new Manna conditioner and everything!"

"I don't think it's that much farther into Preston," said Colleen, fingertips cupping her chin. "Which exit was that?"

"If we were looking at the map back in class, you'd see us moving out of the beige biome, where we've spent our lives, into the dark green," I said. "Think of that."

"Mom," Megan called softly from the back.

"What's happened? You okay?"

"I just remembered about Dad again," said Megan.

Colleen slid her fingers through the window to the back and must've taken hold of her kid's hand. Me, I had Lydia's passport pictures in the wallet in my pocket, and I could feel that strip of paper's distinct weight. I never wanted to not feel it.

"Agh!" Franny yelled behind my head. "I didn't check my texts. I've got texts! A whole bunch from Amber! Aw, damn."

"What?"

"She says, 'Grace is so fucked up right after you left.' Here's the next. 'Both arms gone and skin off her forehead. In the cooler with Craig.' That's it, that's all she said."

"I hate texts," said Colleen.

"Me too," said Megan.

We stared out at the Ohio brown-grass medians and the huge square trucks thundering toward us in the oncoming lanes.

AT NINE O'CLOCK I filled up at a Pegasus station, alongside a little yellow Nissan 350 which I chose to ignore—no spoiler. Inside I asked how far it was to the 91a turnoff.

"An hour," said the blue-smocked girl behind the till. "That lady still out in the parking lot? Maybe you could check her blood pressure or something."

"I don't know who you mean."

"Well, if she's gone it's totally for the best. She wanted bacon to eat, bacon, bacon, bacon, and I was like, 'We just have candy bars, it's not a grocery store,' and she freaked *out*, started screaming and—"

"But you know," said the fuzzy-moustached kid stocking WD-40, "in a way she was kind of awesome. She was so full-on."

"Holy!" the girl yelled. "Another one going off on somebody!"

The stockboy and I collided at the door, but I let him through first because he had a pricing gun in his hand. Outside, an African-American guy in a Redskins cap stood panting behind the Nissan's back bumper, while Colleen swayed at the front, showing her teeth and holding her telescoped stainless-steel baton in front of her like a lightsaber. She took one step as if to come around the car after him and he took a corresponding step to keep it between them. Damn, damn.

"Holy Christ, lady," he yelled, "this car never ran anybody over!"

The stockboy held his hands up like Moses. Maybe that was the Pegasus technique for allaying crises.

"Colleen," I called, "it doesn't have a spoiler. Take a look at it."

She lowered the baton, pulling in a deep breath.

"It's the right color," I said, "you're right about that, sure, but that's all. Let's keep driving."

Still squinting at the poor panting guy, she twisted something in the handle so the baton went back to the size of a flashlight, then she stalked between the pumps toward the ambulance. Her door still hung open.

"Okay," she said.

The Redskins guy leaned against his trunk and looked sideways at us, shaking his head. I jogged past him on the way to the ambulance.

"Really sorry, sir," I said. "She's not well."

"Put a leash on her!" he screamed.

I jumped up into my seat and started the engine. Colleen still hadn't shut her door and had the baton extended in her lap like a piece of expensive plumbing.

"What the shit is happening?" the kids yelled from the back. "Can we get out?"

Colleen looked me in the eye, her face all crowsfeet. "Sorry," she muttered.

I said, "That's—"

Then she was out her door, the baton flashing over her head between the gas pumps before she brought it down on the Nissan's windshield. I heard the thump, then yelling. I let the ambulance roll across the pavement. I heard three more thumps then a final shattering, and by the time I'd rolled twenty feet Colleen had flung herself back in, slammed the door shut and fastened her seatbelt. We roared across the service road onto the on-ramp, getting up into third before the engine was ready. Another crash behind us as the kids were flung against the back doors.

"Hey, shit!"

"Who's driving?"

"Um," I said, once we'd passed a line of dump trucks, "he had it coming?"

Colleen lowered her window a half-inch.

"Somebody did." She picked cubes of greenish glass off her sleeve and dropped them through the gap, her face placid as if she were rolling out pie dough. "Somebody somewhere had it coming."

"You guys need bacon?" Franny said through the window. "Is that the trouble?"

"Give me ten or twenty," I said. "Jesus, yes."

"No, thanks." Colleen glanced at me, bit her lip. "Never mind, I guess I'd better."

"Sounds like there's another one of us wandering this neck of the woods," I said while I chewed—because why belabor Colleen's little quirks? "Some poor woman screaming for the good food, so they threw her out."

Colleen sported a strip of bacon between each finger. "God, the poor girl."

"Might be a good sign as far as we're concerned. Maybe a scientist who—"

"Should we look for her?" Harv asked from the back. "Try to help her?"

"Nope," Colleen and I said together.

I WAS COURSING with so many nitrites by then that the fact I'd been awake for fifty-plus hours didn't even faze me. I watched the used-car lots flicker past and chewed my bottom lip while I went over the plan I'd constructed for when I actually had an unflappable Penzler executive staring at me from across his or her desk.

1. *I did not need Penzler to admit that the industrial mishap in Velouria had brought about—how best to phrase it?—long-term medical difficulties. In my paramedic persona I would present that information as a given.*

2. *I'd describe the Dockside workers' kids who were even now watching their daddies dissolve before their eyes, and in the name of humanity I would request access to the cure for these daddies. The goo could not have gone into production, by anyone's reckoning, without a cure. Or thoughts of a cure. I would describe the kids more than once, if need be, and their little sweaters wet with tears. My fists like hammers beneath the lip of the desk.*

3. *And if forthright beseeching did not produce results, I would take meetings until someone gave me a name I could use—"The gal you really should talk to is Dinah Shore in R&D, she's a big fan of the hippie doctors," something like that. And if not a name then a*

place, because the research had to have happened somewhere and I wouldn't need an invitation to walk into that place, wherever it was. I could knock down walls, I could flip guard dogs off bridges, I could put my hand clean through a person's chest so that fragments of vertebrae lodged under my nails.

4. *But before that, I'd be painfully civil.*

"Do you still have Rob's number?" Colleen asked. "For an emergency?"

I prodded my pants and felt the crinkle of George Reid's fax.

"Hey, G!" Franny called. "Megan says snow is still H_2O, but that's messed up, right? It's got to have nitrogen to be so cold!"

"No," I said. "Snow's water, only slower."

Like zombies are people only slower, and also gradually melting.

"Mr. Giller?" This was Harv. "Did you ever read *The Sneetches* by Dr. Seuss?"

"Maybe eighty or ninety times."

"Okay, but you know the Sneetches, right? Because I said we were kind of excluded but we're actually more like the Star-Belly Sneetches because we get to hang out together and have the weenie roasts—"

"Except it's bacon marathons," Clint added.

"Yeah," said Harv, "and it's everybody *else* who has to sit out in the dark on the beaches, that sounds good, right? But Amber says the difference between us and the rest of the world is *less arbitrary* than if we've got belly-stars or not."

"Though it'd be cool if we did," said Clint.

"Amber's a very bright young woman," I said.

"Yeah," murmured Harv.

At 9:15 I found the pine-shadowed turnoff for 91a and felt my stomach knotting. We passed rows of long cowsheds, then, inexplicably, corporate headquarters: Shell Oil behind a tall fence, Toys "R" Us without any fence, an outfit called American Leaf built right against the road. Smoke drifted across the landscape, probably from farmers burning cornstalks in their fields. A sign advised that that particular stretch of 91a had been adopted by Penzler Industries, and the next sign advised that Penzler Industries was fifty yards away. A tall cedar hedge sprang up alongside the road, then distant granite pillars showed where we'd be turning in.

"How are you going to do it, Gillbrick?"

"Should I get into the back?" Colleen asked, zipping her tracksuit to her chin.

I didn't have a paramedic costume for her, so that seemed like a good idea. I pulled over beside the ditch and she slid down from her seat. A long black helicopter rose above the hedge, then descended again. The hippie doctors?

"Okay," Colleen said from behind me. "Do your thing."

"Think like an ambulance driver," said Franny.

"Will anyone be working on a Saturday?" asked Harv.

We drove on, and under an x-ray my stomach would've resembled a complete pretzel. I intended to make my entrance as an upright citizen. I hit the turn signal with philanthropic gravity.

But then I had to brake hard because an ambulance was already parked in the entrance lane. The back doors stood open and an African-American woman lay strapped on the gurney, her arms swathed in bandages while the attendant lifted a saline drip. I managed to squeeze between the ambulance and the pillar onto the Penzler grounds—yes, *at last*—only to discover a dozen more ambulances lined up in front of the first, their top lights quietly flashing, while far across the green-turfed grounds a mob of fire trucks sat in front of what looked like a smouldering football field, that helicopter hovering overhead.

"The hell?" asked Clint.

If Penzler HQ had been leveled then I had no plan, and my new plan would have to be to keep Josie and Ray in my rearview mirror permanently. A female cop in an orange safety vest waved me into the front of the line of ambulances, and I shut off my engine. Her nametag read HOLMES. She had freckles across the bridge of her nose, and as she walked past she put her hand on my door

"The triage people will bring you someone to run into town, okay? Sit tight. Plenty of customers."

I guess I must've looked pretty forlorn hunched behind that wheel.

"I know," she said. "Just keep your chin up."

"What happened exactly?" As though I already had a pretty good idea.

"Accident," she shrugged. "Explosion. But not a ton of people here on a weekend, thank God."

She hurried away up the line—a black TV news van was trying to get past the pillar. Holmes waved it back.

"When the situation's not so critical!" she yelled.

Frantic whispers from behind my head.

"Mr. Giller," Clint murmured, "do you think this was where they brought those guys who got bailed out of jail?"

"How should I know?" I squealed.

A woman screamed from an ambulance behind us, then a big black sedan with tinted windows steered around the news van on its way toward the smoke, down the hill. I'd have to go down myself, despite orders—maybe some sad-dog-faced researcher in a lab coat was waiting for me with a file marked PINK GOO, I'd never know unless I had a look.

"Back in a while," I said.

I slid to the pavement, quietly shutting my door, and started down the driveway. I wore the white paramedic shirt but not the really-conspicuous fluorescent jacket. I didn't want anyone else's life placed in my hands. The driveway dipped so the fire trucks disappeared below the horizon and for a minute I walked in silence amidst the weird Penzler topiary: shrubs shaped like mermaids, like Pegasus himself, like whatever you call a lion with wings and an eagle's head. The smoke gusted over them all.

I climbed the rise. Guys in polo shirts lay dazed on the grass, firefighters yelled through bullhorns and ran, hoses sprayed haphazard water, men in dark suits shouted into each other's ears, dressed-up women cried on their knees, men with flapping ties wiped their eyes at the edge of the lawn, a table stocked with water and mini-bagels. A plastic tarp swayed over an ad-hoc hospital where a red-haired doctor pressed the heel of his hand against a charred woman's chest.

"Just wait for your call on the radio, okay?" A woman with thick black glasses waved a clipboard at me, her hair escaping its ponytail. "Just go back up and wait, we can't have so many bodies running around down here."

We watched as the red-haired doctor closed his patient's eyes. Blue body bags lay in a row on the lawn.

"Okay, bad choice of words," the clipboard woman said.

I nodded meaningfully to the woman, started back up the driveway then darted around to the back of the hospital tent where I hoped she wouldn't notice me. The helicopter shuddered down onto the grass, its blades dispersing the smoke from our immediate vicinity, and only then did I finally get a good look at Penzler Corporate Headquarters, 1616 Highway 91a. It looked like our house had on the arson morning, only the back of the HQ's foundation was too far away to even see and a team in yellow hazmat suits walked through the wreckage, holding flashing rods in front of them.

A cluster of guys in black-visored SWAT outfits held a conference beside the remains of the wide front steps. A man in a pinstripe suit and hard hat climbed out of the helicopter, then I realized that one of the SWAT guys was walking toward me, swinging what looked like a cattle prod. I took one step into the tent, found a clipboard on top of a cooler and immediately started checking boxes with a pencil. The SWAT guy stomped past, his whole face hidden behind the visor and gas mask, and, by God, did I want to kick him in his bullet-proof belly just to show him I was indestructible. According to the boxes I'd checked, my patient was female, of Asian descent, 64–69 years, suffering from arrhythmia and spinal damage.

I carried that information across the lawn to where Penzler staff, ID tags flapping on lanyards, stood with their arms around each other.

"Excuse me!" I called to the cluster of dark-suited men—hopefully a powwow of the Penzler brain trust. "Are any of you in charge of this entire operation? Is there a Mr. Penzler here?"

"Penzler?" asked a heavyset guy with a white moustache. "He never comes *here*, thank God. If you've got a specific concern you can take it to his secretary—that's her over there, with the pearls on."

The men who weren't yelling into each other's ears looked out at the wreckage and whistled sombrely. I consulted my clipboard and furrowed my brow.

"There's no way to get a hold of him directly?" I asked.

"Is this about insurance?" A tall woman with glasses leaned in.

"Uh, no, not exa—"

"We'll collect paperwork today, but we have to convene a meeting of shareholders before we can submit anything."

"But this form says I should speak to someone affiliated with Dockside Synthetics—can you tell me who that might be?"

"Dockside? Nothing to do with us, I don't know it," said the heavyset man.

"Well, does this Mr. Penzler live in the area?"

"Hell, that's why we built out here in the first place!" he said. "Values his family's privacy."

"And what business are you *in*, exactly?" I asked. "These forms have to—"

"Plastics!" hissed the woman.

I wrote that down and trotted away before I caused any real alarm. I found the gray-haired secretary talking into her cell phone, but she snapped it shut as soon as she spotted me coming. Along with her pearls she wore a pristine yellow overcoat. The bigwigs were all too clean to have been on-site when it happened.

"Excuse me," I said, "the gentleman across the way indicated that you'd be able to supply Mr. Penzler's home address. We need it for the forms."

She just stared at me, big-eyed like a harp seal.

"I don't *know* Mr. Penzler's address," she said. "The man likes to be left alone."

"Fair enough," I smiled. "Who might I ask about the contracts the company carried with the US military?"

"Hey!" The clipboard woman grabbed my arm. "They're *radioing* you! Get to your vehicle!"

"Oh. On what channel?" A bona fide question, I thought.

"Channel *nine*—how did you get called *in* if you weren't on nine?"

"Well, I *had* been on nine, but—"

Clipboard put her hands on her hips. The woman with pearls narrowed her eyes as she reopened her phone. I turned and jogged back up the driveway. What had my entire undercover operation uncovered? Penzler himself lived in the area, which might've meant "in Ohio." And what would he know? Guy probably played tennis and signed the odd letter. I needed a research guy with a beaker in his hand, but he and the beaker had probably had their molecules combined. I should've asked for the mailing addresses of all secret labs.

Holmes, the freckled cop, stood beside my ambulance as I hurried up. The other vehicles had gone. *Who are all these people in the back?* she was going to ask.

"Don't worry about it," she said. "Finn took your call."

"Oh," I said. "Okay then. I was helping out down in the tent. Doctors were asking *me* what had happened here, as if *I* would know!"

"You must have that kind of face," she said. "People always ask you for directions?"

"Yeah, they *do!*"

I bounded up into my seat. I hadn't been so enthusiastic about anything since the kids were babies, not even feigned enthusiasm, but

I'd figured I needed a new tack. And Holmes was the cutest cop in the world if that wasn't too condescending an assessment. The ambulance was so quiet that I wondered whether they'd gone on a reconnaissance mission of their own. I grinned and lifted a handful of bacon out of the mixing bowl between the seats.

"You want some?" I asked.

"You have Nebraska plates," said Holmes.

"Oh, of course!" I imagined I was Clint in mid-improvisation on the theater sports stage. "It's the driver exchange!"

"Who'd you exchange with, somebody here?"

"Oh, I don't know yet. I was just pulling in off 33 when I got this call!"

"But where are you staying?"

"They said to find the motel and they'd call me there. There aren't many motels, are there?"

"No," said Holmes, "just the one."

A gigantic fire engine purred up the exit driveway and out onto 91a. The driver nodded at me and patted the outside of his door, just like they'd done in Hoover.

"If you're done here," I offered, "why don't I run you into town?"

Because maybe she'd feel like talking. She nodded, but then wandered around to the front of my ambulance and murmured into her radio while she looked down at my license plate. Then she holstered the walkie-talkie and climbed in.

"Seat belt," I told her. "Such a treat to have a passenger who's not in shock."

This last bit was to discourage my other passengers, if they were even back there, from staging *Oklahoma!*

"This seat's so warm," said Holmes.

"You must have got a cold bum, standing out in the cold!"

I turned right onto the road. Fifty yards ahead the fire truck had pulled over and the driver stood beside the ditch as he was interviewed by the TV-news people. He waved his arms as though miming large explosions.

"He'll catch hell from Penzler," said Holmes.

"How's that?"

"Old Man Penzler put a gag order on everybody working the site. He throws his weight around this county like you wouldn't believe, but you'll see that by the end of your first shift."

"Ah, he must be the one they were mentioning." I lifted my eyebrows and swayed my head, peering at the ditches on either side of the road like the glorious act of *driving* was all that my mind really had room for. "Must not be a union shop, if he didn't even come down to lend a hand. Where's the guy live exactly?"

"Just out of town."

"Probably some fancy neighborhood," I muttered.

"No, that's the weird thing—he's out on McCauley." She waved a hand vaguely over her shoulder, which meant east of town if I had my compass properly aligned. "I had the honor of driving his daughters home one night, even the one who can still walk. But I guess it wasn't too pretty when their mom died, that might be part of their problem."

"Uh-huh. This morning he must've been making them breakfast," I said. "What kind of house does a big executive like that live in? Just out of curiosity."

"Rambling, I guess you'd call it. Seemed like there were a lot of little buildings."

I figured that asking for the exact address would be too much.

"Pink marble or something?" I asked as I peered up the road, as if the conversation didn't have any relevance for me or the people riding in the back.

"No, no, just wooden. White. Why do you ask?"

"You have a lot of family in Preston?"

"Just my sister and her kids," she said. "You have a suitcase and stuff in the back? How long you staying again?"

"Fourteen days."

"That's not long."

"It's a pilot project."

Mobile home parks huddled on either side of the highway.

"I guess your sister's kids will want to know all about what happened out there."

"No," said Holmes, "it's their *mom* that'll want to know. She works the deli counter and she needs to know everything. I was just talking to the captain, but I can't pass a word of it along to Susan."

I slowed down for a school zone even though it was Saturday.

"Pass what along?" I asked quietly.

"Well, they've confirmed arson." She took off her cap to scratch above her ear. Her hair was in a French braid. "The jumpsuit guys found incendiary devices, something like twenty-five of them. Went off at seven-thirty when only the insane keeners were at their desks. Horrible."

Incendiary devices. No wonder it had reminded me of my own house—but why would Penzler do to themselves what they'd done to me?

"Poor suckers," she said. "As if writing up one more memo about plastic couldn't have waited until Monday. Should've been home watching cartoons!"

You can guess which two people that got me thinking about.

"And that was all he said?" I murmured. "Your captain?"

"Some people aren't as forthcoming as we'd like." She put her cap back on. "Here's your motel."

"Nah, I'll drive you to your station."

"Pull in, I want to see that you get checked in."

"You don't have to."

"Look, I'll happily do *anything* before I have to start knocking on doors to tell people their husbands and wives just died, all right? Humor me."

She got out and walked across to the Lamplighter Motel's front door, its gold lettering faded from too much sun.

"Be right back, ambulance," I said flatly. "See you in a minute."

I glanced over my shoulder and saw Clint's hand giving the A-OK sign—man, his thumb had reattached just seamlessly.

With Holmes I strode across the cramped lobby to the front desk, trying to make myself as attractive a prospective guest as possible, though I'd seen my reflection in the office door and realized I still had black patches around my eyes like a robber in a kindergarten play. I smiled up at the potted palms and the brass clock tacked to a piece of driftwood.

"Single room, please. Be staying fourteen nights to start. You have any kind of limit on length of stay?"

"No, sir!" The woman behind the counter left off watering a spider plant and slid the register in front of me. "Sign in, if you please."

She was that long-nosed, eyebrowless sort of woman that winds up as either a drunk or a basket-weaver but seldom both. She stood picking lint off her cardigan. A lanky boy with braces, probably twelve years old, sat beside her with his feet propped on the edge of a drawer, drawing a fairly intricate Frankenstein on an Etch A Sketch—

Frankenstein's *monster*, to be accurate. Everything his creator's fault. I wrote *Rory McAvoy, Hoover, Nebraska* in the register.

"You drive the ambulance?" the boy asked.

"Yes, son, I do."

"Chad," said the woman, "he's entitled to *some* privacy."

"Cool," he nodded, as though she hadn't said a word.

Holmes knocked me with her elbow. "Everything kosher with this guy, Ange?"

"Joanie!" the woman smiled. "Didn't see you step in!"

"You might get busy," said Holmes. "Terrible business down at Penzler, terrible. Lot of out-of-towners'll come zooming in."

"Oh, I didn't want to ask you." Ange shook her head. "I reckoned I'd find out all about it on the CNN. They just called and booked three rooms."

"My friend Hunter's dad works there," said Chad, screwing the cap back on his orange juice. "But he *never* goes in Saturday—he says working weekends will lead you to the grave!"

"Sickening." Ange offered me a key dangling on a cork. "Here you are, Mr. McAvoy, you're in 17."

"Should I park it around the side?" I asked. "Sometimes there's a minor panic when people see an ambulance out front."

"Well, 17 *is* around the side."

Smart-ass! I figured I could grab the Etch A Sketch and knock her and Chad cold in all of three seconds, even with that gun strapped to Holmes's hip, but that would erase poor Frankenstein. Frankenstein's monster.

"I should be getting a call from dispatch," I said. "I guess the hospital—"

"If Gabe calls I'll put him through. Help with his bags, Chad."

The kid loped around to the door and held it open for us.

"So, I guess you're set," said Holmes. "Now I can go tell Nestor Solomon his wife's passed away. Lucky me."

"Oh, no," I said, my hand on the ambulance's door latch—and for a second I saw this poor Nestor Solomon on his doorstep, squinting hard at Holmes before his face crumpled. Grabbing the doorjamb to hold himself up. Their empty kitchen with her egg-streaked plate still in the sink. I knew what Nestor Solomon's future held, though with Lydia we'd at least had those weeks when we'd known she was going and could talk about it. Nestor just had Holmes on his doorstep, he—

I'd hit the fucker so hard he'd fly through the back of his house, wind up like a smashed watermelon!

"Just down by the school—I'll walk," said Holmes. "I might check on you later."

She turned across the parking lot, and I didn't say a thing after her. She really was cute as hell, with really wiry-looking hands, I loved that, and terrific as it would be to screw her, staring down at her sweaty forehead as I gave it to her, I didn't want to find myself knocking her block off if she happened to fart. I sounded like Amber sitting on Cam Vincent's desk. And what was the point in giving us any urge to reproduce in the first place? Very sorry, Lydia, my brain tried to say.

Our ambulance smelled more like sawdust than I'd realized.

"G," Clint asked through the window, "are you going to have sex with the police?"

"Five dollars says yes!" hissed Franny.

"How'd you like a ride straight back to Rob?" whispered Colleen.

Mom was getting tough. I drove around the building and backed into the space in front of 17.

"You wait for me to let you out," I said to the ambulance. "You do not move."

"Carry your bags in, mister?" asked Chad.

He leaned against the room's green door, his hands pressed behind him. The sun broke through the clouds all of a sudden, glinting off his braces like a carnival ride. I brandished my key.

"I'll sort that out later," I said. "Right now I have to sleep."

"Drove all night from Nebraska, hey?"

He stepped aside as I unlocked the deadbolt and stumbled into the room. I saw a brown pole-lamp, a television, the bed yawning in front of me. Then my face was on the white pillow, and somewhere behind me the door clicked shut.

"Oh," Chad said from outside. "Okay."

But after a couple of minutes—maybe two hundred—the need to talk to my kids woke me up. I sat up and my intestines tied a knot around my belly as I looked across at the beige telephone. All I wanted was to hear one of them say "Dad" in my ear, and I just hoped that whatever vague explanation I gave of what I'd been doing wouldn't sound too hollow.

I dialed. The ring from the other end sounded like a good old Nebraska ring. My arms felt weak despite all the PBF bacon.

"Hello?" Deb said, matter-of-factly, like she didn't figure her line was tapped.

"It's Peter," I said.

"Oh, I knew it. Call display said 'Ohio,' and everyone I know in Ohio's passed on—oh, what a thing to say." Her voice got faint. "Kids! It's your dad!"

"Everything all right?" I asked.

"Oh, sure. The drive was fine the other day, and I signed them up to start at Parkview down the road tomorrow. Does Josie really take size eight shorts for gym? They look awfully short on her."

"That's what she had in September," I said, "but I thought she could've had nine or ten. Get twelve if you want, she'll grow into them. And keep track, I'll pay you back."

"Oh, it's my pleasure, Peter. This has just been lovely. Here's Ray."

"Hey, Da-ad?" he asked.

"Yessir." I smiled. "What is it, Ray?"

"Are you in bed?"

"I was, yeah. Because I'm not feeling well, you mean?"

"Yeah," he said. "I can't fall asleep if it's during the day."

"Yes, I've heard that."

"Dad?" This was Josie, on the other line.

"Hi, Sweetheart," I said.

It was a mistake to have phoned. I needed to touch the backs of their heads.

"Are you feeling better?" she asked.

"I *do* feel better, a lot better, but there's still a few things to sort out."

"How, um, how come you're in Ohio?"

"Hey, MacArthur has Ballocity! But you have to keep your socks on," said Ray.

"Well, I can be there in time for your birthday," I said. "I'll take you then."

"My birthday's after Easter."

"Grandma says I'm going to need braces," Josie said solemnly. "She said my bite looks weird."

"Do you want braces?"

"No."

"I'm not allergic to cinnamon anymore," said Ray.

I watched my oblong, reflected self in the turned-off television screen—if I'd bothered to wash my face I might've looked like someone's father.

"Okay, I should talk to Grandma again. I love you so much. Have fun at your new school."

"Okay," they said together. "Bye!"

Then a clatter of handsets. Somehow in the TV reflection I didn't have any ears.

"I'm still here," said Deb. "They really are fine."

"You're all relaxed, hey? Nobody strange coming by the house?"

"No, no, everything as per usual. We raked leaves. The house across the street, do you remember the one?"

"With the fountain?"

"It was on the market *two years*, then on Saturday it said SOLD, and this morning somebody moved in."

"Uh-huh." My gut re-knotted—I pictured gas-masked Penzler guys unloading houseplants from a moving van. "Is it a, uh, a whole family?"

"No, just one fellow so far. He's on the plump side so the girls and I may have to get him out walking."

All was well in MacArthur, so my unconscious suddenly reminded me to let the zombies out of the ambulance. Had it been hours?

"Peter?" Deb called from my hand.

"Sorry, I'm right in the middle of wending my way back to you," I said, angling the phone toward its cradle. "Love to everyone."

I staggered to the door. The sun was significantly lower in the sky. The rest of the parking lot was empty, and as far as I could tell no one was spying from behind curtains. I opened the ambulance's back door an inch. The sawdust smell was getting pretty rank, and I could tell by the absence of its smell that they'd finished off the bacon.

"Anybody got to pee?" I whispered.

"Holy crap, it's him!" said Franny.

"Holy crap, were you asleep?" asked Clint.

"Too late, you bastard," said Colleen. "I peed in the Rubbermaid."

"This thing seemed a lot roomier when it was moving," said Harv.

"Harv said you got clubbed to death!"

"I seriously thought you'd left for California once and for all," said Clint. "Didn't I say that?"

They managed to assemble their five faces in the crack, like on an album cover.

"How big's the room?" asked Franny. "Lots of beds?"

"One double. But if we—"

"I'll go check us in," said Colleen. "Then we won't have to keep peeping and hiding."

"Oh," I said, "okay." That did make sense—I'd pictured propping a kid in each corner. "Aren't they going to wonder how you got here?"

"Let us out. My boyfriend dropped me off."

I took her small hand and helped her down to the pavement. Beneath the angle of her eyebrows she squinted at me in the bright afternoon.

"Did the cop say anything when you were inside?"

"I wasn't inside her," I said by accident.

"When you checked in. Has she come across anybody like us?"

"Didn't mention."

"Go in and go back to sleep, I'll see if we can get next door." She touched her toes, did a revitalizing jumping jack. "You'd better dump out that Rubbermaid."

MY DOORKNOB RATTLED a while later, and I was on my feet opening it before I really knew where I was. Colleen stood yawning into the back of her hand.

"We're next door. They want to watch TV," she said. "But I don't."

I could hear it through the wall—sirens and explosions. She dragged her feet across the room, lay down on her side across the bedspread and folded a pillow under her head.

"After dark we go find Penzler's house," she said to the wall.

"Uh-huh." I chained the door, suddenly envisioning the disaster-area SWAT team, then followed her over. "They get another text from Amber?"

"You can put your arms around me," said Colleen.

I lay down next to her, tucked one arm under her head and wrapped the other around her ribs—if she'd been my Lydia, that hand would've found her breasts and I would've pressed myself against her behind, but I kept a quarter-inch of distance down there. I lay staring at her ear, breathing on the back of her neck. Josie and Ray were happy and healthy, I had that for consolation, though something in their neighborhood sounded weird.

"Go back to sleep," said Colleen.

I WOKE UP with her hair in my face—it smelled of tangy, unwashed scalp. Dark outside, and cold in the room except for where I was pressed against her—I'd have to stumble around and find the thermostat, probably had electric baseboard heaters. We'd had them in the rental house in Champlain but in Josie's room they'd been on the fritz so I'd had to bury her under a pile of blankets—I'd felt like shit about that. Now the wall reverberated with thudding bass from the TV in 18, and a scratching from somewhere around the foot of our bed. A mouse woke me up?

I sat up, and sleeping Colleen smacked her lips. It *was* cold in there, enough to see my breath by the neon filtering through the blue drapes, though I was more *aware* of the cold than anything. Captain America's super-soldier serum had set me above such trivialities. My hands felt ready to crack walnuts.

The scratching came from the door. I bounded across to open it and my legs were vaguely stiff, maybe from stomping Lonny's head in. So many golden memories.

I opened the door a crack. Chad and another kid—also goofy looking, with blond hair that was long in the back and possibly permed—crouched at my feet, lower than the hoods of the parked cars, like no one was supposed to notice them. Which would explain their scratching instead of knocking.

"Mr. McAvoy," whispered Chad. "You got trouble."

"What in hell you doing?" I said. "Get in here."

They crawled inside like it was a scene from *The Great Escape*, and once their high-top sneakers dragged across the threshold I clicked the door shut. Chad got up and ran across the dark room to the pole-lamp, where he started clicking through the various tri-light settings: dim/regular/very bright/dark again/dim/regular, which took me back to Champlain Middle School's Diagnosing Autism seminar.

"What?" Colleen sat up, shading her eyes.

"I don't know," I told her.

"I'm Pat!" The blond kid leapt up like a jack-in-the-box beside my shoulder, then knelt again to tighten the Velcro on his shoes.

"Holy crow!" Chad whispered. "You're the mom from 18!"

"It's cool," I said. "You didn't walk in on anything."

"Oh. Are you brother and sister?" asked Pat.

"Yes."

"Mr. McAvoy?" Chad whispered. "One of the guys from Penzler was just at the desk, and he said, 'Who's from Nebraska? *Who's* from Nebraska?' But I didn't tell him, I was like, 'What? Nebraska?'"

"You *totally* were like that!" added Pat.

"How do you know he was a Penzler guy?" asked Colleen.

"He had the hat," said Chad. "One of the big guys!"

"And, uh, why should that bother us?" I squeezed my left earlobe between thumb and forefinger. "I'm just here to drive an ambulance."

"He was *mad*," Pat said.

"Yeah, he *was* mad," said Chad.

"We go in people's rooms all the time!" offered Pat.

"Shut *up*, man!"

"Did he see the register?" I asked.

Chad shook his head, still clicking through the settings. Very bright/dark/dim.

"I put that the five of us were from Loogootee, Indiana," said Colleen.

"Should've put French Lick!" said Pat.

"Are you signaling to him with the fucking light, is that it?"

"No, no!" Chad jumped back like it'd given him a shock. "I was just—"

"I'm going back," Colleen said, and went out the door in a half-crouch.

"Stay in here a minute," I told the boys. "Help yourselves to the ice bucket."

"Really?" asked Pat, eyes wide. "We can?"

I ran out and jumped into the ambulance. All the other parked vehicles looked dark and still—nobody watching or waiting that *I* could see. Even if the gentleman in the Penzler hat hadn't read Nebraska in the register, he could still read my plates. I gnawed the last cold strip of bacon from the mixing bowl as I drove around to the back of the motel and parked in front of twenty-six. Blue television light flickered behind its curtain and I could hear sneaker-squeaks and whistles from a basketball game—anybody with their TV turned up that loud deserved to have Penzler knock down their door. Of course, I was undertaking these misleading machinations while wearing a VELOURIA MEDICAL shirt.

I sprinted back around to my unit—and realized how *fast* I could run if I really wanted to—and there were the two idiots rubbernecking at the curtains. But I ran past them and knocked on 18.

Franny opened up. She wore a blue bra and yellow panties—a little chunky around the hips, but not bad. She had a Sharpie in her hand

and black writing up her arms and legs. Clint jumped off the couch in what looked like multicolored *Justice League* underwear. I shut the door quickly but quietly.

"What the hell?"

"It's not a kinky thing," said Franny.

"That's what they keep saying," Megan announced. Hunched over the mini-fridge, she tore open a foil packet of coffee—she'd only stripped down as far as a pale pink NORTH PLATTE CERAMICS GUILD T-shirt.

"Preventative measures!" The back of Clint's scrawny right triceps read THIS IS CLINT'S RIGHT ARM THANK YOU. His armpit smelled of sawdust. "It's going down like Velouria all over again!"

"Did those dumb kids come tell you first?" I asked.

"What dumb kids?"

"Harbinger Harv's wandering around out there." Franny sidled up to the window. "Harbinger Harv says there's guys in black."

"If he comes back, tell him to stay in here." I had both hands gripping that left earlobe now, and I really did feel calm despite whatever shit was unfolding. "Assholes don't know we're all together, so even if you hear me shitting myself, you stay *in here*. Where's Colleen?"

"Shower." Clint studied his labeled limbs in the mirror. "She's of the wear-clean-underwear-to-the-hospital school of thought."

"She has clean underwear?"

"In her purse," said Franny. "Oh, actually, if and when you do pin us back together, if my knees are like in a million pieces?" She bit her lip while she bent to write on Clint's back. "Harv has pretty nice legs. Just sayin'. Oh, and there's another text!"

I opened up her pinging phone. The keypad was sticky.

CRAIGS ONLY IN THE COOLER ONE MORE NIGHT JOCK PROMISED!

As I crawled back into 17 the two boys ducked under the table.

"I turned your thermostat up to seventy-seven," said Chad. "Right here above the table, see?"

Pat held the empty ice bucket accusingly—I'd robbed those boys of such a terrific good time. I hunched over in the corner beside the pole-lamp and unbuttoned my shirt—I could at least wear it inside-out to hide the Nebraska associations.

"Was it possible this guy in the Penzler hat was just affiliated with ambulance dispatch?" I asked.

"Maybe," said Chad. "Mostly the one guy paced around and talked on his cell and said, 'I'll teach *him* a lesson.'"

"It wasn't exactly a hat, either," said Pat.

"What do you mean by that?"

But they didn't answer. They were too busy staring at me.

"What?"

"There's a big hole in your shoulder," murmured Pat.

"Hey, the light's goes right through it!" said Chad. "That's awesome!"

"It's no big deal, fellas." Really, as far as I could tell it seemed to be healing nicely. "I was just in a, uh, a war a while ago, that's all."

"Which one?" asked Pat.

"War of 1812," I said.

"Awesome."

I put on the inside-out shirt but found it difficult fastening the buttons that way.

"What did you mean that he wasn't *exactly* wearing a hat?" I asked.

Chad was on his knees by then, peering under the couch.

"It was a gas mask!" said Pat.

I buttoned faster.

"Yeah, but pushed up on his head—like he was on his lunch break or something."

"This was at lunchtime?"

"Naw!" said Pat. "Ten minutes ago."

"And the little, the little canisters for breathing said PENZLER on them," Chad explained, his face still on the carpet. "Hunter's dad wears one to work. You know what? Hunter said his dad was going to sign up to be one of the plastic soldiers, and they'd have enough money to go to Hawaii!"

"Lucky!" said Pat.

"So this guy in the lobby ranted and raved and then ran out to his car?"

Pat stared into the empty bucket as though ice might materialize.

"Not exactly a car."

"No way!" Chad sat up, holding an orange ping-pong ball aloft, his braces gleaming triumphantly. "Guy got into a *tank*!"

"Boys," I said. "You need to—"

Someone knocked on our door, a solid *knock-knock-knock*.

Good, I thought, grinding my back teeth, *let 'em come in.*

"Shit!" Chad hissed. "My mom!"

He shoved the ping-pong ball down the front of his pants like it was a baggie of weed. Pat leapt for the pole-lamp and clicked it from very bright to dark, and then I could only make out the door by its dim outline. I took a deep breath.

"Yes?" I called, innocently enough. "I'm just getting out of the shower!"

"I'm from around in twenty-six," a man called back softly. "I wanted to ask if you could please move your car. Your *ambulance*, I guess."

"Be right there!"

I crept to the window and put my eye against the curtain. Through the blue weave I could see easily enough that the speaker was not a meek little guy from twenty-six. It was one of the SWAT team guys from the Penzler site, gas mask and inscrutable visor and everything, standing under the 40-watt bulb with his shoulders back, and what looked like a black cricket bat gripped in his leather gauntlet. It looked less like a cattle prod now but probably worked on the same principle. I flexed my jaw and thought, *These poor bastards*. Didn't their job descriptions involve preventing their headquarters from being flattened? I couldn't see whether another guy was standing outside 18, but I couldn't hear any knocking. Tiny green and yellow lights blinked along the length of the bat, and I swallowed hard. The lights were sickening.

I shuffled back toward the bed. I could barely see the boys, crouched at either end of the sofa.

"Just getting my shoes on!" I called out. "I'll come take care of it, not to worry!"

The lamp's pull chain still clacked against the pole.

"How do we get out of here?" I whispered to the boys.

"Climb on the bed and push the air-conditioner out the window," murmured Chad. "But don't smash it, they're super-expensive."

"We have to sneak out of rooms all the time," whispered Pat.

"Sir?" Gas mask called softly through the door—now I could hear that through-a-gas mask quality in his voice. "I felt real bad about having to bother you, so I've got a six-pack here for you if you could open the door."

Pretty ballsy to stand on the doorstep in that get-up for all the world to see, but that probably meant he was coming in whether I liked it or not. Up on the bed, I pulled the curtain across and there sat the lonely air-conditioner, cardboard taped around it for the off-season. I put my shoulder to the corner but on such a springy mattress I couldn't apply much pressure.

"Oh, wait," Chad said from the dark. "Is this seventeen? You've got a new one, with the bolts. Do you have an electric drill?"

I *did*, out in the ambulance.

"What's that noise?" hissed Pat. He was teetering beside me all of a sudden.

I heard a brief mechanical clatter, maybe a diesel tractor, then the door flew off its hinges and thudded against the foot of the bed. A three-foot black square on a horizontal boom followed it in—in the gloom I could only see outlines—as the tractor came rolling across my parking spot. But not a tractor, it was a tank with some kind of battering ram.

I flattened Pat against the mattress as four SWAT guys' silhouettes tip-toed in at the edges of the doorway, their reflective visors down. Oh, it was *good* that they'd come. I flexed my walnut-cracker fists.

"Pretend you're not here," I said into Pat's ear.

I vaulted over the broken door onto the shoulders of the nearest guy, ripped the gas mask off his head and threw it out the door. He didn't like that—he spun his body and swung his elbows at me but I kept my legs wrapped around his belly and my hands underneath his jaw, trying to force my fingertips into his glands. Every time I shaved I imagined how vulnerable we must be under the jawbone there, and after a second his skin broke and my right middle finger slid in up to the base of his tongue. Blood spattered across the back of my hand. The SWAT guy was really screaming then, and even if this *was* Hunter's dad, some poor working stiff, I justified it in that I'd never much liked the name Hunter. Anyhow, if I'd kept myself from crossing a particular line at the 7-Eleven, now I'd overthrown it by fifty yards.

"Light 'em up!" the other guys shrieked. "Get him off!"

As the first SWAT stumbled forward I heard electricity crackle and figured the cricket bats had come out. I rolled off him across the floor, then balanced on one hand and swung my legs sideways into the next guy's knees. Maybe something I'd seen on TV. He thudded to the carpet beside me just as the other two started to hit me across the head and neck. I felt a whack and a *sizzle* every time—the things were burning me, my neck, the back of my arm, my ribs and thighs. I could hear them huffing behind their masks from so much hard work, even as the first guy slumped and gurgled beside the door. The places they'd cooked me smelled exactly like overdone bacon, but it felt a lot worse than when I'd been shot through the leg in Velouria, and I figured they knew it.

"Shitty!" I squealed, and rolled into a ball.

I took one more good thwack across the small of the back, then managed to get one foot under me and launch myself over the sofa. Chad sat back behind it with his knees to his chest, his eyes big as headlights.

"Staunch the bleeding!" an unseen SWAT guy ordered.

"Know what Hunter's dad said?" Chad whispered to me. "He said in the plastic army a severed limb can survive for five minutes!"

"Think I don't know that?" I whispered back.

"Release!" the SWAT guys called.

I never heard the canisters fall but a second later my eyes were burning like I'd rubbed them with a cat, and I wanted to puke though I knew my body couldn't afford to lose a single nutritious carcinogen. Three big guys couldn't just pull a couch away, they needed tear gas?

I tried to breathe through the front of my shirt and remembered that you can supposedly make a half-decent gas mask by peeing on a cloth—when I'm losing them in Science 9, I always mention that—and though my own bladder felt like the Mojave Desert, I figured Chad must've been ready to pee about then.

"Kid?" I managed to say.

I prised my eyes open to peer at him and realized he was trying to get to his feet.

"No, kid!" I croaked.

"There!" barked the SWAT guys.

Then a flash of light as a truncheon arced above my head. Chad thudded down beside me, limp as a noodle, his head propped against the moulding. A piece of skin had been lifted off his forehead and blood steamed down his face, but worse yet was the snot pouring out of his nose. A thousand times I'd held a Kleenex to Ray's nose and told him to blow.

"See that?" they said from beyond the sofa. "That wasn't even him!"

I kept blinking and realized the tear gas had stopped bothering me. Maybe the goo was helping me adapt physically as well as to increase my mastery of bizarre improvisation. I lay down on my back, Chad's lap the only place to put my head, and lifted my hips to slide my belt off. It was all I had for a weapon. My burns still throbbed.

"Man," Pat groaned from far off. "Get me out of here!"

"There's a kid on the fucking bed! What kind of sicko fag—"

"Just get him outside!"

They sounded distracted just then, so I threw myself over the back of the couch and kicked the first guy I saw in the chest. He collapsed on his back, waving his bat from down there before I stepped on his throat. His gas mask went *crack* and his hands dropped to the carpet. Misty crap still gusted from the canister at my feet, and Pat, bent over and retching, was being guided out the door. The next Penzler guy flailed out with his truncheon and it crackled like a bug zapper as it breezed past my chin, then I wrapped the belt around the thing and wrenched it from his hand. It clattered against the TV.

"Grandma," I whispered, "doesn't like this kind of behavior."

What the hell was I doing? I kicked the dude in the side of the knee, then my big elbow to the side of his head, like I was filming the kind of movie Lydia had hated. A final knee to crush his testicles against his pubic bone and the third SWAT guy went over like a stack of dimes. Ought to have worn a cup.

And the room was empty of conscious people. The fourth muscle-head had got Pat clear, the guy with the hole in his throat too, that was good, but I figured Ange might never find him back there if I didn't pull the couch out, so I dragged it eight feet. I had a hard time doing anything with delicacy.

I turned Chad on his side so he wouldn't choke on his tongue, and when I stood up, the tank's treads were flush up against the door-frame and the eight-foot barrel was pointed right at me. Could they shoot through that battering-ram thing? If it pegged me I'd never even feel it, I'd just be in pieces—but that meant Josie and Ray believing, even when they'd retired to the Caymans, that maybe their father had never intended to come back—so I did a somersault and ended up across by the TV, and the end of the barrel followed me, whirring like a blender, so I shuffled back onto the door by the bed, and then whoever was aiming the thing must've got tired of that particular square dance and the whole tank pushed right in through the wall, sending plaster and two-by-fours flying at me like I was a dartboard. In the top corner of the gaping hole it'd made I glimpsed a square of greenish evening sky, and I figured I could fling myself through that square if I hustled. But in the second I spent thinking that, the barrel shifted.

All I saw was the flash of orange, but the noise was like an ocean flattening my head against a gravel beach. The concussion of air sent me flying against the couch and I lay there for about four heartbeats wondering if the tank was going to keep rolling in and squash the guys still on the carpet. Then through the smoke and falling plaster I saw that the wall behind the bed had disappeared, though the air-conditioner still dangled there in its bracket. I stumbled to my feet and dove out into the night, landing with my bare elbows on broken glass. The tank's shell had also taken the roof off a white hatchback and caved in the side of a dumpster, so I realized I was behind the motel—not far from twenty-six.

I ran into the dim glow of those units at the back, all of the guests outside, shouting, "What in hell?" And there was my ambulance, praise God. Moving away from me. A tow truck—white with fluorescent strips down its mud flaps—was pulling it away, and I heard the driver gun his V-10 as I lifted my knees and ran after him.

But then a bluish shape ran out from between the parked cars to my left, throwing itself at the side of the truck—the driver's door flashed open and something tumbled onto the pavement. I couldn't check my stride in time and tripped over it, heavy as a sandbag, so I skidded across the parking lot on my back. Then I was up again, ready to keep after the tow truck, but it had stopped thirty feet away, its right blinker on like it was turning onto the highway, our ambulance dangling patiently behind. It looked like I'd tripped over the truck driver, stretched out unconscious behind a red Honda Fit.

I trotted to the tow truck and found Harv, resplendent in his HOOVER HIGH sweatshirt, fiddling with every knob beside the steering wheel. Gave me a harried look.

"How do I set it down?"

"It's just a Vulcan 810!" Colleen said from behind us. "Watch your feet!"

She hauled on a lever behind the cab. Women were resourceful— once at Toddler Storytime, Lydia had produced a library card from her bra. The ambulance came down and Colleen disappeared under the front of it, chains clanking, then she hopped up, face blue from the Lamplighter's neon sign.

"Don't you have keys?"

She hopped in the passenger side as I climbed into my regular seat, then Harv slid in next to her so she fell across my lap. He slammed his door. Keys were in the ignition. I backed away from the tow truck in a half-circle so I didn't flatten that sad-ass driver. Black shapes darted across my mirrors.

"The other three!" I said.

"They've been in the back for like ten minutes!"

"Please drive," Franny whispered behind me.

Sunday, October 30.

THE FIELDS LOOKED crinkled with frost. We must've still been driving east, because the sun was coming up through the trees ahead of us. We'd driven for an hour, not finding enough road signs to be able to connect our blearily lettered Preston Chamber of Commerce map to the actual landscape, so we'd pulled over and slept, Harv and me in the front seats, and Colleen and the rest in the back. I suspect we all farted in our sleep. I woke up in the dark to doctor my burns again with antiseptic wipes, but they'd scabbed over—a medical marvel, sure enough. Colleen staggered back up to us as soon as I got the engine started.

I looked up at the sign again—the white letters said we were on Hutchens Road but could fork off onto gravel McCauley Road if we gave a damn.

"Go slow." Colleen peered at the map. "Looks like the road's pretty short."

"What'll we do when we find it?" asked Harv.

"Find a place to park," I said.

"We're awake back here," yawned Megan.

"So don't talk shit about us," Franny said.

Used-up orchards appeared on either side of McCauley, row after row of upended trees in craters of black soil.

"Looks like somebody's grandpa's blowing them up as a long-term project."

"Really?" asked Colleen. "Yours too?"

"Exploded half of Pawnee County. He was missing a finger too, come to think."

I flexed my four-fingered hand on the wheel.

"You're genetically disposed," said Harv.

"Hey, G," said Franny, "listen, we got another text from the God of Thunder."

"Who?"

"Amber. Sent at three-thirty AM. 'We danced in the cooler for Grace but she didn't notice. Sucks ass!' she says. That does suck."

"But then they got to eat," Clint said. "Where's our breakfast at?"

"Okay," said Colleen, a shudder at the back of her voice. "I think this is it."

I braked and we squinted to our right through the trembling aspens, the ambulance shuddering beneath us. A rambling white house stared back at us—peaked roof, windows, chimney. No cars or people in sight, but the tire tracks frozen in the mud made it look like vehicles came and went on a regular basis. A white picket gate and a path of overgrown bricks. A shed in the side yard, and what looked like a blue barn in the back—that lined up with the cop's description. No chimney smoke, and though I could hear dogs barking they sounded far away, maybe at the next property. Harv unglued his eyes from the side window to look back at me.

"What'll we do?"

"Um. Go in with my paramedic routine, play on the man's sympathies."

"I'll come in with you," said Colleen.

"Aren't we all going?" asked Harv, eyes large.

"Well, hold on," I said. "We've got one chance to do this with some kind of legitimacy, and I'm the only one who's dressed for that."

"Fuck that," Franny hollered from the back, "we came to rip heads off!"

"Yeah," Megan said faintly.

"I'm the only one," I went on, "who's dressed like he could legitimately, um." My mind went blank. "Inquire. If he kicks me out, I guess *then* we'll start breaking windows and screaming we want a cure and we want it now."

"Man, I thought you were serious about this!" said Harv. "Don't you want to get fixed up? We came out—"

"I am serious. This is my whole thing, kid. I've got nothing else."

"There's another jacket in the back you should put on," said Colleen. "You look like something shat you out."

"I appreciate the advice."

We drove another fifty yards until we found a faded old driveway between the trees, and it led to a clearing full of brown weeds, surrounded by a collapsed wire fence.

"All right," I said. "I'll walk back and knock on the front door."

"I don't get this!" Harv glared at me, mouth half-open. "Are you going to tell him you *walked* from Nebraska?"

"I know it might seem weird but—"

"Yeah," said Colleen, "I think it's better if—"

"What if they don't buy the act for a second," I said, "so he sends one of his boys out to, I don't know, throw a grenade at you guys? At least if you're squirreled away over here then you'll be able to get me out if it all goes south."

They glanced at each other, tense as a couple of broomsticks.

"I'll take the shovel," I offered.

"How long do we wait?" asked Colleen.

"Five minutes," Clint hissed, the ambulance swaying. "Then we're going mad scientist!"

A PATH STARTED through the woods in the direction of the house, thick with thistles in spots, but what was the harm in staying out of sight for as long as possible? The long grass was stiff with cold and the birch branches creaked around me, but it felt more like I was running across the high desert with the wind in my hair, because I was on a righteous mission with my shovel in my hand—though the path seemed to wind too far to the left to be taking me to the house. I hopped one log after another and waited to glimpse white walls between the branches.

Instead the underbrush crackled in front of me and two dogs crept out—dogs they've always got at the pound, skinny-hipped shepherd-crosses, but even Josie wouldn't have adopted these. They crept between the thistles, growling and bristly, each with a square patch shaved off its hip like they'd escaped from the vet's. One circled a tree to get behind me, like I was a baby goddamn zebra, and a chill went up me—I could take a bullet, sure, but what the hell good was I against teeth? I waved the shovel.

"Get out of here!" I shrieked. "Go home!"

Genius, right? The one in the path bent low then jumped, and I swung the shovel to intercept him but missed by two feet. He took my forearm between his teeth and shook the hell out of it, gummy saliva spraying my face, his back feet dragging through the twigs, and I brought the handle down across his snout as I felt the second dog sink its teeth into the back of my right knee. And pull. Something snapped back there, I felt it, but instead of real pain I felt pins-and-needles as though its teeth were hooked to a car battery, and I kept yelling "No!" because dogs obey commands, right?

"Yah, yah!" someone yelled behind me. "Yah, yah!"

There was Harv with a fire extinguisher in each hand—he brained the knee-biter so it staggered into the bush with a hunk of me in its teeth, then I raised the shovel as the other one leapt for my arm but one of Harv's extinguishers hit him so hard across the jaw that he thudded onto his back then twisted to dart up the path toward the ambulance.

"I got him, you go!" Harv shouted, starting between the trees after the poor dog. "I was only checking—promised Colleen I wouldn't go with you!"

"Oh," I said to the suddenly empty woods. "That's okay."

Though there didn't seem to be much holding my right knee together. It couldn't take any weight, so I put the end of the shovel under my armpit for a crutch. My wrist looked like it had gone through a lumber mill but maybe that was just cosmetic.

I started back for the ambulance. The Penzler Mission: over before it'd begun. Each of my medical-professional pant-legs hung in shreds, like the Incredible Hulk's clothes after he turned back into Bruce Banner, who then had no choice but to carry on with his fucked-up life, tattered pants or not.

I *fell* along the path more than I walked it. Car-battery sparks snaked up and down my thigh, telling me I was about to lose the knee for good if I didn't get in the ambulance and find staples—five minutes total, Rob had said. Saplings whipped my belly. Then the house's white gables loomed over me because I'd gone the wrong way.

The crimson front door was fifty feet ahead of me and my stumbling momentum could have taken me straight through, but immediately in front of me stood that side-yard shed, with a Gemtop truck canopy leaning against it and STP stickers across the door. A workshop. Padlocked, but I popped the hasp off with the shovel and hopped inside.

The shed was crowded with dusty shelves and a decade of John Deere calendars sagging off the walls. Down to thirty seconds and I didn't see a staple gun, and though there were spools of fishing line and a pair of needle-nose pliers there wasn't time for sewing. I heaved myself onto the stool, lifted my leg onto the workbench and dumped out a jam jar of four-inch galvanized nails. Between the shreds of pant-leg I set the point of the first nail against the top of my kneecap, then I grabbed the hammer from its hook and brought it down hard on the nail head. Viscous blood spurted out across my hand. The angle wasn't perfect and I had to hit the nail eight more times, but I figured that at least meant it was finding the tibia at the other end. The rest of my body made its opinion known by bucking like a mule with every whack.

"Quit it," I whispered.

Then I lined up another nail to the right of the first—I figured three would be enough. I raised the hammer again.

When I was finally done I leaned against the counter to keep from falling on the floor, and after a minute I was able to wipe up the beads of blood with paper towels, a single-father habit. Behind the roll of towels, a cardboard box sat stuffed with coils of blue and yellow wire stuck to finger-size metal tubes—blasting caps, maybe for blowing out those stumps. They gave me the creeps somehow. As I grabbed my right ankle and lowered the foot to the concrete, nausea submerged me like I'd plunged into a bathtub of the stuff. I grabbed the empty nail jar and puked into it. Then I set both feet on the ground and took a lot of deep breaths, my forehead against the oily bench.

Another minute, then I'd head back to the ambulance and whatever new plan of attack they'd concocted. Colleen would coo over my hardships, Harv could gape at my saddle-leather toughness. I took comfort, really, from that jar of vomit—it seemed a very human reaction to nails through a kneecap. How often did zombies throw up in the movies? Were self-inflicted nails so much worse than a bullet?

Then, behind me: "Mister?"

A woman's voice, raspy but young. She must've been in the doorway, the padlock's busted hasp dangling beside her hip. If she was one of Penzler's people I'd have heard the gas mask in her voice and she'd have recited corporate dictum concerning we victims of pink goo, *The brood of folly without father bred*. That was Milton, from English Literature 12—funny how the brain works. If I'd thought she was one of Penzler's I'd have thrown the jar in her face then fired up the electric drill and aimed for her bladder. But I left the jar on the bench and turned around.

"Sorry to have busted in," I said.

She had dirty-blond hair braided into pigtails and wore gray sweatpants and a white T-shirt that said FLAVA. She held a frying pan down by her side. She had that overripe look around her eyes like she'd been crying, though there was no evidence of tears and her eyes weren't red. She was somewhere between nineteen and twenty-six, and barefoot. Your basic Ohio-style country girl, I figured.

"I'm Alice," she said. "I heard a noise."

Her breasts were small. She wasn't wearing a bra and it was a cold morning.

"Yeah, sorry," I said. "I can fix your door there, promise." I felt flecks of vomit at the corners of my mouth so I wiped them with my sleeve. "Some dogs went after me in the woods and I had to stitch up my leg in a hurry." I stood up from the stool. "Look at that now," I said. "Weight bearing!"

"Those must've been the Ogles' dogs," she said. "I guess you're a paramedic." She spoke with little intonation while she studied my shovel. I'd propped it blade up, crusted with blood and fur, against the bench. "Has there been an accident around here?"

"So far just this one," I smiled. "The Ogles friends of yours?"

"I went to school with their boy." Alice switched the pan to her left hand so she could scratch that shoulder. "Their dogs went after me and my horse once, and we didn't get clear of them 'til we hit the pump house."

"I don't know the pump house."

"It's a long way away."

I made myself smile again. If the Penzler apes weren't there already then maybe they weren't coming at all. Alice leaned to one side to peer at the jar on the bench.

"You sick?" she asked.

I picked it up, ambled forward a couple of steps and the knee held, but with my nitrite levels dipping into the negative I was pretty woozy. The jar was warm, like it was full of hot chocolate.

"Anywhere I can dump this out?"

"Just out here on the grass," said Alice, and stepped back to let me by.

Tall dry wildflowers that I hadn't noticed before swayed beside the shed. I threw my sick over them in a long arc.

Then I felt Alice's frying pan connect with the back of my head, and for that eighth of a second, as all light faded to a pinpoint, I could smell what she'd been cooking.

Bacon, my lips nearly said.

I LET JOSIE and Ray ride yellow bicycles across the blankness. But then Josie rang the silver bell on her handlebar, and that sent a message: my wrists were tied with prickly ropes, and my ankles with a smooth nylon polymer, all four with sufficient tension for me to know, even before I opened my eyes, that Alice—if that was really her name—had me royally incapacitated. I heard a distant whinny, then another, but she'd said she had a horse, and it wasn't even strange that she should treat blatant intruders so unkindly. The back of my super-soldier head felt a glassy calm.

I blinked up at a white plaster ceiling embossed with twining-rose patterns, then looked above my head at my wrists and followed their ropes eight feet across the room—Alice didn't suffer from any scarcity of rope—to the legs of an old carved piano that looked heavier than my car. In that pose Josie would've said I looked like Superman. I lifted my head to look down: I was on a dining table, heavy oak or something that didn't wobble in the slightest, with my knees hanging off the edge. Those fresh nail heads glimmered at me. My ankles must've been knotted to the table-legs.

"Any time now, team," I muttered.

Light came in through thin gray curtains—the house probably ran off a propane generator, out there in the sticks, and the Penzlers must've been thrifty types who didn't fire it up until dark—but even so, it was bright enough to watch Alice saunter across the room and stare down at me.

"Hi," she said.

"Any time now," I said again.

Then she was busy around my middle. I lifted my head and saw that she'd pulled my shirt up and stuck the tip of her third finger into my belly button. I hadn't even felt it go in. She gave a tired sigh out her nose. Her finger looked to be wiggling. Cattle started lowing outside, not far away.

"I need help," she finally said.

I looked back up at the plaster roses. Whenever I wasn't in a fist-fight I was thinking about my kids, so it occurred to me then that I was farther from them geographically than I'd ever been.

"Your dad here?" I asked.

"Oh," she sighed. "He's not well, he's in a wheelchair. I've looked after him and my sister, so throw-up doesn't bother me, all right? Barf all over yourself if you want."

I stretched my arms out as far as I could, to keep the ropes from cutting so deep, because I knew those tendons wouldn't hold together the way they used to. It looked like my dog bites had nearly healed, using up resources, so I'd need bacon to rectify myself.

"What sort of help you need exactly?" I asked. "Hired hand?"

"Bigger help than that."

"Why'd you tie me up?"

"So you won't take advantage of me."

Had she been saving up dialogue for the first XY chromosomes to happen by? She lay both hands over my belly button, and that finally got me thinking about her like I'd thought about Holmes with her freckles, or Colleen the odd time. No, Colleen was more nuanced. Jesus, could I ever focus on where I was?

"I want you to go look for my sister Natalia," Alice said. "She looks like me but with red hair. Think you can remember what I look like?"

I nodded. Her cheekbone formed a perfect line back to her ear.

"I know exactly what you are. Nailing your leg back together, are you kidding me? And you smell like chopped kindling, you know what that means?"

"I'm hungry," I told her. "You have meat or anything in your fridge?"

"We got a telegram from California that said not to expect her back, and she was only supposed to be out there for the *cure*!"

"Cure from what?" I asked quietly. *Holy shit!* I thought.

"Before you leave I'll show you the telegram." She framed my navel between her hands. "I apologize if this is too much. I just love belly buttons, they're what I miss the most. Brad's was good, he had a *good* belly button. Not too deep."

"Your father must have one."

"Don't be disgusting," she said. "I *know* what kind of thing *you* are, anyway."

She bent and kissed my navel. I saw her tongue dart into it, but I didn't feel any sensation except my armpits stretched tighter than harp strings. From another room I heard a clatter like a spoon dropping, though I couldn't twist my head enough to see beyond the piano. So I looked back down at her. She'd lifted my shirt and kissed her way up to my sternum while her hands busied themselves unbuckling my belt. She stopped kissing long enough to unzip my fly, and from the top of my knee I could see those nail heads wink at me. *Good luck!* they said.

I lifted my behind so she could tug my pants down.

"Technically," she said, without looking up, "you aren't even human."

She pulled down the underpants I'd worn for three days, and I could *see* that I had an erection though I couldn't feel it. In her hand my cock didn't look as long and magnificent as I thought it should have, but it did look fat. She got her mouth over it and moved her head up and down, bit by bit it went further into her mouth. Her blond pigtail dragged across my bare stomach. And suddenly her mouth over me felt hot as an oven, and a 100-volt current jolted straight up my spine to flare behind my ears. For once my kids flitted out of my mind—without kids, Jesus, a zombie could have a lot of fun. I gasped and she kept me in her mouth and started yanking on my balls like she was ringing for the night nurse, and if she knew so much about my condition she should've been more cautious. Her bottom teeth moved against me and I shut my eyes and came.

Then my cock shrank to the size of a peach pit.

Her puffy-eyed face appeared over me. She took hold of the back of my head and kissed me hard, her tongue against the back of my incisors. Her hands smelled like oats and molasses. She looked me in the eye, a lovely moment, then kissed the tip of my nose. I imagined Lydia doing that, then I imagined Colleen. I couldn't decide which to think of.

"You taste like creosote down there," Alice said.

"How old are you?"

"Twenty-five. If I look younger it's because Dad's a biochemist."

"Experiments on you."

"Breakfast supplements."

I needed nitrites but there was no sense starting a fight while I was tied up.

"You got bacon in your fridge?" I asked.

"Alice!" a man's crackly voice called from another room.

Sounded like he was coming over a radio, or maybe just upstairs—and who did he sound like? Just like my own hard-bellied dad.

"That guy ready for transit? The boys phoned me they're down the road!"

I tried to sit up but that just wrenched the tendons in my armpits. Did he mean cops? In any case, my cock was hard again. *You never know*, it must have been thinking.

"That's your dad?" I asked through my teeth.

"Listen," Alice said. "My sister, Natalia, got sent to California, and I want her back. You heard of Pismo Beach, with the albatrosses? San Luis Obispo?"

I was twisting like a snake, trying to get leverage. It was time for Colleen and the kids to drive in through the wall, tank-at-the-Lamplighter-style.

"Don't bother," she said. "José tied you up, and I can't get the knots undone."

"You're the one who hit me with the fucking pan!"

"That's protocol around here. Have to know the rules to break 'em!" she smiled.

"Cut the things!" I said. "Before they get in here!"

She shrugged and her breasts shuddered, which was obliging. Had Lydia's breasts ever moved quite like that, in a bikini or anything? I remembered them as still pictures, not moving ones. Not a great time to get melancholy, but the preceding five minutes had set my mind down certain paths.

"He giving you trouble?" The man sounded so tinny—an intercom?

"No, Dad!" she yelled.

Alice ran past my right arm and out of view. Even if I did get loose, I wasn't going to make it fifty steps unless her fridge was packed with the good food.

"They say they're at the door!" her dad called. "Be hospitable now, Alice! I can't quit what we're doing here, so go be hospitable this one time!"

Now she was waving a bread knife above me. She leaned over and sawed away beside my left wrist, giving me an enviable perspective for watching her T-shirt in motion. Bacon, fistfights, sex—since Dockside it'd been feast or famine in all things.

The last strand finally gave and my left hand was my own again. I curled the poor thing onto my chest and let it rest a minute. She started on the right arm, but her pigtails were unbraiding and she stopped to push the hair out of her eyes.

"Keep going!" I said.

"Something's up with this rope," she said. "I'll do your legs."

She gave my cock a friendly squeeze as she hurried down the table. I could hear footsteps pounding up a flight of stairs.

"Quick," I whispered.

"Oh, hell, *this* one I can untie. And don't stress anyway, they're just going to drive you twenty miles and dump you. California doesn't need any more subjects, now they have Natalia. She smelled just the same as you, and I bet *she* could snap these."

"What?"

The boys yelled at each other from a landing somewhere, and I realized I had one hand free and could at least greet them with my pants on. By the time my zipper was up she had my legs free, but they were too stiff to even lift.

"If you're going anyway, I want to watch that butt run out of here." She knelt beside the table, picking strands off the knife. "Curious to see if that knee'll hold, too. Three *nails*—this could be interesting from a technical perspective."

"Get this other arm loose," I said.

She put a warm hand on my right wrist but it was already too late. Four guys in black Kevlar and gas masks marched in from behind the piano. Penzler boys.

"Step back, young lady!" the first one ordered through his respirator. They weren't wearing the visors, so maybe they were new at the job. "That's the living dead."

She hid the knife behind her back. "More like the living end."

She'd been saving that dialogue too. My right arm was still tied but I rolled off and slid underneath the table. Alice scuttled away into a corner. I gave the rope an almighty tug but that piano really did weigh half a ton. Beyond the table legs I could only see the Penzler apes' feet across the room but I heard their truncheons crackle to life and my stomach flip-flopped and the burns on my back felt hot again. My new knee felt no pain but I was soggy through every joint—maybe that was how Donny Brown had felt before the end. And had she said Natalia had gone to California to get *cured*?

"Remember, no live rounds!" Alice's father called. He didn't sound like my dad anymore, he'd have never said that. "That's our home in there!"

"Get around behind that table," a respirator ordered.

I yanked on a carved leg to break it off for a club, but it didn't budge a hair. The apes' black legs surrounded the four sides of the table and a burning-plastic smell wafted from their truncheons. I was like a lassoed calf under there.

"Go to it," the respirator said.

Away in the corner I heard Alice giggle.

I dove out quick. A truncheon seared the back of my neck but I rolled to my feet and ran, straight past that piano I was tied to and into the next room—the kitchen, with a green fridge and flowery curtains. At the far end a sack of potatoes and two mason jars sat beside a closed door—had to be the basement. I knew I'd only be able to run eight feet beyond the piano, but I galloped like a streak of lightning and hit the end of the rope as hard as I could, hoping either the rope or some part of me would give, though I nearly lost my footing on the throw rug by the sink. The rope went taut so my wrist burnt like a branding iron but then it was my *shoulder* that came away—I'd torn all the ligaments at UC Denver, of course, then trashed it on that rebar. The joint ripped in two like a towel torn into rags, then the whole arm flopped onto the yellow linoleum like ten pounds of potatoes. Specks of blood splattered the cupboards, viscous as paint half-dried on the roller. I felt suddenly lopsided. I heard apes' boots. A coupon stuck to the fridge read AWE-SOME HOT DOGS.

"Can I get some progress, please?" Alice's father shouted.

"Shut up, Dad!" she yelled.

All in less time than it took to tell. A meat cleaver hung on a hook over the cutting board, and country people keep their knives sharp. I'd wear the apes down before they could corner me in that basement.

I grabbed the cleaver, lopped off four feet of rope, then shoved the cleaver in the waiting hand at the end of my right arm and closed the fingers around the handle, tight, and all in a goddamn *hurry*. I picked up the rope and started twirling the whole works over my head, arm and cleaver, like a cowboy at a freak show—they couldn't chase me off the property until I had some idea of the cure being given to this Natalia.

The first ape stepped into the doorway and I let the rope play out through my fingers. His eyes went wide for a split-second, then the warm knob of my shoulder-bone crashed into the bridge of his nose—my detached arm had ten feet of reach, thanks to the rope, and a hell of a lot of torque. He dropped like a slaughtered steer and his sizzling truncheon bounced in front of me, burning a barbed-wire pattern into the linoleum. The next ape barreled in.

"Keenan!" he yelled.

I picked my arm up and flung it at him. The cleaver lopped his gas mask in half so he dropped his truncheon, brought his hands up and staggered against the doorframe like he thought his whole head had been chopped in two. He would never have made it as a zombie—he'd have coughed up his nitrites first time he lost a finger.

The next ape pushed past the first two, leading with his truncheon out like a fencing master. No time to collect my arm from the floor. I dropped the rope, stepped beside the fridge and unlatched the freezer. As the fencing ape lunged I sidestepped his truncheon and swung the freezer door toward his head. He ducked, the door banged against the cupboards and he straightened up, eyes crinkling at the way he'd outsmarted me. My joints might have been jelly but I was still fast—I sprang past him for the edge of the door and closed it as hard as I could, smashing his face into the frozen casseroles, then I jammed my knee into the small of his back so I could slam the door on him three more times. I felt like Harv would've enjoyed all that. It was a heavy goddamn door, too—fridge must have been cast iron.

"Hey, zombie. Over here."

It was the last ape, their sheriff who'd been giving orders at the start, leveling an automatic pistol at my chest. He stepped in front of the first pair as they climbed to their feet. The gun, I didn't mind. It was the numerical disadvantage I didn't care for, because I didn't even have a warm jar of vomit to throw.

"I'm no zombie," I hissed. "Look at *yourselves*, man."

I took my knee down and the ape in the freezer clattered to the floor. His truncheon still hummed between my feet and beside his shattered gas mask a copper valve protruded from the base of the fridge.

"Let's get a goddamn report!" Old Man Penzler hollered. "We have to get back to what we're doing!"

The sheriff took another half-step toward me. Didn't fire. I looked to be unarmed, of course, and his fantasy must've been to cold-caulk me with the butt of his pistol. Guys in the country love the action movies. No sign of Alice through the doorway—she must've hunkered down in a corner. I nodded toward the apes.

"Get out of here, Alice," I said, "you don't need to see this."

Each of them glanced over his shoulder as if Alice were behind them, and the sheriff didn't exactly turn but for a heartbeat his eyes flickered off me. I scooped up the truncheon then brought it straight down again, snapping the propane valve clean off. How much gas would escape from the little black mouth of broken pipe in a couple of seconds? Hopefully not enough to blow up the whole house. I gripped the end of the rope between my heels, started to jump backwards and hoped like hell the basement door was as flimsy as it looked.

"Goddamn it, zombie," said the sheriff, "I said to—"

Whether or not he meant to, he tightened his index finger. Maybe the propane smell panicked him, but in any case people should only point guns if they're prepared for the thousand different things that might happen when they pull the trigger.

I didn't much care if the bullet hit me in the chest or the belly or the groin as I jumped, the important thing, once the igniting gas helped throw me backwards, was that I hit the *top* half of the basement door so that I'd be lying across it as we plummeted downstairs and not the other way around. Oh, and to keep my heels pressed tight enough together for my arm-on-a-rope to get dragged down with us. That was the horrendous plan that I wouldn't have needed if Harv and Colleen had come to my rescue as scheduled.

The primer sparked at the back of the sheriff's bullet, the bottom of the fridge detonated, and as the purple explosion hurled me backward I saw the freezer-ape skid across the floor like a rag doll with cotton spilling out of it. The back of my ribs crashed into something then I plunged backward into the dark.

I WOKE UP with my own severed arm across my chest, its rope tangled around my neck, staring up at a yellow rectangle of kitchen doorway, and while the breath was already knocked out of me it wasn't easy to unwrap the noose from my windpipe one-handed. It's possible zombies don't even need oxygen but I didn't want to be that test-monkey, and by the time I'd thought that through I had the rope clear.

Like a one-armed crab I scuttled out of the light from upstairs to sit behind a cobwebbed column, so to lay eyes on me the apes would have to creep right down the stairs. If any of the Penzler boys were left. I could hear wood crackle, and smoke wafted down the stairs, but for the house to still be standing there had to have been a shut-off somewhere in their propane system.

Oval shapes hung above me. I squinted and saw they were dozens of *hams* hanging from the rafters. Two hundred parts sodium nitrite per million. Manna from heaven like in Exodus 16—my brain had gone back to Knudsen First Lutheran. In the meantime I still had a *severed arm* and the meager hope that five minutes hadn't gone by.

A couple of big bent nails were stuck in the post—useful, but how the hell would I pull them out? With all of that stuff out in the shed they wouldn't have a tool bench in the basement too. A tall white shape stood in the corner: hot-water heater. I propped my secessionist arm against the post, then crept to my feet, stiff as a rusted faucet. Without that right arm, I listed to the left like a ship taking on water.

A man coughed somewhere upstairs—big, wet hacks like he had a milkshake in his lungs. "Fuh!" he muttered, then coughed again. Must've been right at the top of the stairs. Footsteps thumped across the boards over my head.

Beside the hot-water heater my foot kicked something metal that skittered away across the bare concrete. I got down on hand and knees to find it—a pipe wrench with a long narrow handle. I hurried back to my lonely arm, the dangling hams taking turns to whack me across the forehead. I slipped the pipe's handle behind the bend in the first nail and yanked back hard, but it didn't fly out, just shifted a little.

"Keenan?" a man upstairs called hoarsely.

"Present," someone muttered.

I pulled again and again until the nail was rattling as loose as a bad filling, then I plucked it out with my fingers. Then I got to work on the next nail. You needed at least two if you wanted your appendage to heal straight, any carpenter would've told you that. Upstairs the men were quiet and I took that as a bad sign.

When the second one clattered to the concrete I knelt and started tapping the nails through the side of my shoulder with the side of the pipe wrench. Just like building a rabbit hutch. The nails were straighter now thanks to the prying-out. I got stupidly queasy each time I broke the skin. "Buck up," that's what I'd always said to Ray whenever I was taking a sliver out of his foot and he started squirming. Buck up!

"Not much left of Danny," they said upstairs.

"Boots and saddles," the sheriff said. "Any exit from down there, Alice?"

She muttered a response.

"Rip the fucker to shreds," a guy announced.

Holding my shoulder against its empty socket was a slippery operation, the nails sticking out sideways like antennae. I backed up to the hot-water heater then ran at the post as fast as I could, hoping like hell the shoulder would still be correctly positioned when I connected. I concentrated on the nail heads striking at a perfect right-angle, then I slammed into the post like De Niro breaking a door down. The thud shook clear into the middle of my chest. I stepped back and saw the nails had been driven in better than halfway, then I rammed the post again. Then they were three-quarters of the way. I let the arm dangle there by itself, and it held! I thought hard about clenching my fist, *clench, clench, clench*, at which point my index finger moved a full millimeter.

As I turned to caress the nearest ham, I saw their black legs on the steps, steps that were so goddamn solid they hadn't creaked so much as a whisper. It didn't look like they'd brought flashlights so I had a couple of seconds before the apes' eyes adjusted. The first stepped down onto the concrete, his pistol thrust out in front of him. They'd given up on truncheons and helmets. Too angry for precautions, which sounded familiar.

I lifted the pipe wrench with the toe of my shoe then caught it in my left hand—the right hand would need another minute. The rafters were too low to swing the wrench overhand so just as the first ape turned to squint at me, pistol wavering, I brained him sidearm across the temple. He dropped. I put the wrench in the back of my pants, scooped up his pistol and slid into the dark under the stairs. I looked up at the second ape through the slats. Why where we bothering with each other? If it hadn't been for that goo from Pipe #9 we might've been sitting together to open a bag of chips.

The second one had stopped but he didn't even holler, like he'd expected the first one to drop.

"Light-switch down here?" he called up the stairs.

If I didn't want Josie and Ray's battered mug-shots in the *Hunter-Gatherer* for passing bad checks I knew I'd have to lead by example, so even though the second Penzler boy was directly above me and I could have put a bullet up his ass and out the top of his head, I waited for him to take another step down, his foot directly in front of my face, then I shot him through the back of the calf. The muscle burst like a water balloon, and as he tumbled to the bottom of the stairs I jumped over him and the first ape, and I started up toward the bright rectangle of kitchen, my feet nearly slipping in the mess halfway up.

The ape I'd shot must've been shrieking but I didn't hear him because my sinuses filled with a smell of gunpowder and blood, and goddamn if it wasn't just like cured meat! I charged up the last step into the kitchen—it was mostly charcoal, the curtains and strips of wallpaper black and swaying, and the real reason for the smell was the freezer guy, cooked to the bone against the cupboard door. Through a hole in the wall I could see a half-dozen low buildings out behind the house. If Colleen and the kids weren't charging through the hole it meant something had happened to them, which was my fault for bringing them down McCauley Road. I put the gun in my belt and hunted under the sink for big garbage bags. No sound from downstairs, so the second ape had either bled to death or fainted. The bags at the top of the stack were melted together but the rest were all right—a flashlight under there too. How soon before more came to get me? If my blood hadn't turned to Vaseline it would've pounded in my ears.

"Nah, I'll be at HQ another half-hour," Penzler was saying. "Place fucking stinks! We didn't deserve anything like this, Christ." The voice came from down a hallway, maybe an intercom panel up at the front door. "Get Jones on the phone."

"Plenty of reinforcements on the way," the sheriff's voice said.

So it was time to load up on hams and hightail it to the ambulance, but then where, if I didn't know exactly where to find Natalia? My highly intelligent penis twitched at the idea of adding Alice to the crew as navigator but while my brain was still running the show I hurried down the stairs to my basement seclusion. If I still wanted Penzler himself he was back at his flattened headquarters, I'd been there a day too early, but in the meantime there was Alice and her sister and the cure, the cure, the cure!

My flashlight beam showed the two Penzler guys sprawled in a pool of blood eight feet across—and it was trickling out of the back of the second guy's leg, not *spurting*, which might've meant his heart was slowing down. I set the flashlight on the bottom step, turned the guy over and unbuckled his belt. His holster kept it from sliding out all at once but after I unsnapped that the belt came free so I could loop it around his thigh. I stepped on the leg to pin it down, then tied as tight a knot as I could manage above his knee—only time would tell if it was tight enough to stop the flow, though I wouldn't be around to see that. But I was confident that my single act of mercy would inspire plenty of clemency when I stood trial for all of the guys I'd killed and/or maimed since Thursday morning.

"Oh," she said behind me. "You *are* still here."

My jellied heart thudded. Alice rolled the flashlight back and forth with her bare foot. Her hair hung loose. I stepped into her and wrapped my arms around the small of her back, which in the long view was nearly as inexplicable as when I stopped chewing the guy's ear off. We kissed each other on the mouth and I was hard within seconds, which should've been impossible since my blood pressure was five over zero.

She squeezed the back of my neck and pulled away.

"Yuck," she said, running her tongue behind her lips, "I guess you haven't brushed your teeth."

"They know you're down here?"

"I told the boys I had to settle the animals in the barn, so we might have five minutes. I said these guys were already out there."

I put my hands on either side of her neck and kissed her again. She used her tongue and the very ends of her lips in equal measure, like she was dancing around my mouth, sometimes hardly touching it. She was up one step so her breasts pressed into my chest.

"Hey," she whispered. "Your arm works."

What kind of people make out like weasels beside two critically injured rent-a-cops? Lonely ones? She bit my earlobe, and the ear stayed on. Of course I thought of Donny Brown's ear then, which ought to have cooled me down to a more human level, but I put my fingers inside the waistband of her pants anyway. She had a warm bum, though my right hand couldn't tell. She reached down and pulled my wrists up.

"Five minutes," she whispered, "is how long you've got to get out. What's the bag for?"

"Hams."

She stepped down into the blood and took a good look at the guys.

"Roll them on their sides," she said, "or they'll swallow their tongues."

I'd done that for Chad, sure, because he was a kid. After that she pulled out a pocket knife and helped me chop down a half-dozen hams, then she used the bottom step like a cutting board and sliced one up—and the peristalsis in a zombie's esophagus must be a determined process, because I hardly chewed even once. I make it sound like an all-afternoon picnic but really we shuffled around and bumped into each other and got our feet sticky with blood and the whole thing took about ninety seconds.

"Nothing I haven't seen out in the barns," she said.

That line-of-dominoes sensation of nitrite-rich vitality flooded back into my limbs. And that feeling didn't make Alice any less beguiling.

"If you're going to find Nat you've got to get going!"

"Hell," I said, "you just like me because I won't be around for long."

"Natalia can tell you how long you have." She kissed me, a flicker of tongue against my teeth. "And it'll be longer than half an hour, because she's months ahead of you. Maybe a year. If she's not better by now she just has to come home. Here's that telegram, and I wrote her mailing address on the back."

"So why doesn't your dad bring her back?"

"We disagree about it."

I glanced at the paper as I folded it in my pocket. A po box in San Luis Obispo.

"But that won't be where she lives?"

"Inside a po box? You'll have to be a detective for five minutes to find that out, all right? Then get her *home!*"

"Are these hippie doctors with beards?"

"The ones I've met had beards. Let's get to the back here."

The head-wound guy groaned through the roof of his mouth, and the follicles across my head crackled.

"Hold on—you said there's a *cure*." My fist tightened around the bag of ham. "But it hasn't ever worked?"

"They don't *tell* me! Go out and get her, you'll be the first to know."

"Why don't you get her yourself?"

"I get as far as Preston and his staff swoops in, it's happened eight times! Must have a microchip in the back of my neck. He's scared I'll get pregnant or drug-addled, plus he doesn't want his only non-zombie offspring out of his sight. So instead I look at the internet all day and make sure nobody's infringed his patents."

These people proved what I'd said at Dad's funeral: families are pointless.

"No such thing as zombies," I muttered.

She really did roll her eyes that time. Then she covered the flash-light with the palm of her hand and we quit breathing as enough foot-steps thundered across the ceiling to be a herd of cattle. I'd given up on imagining it was Harv and Colleen.

She took my wrist—I nearly had feeling back in that right arm—and led me behind the hot-water heater, the flashlight trained on our feet, then through a wooden door that she barred behind us by quietly lowering a waiting two-by-four into iron brackets. Who'd have a room like that in their basement? The air smelled like rank washcloths. She kept me moving between two brick walls, and so many boots thudded over us I thought the ceiling might come down. The cobwebs wavered like kites.

"Kirk's away in town!" the sheriff hollered above us. "The kid's in the stable!"

I stopped walking.

She shut off the flashlight. "What?"

"You're a Penzler, and you folks have fucked up everything in my life." Everything since Lydia.

"But you're still going to get my sister?" Alice's voice asked.

I listened to the dark. Boots were thundering down those basement stairs.

"I'll give you five million dollars," she said. "How does that sound?"

The last Walgreens flyer I'd seen had advertised bacon at $3.29 a pound for the really good cheap stuff that congeals a half-inch deep across the pan. I could feed Amber and the rest for a decade.

"And I'm qualified because—what?" I whispered. "I broke into your shed?"

"Am I supposed to phone up a soldier of fortune, give him a credit card number?"

I remembered from Lydia that when a woman adopts a certain tone she isn't expecting a response. Alice flicked the flashlight back on. She found the knob to another door and we passed through into fresher air, with steps against the far wall that climbed to a set of root-cellar doors shaped like shutters. Sunlight filtered through gaps in the wood. She stepped up and put her eye to a crack.

"Stupid armored vehicles circling around," she whispered. "He leased them all yesterday after the explosion. I told him they'd suck, listen to those carburetors!"

"You sound like you're pretty tight with your dad."

"Until he decided my sister was *really* sick." She kept an eye outside but I saw a shoulder droop. "Took matters, as usual, into his own hands."

"You're serious about that money."

She jumped down and straightened out some musty blankets that had been balled up on a shelf. She lay down with her head against the water-stained foundation.

"Come stretch out," she said. "The trucks'll head cross-country in a minute."

"Why wouldn't they think I was still down here?"

"I threw a strip of your pants out the hole in the wall."

I set my gun and wrench on the step then lay down beside her warm arm. She laced her fingers through mine. I could see in the gloom that she'd shut her eyes, so I shut mine too. I felt tired like I was still tied to that piano—must've been the strain of putting my limbs back on.

"How'd your sister get to be a zombie exactly?"

"Long story," she murmured.

"Why do you live out here if you're the multinational Penzlers?"

"Oh," she said softly. "Our mom grew up here."

I touched the tip of my thumb to the tip of my pinkie. Worked like clockwork.

"Have you ever been on a horse?" she asked.

I had to think hard about that.

"At my grandparents," I said.

"Can you do it again?"

"I'll carry it on my back if I have to."

"I'll put you on Shamanski, they'll think you're a neighbor. Who ever saw a zombie on horseback, right?"

"Ever heard of one that throws up?"

"Careful your nails don't catch on anything. Wait here a minute."

She got up, climbed two steps, unlatched the bolt and pushed the doors up in a burst of shredded cobwebs and white light. Her sweatpants started up into the yard. *Christ, no!* my baffled penis called after her.

She turned to drop the doors back into place. I peered through a crack as she jogged away across brown grass then through a low door into one of those peeling-paint blue sheds. A goat bleated somewhere. This was the start, we were on our way indisputably to California. Clint had been right.

But why way out west? Even if Penzler kept a lab out there, couldn't they have sent a vial back to Ohio in a courier envelope instead of flying a dissolving girl all that way? No, it had to be bullshit—*Out to California for a cure* was probably a line from F. Scott Fitzgerald. Which reminded me: there was that telegram. Who the hell sent telegrams anymore?

MR K PENZLER

N'S PROGRESS LESS DRAMATIC THAN FIRST HOPED STOP
OTHER WORK WILDLY SUCCESSFUL WILL INCORPORATE

N IF YOU ADVISE STOP WILL TELEPHONE IMMEDIATELY
WHEN CELL TOWER REPAIRED STOP

DR Q DUFFY

A science outfit, and it couldn't even send e-mail? Fishy as Charlie Tuna. And why was I leaving Preston before I could throttle her old man? Because if he'd *had* the cure he would *not* have sent Natalia to California. Though if we were really reanimated corpses like they'd said on the radio, would it just cure us of being alive?

The cellar doors flew open again, blinding me. Alice, back already?

"Seriously," whispered Colleen, taking the front of my shirt in her hands, "leaving the girl to wait is bullshit! You raised on Enid Blyton?"

"Holy shit," I said, "you can't be down here, there's—"

"We saw her run out and figured this was it! Harv's bringing the ambulance!"

Blinking like hell, I dragged my plastic bag and climbed up after her, tucking my tools in the back of my belt. Did the gun even have bullets? From the front of the house I heard gears grinding, an engine.

"It's California from here," I told Colleen. "I've got tons of hams."

But on the grass a big pink pig looked at us and wagged its tail—a black furry tail with a brown tip like a German shepherd's, attached with the spike that Christopher Robin used on Eeyore. My fingers, unbidden, went to the nail heads in my shoulder.

"Oh," said Colleen. "Good dog."

Then gunshots clapping on our ears—a broken roof shingle hit the ground in front of us. Apes, but where? The pig turned, chasing its tail, and fell down. I pulled Colleen low behind a woodpile, then we ran like hell along the side of the house. Our ambulance roared up the lawn from the front, tearing up turf, sun glancing off the windshield, turning in a tight circle so it'd be ready to make an exit, then twenty feet from us it lurched to a stop and the back doors flew open. And Franny and Megan reached out?

"Zombie!" a man's voice barked out. "Line up for attendance!"

I knocked against Colleen's shoulder and peered into the ambulance: our gurney had disappeared and the four kids lay on their faces on the rubber floor. None of the kids so much as wiggled. A hefty guy, with wavy salt-and-pepper hair, grinned at us as he crouched over them in his tan suit.

"I'm James Jones, Mr. Giller. Put down the hams."

The kids were ants and Jones was the jerk with the magnifying glass—I ought to have come to Penzler alone. I'd always cleaned up messes by myself, right? But my legs were cemented like fence posts, and I couldn't make my fingers let go of the hams. I'd been ready to hop to California on one foot, but this bullshit dropped a blanket over me.

"Two-by-four," Colleen murmured. "He's a dead man."

Jones lifted Megan's hands behind her back—her wrists had been cuffed together with plastic zip ties—then he dropped them like over-cooked asparagus.

"High school kids, they love their Rohypnol. Here, maybe this'll calm *you* down." He pressed a black handgun to the back of Megan's neck. "I said drop what you're carrying."

"I am calm," I said, dry-mouthed. "You don't need to do that."

But Colleen only made fists, and I thought of the Preston gas station and how many different ways she was going to get shot. Behind me, an ape on hands and knees reached up to extricate the plastic bag. The wrench and gun were lifted out. There was more movement and I felt a pinch in my neck, but I didn't twitch because point-blank to the back of the neck might've been more than even Megan could take.

"That's the first of them!" said a gas mask at my shoulder.

My legs went woozy. The apes turned to Colleen.

"That's real good," smiled Jones. "And let's maintain that perimeter."

"Megan?" Colleen called, though Megan was unconscious. "Stay there, baby!"

She did a dive roll beside the woodpile and came up with a two-by-four in her hands. She bounded toward the ambulance and I figured Jones had eight seconds to live—he threw an arm up in front of his face like he'd forgotten the gun. As Colleen whooped like a baboon, two guys materialized on either side of her, one grabbing the board, the other jamming something into her shoulder. She shuffled forward a step then pitched forward onto her face.

"The excitable type," said Jones.

Her back arched then she lay still. Jones wiped his palms with a hankie.

"Giller, you stroll around front, we'll strap you in up there. We doctored this cocktail for you zombies especially, so you've got thirty seconds before you zonk out."

I set one foot in front of the other. Couldn't risk the kids getting hurt.

"Something moving back there," a ventilator announced.

"All right, all right!" Jones was taking Colleen's limp elbows as they loaded her in the back. "Keep that perimeter solid! They might've brought fifty of these people!"

I must've had a different angle than the apes, because I looked toward McCauley Road and there was Alice astride a big black-and-gray horse, the famous Shamanski, trotting up from beside the ditch. Tendons flexing in her arms, Alice looked so beautiful with that blue sky behind her. Here she came to swoop me away.

The air cracked. Shamanski reared up, baring teeth.

"Shit!" yelled the ventilators. "Hold your fire!"

Alice had fallen below the skittering hooves, her whole belly suddenly a wondrous tomato-red. Black elbows flapped as apes raced toward her.

"All right, zombie shit," Jones said pleasantly. He gripped my arm to guide me onto the passenger seat—my wrists had been cuffed. "Let's get you someplace private."

I watched an ape take Shamanski's reins and another sit beside Alice and lift her head into his lap. She stared right at me through their grove of legs. *The deal stands*, she was saying, because why else would she have kept staring?

"Hey, there, man!" Some kid behind the wheel with a PENZLER ball cap and a scar cut across both lips. He grinned like a fellow son of Nebraska. "Welcome aboard!"

WE DROVE BETWEEN muddy little farms and small-engine repair shops with yards full of rusting crap. Jones was hauling us away from Penzler's so he could kill us anonymously out in the boonies. I could picture it so well that my chest got tight, right out to my armpits, but all I could do was simmer like a pan of onions.

It was 905 miles from Preston, Ohio, to the pale-blue bedrooms where Josie and Ray slept in MacArthur, Nebraska, but I would never drive that distance. It was over.

But it wasn't going to end in the boonies—we turned onto 91a and slowed down at the Lamplighter Motel, rolled past the black tarp and yellow police tape that covered the front of seventeen, then drove all the way around the back to twenty-five. The day was steel-gray overcast now, and the air flecked with snow.

"What're you doing to the kids in back?" I asked. "You going to hurt them?"

The driver shrugged; he'd be happy with anything he got for Christmas. I was breathing through my front teeth like an incensed mother badger.

Three Penzler apes opened the passenger door, grabbed my shoulders and hauled me down to the pavement. The line of parking spots was crowded with pristine pickups and SUVs but without any sign of people—not even Chad and Pat creeping along with knives clenched between their teeth. The door to twenty-six opened and they shuffled me in. Instead of a double bed, a desk sat in the corner, and the spinning titles for WNBS-10 News flickered on the silent television.

Jones hustled in past me, lighting a cigarette.

"Come sit down, Giller."

They uncuffed me and I staggered a step—the sedatives made me feel like I'd been hit with the flu. I wouldn't be bursting through the roof.

"We'll hash it out right after this," said Jones, settling his backside on the desk.

He was addressing a lean Asian guy in a black tracksuit who was lounging on the couch, a Penzler guy scowling on either side of him. Maybe he was in trouble too. My apes sat me down in a steel-frame chair, then threaded my arms through the back somehow and cuffed my hands again.

"I only ever let girls tie me up," I said.

"You sent me a fax," said Jones, getting up from the desk.

"Yeah!" I tried to keep my head upright, my eyes focused on him. "You're the douche who sniffed around my school. Probably pissed on my front door."

"I'll read you the fax." Jones sat up on his desk—he was pretty spry for a heavier guy. "The handwriting's awfully shaky but it appears to say, 'Mr. James Jones. What the fuck do you want from me? Peter Giller.'" He lifted the paper over his head like it was a winning ticket. "Classic, isn't it? That's going in a 'Do Not Destroy' file, definitely. It came in three days ago, Thursday, but I just got it this morning. I went sailing on Thursday."

"No," I said. "You faxed me back."

"Good God, you're sharper than most! I've never sailed in my life, not one fathom or whatever those assholes would say. No, I only read you that because by now I bet you have a pretty good idea what it was that I wanted on Thursday. It's obvious, right? I wanted you and your family to disappear so we wouldn't have to deal with you the way we're dealing with you now. And it would've been for the best for you if you *had* disappeared, it certainly would. You could have dispersed with some dignity then. Messy either way—fatal!—but you could've at least had the dignity."

"Sorry, Chief," said my scar-lipped driver, tiptoeing past me. "These came."

Jones took the thick yellow envelopes and ripped the first open with his thumb. As he read, he rubbed the cigarette's filter against his temple. The driver gave me a dimply smile as he went out, then my sluggish eyes lingered on the silent TV. DID U.S. PAY LRA $10 MILLION TO DIVERT KINSHASA SUPPLY-ROUTE ATTACKS? The screen showed dusty palm trees, and a jeep so crammed with men and rifles it looked like a porcupine.

Then NEBRASKA SQUATTERS: NO SURVIVORS FOUND. It cut to a long building on fire, framed by shards of night sky, the wet ground in front reflecting such a brilliant orange that it must've been painted for Halloween. Nebraska. The building's silhouette could've been the PBF dormitory. It felt like all of my blood was moving into my face, and the cuffs stopped hurting.

4 AM EXPLOSION. VOICE OF LINCOLN, NE FD CHIEF:

The shaky camera panned left to show a fire truck parked a couple of hundred feet away, just hosing down the ground—no effort made to save the building. Or anyone, my muddy brain calculated, who might've been inside. Firelight catching the airborne water looked like clouds of bugs.

BODIES FOUND IN CONVERTED PIG BARN AS WELL AS NEARBY INDUSTRIAL BUILDING

I continued swallowing Jones's cigarette smoke, sludgy pulse throbbing in the tops of my ears, just staring. What else could I have done? All of those PBF faces blurred together in my mind into one small frightened person.

VEHICLES ON SITE TRACED TO BURROUGHS COUNTY, NE

The camera panned right as an orange burst spilled out of the dormitory and across the horizon, then the person with the camera must've turned away into the blackness, giving us occasional glimpses of his running legs. Flickering orange shapes dropped across the screen, and after a second I realized they were burning shingles.

Guys smelling of sour coffee strolled around the room, and I chewed the inside of my mouth and forgot any plans, any ambition, or Lydia, bacon or even my kids. I only watched as the shingles dropped like poisoned birds.

The picture cut to a grave-looking newscaster in a red blouse. The graphic over her shoulder showed a smoking barn, with the title LAN-CASTER CO. DISASTER.

When had Amber last sent us a text, three-thirty?

After I'd told her, "It's better you don't come."

But at least you drove five of them away with you, part of my brain whispered. *Get out of this room. They need you now.*

Strategy. Maybe if I got Jones mad it'd confuse him. My drugged neck had turned into a Slinky.

"You're *so* concerned with keeping secrets," I announced.

"Hey?" Jones set his envelopes down. "What's that?"

"So." I swallowed hard, trying to remember where I was and to not imagine the charred skin of Amber or Grace or even Arthur's stupid dog. "Why'd you let a lot of schoolkids into your top-secret facility?"

"My gosh," smiled Jones, shifting his backside, "that does seem like a contradiction, hey? You're sharp as a…as, man, I don't know *what*!"

"*Shuriken*," the Asian guy suggested. "Sharp as a *shuriken*."

"Sure, that sounds just fine!" Jones rubbed his jaw. "What is that, a *shuriken*?"

"Throwing star." With a flick of his wrist, he mimed launching one. "*Fwip*."

"My gosh, Gary, you know a little bit of everything," said Jones.

"Jack of all trades," the Asian guy agreed.

The TV had already cut to a dreadlocked Red Sox batter striking out, then spitting.

"What're you doing to those people I was with?" I asked.

"Say, this is interesting for *you*, Giller—Gary here is the guy who burned your house down, isn't that something? Now here you are like bugs in a rug!"

Jones grinned as though my dad and Gary's had come over together on the *Mayflower*. Gary stretched his legs out and stared at his feet—he wore black Converse All Stars just like the high school kids. I forgot the dormitory burning down and remembered my own house.

"Gary," I said. "Thanks for rigging them to go off when nobody was home."

He glanced up at me a second, his mouth stiff as a slide rule.

"You're welcome," he said.

"All right, a pair of kidders." Jones slid off the desk and slowly circled my chair. "I haven't answered you, Giller. Why'd we let schoolkids into Dockside if the product was so volatile? Because when you *stop* letting schoolkids in, *that's* what a competitor notices—certainly *we* would notice if DuPont or 3M suddenly barred *their* gates—and *that* is when uninvited people start to poke their noses in."

I was maintaining good posture but my eyelids felt heavy as sidewalks.

"But not people like me, supposedly. Like us."

"Ah. You all must be the exception that proves the rule."

"That expression's never made a lick of sense to me."

"Me neither. And yet..." He brought his fingertips to his lips, then spread his hands dramatically. "Here you are!"

He could've been a French 12 teacher, he liked to talk so much. He lifted a wallet from his desk—it looked like mine. Was Lydia still squirreled away inside? Jones held the driver's license up, maybe comparing it to my present face.

"Taken just last March." He grinned, which spread a roll of fat over his shirt collar. "Eighteen months ago you were a handsome man." He dropped the wallet into a ziplock bag. "Yet three days ago you received my fax and promptly tried to bite off a gentleman's ear, and seventeen hours after that you torched our head office and murdered thirty-five people."

"I didn't murder your head office."

"I have footage of you at the scene. Helicopter cameras."

"An hour *after* your place got murdered, I was still driving east across Indiana."

"I really believe that with all of my heart."

"You've got my ambulance, right?" I squirmed against the cuffs while I had a minute. That had to be the reason I was arguing. "Ashtray's full of gas receipts, look—"

"Barney Jordan died that day. Our head of marketing. Twenty years with the company, right from when Kirk Penzler came back from Kuwait. Every year we show the staff an exceptionally good time at our

Christmas party, and do you know what Barney wanted to see, ever since the 'Enhanced Personnel' project started sliding off the rails? He wanted to see one of you zombies fight a *shark*. Get a big tank of water, drop the two of 'em in, right there in the Ramada ballroom. HR never finished the paperwork but plenty of bets had already changed hands, so you know what? We're still going to do it, zombie versus shark, in memory of Barney."

Guys in dark suits started to wander in from all sides, slim guys and heavy guys, crowding. Maybe they'd all established their offices at the Lamplighter.

"You've been nominated to represent your species," said Jones.

If I peered through the crowd of potbellies and three-button jackets, I could still glimpse Gary on the couch, staring at the ceiling and moving his lips like he was trying to remember his state capitals.

"Another two-fifty on the shark," someone called.

Maybe it was because Gary was the only other guy not wearing a flack jacket or a business suit, but I *liked* the fucker. Even so, I figured if I had a card to play I'd better go ahead. Jones and a bearded guy stood over me, corners of their mouths twitching as they fought between poor grieving Barney and grinning at the prospect of seeing me chewed apart. Maybe there'd still be a finger and thumb left for them to mail to my kids.

"I spoke with an officer at the scene yesterday," I announced. "Your office was torched with a series of explosive devices set the night before, which is exactly what happened to *my* house. And to all the houses torched in Hoover. Maybe even this place that burned down on the TV." I nodded in that direction, my spine feeling more solid by the minute. "I wasn't *here* to blow up your office and I wouldn't have known *how*, right? What am I, special ops? So maybe you ought to look closer to home."

Jones lost any semblance of a grin. He and the bearded guy narrowed their eyes at each other, then at Gary. But Gary wasn't on the couch anymore. The Penzler guys who'd been on either side of him sat slumped against each other, sound asleep with their mouths hanging open.

"The fuck?" said Jones.

In a heartbeat the Christmas-party enthusiasts quit crowding me like a soft-serve dispenser. They backed toward the walls. The apes who'd dragged me in stood in a corner, pistols drawn.

"Remember?" whispered the bearded guy. "I said, 'Don't meet him in person.'"

Jones was staring up, an unlit cigarette between his lips, so we all looked up. The ceiling panel above the couch had been removed and the resulting black rectangle wasn't telling anybody what Gary was planning.

"Fucking contractors," muttered Jones.

The overhead fluorescents blinked off and even though there was light through the curtains, the unnerved businessmen turned the air pretty blue, as my grandma used to say. Suddenly I was the one who couldn't stop grinning. My body had woken up. All my pointless talk had accomplished something.

"Open the door!" someone yelled from behind the desk.

But nobody wanted to see what would happen to the first guy through.

Then my eyes were streaming from the rotten-egg smell permeating everything. I wiped my nose on my shoulder while the suits coughed and gagged. And *then* the door got opened! I could barely see through my own eyes, and on their way out the businessmen stumbled against me.

"Keep a hold of Giller!" Jones barked from the corner.

I realized that my cuffs had somehow separated from each other. I leaned forward and my arms came free of the chair.

"They're in 28," a quiet voice said in my ear. "Get up and walk out."

I stumbled forward until I bumped into Jones's desk, groping around until I found the ziplock bag. Then as a couple of suits stumbled for the door I threw my arms around their shoulders like we'd been dragging each other out of bars for years.

Outside I squinted at the parked cars and the businessmen leaning over to gag, wiping their eyes on their shirttails. Room 28 had to be to my right so I lurched along the stucco wall, coughing my guts out, until I looked up and saw the brass number. I twisted the knob but it was solid as brick.

Every half-bald guy in sight was hunched over his cell phone or retching beside the bumper of a car. I coughed for another second, for show, then drove my elbow into the faceplate where the room key was supposed to go. An ache flared in my new shoulder. I tried the knob. It didn't turn but the door opened, the deadbolt swinging out from its splintered doorjamb.

I slid inside, nudging the door shut behind me. The room smelled like mildewy towels. At the foot of the bed my people lay blinking on the taupe carpet, duct tape over their mouths, all zip-tied together—Colleen's ankle zip-tied to Harv's, whose other ankle was zip-tied to Franny and so on—crammed together like a package of hot dogs. Their eyes followed me.

"Sorry," I whispered. "I'm sorry."

I got a steak knife out of the kitchenette drawer, cut through all their ties.

"Arms and leg still attached!" I whispered. "Must be a well-fed bunch!"

I let them rip off their own duct tape. I went to the curtain and saw apes peering under vehicles in the parking lot. Colleen got to her feet, swaying, and before Megan could reach her Mrs. Avery threw up on the bedspread.

Since when was she the least resilient?

"Oh my god," said Franny, fingers to her scalp, "I want to go home so much."

"We can get out the bathroom," said Harv at my side. "I kind of kicked the window out when they brought us in."

"Way to hop."

I stood on the back of the toilet and lifted myself through the window frame—the lane was strewn with Yuengling beer cases but there were no apes to be seen, not yet. Nothing but pine trees across the lane. I dropped down to the asphalt and broken glass, gripped Colleen's foot and lowered her down, then she went limp again so I kept my arms around her shoulders while she butted her forehead into my collarbone. Her breath was all stomach acid. The kids dropped to the ground then stared at me, big-eyed, blue-lipped.

"Straight back in the trees," I whispered. "These guys are too fat to run."

I didn't need to horrify them with the PBF news to get them running. There'd have to be a better time to tell them our fellow zombies were dead, though I couldn't imagine what that time would look like.

THE WOODS WERE invitingly thick, like they'd been planted express-ly for us decades before. I ducked under the first branch, disturbed a couple of crows sharing a hamburger bun, then kept low as I heard the five start through behind me, dry pine needles crunching. I felt steady enough on my feet by then to run a hundred steps, then I went two hundred more.

"They'd need helicopters to catch us now," Franny whispered behind me.

"Mrs. Avery's not used to running, she's tired," said Harv.

"No, I'm not." Colleen's breath dissipated between the pine branches. "Doesn't the air feel like snow again?"

Once we stepped onto an actual path, cut by hundreds of bike wheels, we really started to cover ground. I didn't wonder what was ahead of us, instead I thought about our savior Gary and how maybe he *had* burned down Penzler's evil HQ—he'd sure acted like it, once Jones clued to the possibility—but he'd also burned down the house where Josie and Ray and I'd been living, and even if Deb did own some of the same pictures of Lydia there were hundreds more I'd never again hold between my fingers. So for that I'd grind a rope of his intestines between my teeth. And I discounted that he'd leveled PBF and everyone in it because Gary wouldn't have had enough time to drive from four AM Nebraska to room twenty-six at the Lamplighter, but then I remembered: he has resources, and there are airplanes. So this one guy had maybe killed all of those people we loved, but were we running *after him*, to snap his neck? No, we were running away.

The trees thinned out, brightening the path, then we stepped out into a backyard with woods on three sides. An ornamental pond and a trampoline led to the back steps of a two-story log cabin, painted blue. No smoke from the chimney. Was it too much to hope that nobody was home? Jones said it'd been three days since Thursday, so that confirmed it was Sunday. A chewed-up *Little Mermaid* Frisbee lay at my feet, but no dogs barked. Man, if it *was* Sunday, I was missing the Steelers trouncing Miami!

"Maybe they're at church." Franny scratched a branch-scraped bare arm that read FRANNY'S LEFT ARM™. "One that has the afternoon tea after."

We tiptoed around the cabin and past a shingled double garage—containing exactly one locked blue station wagon and an oil stain from an absent vehicle—to the more-respectable front door, where I opened the screen and knocked. Stray links on my broken handcuff rattled against the panel of stained glass. Still no barking. *Pardon the intrusion, does this road out front lead to Highway 33?*

"Maybe there's buses to somewhere," said Megan.

There was no sound at all from inside.

"How likely that they're right behind us?" asked Colleen.

"Superstars like that could be out with infrared scanners." Clint tottered a plaster goat-boy figurine beneath his pointy shoe. "Maybe we got microchipped."

Harv loped around the corner from the far side of the house. I hadn't noticed he'd been gone, which wasn't the first or last time my leadership would be shitty.

"I hunted around behind the lattice," he beamed. "They've got five bikes. One of them only comes up to my knee, though, and it's got a pink basket."

"Clint," I said.

"Har, har," said Clint. "Here's something pink that goes down to my knee."

"Seriously?" asked Megan. "Like *bright* pink?"

"Gillbrick." Franny stalked up, twisting the hair around above her ear. "That back door isn't even locked."

THEIR KITCHEN SMELLED of bacon and overripe bananas, and a dozen gap-toothed faces smiled down from the fridge. So, grandparents. A pixelated snapshot they'd printed off their computer showed a grinning, squinting young man in green camouflage, an M-16 over his shoulder as the wind tossed the palm trees behind him. A bag of Purina Pro-Plan Small Breed Formula sat on the counter, so they'd clearly chosen to save their yappy dog's life by carrying it away.

More importantly, Clint started two frying pans and a stewpan's worth of bacon cooking on the range, tenderly lifting each strip to peek at its underside before committing to turn it over. He wiped the spat grease from his face with a paper towel. Franny hovered over the pans with a teaspoon, scooping up the grease as it became available.

"Whoever needs Band-Aids," I told the room, "now's your chance to look for Band-Aids."

I still didn't tell them that Amber and Grace were dead. I reassured myself that I'd imagined it. I felt like the back of my head was missing.

We each fall apart in our own time and in our own way.

"Peter," Colleen said from the hallway. "In here."

"G," said Franny, "you want to try the juice? It'll grow you a new pecker."

"Someone ought to slap your face," said Colleen. "I mean it."

Franny shrugged. "Whoever tries it'll get fucked up."

I put my head back like a baby bird, and she tipped in the bacon grease. It seared the back of my throat but its sheer deliciousness curled my toes inside my shoes.

"Now your turn, Mrs. Avery," said Clint.

"No, thanks."

Colleen led me into a narrow bedroom, toward the big bed with its orange counterpane, then past it into the closet.

"You look like one of those plane-crash soccer players who ate all the other guys," she said.

"Well, it's all how you carry yourself."

The old homeowner had a lot of red plaid shirts with snaps, Lee blue jeans, long gray socks. Wool used to itch me but those socks didn't, probably because I was a different species from what I'd been. I spent a good minute at the mirror, inspecting my right shoulder where it had reattached—white tendrils of tissue had grown across the gap.

"Feels like fiberglass insulation," I said.

She ran her fingertips across too, stopping on each fiber like she was playing a harp. My penis filled with sluggish blood. The skin was puckered and purple around the nails in my shoulder.

"Wow," Franny said from the doorway, "you look so retarded."

I snapped up the shirt and we followed her into the kitchen. Clint was transferring the perfect bacon onto a platter painted with ducks. Maybe I could've fed and clothed myself without my bevy of helpers, but they sure ran things smoothly, and what had I offered them? Twenty-two hours in an ambulance and one more day alive.

"Eat outside," I said, "so we can go into the woods in a hurry. Where's Harv?"

"By the garage." Megan dropped pans in the sink. "He wants to start that car."

"What're *you* doing?" Colleen asked as they all filed out.

"Gotta pee."

Though since Pipe #9 burst I hadn't actually needed to—but my intestines felt distressed as I reached for the beige kitchen telephone. To phone Deb I had to call collect. Still hadn't forgotten the number!

"Will you accept the charges?"

"Yes, *yes*," she said. "Peter, where *are* you?"

"Still in Ohio. I'm heading way out west for a day or two, but then straight back to you guys. Promise. The kids there? Everything still all right?"

"You just say where you are, we'll come get you. Just come be with us then go do what you have to do. Say where you are, we'll be there."

"That would be nice. That would be nice. The kids there?"

"Sure."

Bacon grease rose in my throat. I trotted to the sink and spat, getting a string of the salty stuff down my chin.

"Dad?"

"Hi, Ray. How's the school?"

"School? Good. Hey, Dad?"

"Yeah, Ray."

"Can we come get you? I'll sleep in the car, Grandma doesn't mind!"

"I've got to ask you something."

"Yeah?"

"How was your birthday?"

"Birthday? Pretty great. Yeah."

"What did Grandma get you?"

"Here's Josie."

"Hi, Dad!" said Josie.

"Was he pretty pissed off at me?" I asked.

"You mean Ray? What for?"

"I told him we'd bowl on his birthday. I'll take you another time, all right? Listen, help me out, what was the name of your teacher back in Hoover? I have trouble remembering."

"My teacher?"

"Mrs. Somebody, with the black hair. Drives a Subaru."

I heard the phone change hands.

"Peter," said Deb. "I don't care how far away the place is, they have to see you."

"I'll tell you what," I said. "I would love that. I would love it. But I can't say, I'm sorry."

"Well, I suppose we've talked long enough. You have your things to do. I have to get them down for their naps now, Peter. Say good night, kids!"

"Good niiiiight!" they hollered.

"See you soon," said Deb.

She hung up, with a click across the phone line like a screen door closing. I kept the phone to my ear in case it wasn't *really* hung up and the kids were going to jump back on with something desperate to convey. Instead I listened to it hum for ten seconds until there was *another* click, like another door closing, then the dial tone came on. Did all collect calls do that?

And the day before, Ray had said his birthday was after Easter. Also, it was only noon in Nebraska, and neither child had napped since they were three and they would've knocked the bastard down who said otherwise. Something fucked-up had happened to my kids, when all along I'd believed they alone were in the clear. On the old people's toaster, my reflected face looked like melted cheese. I clacked my jaw shut and shook the numbness out of my fingers. I found plastic cups above the sink and filled a pitcher with water. I couldn't hear Franny's guffaws on the porch, so they'd probably gone to sit in the wading pool.

"Okay," I called, swinging out the back door. "Harv got that beater started?"

The four of them lay all over the porch like they'd been dropped from a helicopter. No apes around, no cops—were they just fooling? Franny slumped sideways in her Adirondack chair, and Clint had fallen out of his. Colleen stretched on a plastic lounge two feet in front of me, looking up at the roof though her brown eyes didn't blink. She was breathing. An inch-long pink dart quivered in the side of her neck. Nowhere to be seen: her telescoping titanium baton.

I dropped to one knee, set the water down silently on the blue boards and looked over my shoulder at the roof. No one. I scanned the pines in all directions and listened hard for ten seconds.

From the woods a bird whistled a loopy tune.

The attacker had come and gone? Where was Harv? Megan had toppled down three steps onto the back lawn, the platter overturned six feet away from her, our bacon strewn in the grass like eggs on Easter Sunday. Her feet were still on the porch and her neck looked twisted as Play-Doh from the way she'd landed, so I slid down beside her, rolled her onto her side, brushed the grass from her face and after a few seconds found the slow, slow thud in the side of her neck.

I plucked the tiny pink dart from behind her ear and threw it under the steps. Looked like the darts had all come from one direction.

I huddled against the steps and peered up at the roof again. The gray sky seemed too bright to look at, but I made out a dark shape crouched beside the old people's chimney, and when it dropped flat to its belly I knew it was Gary.

Part of my brain thought *Good, now all of us will be dead. Very neat and tidy.*

I rolled away from Megan, and ran sixty steps across the backyard toward our path, then got ten steps into the woods, fifteen, hoping that I was behind decent cover by then. A starling flashed past, brushing my eye. I ducked under a branch, blinked and blinked—my eye could still see. Something had landed on my shoulder—had the bird taken a dump? No, too solid to be bird crap. I squinted at the thing.

It was my ear. *Sharp as a shuriken*, he'd said.

I slipped the ear into my shirt pocket and slid backwards under some kind of wide-leafed bush, then folded my feet under me. An earwig dropped onto my arm, skittered under my sleeve. I dabbed my sleeve against the sticky stuff dripping down the side of my head. I could still see a strip of green lawn. Was he coming from the cabin or was he in the woods already?

"You're a riot," Gary said from somewhere above me.

He didn't say anything else. The roof of my mouth felt hard as a hatchet. I peered up at the trees but every shadowed branch swayed the same gentle fraction of an inch. I committed my heart to waiting him out, years, staying silent as snowfall.

"Come out of there," he said, "let's throw down. See, there's other dudes I work for. These dudes want to retain a sample, exclusive of Jones." He seemed to talk from one side of the path then the other— some trick he'd picked up at ventriloquist camp. "I see your name on the target list, five minutes later you walk in the room, I was, like, 'I need to buy a scratch card.' So come on out, okay? Let's throw down."

A happy prickle went up my spine because we were going to fight, ninja versus zombie, and prove that I was indestructible. I wriggled right back against a tree trunk and branches pinched the side of my neck. I reached back to push them away and grabbed a hand. He'd reached from between the trees to knock me out with some kind of nerve pinch—who'd told him I even *had* nerves?

"You're such a fucking sissy!" I rasped.

I squeezed his black polyester wrist as though toothpaste would squirt out his fingers. Crows above us shrieked, but Gary didn't make a sound, only hacked at my hand with some kind of blade! So I grabbed his free arm and dragged him onto the path. Under that gray sky his face looked white as paste but his crooked bottom teeth grinned like he'd won a trip to clown college. He wanted to see who was indestructible too. He slashed my forearms until I got a hand on his other wrist and squeezed the shit out of that one too. An X-Acto knife fell from his hand into the pine cones, then he drove his knee up into the side of my head but I didn't care because I'd twisted him flat against the ground so he didn't have any leverage to commit his sneaky spider-in-a-tree bull-shit. I sat down hard across his legs, pressed my thumbs into his larynx.

He thought a nerve-pinch would take me out? Decapitation would've been too subtle.

"*Heh!*" Gary gasped.

He writhed, clawing at my arms. I kept my thumbs where they were, my arms sliced up like coleslaw, and drew serene deep breaths. Christmas Eve, two years before, Ray had asked for a fireside story about a ninja, of all things, and Josie had started telling him how good kids get a visit from Santa Claus but *bad* kids get the Christmas Ninja. "And on Christmas morning the good boys and girls wake up to oodles of presents," Lydia had finished. "But bad kids *don't wake up at all.*"

I smiled about that while Gary dug his stone fingertips into the insides of my elbows, and my hands suddenly let go like he'd found their off switch. I was still sitting on him but just like that I'd lost all momentum. I stumbled to my feet so I could kick him, arms dangling, but I lurched down the path instead, back toward the Lamplighter six miles away. If I could keep him away from the kids for an hour, maybe they'd crawl away under their own power. Would I still be *valuable as a sample* if I was in fifteen pieces?

"Don't bother," Gary wheezed behind me.

I ran, my legs lifting like a stiff antelope's, but after twenty steps I was in the backyard again, looking across at Colleen and the kids sprawled behind the blue cabin—I'd been turned around on the path.

I ran again anyway, sprinting for the garage, because if I drove away, maybe Gary would chase me and forget the others. I was the best sample! Branches snapped behind me, so in mid-stride I glanced back over my shoulder. I didn't even glimpse the path in that split second but it was long enough to catch my shin on the lip of the green plastic wading pool and tumble in, splashing into an inch of water.

I twisted onto my back, wet leaves stuck to the side of my face. Gary swayed at my feet, loading some kind of dart into a pistol, the black wall of pines behind him.

"*You're* the fucking sissy," he croaked.

Monday, October 31.

EVERY YEAR WE lived in Wahoo, a farm across the valley hosted its Olde-Fashioned Sleigh Ride. The sleighs used hay bales for seats. Our last year, we squeezed together with Josie on my lap, Ray on Lydia's, and piled on red blankets against the evening cold. Before the horses started to pull we sat staring at a Massey Ferguson tractor bedecked with twinkling lights, and every half-minute I wiped Ray's nose with a handkerchief recycled from a cowboy pillowcase.

"Coldest one yet," said Lydia.

Her collar was zipped to her nose, and she sat in a sleeping bag beneath the blankets because the chemo drugs had destroyed her circulation. She called her hands her frozen fish.

The black-bearded driver called, "Giddy-ap," reins slapped, bells jingled and the wedges of snow moved past beneath our toes.

Away from the electric halo of the barn the air seemed even colder. Women behind us cooed over the snowy pines. Lydia just sat up straight, smiling, one hand perpetually rubbing Ray's back.

"Might be hard to imagine," she said quietly, "but in a while you two'll have to look after your dad."

We were jangling up to the first carolers: three guys and a little girl singing "God Rest Ye, Merry Gentlemen." The week before, we'd been to Pawnee for Evadare's birthday, and with her latest diagnoses I'd half-expected Lydia to say over the cake that it might be the last Evadare's birthday she'd ever see, but in front of my mom she never gave bad news. Now here she was taking the bull by the horns. Josie and Ray glanced up at me like I might need looking after in the next few minutes.

I flexed my toes inside my boots—it was that cold—and pictured our sleigh as if I were a caroler, watching the passage of wet-nosed passengers. Only Lydia wasn't there.

We jingled past the three guys and the little girl, and the singing faded.

"You'll think of ways to cheer him up. All right, Jos?"

"Okay," Josie said through tight lips. Her scarf covered her chin.

"And still have dance parties," said her mom.

Josie nodded, one little jerk of the head.

"Even the songs no one likes but him," said Lydia.

"Okay," Ray said automatically.

"You too, Peter—you'll still be happy, right?"

She blinked at me over the pom-pom of Ray's toque; she'd spent many months not saying anything like this. Her eyes were yellow from the jaundice, and though her eyebrows had grown back they were mostly gray. She was thirty-two years old. The trees looked knotted together—the low branches brushed our toes.

"Sweetie?" she said.

Her next appointment with the oncologist was two weeks away, but her distended abdomen had already told us that tests were going to lead to more tests and a hospital bed she wouldn't climb out of.

"Sure," I said, my voice like a paper airplane.

I grasped her hand, wrapped in its three mittens, and struggled, as I did daily, to say something meaningful that wouldn't also sound *final*. I said what I would've whether she was sick or not.

"I love you."

She leaned over Ray and we kissed. Josie's teeth chattered against my collarbone. Lydia and I leaned our heads together. Her forehead felt like a furnace.

Then the sleigh stopped next to a table lit with tiki torches, where men in top hats and scarves handed out Styrofoam cups of hot chocolate. Josie slid off my lap and down into the snow, then she turned to help Ray down while the teenaged riders bounded off from all sides. In his snowsuit Ray looked eighteen months old again—he wouldn't be able to orchestrate hot chocolate by himself.

Lydia withdrew her hand. "Off you go."

I jumped down and the three of us stood together in the line, Josie pressing her cold fists under her chin, Ray clicking his flashlight off and on.

"I guess she means 'Indiana Wants Me,'" Josie said. "It's too slow for a dance party."

"It's too slow!" Ray's teeth chattered and his lashes were crested with frost, but he nibbled snow off his mitt anyway. "I can't do my crab walk." And he swayed to the song in his head, which he'd said was always "The Kids Are Alright."

"We'll be right there!" I called, stamping my feet.

Lydia smiled back, regal on her hay bale, alone with the driver and horses like she'd planned a daring escape.

THEN I WASN'T in the snow. I'd been sitting in a chair for too long, my legs asleep from the knees down. My wrists felt tied down and I had such a crick in the base of my neck that maybe I'd been strapped into a car crash, feeling what Bill Giller had felt.

Then I remembered Gary, the blue cabin, and felt hollow as a toilet roll. His tranquilizers must've acted on the nervous system because if he'd relied on my circulation it would've taken a week before I'd even stumbled—hell, if my crew drew the diagrams big enough that idea could win them the Burroughs County Science Fair. If Gary had left any of them alive. Sixteen years old, just starting to have their own brains.

My eyes tried to open.

I was under fluorescent lights. A clean-cut guy in a tie and short-sleeved white shirt sat in a chair in front of me. He wasn't handcuffed to his, just a blue binder open in his lap. A gun in his shoulder holster. He had salt-and-pepper hair and lots of eyebrow.

"Ah! The ambulance thief." He glanced up from what he'd been writing, working his lips like his spit was too sticky for him. "Brother, you have done some traveling, and you slept through the lot of it— thought I'd have to go find a book to read! All this time chasing after you and I never realized you were such a sleepyhead!"

He squinted hard at me, then ticked a couple of boxes on the page in front of him. There was a bare table behind him and a red door behind that. The floor was linoleum, and the walls looked like steel.

"You going to kill me?" My teeth were sticking to my lips. "That the plan?"

"No, Mr. Giller."

I stretched my legs, trying to work the prickles out. Long pink welts ran across my hands and arms from that forest-floor tussle with Gary. Aw, shit—I remembered the flash of orange from the TV. A stupid tear welled up in my left eye. I shook it off while my inquisitor went on initialing the corners of pages.

"Where's my ear?" I asked.

"Right there on the side of your head," he said. "Someone was kind enough to staple it back in place for you. I think it lined up perfectly."

"So what do you want?"

"Well, that *is* the question. You're in the custody of the US military. Suffice to say—"

"Which branch?"

"Jesus, 'Which branch.' You weren't a, a lawyer, were you?" He flipped back a bunch of pages. "You weren't." He scratched the side of his head with the pen. "I can inform you that I'm here on behalf of the Joint Chiefs of Staff and that there'll be a discussion on Thursday or, at the latest, Friday to determine whose jurisdiction you're under—to be honest, nobody's too keen. My name is Carver, by the way, C-A-R-V-E-R. We're going to be seeing a lot of each other."

"And you're not from Penzler?"

"Definitely not."

"And now Gary's not from Penzler either?"

"Gary?"

"I want to see my kids."

"Yeah! Huh. *That* much is clear as crystal."

He flipped to some yellow loose-leaf pages and started writing like crazy.

"Listen, Mr. Carver," I said, "you ought to put me on a nitrite drip if you plan on keeping me alive any length of time."

"Uh-huh."

"I don't feel good, Mr. Carver, and if I *really* don't feel good you're going to need a wet-vac, not a stack of papers. If you know anything about this Penzler stuff, you—"

"We have calcium nitrate fertilizer as an experimental ration. You like some?"

"Does it work?"

"It has side effects."

He gave me a hard look then went back to writing, and every seven seconds his free hand brushed the butt of his gun—he wanted to be sure that our balance of power wasn't going to shift within the next, say, eight seconds. He flipped forward to some typewritten pages.

"Mr. Carver?" I asked.

He held a fingertip to his spot on the page—maybe he'd been marveling at a transcript of how I once defended myself with nothing more than a propane fridge, though it wasn't likely anyone outside Penzler knew about that.

"What's on your mind?" he asked wearily.

"Where are we?"

"We're on an armed forces base in the state of Virginia, fifty miles from DC. According to this morning's roll there are 1,855 personnel beyond that wall."

"You know Gary?"

"I know *a* Gary."

"Is he like a double agent in all this? It doesn't make sense he'd blow up that HQ in Preston too if he—"

"Possibly we don't know the same Gary."

"I'm not the only one left, am I? Besides Natalia or maybe—"

He lifted his pencil from the page. "Natalia?"

"Never mind."

"Never mind, exactly. Suffice to say our ladies in the lab up in Albany think your tissue will make for fascinating analysis. But before that I want to know if the psychological effects are anything like what we paid for. We didn't *develop* this formula, you understand, the manufacturer brought it forward and we entered into an agreement for full rights of distribution, et cetera."

"Out of their lab in California," I ventured. "The big bosses."

"That's a given. But the manufacturer's stipulations didn't allow time for our usual due diligence which, after this experience, is not a protocol we'll be forgoing in the future, regardless of the beautiful application this product might have had overseas."

"So why'd you have to blow it up?" I asked. "Whole shed full of kids."

"With their whole lives ahead of them, blah, blah, blah? You tell me."

"What?"

"You're supposed to be this smart guy." His bottom lip hung in a pouch, disappointed like I'd missed curfew. In what possible sense had I been smart?

"Okay," I said. "I'll guess that you have a phobia about people being alive."

"I just about do. No—it came down to covering our tails. Enemies of democracy, the LRA, any of them back in Rwanda, they'd kiss their own behinds to hear about this kind of innovation, even if we *are* in the middle of discontinuing it."

"Killing us all still seems excessive."

"Really? For the US military? Maybe you've heard of Laos in the

1970s?" He jammed his fingers under the holster to scratch his armpit. "I mean, do you have any idea how many bums I had to wipe to clean up your Velouria bullshit? No, I'm tired of pussyfooting around."

"Sorry," I said. "Hadn't realized how badly you'd been inconvenienced by the piles of kids."

"Really, yes!" He nodded like he'd finally found the one guy who understood him. "I mean, worldwide, civilians get offed by internal conflict every day in the week—only reason we went into Congo was that bleeding hearts wanted to save the chimpanzees! But if we evolved from monkeys, then they had a shelf life already, right? They're on the way out, natural selection."

"The zombies'll say that about you, Carver, and we'll see how much you like it."

"They eat chimpanzees over there, even in Kinshasa, call it 'bushmeat.' But you'll never do that to us, right? Promise?" He clicked his pen happily—this tied-to-a-chair debate was his kind of party. "Anyway, to say this Penzler contract has been the biggest fuck-up in the history of this administration would—well, it actually *would* be an exaggeration, but it's definitely top ten. So..."

"You've left me alive to hit me with that binder."

"In a manner of speaking!" He rubbed his nose ecstatically. "Hah! Sure, now having formed some impressions, I'd better order the questions for your work-up."

He bent to his labors. If I'd had an elbow free I would've caved the top of his head in like a coconut husk. "I'll answer anything you want," I said. "First, tell me where my kids are and exactly when I'm going to see them. Exactly when. If you're really from the Joint Chiefs of Staff you can fly them here in a helicopter."

"All right, okay. I'll never conduct an interview under false pretenses."

Though he'd set fire to a hundred people who'd never understand how or why. He lay his binder on the table, spun the chair and straddled the back of it like he was all relaxed now, my buddy. "Yesterday," Carver said, "when you telephoned your kids, you in fact spoke with three voice actors that I'd had stationed at your mother-in-law's house since Saturday night—two of them used to work on *The Muppet Show*, believe it or not. Times are tough all over."

I expected my gut to give an anxious kick but I was still so dumbfounded just to have woken up that I was willing to sit and listen.

"So tell me where my kids really are."

"Where they *really* are?"

So here it was—with his fifties-sitcom crewcut and short-sleeved shirt, he was going to break the news to me. The news that had been inevitable all this time. A vein throbbed sullenly in my neck.

"We don't have the slightest idea," said Carver. "By the time we got the full list of those affected and started sniffing around for you in MacArthur, your mother-in-law's house had been deserted. Kids' clothes in the drawers, though, and every sign that the three of them might be back any minute. Her neighbors said they'd left an hour before and had probably gone back to Hoover—but what *really* seemed to upset these neighbors was that the man across the street had evacuated too, and *he'd* only moved in a couple days before, telling anybody who'd listen he had a nine-to-five downtown. You look bored, are you bored?"

I shook my head. If Carver really hadn't known the guy across the street then that guy must've been from Penzler, the unreliable goop manufacturer, and he'd taken my family to San Luis Obispo to jam steel shafts in their sinuses.

"Anyway." Carver tapped the pen against his cheek. "In the meantime we manned the phones in case you made contact, and of course that paid off fine. And now that we've got you, we don't much care about the whereabouts of daughter, son or mother-in-law—*they* didn't come in contact with any product, that's for sure. But I will tell you *one* thing that might sort this out, then you'll know where we stand so you can cooperate wholeheartedly without me having to dial up the torture and duress. Clear?" He showed plenty of eyebrow. "I don't think I ought to tell you too much before I chart your reactions, but, man, pretty soon you're going to be wondering why in hell you ever left home. Really, leaving your kids with your mother-in-law?"

"I just wanted so badly to meet you."

"All right, okay, I do what I'm paid to do, change what needs changing, but on this totem pole I'm so far down I'm the dirt, so leave me out of it."

Change what needs changing? Why was that familiar?

"So," he said, "the whiteboard on her fridge. One word was written on it, 'camp,' C-A-M-P. Mother-in-law's printing, we confirmed that. We checked Rock Creek and every commercial campground in Dundy County even though ninety-eight percent are closed for the season, but no trace. We'd still be canvassing but the protocol is to not extend outside the originating county without substantiating intel. Could be Penzler *made* her write that, they caught scent that we're dissatisfied with the product, but—"

"Camp?"

"Mean anything to you?"

Of course it did, yeah.

"No," I huffed.

He got up, spun the chair again and sat down with his binder. He unfolded a legal-size page and signed the bottom. Right then I could've floated away over the linoleum, because *camp* meant they ought to be fine.

"Their voices sounded exactly right," I said. "How'd you figure that out?"

"Well, it wasn't—"

"That *was* them on the phone. You're screwing with me."

"Your mother-in-law had videotaped every Christmas and birthday since the dawn of time, right? For a couple of hundred minutes we listened to those things, and you, sir, are *not* a singer. Okay, first question—and keep in mind that I'm not interested in the details of your answer so much as the way in which the product affects the way you *give* an answer, understood?"

"Sure. The truth is somewhere in the middle."

"First: Since your exposure, have you had cravings to eat one or two particular things? I won't specify 'food' as I don't want to limit your answer."

"Bacon."

"Not brains?"

"Do I look like I've eaten brains?"

"Couldn't say." He jotted down some bullshit. "The only confirmed brain-eater I've encountered face-to-face was a legal-reference librarian and looked the part."

"My turn. What kind of car do you drive?"

"Dodge Charger," he said.

One of the makes we'd been after. That vein bubbled in my neck.

"What color?" I asked.

"Second: Which affected subjects were *not* present at Prairie Corners Road?"

"At the where?"

"That's Aiken's freak factory! Remember, just respond naturally—the wording of your answer doesn't much matter."

"Huh," I said.

Because that *was* a good question. Maybe Scotty Barnes, the compound fracture kid, maybe he was still at large. And maybe Penzler really had created a heap of plastic soldiers—Hunter in Ohio's idiot dad. And of course Natalia.

"Why do you still give a shit about the product," I asked, "if you blew up all those kids just to get rid of it?"

"You misunderstand." He scratched his top lip with a thin pinkie. "By torching our subjects' houses, among other dubious tactics, Penzler made itself a liability. They felt they had to cover their bases, security-wise, I appreciate that, but even so. They're out. The US military does not consider itself or the product a liability, so in our hands solely the project will move forward."

"What happened to the woman and kids I was with?"

"We have seven more subjects from diverse sources but you aren't going near any of them until your parts all get thrown on the pile."

I swallowed hard.

"What are the names of these subjects?"

"Don't worry about it."

"You feeding them this fertilizer crap?"

"Don't worry about it. No one exposed to the product has lasted long. After that we send the remains to Albany."

"Oh," I said. "Huh."

I lunged at him, but of course the cuffs kept me pinned. He sat watching me, the pencil between his fingers. I lunged again, flashing canines like a pit bull tied to a tree, then something felt wrong so I stayed pitched forward, waiting to pass out or puke. He'd doctored me with something. And how long had it been since my last strip of bacon? Carver gripped his gun in its holster and squinted like he was inspecting my undercarriage. I hiccuped, hard. My ears produced a hiss like a beer bottle opening, then my lower jaw detached and fell on the floor with a thud like a T-bone falling into a tub.

It lay beside my left boot, my goddamn jaw: two half-hinges of grisly bone at either end, a fringe of beard, scabbed bottom lip, then yellow teeth, tongue like a raw cutlet. The tongue's pink tip quivered like I'd had something to say.

Carver's face went gray like it was a hunk of *him* down there.

Syrupy blood migrated down the front of my shirt—now I was half a head over a drooling spigot. Carver squinted up at the part of my face that could still blink, his lips a little blue, so I took a deep breath and looked at him meaningfully.

"Aaah-ghaa-ghaa!" said my mucousy throat.

He bent and puked into his hands. Yellow bubbles seeped between his fingers, then I was on my feet in the middle of a 180-degree turn. Painful on the arms, but the flying chair legs must've flattened him because there was a crash like a shopping cart falling down stairs, and when I finished turning, his own chair lay on its side, casters still spinning, and he was halfway under the table with a gash across his temple.

I stepped gingerly over my jaw and around his smear of puke, the chair prodding the backs of my knees, and studied Carver for a loop of keys. None visible. I got my toe under him and rolled him onto his front, but there weren't any on the back of his belt.

I sat back down to think it over. No klaxons were ringing, no sleep-gas fizzing in yet. Five minutes to get the jaw back on. Carver's foot twitched in its loafer, which either meant he was waking up or just died right then. Thanks to unfettered salivary glands my top half was sopping wet. I noticed his gun in its holster and cursed myself for a full-blown idiot.

"Yaah huh-huh yah-yea," I muttered.

I stood up and shuffled forward. As long as he was under the table, I couldn't get near his holster, so I put my shoulder against the table leg and pushed so it *mooed* across the floor. Then I knelt beside Carver, the edge of my chair really cutting into the backs of my knees, wrists straining at the cuffs, and managed to wrap the fingers of my right hand around the butt of his pistol. Ropes of my mucous drizzled his cotton-blend shirt. I tried to straighten up with the gun in my hand but the chair tipped left instead and I toppled onto my back.

With four minutes to get my jaw back on I stared at the particle-board ceiling. Seven prisoners? Colleen, Harv, Franny, Megan, Clint, that made five, but if Carver had two more from someplace else maybe the last two were Amber and Grace. Or maybe none of the seven were from my gang.

C-A-M-P, I reminded myself.

I bent my wrist far enough for the barrel of the gun to point at my left hand eighteen inches away. I pulled the pistol's hammer back with my thumb. The cuff dug so hard into my right wrist that I had to concentrate to get my trigger finger to tighten while drool ran down in my ears—could I even aim? I lifted my left hand so a single steel link appeared, vulnerable, between my wrist and the arm of the chair.

Before I was entirely ready I pulled the trigger.

THE RECOIL ROLLED me onto my right side, my feet across Carver's chest, but my left arm flapped free! It didn't look right, though, because the wrist was raw hamburger and because my hand was *gone*. People should only point guns if they're prepared for the thousand different things that might happen when they pull the trigger.

I rolled most of the way out of the chair onto the purple-spattered linoleum. My left hand lay exposed on its back five feet away, fingers outstretched like it was waiting to catch a baseball. I lay down with the runaway hand against my left hip, and tried to push the thing onto my belly but my stupid stump was too slick to steer the hand up off the floor.

"Ga hoo," Carver sighed.

My faithful right hand laid the gun on my chest then reached across, dragging the hard corners of the chair over me, patiently set the left hand on my belly then spun it and turned it over like it was a specimen we'd found at the beach. That put the severed hand in position to hold the gun. One by one my right hand uncurled the left's fingers and let them snap closed around the handle. I set the index finger around the trigger. What was I down to, two minutes? Less than that before Carver sat up shrieking.

I tried to breathe easy through my flaps of throat. With my right thumb I cocked the gun, then banged the chair down to get the right handcuff into position. The fluorescent tubes glared down at me. I set the wet stump of my left wrist against the toothpick bones at the back of my left hand. Maybe with the barrel pressed against the handcuff I could apply a modicum of pressure to the hand before the wrist went sliding in another direction.

I glared at my left hand—it had done everything I'd wanted for thirty-four years, right? Its thumb twitched.

Then my left hand, gun and all, flew across the room, and my right hand lifted away from the arm of the chair like they'd never been more than passing acquaintances. The gun had fired. My body was missing two crucial pieces, but I was chairless!

"Zah," said Carver.

I clambered to my feet, dropped my dripping jaw down the front of my shirt then scampered across the room and did the same with my heroic left hand. Carver's gun slid into the back of my belt. The steel door only had an opening for a key card. I ran back to Carver and noticed a pivoting security camera, green light blinking, in the corner of the ceiling. So why hadn't those 1,855 troops stormed in? I knelt over Carver, feeling his shirt pockets.

He smacked his lips then opened one eye, just halfway, calibrating. He said, "Yuh!"

As his wiry arms flailed up at me I gripped his whole forehead in my one hand, lifted his head six inches then drove it into the floor. Both of his eyes flew open, then stayed that way, like he couldn't comprehend something written on my forehead. A pool of blood spread around his head like a sombrero, then a rope of my drool draped his eyebrow. My jaw had one minute left and the other subjects might've been dead already.

I rolled him over and checked every pocket. No key card. Even as dead guys go he was useless. I stood, breathed deep up my nose, then ran at the door and kicked it as hard as I could with the heel of my boot.

It flew open, banging the wall. Not even locked. The light from the interrogation room was enough to show a hallway, a wire wastebasket, a space heater plugged into an outlet, a heavy yellow door six feet in front of me, another red door ten feet to my right, and a rolling garment rack with six wire coat-hangers dangling from it, one displaying a satin turquoise Florida Marlins baseball jacket. No pimply sentry cradling an M-16, that was good, but no useful power drills or wood screws either. I threw the yellow door's deadbolt in case that stopped anybody coming in from outside. Frightening them with my dripping head might buy some time too.

I laid one of the coat hangers on the floor, and stepped on it while my good hand unwound the top hook then straightened the whole thing out. The hanger squirmed like it was dipped in Vaseline and my right hand kept expecting the left to pitch in, but eventually I had a shape like a C. Five minutes had been and gone. But old Arthur had heard on NPR that the brain believes moments of stress last longer than they really do and normal humans think a twenty-five-second roller coaster ride lasts three minutes.

I dropped on my back again, twisted the top of my head against the beige lino and balanced the jaw on my neck. That left enough of a gap to fit half my hand between the bottom teeth and the top, so at age thirty-four I'd inherit Great-grandma Giller's astonishing underbite. With my stump I pressed one end of the wire against the side of my head then used the good hand to wind the rest of the hanger under the point of my chin then tight across the top of my head. Then I was out of wire. I had no idea if the jaw would stay on my face when I sat up, but at least I had contact. I twisted the ends of the wire together, then held the jaw and sat up.

My chin must've been a good focal point for the upward pressure, because nothing seemed to shift. But could I cram my left hand back on before the 8th Airborne Division rammed the door?

A much-beloved to-do list:

1. *Pull Carver's baseball jacket off its hanger and into your lap.*
2. *Tie a knot in end of left sleeve. You only have one hand so pinch armpit of jacket between your heels.*
3. *Form left hand into fist and drop knuckles-first down the closed sleeve.*
4. *Put left stump into left sleeve, aligning wrist to back of hand.*
5. *Put right arm through right sleeve so that you're wearing the jacket. Shortened left sleeve causes jacket to bind painfully under right armpit but also creates beautiful pressure at left wrist.*
6. *Palpate left sleeve with right hand—does the hand sit against the arm the way it used to? Wish that you'd palpated your left wrist more often in the old days so you'd know for sure whether it felt all right? Yes, if it heals the* arm will *be shorter, you've lost body mass, but that doesn't matter a good goddamn.*

Then I was light-headed from loss of viscous blood or cough syrup or whatever. I swayed to my feet and took down another coat hanger and yanked it into a sort of diamond. I tucked that under my chin too, dragged the top up over my forehead, and the thing fit perfectly after all of ten seconds' work.

And it was a good thing I'd doubled the pressure on the jaw because then I knelt and vomited into that useless wire wastebasket, though my mouth couldn't open more than a quarter-inch. My jaw stayed in place.

So I stepped back to that big yellow door and put my hand on the cold latch.

COLD AIR BATHED my poor face and shook those structural coat hangers. I looked down at a set of three wooden steps, then a tall chain-link fence, white windblown prairie and gray sky beyond it. Just looked like Nebraska as far as I could tell, but I'd never been to Virginia to be able to say if it looked any different. No sign of friend or foe. Left alone to mop up as usual.

I shut the yellow door, tiptoed down the foyer and clicked open that other red door. By the light of a spastically flickering fluorescent I saw twenty feet of bare hallway, with a blue door at the far end this time, and chunks of cement spilled across the floor from a hole in the wall. With the red door open an inch I could smell sawdust, so this seemed right—still no clatter of grenade belts. I shut the door silently, and behind it found a green-and-white fifty-pound bag of fertilizer, showing grapes and watermelons, just like farmers buy in Velouria.

"He-oh?" I called to the knee-level hole in the wall. "Ih Heeda." It's Peter, who's in here? "Who ih he-a?"

Five seconds of silence. A noise from the hole like a cat coughing up hairballs. None of my crew had ever made that sound. Gingerly I dropped to one knee and peered in. Just blackness, and a bare patch of cement floor lit by that sporadic fluorescent tube.

I went back to the bag—it was open but mostly full, with a Pyrex measuring cup on top of the white pellets. I dragged the bag over to the hole.

"Aw? Jock?" *Rob, Jock*—funny the words you can still say even when your tongue's on hiatus. "You guys ungry? Ih Heeda."

I threw a handful in ahead of me as I crawled through the hole. It was dark and smelled like *smouldering* sawdust. Crawling across the pellets didn't feel too pleasant on my kneecaps, so with my good right hand I dragged the bag in after me.

"Who in heah?" I asked.

Straight in front of me I heard the coughing-cat noise again, and to my right what sounded like a guy muttering in his sleep. Where the hell was I?

Suddenly enough light came through a window in a door on the left to throw a weak square onto the floor, and from that I could make out two guys sprawled to my right and one in front of me. Then the square of light went off again.

I crouched and waited to see if the bodies would get violent. I was in the mood for that, to be honest, until something else occurred to me.

"Hey," I whispered. "You guy know 'Onny 'Own? Ih 'Elouria?"

No response.

"I was at 'Ockside doo, at day. I was da deccha."

The coughing-cat sound turned into indisputably human gagging, loud and wet, and somebody else started to slowly hum. I recognized it. *Well, East Coast girls are hip, I really*—"California Girls."

"Wha you know about Dockside?" asked a guy to my right. Sounded like his mouth was full of paste.

"I know na-hin. Any kids in heah? Ha do ged dem outta heah!"

"What's in that bag?" someone else whispered. "Smells good."

"Why's id so dah in heah?" I asked.

"Tim smashed the bulb," said Pastemouth. "Tired of looking at each other."

"Give me some of that to eat," said the whisperer.

I scooped a cupful of pellets out of the bag and held it out to the dark. I couldn't see exactly who'd been talking.

"What's he s'posed to do with that?" asked Pastemouth.

"Ih calciuh nidrade."

"He cand reach it," said Pastemouth. "You a retard."

"You got to put it in my mouth," the whisperer agreed. "Please."

On my knees I shuffled toward his voice, handful of fertilizer extended.

"Tell him where you are, Lars," said Pastemouth.

"Nah, I'm down here," said Lars, the whisperer.

The light flickered on again. I was kneeling over Lars's bare leg but the leg wasn't attached to the rest of him, which was propped in the corner dressed in a T-shirt and underpants. Just below his right elbow his head lay on its side. Only the head. His eyes looked up at me, blinking as the pupils dilated to pinpricks in the light.

"Oh," I said. "This stuh is dry."

"Just cram it in," he whispered. "I'd like to choke on it."

He opened his mouth wide like a child in a high chair. I set my hand on his forehead to roll his head back so the stuff wouldn't fall out of his mouth.

"Pour it in," Pastemouth said—I saw now, he was a fat bearded guy with his left hand lying by itself in his lap.

I dropped the pellets into Lars's mouth. He shut his eyes and said, "*Mm-nn*," as he tried to swallow, trying to get his throat to work even though it was a couple of feet away. He made a wet, determined sound, "*Mm-nn!*" Then he tried to get a breath in through the stuff and his eyes opened wide.

His eyes shut again and didn't move. I figured he was really dead then. I brushed his hair out of his eyes. Must've looked like I was petting a football.

"He had a girlfriend in Velouria," said the hummer, his voice warbling like a flute. "She had sex with him in the interview room in jail."

"Whad were dey gi'ing you to eat heah?" I asked.

"Chicken breast," Pastemouth mumbled. "Fuckin' salad."

"We just have to wait," said Colleen.

I quit breathing, waited for her to say something else.

"Whed da hoice cah rum?"

"Vent up dere," said Pastemouth. "We dought they were on that side, hey, made a hole, but we guessed wrong. I don't figure I'm intact down below anyway. Crawled back in here for a rest."

He tugged at his handless forearm. It was tattooed with a bare-breasted mermaid, the fucked-up product of science gone wrong.

"Delicious *salad*," the hummer said.

"I tole hib we need bacon. Dockor saib, 'Human body dond need *bacon*,' I saib, 'This *in't* a human body, fuggin' *asshole*.'"

Pastemouth's shorter arm dropped away at the elbow. We both sat looking at it. A single drop of blood trickled sluggishly across the mermaid.

The hummer started into "My Bonny Lies Over the Ocean."

"We said we'd wait," Colleen whispered out of the vent, "so we'll wait."

"*I* never said I'd wait!" Megan yelled.

"Toby?" said Pastemouth. He prodded the hummer with his toe.

"He's aslee," I said. "Ow do I ged negt doah?"

"Toby ain'd *adleep*," said Pastemouth.

I felt hungry as hell, I realized, a real emergency, so with nothing else in front of me I scooped a half-cup of calcium nitrate past the coat hangers and crammed it into my *own* mouth. Tasted like chalk and tonic water.

"You smed like Sunday ham!" Pastemouth announced.

"Oh." I smelled like Sunday ham?

I jumped to my feet and, before he could do the same, I swung the bag of fertilizer and walloped him across the side of the head.

"Gah!"

He reared up and clubbed me across the face with the back of his good hand. I fell down across his old hand and arm, and it seemed like a good idea to throw them at him, but his hand flew out the hole into the hallway.

"You hear something?" asked Colleen's voice. "Fighting again."

"Collee!" I shouted. "Ih Heeda!"

Pastemouth kicked me in the sternum and I went down on my behind, but even with my left hand tied in a sleeve I was still strong from eating fertilizer, though it was kicking my intestines like I was nine months pregnant.

Colleen asked, "Did he say Peter?"

Pastemouth blinked his Doberman eyes then jumped at me again, so I tugged Carver's gun out of my belt and buried the butt in the top of his head. His skull was soft as cheese. He dropped to the floor beside Toby. "Collee?" I yelled at the vent. "Kick da wah!"

"The what?" That sounded like Colleen and *Clint.*

"De wah!"

The wall above Pastemouth gave a dull thud.

"Okay," I said. "Ih kahing!"

As I crawled out of the hole, I felt something hot trickle down the inside of my thigh. I'd crapped myself. Commercial fertilizer was not the zombies' great way forward.

"Giller!" yelled Clint's tinny voice. "Franny has to get out of here!"

"Yeah," I called meekly.

I'd been unfazed by the demise of Lars's whispering head but figured the world had ended because I'd pooped my pants. Why does diarrhea need to smell so sour? Pastemouth was too big around the middle but I managed to get Hummer's pants off without his legs coming too. In the gloom, I got the guy's underpants too, then wiped myself with my former trouser leg. A minute, two.

Then I remembered to pull the gun out of the twenty pounds of butter that was Pastemouth's head, because I was going to need it to fight the United States Army.

"Peter," I heard her say through the vent.

The blue door led to a corridor lined with four steel doors with a square window in each, and Colleen, Megan and Clint had their faces flat against the second one like they'd been pressed onto a slide for a microscope. I might've worried they were asphyxiating if it hadn't been for all the yelling.

Franny, they were all saying. They were gray skinned like they'd been painted with grease.

"Jesus Christ!" choked Colleen. "What happened to you?"

"I'd okay." I put my hands to the glass. "Where ih she?"

"Here!" Megan had two black eyes. "Get her out of here!"

I tugged the big metal handle but the door felt welded shut. A black plastic slot sat against the doorframe.

"Key card!" yelled Clint.

"It needs the key card." Colleen put her hands against mine, just the glass between us. "One of the beard guys has it!"

"Where dey?"

"Maybe out in that yard!"

I ran out through the blue door. So long as one of them was dying I couldn't be excited that three of them were alive. I barreled through the flickering red door, leading with my shoulder, then in the dark hallway I could see the yellow one ahead of me. I threw the deadbolt back and opened the door a quarter-inch. Light burst in. Blinking hard, I reached back to tug Carver's gun from my belt.

Snow at the bottom of the wooden stairs, and every footprint walked away to the left—the path just led around the corner of the building. It sure didn't seem like 1,855 personnel were on-site, but Carver hadn't been all by himself. Was that a dog barking? I closed the door gently because somewhere there was at least one guy with a beard.

Wind whistled through my coat hangers and the snow under my boots crunched as loud as potato chips so I made sure to step in the icy, silent tracks that had been stomped down already. I was hurrying for the key card but had to keep from being disemboweled in the meantime. I peered around the corner—Carver's building was only eighteen feet wide like the portable we'd used for drama class at Champlain High.

I tiptoed the eighteen feet and looked past the next corner. The building formed one side of a compound, along with a beat-up green pickup truck with Nebraska plates and a camper on the back, a mobile home with smoke rising from its tin chimney, and the chain-link fence meeting at a padlocked gate. A road ran past, dusted with snow, and barking dogs were very nearby.

"Got out, did you, little *terrorista*?"

Two burly guys in camouflage vests strolled up behind me, shotguns over their elbows—they'd been walking the perimeter after all. One definitely had a beard.

"Ouch!" he said. "What'd our boy do to you?"

"You ha do o'en da doah!" I yelled.

"Don't be funny," he said. "One day you'll get a fair trial, 'til then—"

I lifted the pistol and shot him through the beard. He raised a hand to his throat as a line of blood squirted onto the snow, like I'd shot a can of soda. The dogs kept barking behind me. Now the key card.

But the second burly guy, with pimples between his eyes, opened his mouth and lifted his shotgun. I threw myself backward past the corner of the portable a half-second before he fired—plastic siding turning to confetti—and landed on my back on the hard snow. I'd lost Carver's pistol. Pimples loomed over me as I skittered away on my back, picturing the chunks of me raining onto the snow. He lifted the shotgun but instead of firing he just *kept* lifting it, then brought it down on my head. That knocked me down on my side.

For Franny I needed to get up and find the key card.

"Your head's fucked up!" said Pimples. "Let's get you locked in here, how about that? Patrick, boy, you all right back there?"

No answer from Patrick. Just the barking, and snow crunching under Pimples' boots as he dragged me by the collar toward the mobile home. Carver's jacket dug in under my jaw and I tried to swallow but totally couldn't. A screen door creaked open. And now a noise like an engine from somewhere.

"Check my amigo, see what the *man* says to do with you," Pimples muttered. He dragged me over the doorframe, then green linoleum, then onto a pile of kindling. "Lay still here a minute, I won't crack you another one. Aw, shit, now what?"

Even over the barking from outside I could hear the clatter of a motorcycle. The greasy ass of Pimples' jeans stomped past me.

"Sleep it off, motherfucker, you've got about two—"

The door slammed behind him then he bolted it, from the sound, locking me in with a fridge and woodstove and a laptop and stacks of papers—this was obviously where the Joint Chiefs of Staff would be meeting on Tuesday. Pimples wasn't familiar with a zombie's constitution. The corner of my forehead throbbed where the shotgun had come down but I shambled to my feet and leaned over the desk to look out the window, half-dead flies buzzing along the sill. Even through the grime, I could see the yard.

A motorcyclist in black had pulled up outside the gate, waving a thick yellow envelope, his face covered by helmet and visor. Pimples, shotgun in the crook of his elbow, shoved a key in the padlock. He unlooped the chain then reached through for the envelope. And did the rider hand it across then disappear down the road? No, he hit the throttle, rammed the gate and came tearing across the yard straight toward the portable. A Penzler elite ape, or maybe just Gary dorking around. He'd nearly passed the edge of my window when Pimples' shotgun coughed a yellow flame. The rider flew sideways off the bike, spraying plastic helmet shards, and the bike skidded away without him. My buddy in black—he wasn't any crony of Pimples'—lay sprawled like a banana peel.

The barking dogs must've been in the camper because it rocked like they had the whole thing between their jaws. Pimples wandered up from the gate, methodically loading a fresh shell into the shotgun's breech.

And I needed the key card no matter what those two did. I reeled to the kitchenette and threw open the drawers but all I found were spoons and a potato peeler, and I wasn't going to chop through any doors with those. I grabbed the peeler anyway and ran back to the window. The tough-bastard rider was sitting up, his arms propped across his knees, while Pimples stood over him, shaking his head like they were talking about the real-estate downturn. The helmet had a ragged chunk out of the back so it looked like the half-built Death Star. The rider flopped sideways onto the snow and I figured that was it, Pimples' work was done, but then the rider sat straight up again, fiddling with the strap under his chin like he had ants in his helmet, while Pimples marched across to the truck without even looking back at him. The helmet came off and the rider threw it away across the snow.

It was Harv Saunders.

"Havvah!" I shouted, slapping the glass.

He didn't budge from where he sat. His head was bloody. As Pimples stood behind the camper I could only see him from the knees down—the legs took a step to the right then three dogs bounded down onto the snow, beelining for Harv. He climbed to his feet but then the first dog took the back of his arm between its teeth.

Down Harv went.

The dogs were all pit bulls, white with brown patches. The other two piled on and pieces of Harv and his clothes started to fly.

I pounded the window, dropped my peeler. I ran to the door, pulling back on the knob, but the thing might as well have been the wall. I unzipped Carver's awful fucking jacket, took it off my right arm then gently extricated the left—the poor hand was still balled in a fist but I thought hard and the fingers started to open. Jesus, how long was Harv going to last? Or Franny? My wrist looked like crushed tomatoes but it had these white filaments running through it. I looked at the kindling and realized there had to be a hatchet, out back, a weapon, so I circled the woodstove and found another door, a bathroom, with a frosted glass window over the toilet. I gripped the sides of the frame—with both hands—and kicked the window out into the snow.

I had to tumble through sideways, falling onto a couple of trash cans. I was out of the mobile home but on the opposite side from Harv. I could hear the dogs still chewing him, and then how long before Pimples blew his brains out? I got to my feet, and under a blue tarp there was a woodpile with a black-handled hatchet stuck into the chopping block. I tugged it out. Its weight in my hand felt perfect. My brain showed me Colleen's gray face up against the glass.

I crashed through flats of beer cans, then out into the yard, around the truck and camper—I had to squint like hell, the prairie was so bright. Pimples stood with his back to me, watching the show while two dogs tugged Harv's arms in opposite directions like they were opening a Dickensian Christmas cracker, and the third darted in to bite his groin. He'd been torn above his right hip so a loop of intestine lay beside him in the snow. He raised his head.

"Screw off," he called weakly. They'd already taken half his face, so no part of him was easy to look at.

"Har-la!" I yelled.

Pimples turned, the gun only beginning to swing in my direction as I brought the hatchet down through his collarbone—the assholes happened to own the sharpest hatchet in the world. As he dropped to his knees, the shotgun pivoted upward and went off. I felt the heat against my elbow, no harm done, but Pimples' left hand spiraled off through the crisp air to slap against the camper door. It left a wet hand-print.

He screamed like he was auditioning. He pressed the stump of his wrist to his chest, then fell flat on his back and lay still. Blood sprayed across his face from his wrist—real, unmodified blood will do that. His groans slowed down like somebody'd unplugged his record player. I tried to pull the hatchet out of his collarbone but only lifted his shoulders off the ground. The bones pinched from either side. So I stepped on his chest, hurrying, and brought the hatchet out with another spray across the snow.

"Carver's the tough fucker." Pimples looked up at me. "He'll gut you."

Then his eyes rolled back in his head. I figured that was shock. After all of the pieces that had fallen off me, I'd forgotten what was *supposed* to happen when part of a person came off. The ground looked like a jam factory had exploded.

"Hip hip," Harv said. "Hooray."

One pit bull had his arm and another his leg, shaking them like they meant to break their necks—luckily for Harv those limbs weren't attached to him. The third dog looked tired as it dragged him by the arm across the yard. So when was I supposed to tell Harv that Amber and Grace were dead?

"Mr. Giller, hey," he murmured.

The dog with the leg dropped it and stood looking at me, its eyes microscopic, his mouth giant and wide—the shark's mammalian cousin—then lowered its purple-frothed muzzle and ran for me and jumped, almost faster than my eyes could follow, lips curled back—it was an *ugly* piece of shit!—and I sidestepped just enough to bury the hatchet in the bone between its ear and eyeball. It dropped to the snow like I'd pulled its electrical cord out of the wall. That left the other two, pink-eyed, running at me from opposite sides. I dropped to the snow beside Pimples and tugged the shotgun out from under him, my good right hand already on the trigger. But my left hand had to pump the stock. All I could see down the barrel was a dog's black mouth. I threw my left elbow back, the stock slid and *clicked*. I pulled the trigger. The dog's head flew apart like ground beef thrown into a fan.

I pumped again and fired the second barrel at the last dog, but nothing came out but a breeze. I sat up and stuck a leg out in front of me, so instead of my throat the dog took my shin in its mouth. I lifted the shotgun high, as Pimples had taught me, then clubbed the thing across the eyes. It just blinked at me with those tiny lashless things and ground me even harder between its teeth.

"Good bie," I reassured it.

I reached back and jerked Pimples' camouflage jacket open—he wore a fluorescent vest underneath, stocked neatly with shells. But they were jammed tight in their loops so I had to lay the gun in my lap and hold the vest steady with my creaking left hand. The dog dragged me across the yard toward the gate, one foot back, another, so while I held tight to the vest, Pimples slid with us too, ridiculously. The dog produced so much drool I was wet to the ass of my pants. I'd loved Keister, but not this dog.

Finally I tugged a shell free, let go of Pimples and lay on my back as the dog slid me across the snow. I slid the shell into the breech then pulled the pump back without any trouble. I set the barrel against the dog's shoulder. Franny was still waiting.

"Here bie," I said.

The jaws clenched tighter as I pulled the trigger, so I wavered to my feet and dragged the half-a-dog and myself over to the first one, with the hatchet through its head.

"Cool," muttered what-was-left-of-Harv.

I stepped on the snout to provide enough leverage to yank the hatchet free. Then along with my pet dog I limped over to Harv. Even his guts spilled in all directions didn't make the sinew and bone and grimacing teeth of his face any easier to look at—I guess the face is a person's main thing. I knelt beside him.

"Hey, kid," I managed to say.

"I'm fucked up," he said softly.

"Nah, yuh be okay. We heal okay."

Though his bare arm still showed those cigarette welts.

I went to work on my dog's jaws, pulling the folds of lip back then prying the slimy back teeth apart with the hatchet's handle.

"Don't bother, Mr. Giller."

"I sure a-heciate yuh co'ing here," I said.

"It's cool."

The hatchet handle was too thick to go between the teeth.

"Car was leaking oil," he murmured. "Took a real long time. I went to get you after a long time and a car was in the yard. So weird. This

Chinese guy put Franny in the back! I jumped behind the tree. She's okay now, she's here someplace?"

"Ranny? She hine," I said.

So he'd somehow shadowed Gary all the way here? I still saw Colleen's face against the glass. Could I fit the *blade* between its teeth?

"Cut off the snout," Harv muttered.

"Oh, hey," I said.

I twisted my knee around so the angle would be right. Of course it would've been a shorter route to have chopped through the lower jaw but he'd said *snout*, I thought *snout*. Funny how the brain doesn't work. With the first chop there was a spurt of blood.

"I had this awesome idea," Harv whispered, "for a movie. Zombies like us are sent to this jail…"

"We art zom'ies," I said. "Don't eat rains."

As I went on thwacking I concentrated on his every word. I was tired of dogs.

"There's zombies and normal people in there. And the zombies don't get bacon so their arms'll fall off. So we take up less space. So more of us can go into one cell. Then a zombie survives the electric chair. Then all the guys on death row want to be zombies. They really want to."

I'd nearly chopped through to the top teeth.

"We cah turn so'one into a zomhie?"

"If my dad came," he said, "I'd mess him up."

I straightened up, hatchet dangling.

"Nah, Harr. You nah lie dat."

"I guess," his teeth said. "Are we the last two?"

"Colleen and guys are insie."

"Oh," he said. He was looking at the sky, eyes wide open. "Good."

Then I watched for a full minute, but his one eyelid didn't flicker.

OF THE MANY dead things on that property, Patrick had to be the tidiest—he just had a hole in his throat and a beard and clothes matted with blood, his camouflage ball cap rolling in the wind beside him. Inside his jacket I found the card on a Farmers Mutual key fob.

I crashed through the first red door, key card in my apprenticing left hand, my right reaching for the next handle, when I stepped on something, slid a yard and landed flat on the back of my head. My coat hangers went *fwannnnggg* like a tuning fork.

I'd stepped on Pastemouth's hand, flattened it, but I could still make out the little centaur tattoo.

I limped through the last door but saw nobody at the window. Something had happened. I swiped the card, a green light blinked, the latch clicked. I tugged the door open.

Colleen stood in front of me, gnawing the end of her finger as tears streamed down her face. Clint and Megan crouched behind her with their arms around each other. Megan blinked up at me, teeth chattering, but Clint kept his head buried in her hair. There was a mound of multicolored clothes at the back of the dark cell, and the place smelled astringent like a cider mill.

"Doo lade," I said.

A bare arm lay between Colleen's feet.

PEACE OUT COPPERS**THIS IS FRANNY'S LEFT ARM

"I guess so," said Colleen. "Don't come in." She extended a gray hand toward my badly wired face. "Is it okay if we touch you?"

I held my arms out and she wrapped her entire body around my ribs. She steered me back into the hallway.

"We've been saying prayers. We knew we'd die in there," she said to my chest. "We knew they'd stopped you. Can we go now?"

"As fah as I know, e'rybody's dead foh fiddy mile a'ound."

"Maybe one of them was the one who killed Doug."

She looked up at me, our bodies tight together from top to bottom. I must've had breath like a bile duct.

"Can you take all that stuff off your head?" she asked.

"Nod yed."

The cell door clicked shut behind her and I had to swipe it again. Clint came out draped over Megan's shoulder, his head down.

"Do you wan do 'ery heh? In da ground?"

"No," said Megan. "We want to leave."

The two of them staggered out through the red door. Colleen kept her arms around my waist.

"I wad do dake all da 'odies away frah heah, so no'ody can do dests on deh."

"What happened to those poor guys who were screaming at us before?"

"All dead. Harr is dead too."

"Oh my god—Harvey was here?"

"Yeh," I said, and I made my throat relax so it wouldn't catch.

"He was."

She walked out ahead of me. We'd have to find some bacon in the mobile home's fridge, before my jaw fell off again.

And my own kids?

THE BIGGER LOGS started to crackle, the iron stove creaking as the heat pushed from the inside, so I threw the bacon in the pan but it wasn't hot enough to sizzle yet.

"Isn't a yellow car on the whole property." Colleen picked something out of her ear, inspected it. "Fuck. I'll take a shower."

"Ight be cold," I said. "Dere's no hindow."

"Those two found a wheelbarrow out there."

As Megan and Clint passed the window, I flopped down at the desk, opened Carver's laptop and fumbled for the power switch. The Microsoft logo and various start-up screens went by, then my breath caught in my throat. Carver's desktop photo showed Ray Lewis stretching for that interception against Pittsburgh from Week 4 back in 2010.

None of the desktop icons said CURE FOR ZOMBIES. I tried a little blue shield marked OPS, assuming that meant secret operations, and a window popped up asking for a user name and password so I couldn't open it. But the heading across the top of that log-in window?

CONTRACTOR INTERFACE

FEDERAL BUREAU OF INVESTIGATION

I spotted a Word icon called PENZLER GILLER which sounded exciting, but of course it wasn't, or it would've been inside the secure file. This was a questionnaire.

1. *Since your exposure, have you had cravings for any particular food?*
2. *Is it conceivable that you might one day be defeated in a fight?*
   a. *Barehanded?*
   b. *With any particular weapon?*
3. *Toward whom is your rage primarily directed?*
4. *On behalf of your country, would you at any future date be willing to jump from an airplane at 500 feet without benefit of a parachute?*

a. *At 2000 feet?*
b. *At 10,000?*

5. *To which enemy of the United States do you feel your aggression might most effectively be directed?*

Whoever had written the questions knew a lot about pink goo, maybe Carver himself, or Carver via Penzler. All phrased in administration-speak like minutes from a school trustees meeting—*that* was the soulless crap that would kill the world, not any mad scientist formula. I heard the shower running then got up to turn my bacon—of course I wanted it to burn, but evenly.

I opened the desk's top drawer and found a bottle of chewable vitamin C, a blue asthma inhaler, a couple of UHU glue sticks and, even better, a white Burger King takeout bag containing my wallet, the mummified pinkie of my right hand and Alice's telegram—all green lights in terms of our getting somewhere.

In the next drawer, I found credit cards and a checkbook issued to Josh Q. Carver by a Capital One in Indianapolis, and his record in the back showed checks written to Andy's Mobile Oil Change, to the Indiana Bell Telephone Company and to Gary Yeung for "FBI chores." Josh Q. Carver had deftly shoved my life up my ass but also supplemented his income with curbside lemonade and light babysitting.

In the driveway Clint and Megan threw dog-parts into the blue wheelbarrow—neither kid vomited, just gathered hairy scraps in their fingers like they were twenty-year veterans of the profession. We were chemically hardened for the battlefield and hardly ever phoned home to Mom.

I noticed a cell phone behind the laptop, then I was typing in 411.

"Ohio infor'ation, please," I said.

I had to concentrate on where my tongue was in my mouth, but I was comprehensible. The Nebraska operator gave me a free Ohio number to call.

"Preston, please," I said into the phone. "Penzler. Is a res'dence."

The mobile home's pipes gave a thud as Colleen shut off the shower. The phone hummed in my ear. I wanted Alice to pick up so I'd know she wasn't still stretched in the dirt.

"No," I told the operator. "No, what I wan is a res'dence. Really? Huh. Okay."

No Penzler. That was probably the same for anybody with a

corporation named after them, but then how were their daughters going to meet boys?

In any case, the world still needed Natalia.

I pulled up the Travelocity website and a blinking cursor asked where I'd like to fly from, then to where. I selected from the list of possible connections between LNK and SLO, then the next cursor asked how many travelers would be flying. I dragged down to 2. Then to 4. Then back up to 1. A screen came up asking for payment and Carver's MasterCard was close to hand, then I wrote the confirmed departure time on a napkin.

Colleen wandered out, her hair wrapped in a *SpongeBob Square-Pants* towel.

"That's better," she said, though her simmering eyes hinted that no longer being a zombie would be better still. "What'd you book?" She was gazing at the laptop. "We going somewhere?"

"California," I said slowly. "Penzler's daughter's getting cured."

"When'd you find that out?"

"Penzler's ouse."

"And you never said?"

"Never ad a chance."

"I guess, okay. Who'd you get tickets for?"

"Everybody," I lied.

Eating bacon would be easier with the coat hangers off my head, so after I showered I wiped a hole in the mirror steam and stared at myself while I unwound the wires. So many plastic tendrils had spread in front of my ears, stitching my head back together, that it looked like I'd grown white sideburns. I resembled Martin Van Buren, eighth President of the United States, with blood spattered all down his presidential neck and one side of his face. I took a washcloth to my boots in the sink, then traded my shredded grandpa's shirt and Hummer's trousers for the charcoal dress pants hanging from the back of the bathroom door. Carver's white Diet Pepsi T-shirt and green button-down were also unblemished by blood. Clean-living guy.

I inspected my right shoulder where it had reattached.

"If we're taking a plane somewhere," Colleen said behind me, "we need to pull those nails out."

I wrapped myself around the doorjamb while she set the claw over a nail.

"Oh," flushed Megan said from the doorway. "You guys are busy."

"Could take a little while, honey," Colleen said through her teeth. "You done?"

"No. But Clint keeps crying."

The nail slowly gave way, sounding like the last of a milkshake coming up a straw. She set the bottom of her bare foot against my hip. Her heel felt like a rasp.

"I can't watch this," said Megan.

"Got three more in my knee!"

UNDER THE CHECKBOOK I finally found the truck's keys. We were fed and ready.

But they left it to me to put the dead kids in the camper—Megan had managed to wrap Franny's head in that chocolate-stained serape, and as I lifted it out of the wheelbarrow I saw where she'd scrawled EVERYBODY WANTS PEACE with a ballpoint, in the sprawling letters of a first-grader. And everybody did want that, but you can't sit in your house in Hoover and wait for it, especially if your house has burnt down.

Her torso was all one piece, still in T-shirt and underwear, and once that was in the camper I lifted out her limbs one at a time, the ends crusted over with what might've been old Dimetapp. I wondered if months of footage out of the Congo had desensitized me to such things or if it was the super-soldier serum, then I wondered whether it would be appropriate to send her father a piece or two—I pictured a wispy-bearded guy cooking in a MR. GOOD-LOOKIN IS COOKIN apron, surprised by the package in the mail. I smiled, which felt crinkly on my Martin Van Buren face. You realize how little you knew a person when you're holding her downy-haired arm and it isn't attached to anything else.

The last piece was her left leg. In his narrow printing Clint had written I LOVE FRANNY'S LEFT THIGH, right on the back where she'd never read it. Unless she'd seen it drop away, and it'd been the last thing she'd ever read.

"Sucks," I said to the dog crap smeared across the table leg.

With the remains of the six adult males stacked in the three bunks, I wrapped Harv in the shower curtain and lay him in the middle of the floor.

I took our last square of bacon and set it on Harv's tongue.

FIVE MINUTES BEYOND Carver's we rolled past the clapboard houses of Inavale, Webster County, Nebraska, then east along 136. I would've bet cash money that the truck's radio would be on a bluegrass station, but Colleen made no move to click it on. We sat in silence as Clint steered with his wrist propped over the wheel, four pairs of unfocused eyes trained on the pin-straight road and snow swirling across the pavement, Colleen clenching Megan's hands, my jaw and wrist recapitulating in the spirit of twenty-first-century military science as I pressed my head against the cold window. It was tight, four of us across the cab, but even after we'd pitched the corpses out nobody wanted to ride in the camper.

"Know what I kept telling her?" Clint steered lazily toward the shoulder, then back toward the line. "I said, 'What happened to the jail guy will not happen to us.' And then ..."

Megan was nodding.

I shut my eyes and felt the drift of snow flatten under us, and for the first time I wondered what I'd do if Natalia refused to come home.

At the end of our second hour we were still inhaling each other's sawdust, but we were coming into Beatrice—19 YEARS WINNER OF THE TREE CITY USA GROWTH AWARD—and saw green signs reading LINCOLN 40 MILES and PAWNEE CITY/FALLS CITY EXIT ONLY. Colleen jerked against my shoulder like she'd stirred from a coma.

"Not far to Pawnee City here," she said. "Oh, and Lincoln! Say again how many plane tickets you bought?"

"Enough for everybody."

Megan extricated her sweaty hand from her mother's. "Don't they check ID?"

"Does *anybody* have ID?" asked Colleen.

"I guess if we have time," Clint murmured, "we could go to the factory and give them our bad news. I dunno."

Because he thought PBF still existed.

"We'll think of something," I said. "We'll manage. What's this coming?"

A plywood sign stood over the highway:

OPEN 363 D YS A YEAR!

YOU WILL LOVE OUR "RIDES"

ZAGAT'S ADVENTURE WORLD

Beside it, a sagging amusement park stood in front of snowy wheat fields—the rides might have been painted fuchsia and teal but under that ceiling of cloud everything was gray.

"Place must be a gold mine," said Clint.

But maybe it'd give me an opportunity—when else would I be able to bolt? Coming west with me would kill them, one hundred percent of studies had proven it.

"Let's stop." I tapped the window with a knuckle. "I want to see it."

None of them said anything, but Clint slowed down and turned his flicker on. He had a yellow shoelace, patterned with JESUS in red letters, twined around his finger.

"I feel like Harv would want to see it," I said. "I don't know."

"Especially if he could throw stuff and win prizes," said Megan.

"But shouldn't we just keep going?" Colleen took her daughter's hand again. "What if there's airport hassles? We'll need time, and we can't get split up anymore. I was so busy trying to kill somebody, I hardly even noticed you were back, I'm serious."

"No, Mom, it made sense that you—"

"No." She got an even better grip on Megan's hand. "I'm not looking to kill anybody ever again, and we need a real plan for the airport."

It was getting too convincing—had to remind myself that they weren't coming. I rubbed my shoulder against hers.

"My brain's too tired for that kind of scheming."

We bumped across a parking lot half-full with trucks and long Pontiacs. A long burgundy van read PAWNEE CITY MASONIC TEMPLE SENIORS EXPRESS.

"Jeez," Clint said blandly. "Almost back to Pawnee City. How far away's it?"

"Probably thirty-odd miles."

"This seems like a lot of customers," Colleen sighed. "It's a Tuesday in November."

A twenty-foot fiberglass figure creaked over us, his fist full of glitter-painted lightning bolts, swallows flitting from under his rust-streaked beard.

KING ZEUS WELCOMES YOU
TO OUR WORLD OF ZADVENTURES
SENIORS DAY MON–TUES

"Must be a lot of old people here on dates," I said.

"That sounds kind of nice," said Colleen.

"Who has money to get in?" asked Megan.

I was the only one with a wallet, but Patrick and Pimples must've helped themselves to my cash. Colleen opened the glove box—a roll of bills sat wedged between a bottle of Famous Grouse and the wet wipes. It was all fifties and hundreds.

"I call Ferris wheel," Megan said quietly.

"Never failed, at the wrecking yard," said Colleen. "Cash in the glove box."

She passed me half the pile and I shoved it in my pants.

"What wrecking yard?"

"We run Avery Salvage back in Hoover. Jesus, the guys must be thinking I've—"

"*And* you run the Farmers Mutual?"

"We'll call our screenplay *Avery Salvage*," said Clint. "That's perfect."

"And *that's* why you know every make of yellow sports car?" I asked.

"Absolutely," she said wearily. "They're the most likely to be wrapped around a telephone pole."

Then she didn't scrutinize a single vehicle, just stumbled toward the park with an arm around poor Megan. Maybe she would be able to go back to living with regular people without kicking their asses. Zeus swayed over us, waiting to rain havoc on the unsuspecting.

Around the first corner we found a padlocked concession stand called the Zucchini Zone, then a little kid's carousel called Zebra Crossing. Toddlers with mullets straddled plastic zebras and blue-assed mandrills while grandparents in acid-wash jeans orbited the thing, taking pictures and hollering.

"You keep a hold now, Tyler! All right, TJ!"

"Here's the ride for you, Megan," said Clint.

The four of us stood staring like we'd staggered out of a crashed elevator, but Clint still had his capacity for nasty—well, we probably all did. THAT'S THE ZOMBIE ADVANTAGE! the billboards would say.

How was I going to make my break? The tattooed teenager running the ride was busy picking his lower lip, so I turned to the grandma next to me as she rolled a cigarette.

"Do we buy tickets around here?"

"Right around the, uh." She motioned with her head. "Ziggurat."

Our two kids had an increasing spring in their step. We walked past the boarded-up Zodiac Hot Dog Stand, horned Aries emerging from a bun on its awning. Floating through an oddball dream, though for once I knew how a dream was going to end. At least I'd be leaving them with a few hundred bucks. Megan pointed out a ticket booth the size of an outhouse, labeled *Zagat Zookeeper*.

"Tickets? How many?" a guy yelled from inside, voice muffled like his head was in a picnic cooler. "Ten rides for thirty-three dollars, that's the special!" Right down to his yellow sou'wester hat, he was imitating a lobster fisherman. "Also popcorn balls, but they're a week old, things'll pull your fillings out!"

I nearly turned and said *You want popcorn anyway, Harv, you hungry?*

"You don't have Zagnut bars?" asked Colleen.

"Good guess, young lady! I used to sell Zagnuts by the caseload, right here on this spot, but the wholesaler can't get them anymore—know why?"

"The *man* won't let you," said Clint.

"No, son, no, it's because they don't contain chocolate. That's a clue. So who do you think is taking them?"

"The army," I said.

"Yes!" said the fisherman. "The United States military takes 'em to the Congo, because Zagnuts do not *melt*! Now you all want tickets for The Zombie, am I right?"

Colleen looked at me from under her eyebrow, swallowing hard.

"Has your brain rested enough?"

"*Three* for The Zombie—me, I'll have to pass," I told the guy. "Dental surgery. Oh, can I borrow that pen a minute? Scrap of paper?"

The PA blasted "Sharp Dressed Man," ZZ Top, as we hurried across the park.

"God," said Colleen, kicking through spilled popcorn. "The Zombie?"

Nobody screamed "Agh!" like when Eric had been alive. We were all tired of that. Nobody said, *I'll be pissed off if it doesn't look like us.*

"Hey, I'm pretty good with those BB guns," said Clint. "Get my brother a killer crocodile."

The Zombie had eight arms that lifted up and down while the whole machine rotated, and at the end of each arm a fiberglass car, made up like a gore-smeared head, held three giggling kids where the brain ought to have gone.

"Is this the line?" I asked.

"No, go right up there," said a pockmarked grandma behind a stroller.

Two hours before, we'd been lab animals, now we were using every fiber of our freewill to line up for The Zombie.

"You dropped something," said a grandpa with a can of Pepsi in each hand.

A wad of keys lay in a puddle at our feet, looking like a crashed helicopter.

"Oops," said Clint.

"Let me hold onto them," I said. "We're screwed if they fall under that thing."

"One ride, then we go." Colleen tucked hair behind her ear. "I don't understand how we can afford to waste *any* time getting to Lincoln, considering—"

"Leave it to me," I said.

"Okay, just blow," said a grandma, holding a Kleenex to a little girl's nose. The line moved forward.

"Oh, and speaking of Pawnee City," I said to Colleen, "this is the number for my mom and Evadare." I folded the scrap of paper into her warm hand. "In case it gets crazy at the airport."

She looked at the paper, eyed me, then put it in her pocket.

"I shouldn't be this excited," Megan said flatly. "Doesn't seem possible."

My three were ushered toward the car that had an airbrushed rat squeezing out of one of its eye sockets. Hand to his ear, the operator made a big show of listening to a question from that fanny-pack woman from the Zebra Crossing.

"What do zombies *eat*? Diesel!" He staggered around with arms extended, lowering safety bars across the riders' chests. "Die-sel…."

"No tongue on the metal!" a grandma called. "Too cold out!"

As they took their first spin past, Clint and Megan and Colleen stretched ecstatic hands in my direction, the arm lifting them six feet in the air while the shrieking car ahead of them dipped down to brush the grass. Hilariously, Clint bit his knuckles in dread. Colleen smirked at me, tucked hair behind her ear again and turned to say something to Megan, whose eyebrows were nearly up in her hair. I took a deep breath up my nose then stepped behind the fanny-pack woman, then a trash can, always keeping low. The last glimpse they might've had of my behind was as I cut through the crowd of wheelchairs in front of Zarathustra's Tower of Silence.

YOU MUST BE THIS TALL, Zeus proclaimed.

I wasn't going to fly the other survivors to California just so they could quit being survivors, but trotting across the parking lot to Carver's truck, my righteous shame took me back to the first night I'd left Lydia to sleep alone in the cancer hospice. The gravel under my feet demonstrated more loyalty than I ever had.

AT LINCOLN AIRPORT I found a men's room and walked into a blur of multicolored tiles, and the mirrors reflecting more multicolored tiles managed to short-circuit something. I dropped to one knee. Guys in suits steered their rolling carry-ons around me as they hurried to the cubicles. Two Congo-bound soldiers in dark camouflage sidled out, poor bastards, duffel bags slung over their shoulders.

"You all right, pal?" asked a guy in a ball cap.

"Uh-huh," I said.

I splashed cold water on my cheeks so the other bathroom guys would think I was nothing more sinister than a nice, quiet drunk. I'd only come into the bathroom to decide how convoluted a story I'd need for when security stripped me down. Half of my sideburns had dropped off, I was only half–Martin Van Buren by then, so I could probably get away with *I just had minor surgery*. But first there'd be metal detectors. Steering toward a cubicle, my eyes down on the unhallucinogenic gray floor, I whacked the corner of my head into some tall idiot's jaw.

"Hey, what the fuck?" he whined.

I squinted up into his face so I wouldn't see the wall tiles. He was pimply, with a steel bar through his *septum*—what a word to remember. Funny how the brain works. He glared like the Whig who'd lost to Van Buren in the presidential election of 1836.

"Here's where I penetrate you in the eye socket," I told him.

"Uh…"

He held his palms out in front of him. Backed into the trash can.

"You're a disgrace," my Lydia said in my head.

Our kids are at camp, I told her. They're fine.

I locked myself in the cubicle and undressed, shoes, socks and everything—we'd pulled those five nails out at Carver's but had there been more? Didn't find anything in the bottoms of my feet. I worked my way up, feeling carefully around my right knee especially. Someone had scratched NEVER TRUST A MAN IN A BLUE TRENCHCOAT in the cubicle's paint, and underneath it a different pen had written NEVER DRIVE A CAR WHEN YOU'RE DEAD. Nothing around my anus. Nothing in my shoulders or elbows, but—ah! Something in my right ear, felt like a staple, but I couldn't even get a fingernail under it. Gary'd patched me together at the blue cabin.

I got the truck key out of my pants pocket while the guys on either side released their various gases, and I tried to jab the sharp end under that minuscule strip of staple. The ear must've grown over it because I had to dig like crazy, and I knew if I slipped a half-inch the key would penetrate my only hemisphere that still worked.

"Aw, man," I muttered.

"You and me both," wheezed the guy in the next stall.

The staple came out slick with purple goo. I flushed it down the toilet. That reminded me that I ought to get rid of the truck keys too in case some workaholic detective used them to connect me to the camper full of dog shit and bloodstains that I'd left parked in the five-minute-only zone. I dropped them in the garbage.

Between the maroon ropes, I tried to look as bored and respectable as your average orthodontist. Only two of the eight x-ray machines were running so all of us stared like oxen at the TV suspended over our heads—it showed a brown-haired woman with a microphone, in front of haphazardly parked trucks and a long trapezoidal bridge surrounded by leafless trees. BREAKING STORY: MARY WARNER IN GAGE COUNTY. If memory served—and did it?—she'd had to quit being Miss Nebraska after a DUI.

"A grisly discovery," she barked over the wind, "made shortly before three this afternoon by a local woman jogging across this bridge two miles northwest of Adams." Ms. Warner's eyeliner really popped the blue in her eyes, but her jaw wavered like Lady Macbeth's at the horror of it all. "The mutilated bodies of three Caucasian males, along with what appear to be three pit bull *terriers*, found here on the western bank of the Big Nemaha River."

The woman in front of me covered her daughter's eyes with her sari.

"Paramedics on the scene estimate the victims were in their thirties or forties, but state troopers say they have no clear leads at present regarding the men's identities. They're confident dental records and tattooing on the dogs ...."

As she went on emphasizing every third word, the Gage County wind wafted her bangs across the journalistic furrow between her brows. A red Acura appeared behind her and Gary, still in his black tracksuit, climbed out and walked across the shot, a cell phone to his ear.

A luggage cart bumped my calf—I needed to move.

I dropped my belt, boots and wallet into the plastic bin and watched it slide between the black flaps of the x-ray machine. The white-shirted security guard waved me through the metal-detector with his black baton, then it crossed my highly scientific mind that the dried-out finger still in my shirt pocket might be high in, say, mercury. I'd dropped eight people and three dogs into the Big Nemaha River, yet only the uncontaminated had washed ashore, from which we can infer—yes, a hand up at the back of the class? Zombies must not *float*?

"No carry-on, sir?" asked a white-shirted guard with a bow in her hair.

"No, ma'am. I'm traveling light."

I smiled and it must've looked gruesome as hell.

Tuesday, November 1.

IN THE LAX food fair the sign above the sandwich counter showed a smiling *bandito*, but it should've been me with my face dripping into my trouser pocket. It was six AM.

"I don't want *sandwiches*," I told the heavily moled woman. "Can't you just sell me the bacon?"

"How much bacon?" she asked.

"All the bacon you have."

"We…we need it for sandwiches."

"Fuck you," I said through my teeth. "Twelve bacon melts."

She and her co-worker exchanged glances, then she adjusted her clear plastic gloves and got to work. There'd been no bacon with the omelette they'd served on the plane. I gripped my left earlobe as I watched them throw pointless vegetables on the bread. I had another day or two before I went the way of Donny Brown and instead of reading Josie and Ray *The Berenstain Bears and the Haunted Hayride*, I was hoping to crawl into a hippie bunker with pink goo in its Slurpee machine.

"Meat and salt remind us we're human," I told them.

"Forty-seven fifty-two," the lady replied.

The twenties I handed her were dappled with purple. As I shuffled toward my gate, two giant candies smiled at me from the M&Ms vending machine, a red M&M and a green one, trying to break my concentration though they'd been created in a CIA lab in South Dakota and were my deformed and unclean brethren.

"Fuck you," I told them.

Just eat the bacon, I said to myself. You need to be a detective.

"I want to go home," I said to the air.

Tanned dads, pushing twisted, sleeping babies in strollers, steered wide arcs around me.

WE LANDED AT San Luis Obispo at 7:19 AM. In the security monitor above the exit doors my nose had melted into my upper lip and my hair looked like a rooster's. Outside I found a Beach Cities cab, yellow, with a surfboard painted on the side.

"Let me guess," the driver said into the backseat. He wore a patchy beard. "Birdwatcher."

"No, um…"

"Nah, I guess you don't have the look in your eyes. Ever since last year, I get birdwatchers at the airport, oh, three times out of four."

"I want to go to the post office in town," I said.

We rolled through the parking lot, hemmed in with palm trees.

"What happened last year?" I asked.

"What?"

"Last year with birdwatchers."

"Oh, those big ones started nesting at Pismo Beach! What, they're… black-footed albatross! Nesting up on the bluffs there. Buddy told me each one of their wings is nine feet long, and they're the only kind of albatross who nests in, like, this hemisphere. Whole bird's black but they call them black-*footed*! Whole thing's B.S."

"Huh," I said.

The airport was out on the flats, of course, but as we rolled into San Luis Obispo the pointed hills sprouted uniformly around us with the tree-lined town nestled between them like the city fathers had snapped their fingers and the landscape had obliged. Nature was malleable.

I shut my eyes and remembered what Alice had done to me two mornings before—I might have enjoyed it even more if I hadn't been tied up like a rodeo calf, but in hindsight it sure seemed like a glimpse of the blessed afterlife. Though now that I knew her slightly better, it made my half a brain a little sad that she hadn't climbed onto the table and put me inside her so we could've looked each other in the eyes. Or maybe she knew that Stage 4 zombies were still capable of getting girls pregnant—hell, if anyone knew that, it'd be Penzler's daughter, right?

Had she told me her dad had *deliberately* made Natalia a zombie?

A top heavy brunette in a halter top jogged across the street in front of us.

"Holy shit, look at that," the driver said. "You say you're from the Midwest so you might have never heard it, but two out of three boob jobs in America happen right here in California. That's fact, that's gospel."

That spirit of anatomical innovation had brought Natalia's doctors to this very spot. Cutting-edge treatments to keep single fathers and their social circles from gruesomely dissolving.

"It's not why I moved out here, myself, but it keeps me hanging around." The driver moved us gradually through the intersection while the girl leaned against a lamppost, stretching a sinewy leg. "All right, let's get moving—the post office, you say. There's more like her in the post office, even. I'm guessing you're unattached, am I right? Lucky man?"

"That's right," I said.

"No kids to feed either, I can always tell that."

A boy and girl ran along the sidewalk, backpacks bouncing. The little boy veered toward the curb but the sister grabbed his hand.

"Fuck you I don't have kids," I drawled.

I was too worn out to sound excited but my heart pounded with righteous anger.

The driver hunched his shoulders and squinted up at the rearview mirror.

"You want to piss people off, keep talking shit about their kids. Asshole."

"I said beg pardon, okay?"

WE PASSED BLOCKS of two-story houses with cedar shrubs and swing-sets. The driver started chewing spearmint gum. Stewing over my kids was not going to help, so I unfolded the telegram and flattened it against my leg.

MR K PENZLER

N'S PROGRESS LESS DRAMATIC THAN FIRST HOPED STOP
OTHER WORK WILDLY SUCCESSFUL WILL INCORPORATE
N IF YOU ADVISE STOP WILL TELEPHONE IMMEDIATELY
WHEN CELL TOWER REPAIRED STOP

DR Q DUFFY

Written by Alice on the back: PO Box 307, San Luis Obispo, Dalidio Drive.

"What's their names?" the driver asked.

I could picture who he was talking about but couldn't answer him just then.

"Thought we'd be there by now," I said. "How big is this town, anyway?"

"Post office's around the other side of the lake here. You mean the new one, right? Because the old one's downtown."

"Dalidio Drive."

"That's right. For sure."

"How busy are you going to be today?"

"Next flight in from LA's at eleven-thirty, then Phoenix, other than that it's hit and miss. Welfare bums buying groceries. You looking for work out here?"

"I'm going to wait for somebody to go to his post office box, then I'm going to see where he goes. I might wait five minutes, might wait two weeks. I've just been to the cash machine. You interested?"

"Here's a rent-a-car place with very reasonable rates."

WHILE I STOOD on the asphalt between silver rental cars, California turned hot as a stovetop even at eight in the morning. I *felt* heat, too, not like with cold. Sweat trickled out my ears and down my neck and I had to keep peering at it on my fingertips to make sure it *was* sweat, not some toxic compound that was government property.

"Mr. Giller?" said young Brian, his wide forehead freckling even as he trotted back out. "She says it's *not* impossible! If you could just get *access* to a credit card number, even if it wasn't your own, the cardholder could give us permission over the phone to use it as a deposit, then we could—"

"Do you use a post office box?" I asked.

"No, sir."

"How often do you go and check it, like every day?"

"If I had one, yeah, probably every day."

I could just watch the post office for a guy with a lab coat, a DRDUFFY vanity plate and a hysterical redhead in his passenger seat.

"What if you weren't expecting any mail?"

"Do you mind if we step inside? I think a drink of water'd be a good idea."

We walked across the shadow of the PAN-AMERICAN RENT-A-CAR sign—did that name make sense if I'd never heard of them anywhere else in America? Maybe I had and forgotten. Funny how the brain works. We each fall apart in our own time and in our own way.

While I sat outside the manager's closed door, the front-desk girl brought me glasses of water as quickly as I could drain them. Brian's voice was just a murmur but the manager seemed to be talking right in my ear.

"Fuck it," she finally said, "for a hundred cash he can take that piece of shit Fiesta, I seriously don't care. Tell him, I don't know, twenty a day."

I smelled something.

"What kind of sandwich is that?" I asked the girl behind the desk.

"Bacon breakfast burrito," she said, wiping her chin.

"Give it here."

I had to take my half out to the parking lot and watch while Brian and his clipboard inventoried the turquoise Ford Fiesta's pre-existing damage, and I was still sucking sublime, nitrite-rich mayo off my thumb when he finally hurried over to show me the fifteen Xs he'd made on the generic-car-body outline he'd been provided.

"Have some sympathy for the old girl, see what she's been through? Oh, and there's a car seat in the back, I'll take that out."

"How come?" I said. "You think I don't have kids?"

"I just thought…"

I handed over the stack of bills for my deposit, and sure I could've *bought* the car for five hundred but I didn't give a shit so long as it got me to the post office—but then he had to hash something else out with the manager and left me with a lot of forms to sign. Instead of initialing the box that waived third-party collision insurance I turned the sheet over and drew a human being's outline on the back of the sheet, then put an X over each place my bodywork had been gouged, going all the way back to the re-bar through my right shoulder. Thanks to Penzler my beautiful teacher-printing had gone to shit.

I imagined the day that I tracked my kids down and the two of them not being able to look at me or talk to me. I could put the drawing into their hands and they'd maybe have some notion of what I'd been through in order to be standing there.

Dear, I wrote at the top, then I had to stop and click the end of the pen a couple of times. My kids' names weren't exactly on the tip of my brain.

"I'll just need a photocopy of your driver's license." Brian wiped his palms on his pants.

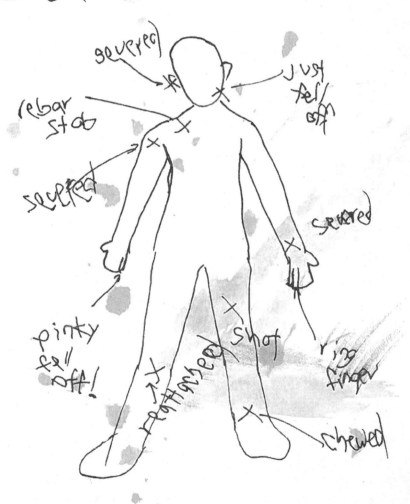

"I don't carry a photocopy of my driver's license."

"Ah, no. I can take your license and make a copy, no problem."

I ought to have used a secret identity on Travelocity—Lee Pert Girl, that was me. Lydia and I had made anagrams of each others' names while we'd shuffled around the maternity ward, waiting for her to dilate. Lee Pert Girl and Lily A. Gilder. Maybe we'd both died and been reincarnated as somebody else. Maybe she'd been in that burrito.

Our kids were *Josie* and *Ray*—screw you, hippie doctors, you hadn't done me in!

I waited in the Fiesta while the DRDUFFY car was probably backing up to the post office. My hair was sweating. I found napkins in the glove compartment to dry off my ears, then Brian swung into the passenger seat and solemnly handed the key across like it was insulin. The engine rattled to life like it had marbles in its fuel pump.

"Well, happy trails! Just give a call if you need it longer than the three days!"

"Hold it—show me how to get this air-conditioning on."

I STOPPED FOR three minutes at Miner's Hardware, then at 8:56 I finally pulled into the post office's parking lot and read on the door that they wouldn't open until nine-thirty. Grasshoppers loped across the hot parking lot. But it looked like anybody with a PO box could probably unlock the front door and check for mail inside the lobby, so I peered in the window on the left and didn't see any cameras. On that side the little steel boxes were numbered 1 to 160. I tried the right and there was lovely 307, right at the bottom near a potted palm.

I drove to 7-Eleven, used their toilet in the back and got to overhear two kids decide that *Awesome Dumps* would be an awesome magazine. Then I bought my bacon dogs and urine-flavored coffee, drove back to the post office and parked outside the front doors like a regular citizen.

I ate while I waited for nine-thirty. I prepared my brain to spend the day staring at 307's window—maybe all day, maybe into December if I could hold up structurally for that long. The Fiesta's turquoise hood shimmered in front of me.

A blue minivan pulled in and a mom and four kids in soccer gear piled out, and my heavy blood beat up in my throat as I watched them cut to the right then crouch down by the potted palm. But they were more in the neighborhood of 267. A kid in cleats slipped on the tiles.

A heavyset woman in a headscarf got mail out of 47 or 48. I watched her in the rearview mirror as she got back into her car and cranked up the Fleetwood Mac—then I sat up straight as a poker when I realized a red Acura had parked beside her. I hadn't seen it pull in. A dark-haired man in the driver's seat. California plate, but maybe Gary had had that all along?

A skeletal African-American in a blue USPS shirt unlocked the front door from the inside then disappeared back into the depths of the post office. I slipped out of the Fiesta and through the front door. The big lobby gate was already up. The USPS guy glanced at me, then went back to arranging the racks of bubblewrap envelopes. I gazed outside and watched the Acura driver put a leg out. A dark tracksuit. I slinked back behind the doorframe.

An Asian kid about seventeen, with horn-rimmed glasses. As he came across the parking lot he bounced a wad of keys in his hand.

I strode into the back of the post office and the USPS guy circled behind the counter.

"How are you this morning?" he asked.

"Just great. What about you?"

He nodded encouragingly.

"I was wondering," I said, "if you carry an express envelope or something where you actually *phone* the recipient and tell them to come get it."

"Well, if you sent it registered we'd take it right to the address and get the recipient's signature, then you see the signature right online. How's that sound?"

He didn't even blink as he talked. The postal service was an intense endeavor.

"I guess I better tell you the whole story, it's a weird scenario."

"Go right ahead. No hurry just now."

He gestured behind me—not even the Asian kid had come in yet. Flutter in my stomach, because where the hell had he gone?

"All right," I said, "well, my friend in Minneapolis gets his mail sent to a post office box there, I think it's the government post office right downtown—"

"Sure."

"And we met at a conference originally, had a bit to drink, you know, and said, hey, friends forever, let's keep in touch, so he scrawls

278 · ADAM LEWIS SCHROEDER

down his information and I get home afterward and all he's given me is the mailing address—no e-mail, no phone."

"I see."

"So I'm setting up a seminar out here now and I'm hoping he'll present, and I wrote him four times but I get nothing back. See, I don't think he checks the box! So if I send something, I don't know, *ultra*-registered, then probably the post office there has a phone number for his box, right, and they can let him know it's waiting for him?"

See? I'd make Dr. Q. Duffy come to *me*.

"I happen to know Eva Dixon at the Minneapolis office." The USPS guy blinked luxuriously. "We can make that happen."

"Ah," I said. "Great! I'll bring the letter and you can phone ahead for me, is that right?"

"We could do that."

"I would really appreciate it. But just for argument's sake, if you *didn't* know that particular girl—"

"She's just about ready to retire."

"All right, woman. Distinguished lady. Is there an envelope that'll do that just as a standard procedure?"

He shook his head minutely.

"Well, shit," I said.

I turned to go and slammed straight into the Asian kid, who was looking down at his iPhone. His glasses got knocked onto the floor. I was so baffled by my plan's not even starting that I couldn't even get mad at the kid—I picked up his glasses and iPhone, dusted off his shoulders.

"I'm fine now." The kid had that ragged pot-smoking voice so well-demonstrated at Hoover High.

"Sir," I said to the USPS guy, "I'm meeting my wife here. Can I just sit in the lobby for a few minutes?"

"Help yourself," he said flatly.

There were no chairs inside the front door, so I balanced against the edge of the big trash can while a well-dressed Hispanic couple emptied the contents of 215 into her handbag.

I shouldn't have told a lie that involved my wife, I should've said I had to wait for my brother because I'd never had a brother.

A flabby-shouldered guy in camouflage pants and a sleeveless black T-shirt hurried in, navigated around the 215 couple, knelt beside the potted palm and opened 307. A Domino's take-out menu. The guy had a red brush cut and triangular red goatee. The Hispanic couple said something and he smiled up at them.

My hands trembled. I glanced at my watch.

"Oh, man!" I whispered, as though time had really flown away from me.

I straightened up from the garbage can, slipped out the front door and had the Fiesta started six seconds later. The camouflage guy was throwing his menu in the recycling bin as I backed out of the spot, then even before he reached the outer door I was driving calmly and efficiently out the exit. The main thing was to stay inconspicuous. This was the start of a lucky streak and I was not going to break it.

I pulled into heavy traffic on Madonna Road, then drove behind the post office onto Dalidio and around the parking lot until I was at the intersection with Madonna, which would be the perfect spot to wait for him provided nobody pulled up behind me. I sat with my right signal flickering and peered over the gray-green yucca plants at Camouflage as he climbed into his vehicle—a black Jeep with no roof. He turned on bleeping techno music and slowly, slowly put on sunglasses.

A beige Ford Taurus stopped behind me so I switched to my left signal and made a big show of craning my neck one way and then the other so the driver would get the idea this might take ten minutes. If I pulled onto the shoulder, it was too likely Camouflage would notice my turquoise glory as he came out and so notice me five miles later and the mile after that. Thankfully I wouldn't be the only conspicuously crappy car driving around San Luis Obispo—a rusted-out Eagle Talon whizzed by and that gave me a lot of confidence.

The Taurus leaned on its horn, so I switched to signaling right and started to creep onto Madonna Road. The Taurus revved its engine four inches behind me. The Jeep thudded and beeped out of the exit and turned right onto Madonna, so I pulled out after him, calmly and efficiently, a hundred feet back.

Then two hundred feet, because he was driving so fast, then instead of turning at the next intersection he cut through a corner Pegasus station like a smart-ass. But I caught up at the crosswalk outside a seniors' center where an elderly woman in a sundress pushed her walker across, a smile surgically installed beneath her floppy hat.

A Central Coast Brewery truck slid between us before a red light, and the hair stood up on my arms—because maybe he only checked the box once a month, what would I do if I didn't see him turn off and he got away from me for good?—but then I turned down the air-conditioning and held my breath and realized that even over the rumble of the truck I could hear the *oonce-oonce-oonce* of his music. God bless the geeks in small rooms who manufactured the stuff.

With every coffee-flavored burp I drew closer to Natalia. She was going to look like Alice, only red-headed, and she'd also resemble Peter Giller, famous for his feathery scar tissue and perpetually dazed expression.

We rolled past farms where horses dozed under the palm trees, then up across hills covered in tall dead grass. It was a terrific road and I envied Camouflage's vestige of hair fluttering in the wind, but at least the Fiesta was keeping up. I kept a hundred yards back because every side road and driveway was dirt, so when he finally pulled off I knew there'd be a beautiful plume of dust. I decided I didn't much care if he caught a glimpse of me, because unless a driver's robbed a bank who really pays attention to whether they're being followed? Camouflage probably drove around thinking, *Hey, I'm helping out Dr. Duffy and he's helping out the world with science and if we get a kitty for the office I'll name him Bela Lugosi in the film White Zombie.*

He went out of sight over a hill topped with an ORGANIC TURKEY SAUSAGE sign, then as I came down the other side, I saw telltale dust rising to the right. I got down to an unmarked driveway and turned in after him as quickly as I could, thinking my dust might merge with his and no one would be the wiser. And if Penzler goons with knapweed stuck to their Kevlar pants stepped out in front of me, I'd ask, "Turkey sausage?" I turned into the driveway too fast, gravel spraying under me, and nearly fishtailed into the ditch.

Then for a quarter-mile I drove up the hill at twenty miles an hour until I came to a pair of closed steel gates, ten feet high. They weren't marked with a wrought-iron *QD* or anything at all. A ten-foot chain-link fence, topped with barbed wire loops, stretched out on either side. I sat in the idling Fiesta, watching through the gate as Camouflage's dust settled. The follicles crackled across my head. From my quest's pool-of-blood basement origin in Preston, Ohio, this was finally the place.

I DROVE BACK to the paved road and down the hill until I came to a stand of yellowish willow trees growing beside a black creek. It seemed like a reasonable place for people to leave their car if they were looking for frogs.

I opened the back of the Fiesta and lifted out the plastic Miner's Hardware bag containing my new hammer, wire cutters and big slot screwdriver. I hadn't thought to get myself a knife or a pistol. I'd have to be the weapon.

Hadn't thought to get a staple gun either. Some strategist.

I tucked the big rental car key into the exhaust pipe so I wouldn't have to worry about misplacing it. Nobody on the road in either direction, so I hopped the ditch into the crunchy knee-high grass and started cross-country for the fence. I still wore Carver's dark green dress shirt, so at least I couldn't have stood out as badly as if I'd still had that red shirt from Preston—this is what I thought as I jogged through the brush, bent low like a baboon with his plastic bag. The air smelled like freshly mown lawns and urinal cakes.

Just as I saw the fence at the top of the slope I tripped and fell on my face, jamming dirt between my front teeth. I looked around for somebody's mouth to punch and just saw the gopher hole. A horse would've broken its leg.

Gophers could mean rattlesnakes, that'd been the case at my grandpa's, so I put my sweat-filled ears on alert as I maintained my baboon lope. And I heard them in front of me, *chicka-chicka-chicka*. I crept up to the fence. Lines of rattling sprinklers stretched fifty yards up the lawn, and buildings with white walls and red roofs stared down at me—a two-story farmhouse surrounded by trees and flowerbeds, a three-car garage, square outbuildings. Camouflage's Jeep sat in front of the garage. No living thing moved, and it was impossible to hear a sound over the army of sprinklers.

I got to work with the wire cutters and wriggled through onto the wet grass. I leaned the triangle of wire back into place against the fence, then loped straight up the lawn for the apple trees below the house. No cover to speak of, and I kept waiting for a face to appear at an upstairs window and start hollering—or maybe a pale girl with red hair who'd silently set her fingers against the glass. But I saw nobody in any window.

I slid behind a tall bed of orange gerbera daisies. Lydia had loved those. Josie preferred cornflowers. I lay on my side and peered through the daisies—there was another stretch of lawn right below the house, maybe a basement door, but I'd have to stand on tiptoe to see. The garage and sheds were away to my right, opposite the house's front porch. I couldn't see the front door. I wiped at my dripping ear with the collar of my shirt and all of a sudden things went quiet. The sprinklers had been turned off, steel heads gurgling like their throats had been cut.

A *huh-huh* panting from somewhere. Maybe a generator in an outbuilding.

"Mikey?" someone called.

A lanky man with a gray ponytail stood on the porch, hands on his hips, facing out to the garage. He wore a pink-and-green tie-dyed T-shirt and I saw the edge of a salt-and-pepper beard.

"Mike?" he called again, his voice high.

"What?"

Camouflage Mike appeared from behind the garage, pushing a black plastic wheelbarrow with a pitchfork balanced across it.

"Where's all the fertilizer?" asked Tie-Dye. "I got salt licks, fine, we got the strawberries, but if—"

"Aw, shit, Doc." Mike put the wheelbarrow down and set his knuckles against the small of his back. "I totally forgot fertilizer."

"Well, go! This might be the last day!" Doc threw his hands up. "I've just got *dregs* in that bag and you know how she is if we don't do the smoothie by eleven!"

Mike nodded, head down, walking toward the Jeep.

"You only have to go as far as Fisher's," Doc called. "Where's Tyrone and Dean?"

"Doin' the straw!" Mike barked, swinging up into the driver's seat.

"How's George today?"

"You know how George is."

"He taking his feed?"

"Not so much."

Mike backed down the driveway in a cloud of dust and slammin' beats while Doc—Dr. Q. Duffy himself?—speed-walked off the porch toward the sheds. Unless they kept their straw in the living room, maybe that meant the house was empty of staff for the minute. There couldn't be a cook if the doctor himself was up to his ears in smoothies. A crow cawed up in one of the trees, once, then everything was quiet again.

I straightened up tall and looked over the daisies, then stepped backward as the hair stood up on my head.

Fifteen feet away, on the oval of lawn below the house, a large tawny animal lay on its side—its underside was toward me so I couldn't see whether its eyes were open or if it was aware of me at all. Its white tongue lolled, its side heaving so blades of grass bent back and forth with every breath. It looked like a full-grown lioness with a slack cow's udder stitched to its abdomen below its twin rows of nipples, its front legs draped under two enormously long black wings that'd been wired to its shoulder, while a pair of black testicles shifted between its back legs and the udder—steer testicles, maybe. I felt a percolating affection for the thing. That labored breathing reminded me of someone I couldn't put a face to. The wings lifted six inches to flap like they didn't have a care in the world.

I climbed over the daisies and onto the lawn. I knelt in front of the animal, fighting the compulsion to squeeze its big paw between my hands. Its eyes were silver, its teeth yellow, and thick as my thumbs, and its hot breath smelled like sawdust. What *didn't* smell like sawdust? Its new wings weren't just wings but lumps of black-feathered shoulder, too, sewn on with copper wire that bubbled with syrupy blood against its golden skin. I saw the telltale shaved patch back on its hip.

"Hello," I whispered to the creature.

Its brown whiskers quivered, once. Its breath collected like dew on my forehead, but the wings lifted again to briefly fan us. Had it crash-landed? No, even if they were nine feet long it wasn't possible that the two wings could've lifted it in the first place. *Four* wings—I could see two from its other shoulder, pressed beneath it. Clear fluid ran out of its ear and down its forehead. Even if I'd had bacon, the thing would've been too far gone to chew. Of the whole sorry mess, that deflated udder was really the most disgusting, and that's from the guy who'd cleaned out Patrick and Pimples' camper.

"You all right out here?" I whispered, and its whiskers flickered again. One paw moved a half-inch across the grass.

I sat up straight to see a bony guy, seven feet tall, ambling across my lawn from the direction of the porch. He was bare-chested, in overalls and gumboots, so maybe the place was staging *Of Mice and Men* in addition to its other fucked-up endeavors. He had small squinting eyes and the rest of his face could've been used to drive nails into concrete. He looked past me at the lion. Had moles all over his shoulders.

"*There* he is," the big guy muttered.

Kneeling beside me, he ruffled the chocolate-brown fur behind its ear. He glanced at the top of my head.

"Penzler sent me," I said.

"Oh," he murmured. "Sorry about this, I guess."

So I had some authority? I stood up—and even then his eyes were only a foot below mine—and folded my arms mightily.

"Are you Tyrone or Don?" I asked.

"Dean." He went on petting, flattening the thick folds of skin each time. The thing's breathing was turning into a continuous hiss, like the end of a record before the needle comes off. "I guess they didn't know anybody was coming."

"What's happened to it?" I asked.

"He's had all the chemicals and everything." Dean shrugged. "Did Dr. Duffy tell you how this happens every time? No matter what. See his grafts? They're all good. None of them work, but they're solid. Now I let him go around wherever he wants."

He gave the neck one final emphatic stroke then clambered to his feet, throwing his shadow over me.

"It's dumb, I mean, how's the balls going to work without a cock attached, right? He's done already and that's such a dumb combination! But I think the wings are pretty, I do, I do. Poor Hopper."

I craned my neck to look up at him, shading my eyes because of the sun breaking from behind his head.

"This isn't an extended visit," I announced. "Take me to Natalia."

Dean nodded, folded his arms around himself and started for the porch, his first two steps taking him eight feet. Then he looked back at me.

"Dr. Duffy should show you," he murmured. "He doesn't think she'll—"

"I don't have time. Mr. Penzler needs me to fly back tonight."

I strode up the grassy slope, stepped for a second onto the dirt driveway then turned onto the porch. A red painted bench ran the length of it, displaying the same big-eyed ceramic kitten Kirsten McAvoy had glued to the dash of her car. Conspiracy of inane shit.

"I'll get that screen door," Dean said. "The handle kind of sticks."

He tried it but the door just rattled, so he gave a yank and the hinges tore out of the wood. He glanced down at me.

"Crap," he said.

He leaned it against the bench and I followed him into the cool house, through a narrow foyer with a bighorn sheep's head on the wall, then down a dark corridor. A rectangle of light showed around a doorframe at the far end, maybe the kitchen, but Dean pivoted left and started up a staircase that twisted to the right every five or six steps. The house smelled sawdusty, but lemony like insect repellent too. On the third step it came to me: the slow-breathing lion was like my mom.

Upstairs was bright thanks to windows at either end of the hallway. Framed needlepoints on the walls showed rampant dragons and such, maybe a family crest. Dean led me across into the first room—the door stood open. The room was pale pink, its ceiling tilting down with the pitch of the roof, flowery dresses spilling out of the closet toward a single mattress smothered with magazines. A stony-faced model on the cover of *Allure*. Rose-tinted perfume floated in the air but it couldn't disguise a sawdust stench so strong it just about turned my stomach, even though the same smell was coming out of my armpits. I burped up a taste of hot dog and coffee.

"I forgot." Dean pressed one great hand against the ceiling. "They put her in the other room."

He wandered into the hallway and tried the next door down, which was a small yellow room containing a pull-chain ceiling light and a toilet. He shut the door, embarrassed.

"I don't come up here much," he said.

We went to the end of the hall where he wavered between closed white doors on either side.

"Why don't you yell her name?" I asked.

He looked down at me, eyes wide. "I sure don't want to wake her if she's sleeping!"

He swallowed hard, decisively, reached for the knob on the right. The door opened an inch and I saw a strip of navy-blue wallpaper.

"Okay." He jumped back. "You go in."

His cinder-block feet clumped down the stairs.

I could've stood there savoring the moment, my trail's hard-fought end, but I swung the door open with the flat of my hand. The room contained an ancient claw-foot bathtub, its enamel striated and yellow. The tub in turn contained a red-haired, white-faced girl, though I couldn't quite make out what she was doing. She looked up at me.

"Yeah?"

"Oh," I said. "Can I come in?"

"You're in, looks like. Did you forget the smoothie?"

"Uh, that might be another minute. Um…"

"Sit on the edge. That's what everybody does."

"You don't mind?"

She dropped her eyes. I perched my behind on the curved lip of the tub. There was no water. The girl's naked body filled the bottom as a shapeless mass, like her bones had dissolved, leaving her head propped at one end of a bag of freckled skin. Her hair, for what it's worth, looked thoroughly brushed.

"You new?" she asked.

"I don't work for Duffy," I said. "Your sister sent me to bring you home."

"Oh, finally." She blew a strand of hair out of her eyes. "Let me get my things and we'll hit the road."

I smiled at her. My jaw ached as though Dean had already hit me.

"She hoped maybe you'd be cured," I said.

"You're Alice's type, definitely. Did she move pretty fast with you?"

I nodded. She had at that.

"God, I love her," Natalia said.

"I don't want to pester you," I said, "but if they have anything *close* to a cure—"

"You see the horse they made me? They killed a lot of birds to make that horse. They worked on it a long time before I even got here, supposed to cheer me up."

"Did it?"

"Huh. I guess you haven't seen my horse. If you have to ask."

"I'll get them to show me."

"There used to be this transmitter tower up on the hill, did you know that? My horse flew into it."

"Flew?"

"I had a bad back for a long time. Like razors," she said. "Then I did such a *terrible* thing to Dad."

"What was that?"

"Our dad's very protective." She chewed her bottom lip. "Maybe Alice told you our mom had stomach cancer. She was outside the clinic in Columbus and got hit by a motorcycle."

"That's terrible."

She didn't answer. Her eyes had glazed over, but then her head suddenly gave a hop and she sucked in frantic breaths, one then another. After half a minute of that she shot me a bored look.

"Dad said if he'd been there he could've saved her life with this thing he was doing with his buddies, and Alice and I were like, 'What the fuck, Dad? You manufacture rubber boots.' That tanked. No Mom anymore, and Dad figured he was on such a roll, he was like, 'I've got this stuff right here, girl, so you never get that pain in your back ever again.'"

"And do you still have pain in your back?"

Her eyes darted down at the expanse of herself.

"No. Problem solved." She gazed up at me. "You better kiss me."

She did have a lovely face. Those brown eyelashes, the creases around her eyes like she'd grinned a lot in her time, her top lip a little upturned like it was *made* for kissing. But I didn't lean across. I looked at the enamel edge of the tub.

"You know Alice pretty well," she said.

"Yeah."

"So pretend I'm her, for Christ's sake. I remind you of her, right?"

"That's why I don't want to."

"Because of where I am?"

I hadn't flown from Nebraska to hurt the girl's feelings. But even so, I nodded.

"You don't want to picture Alice all melted down in a bathtub," she said.

"No."

"All right, mister, that's fair."

She was looking out the window, her green eyes open wide like she was studying hummingbirds and all the acrobatic things they could do. I could gleefully crush Carver's skull but I couldn't kiss this girl? Sure, I could.

I knelt on the floor, the tub's edge digging into my belly, leaned across and kissed her on the lips. They were soft as a Kleenex. I kissed her for about two seconds but she didn't kiss back. I opened my eyes. Her gaze was still on the window. No breath was coming out of her.

I put my hand on her cheek, rocked her back and forth. Her red hair swayed across her white skin, but she might've been moulded out of plastic. Natalia Penzler was dead.

I SAT ON my behind, laid my hands on the floor, and for a minute just studied her. It was easy to imagine that she'd *never* been alive, that the people-manufacturers had fouled up her components too much to ever bother plugging her in. One day I'd be looking out of a dry tub myself, wondering how such a pool of meat had ever been alive.

Every thought I'd had for the future dissipated because there was no cure.

My arms shook and I covered my face with my hands, and pinkish tears as thick as pancake batter trickled between my fingers. PBF, my kids, Styrofoam containers of bacon.

I sat up, gasping for air.

"Huh," I said.

Hairy feet in a pair of ragged Birkenstocks stood in the doorway. I closed my eyes and gulped back snot.

"Hello, Dr. Duffy," I murmured.

"Did she pass?" he calmly asked.

"Obviously."

A dumb teenage thing to say, sure.

"I *thought* it would be today," he said slowly. "I'm sorry I wasn't up here."

"What for?"

"To comfort her."

I sat up on the edge of the tub. Duffy was leaning an elbow against the doorframe, one foot cocked behind the other like he was posing in hunting garb with a pack of beagles.

"What's your name, sir?" he asked.

"Lee Pert Girl," I announced. "Peter Giller."

"'Giller.' Dean said that Penzler sent you. I've just phoned him and he can't—"

"Not the father. Alice."

"No, he told me *very* clearly that she didn't—"

"I'm here, aren't I?"

"But where's your vehicle? Who let you through the gate?"

"Walked up from the road. I'd been sitting in a car too long."

"And the gate?"

"It was open." I held up my palms, helpless to the fact. "I came on through."

"But what do you want here?"

"Alice Penzler wants me to bring back a cure."

He brought his elbow down and stared at me.

"But how are you here already?" he asked. "We only learned this morning that Alice was affected."

I stared at a diagonal scar that crossed his hairy knee. Sweet Alice in her T-shirt, a zombie. Thick blood simmered in my lips and I raised an eyebrow at him—that had always been my fail-safe for ninth-graders mouthing me off.

"That right?" I asked. "Are you usually the first to find out about anything?"

With his bottom lip he smoothed his moustache. Dropped his eyes to Natalia.

Something kept flickering across my peripheral vision like a fly buzzing in the room, but when I focused on a corner of the ceiling, where blue wallpaper rose to the white crown mouldings, there was nothing. I'd wasted the final days of my life like so much piss down a urinal. But I'd been a monster in Hoover, unable to so much as live with my kids. Piss down a urinal was what I deserved.

"Have you found anything remotely like a cure?" I asked.

"I have no clearance to tell Alice anything," Duffy said quietly. "And that connective tissue under your ears gives you more than a professional interest."

I raised a finger to feel down the edge of my jaw, but stopped. Duffy relaxed his posture, smiled his beardy smile.

"We never found any procedure that arrested the process completely. Radiation seeding had her back on her feet for almost a month, but that's prohibitively expensive, and who knows what it did to her cells long-term—look at her. Nobody else had degeneration like hers."

"Never thought to put her in a fridge?"

He raised his shaggy brows, eyes wide as petri dishes.

"Why would I?"

"Subjects in Nebraska preserved indefinitely," I said, though now every one of them was dead.

"And no ill effects, seriously, in a fridge? None of them died?"

"Sometimes yes and sometimes no. Wasn't the fridge's fault in any case."

"Lord a'mighty," said Duffy. "And all our subjects ended up—"

"Reminds me of when we were first going into space." I had to distract myself from PBF. "NASA says, 'Ballpoint pens won't write in zero gravity, we need a space-age pen,' we spend x-amount of money, meantime—"

"Russians used pencils," he said quietly. "I get it."

He walked across the room and leaned against the window sill.

Looked down at the lawn for a minute. I knew it was time to formulate spectacular plans but then my eyes fell on Natalia's waxy features, and vestiges of thought evaporated. Someone else I hadn't reached in time, like Franny.

"Oh, well," Duffy finally said. "Kirk's been having trouble thinking long-term."

"Kirk jumps through hoops," I said. "I know that. This is all your show. Penzler's just the means of production."

He rolled an eye back at me. "That's what you think, hey?"

"Everybody points to the hippie doctors in California."

"Hippie doctors."

"So where's the other one?"

"Ah, those gentleman in Velouria, that's who you talked to. They must've meant George. We have a minute before Dean comes up. Let me tell you a few things."

"Talk away." I noticed my left wrist—the filaments had nearly dissolved back into the skin. "I'm an empty vessel."

"Twenty-five years ago." He turned to the window, hairy knuckles folded behind him. "Twenty-five years ago, three guys got Chemistry degrees from Michigan, and the army paid for that, provided we were infantry medics every summer and for a couple of years after, so bright futures for all, mothers and fathers proud as peacocks."

I swallowed hard. "I want no one else to die from this crap."

"We don't want a *cure*, all right? We want a compound that works properly from day one! You see this?" He gripped the edge of the window and bent his knee so I could stare at his scar. "First year after college, Bush Senior takes us over to Iraq, and here's what I get. Friendly fire, too, but that's not the issue—after triage I had a ligament and three arteries still intact, and an artery is not load bearing, you understand? But Lieutenant Kirk Penzler, my buddy, had this *stuff* the Kuwaiti medics left with him before their unit withdrew, some Bedouin cure-all no one had heard of, a kind of *gum*, a sap, and it took eighteen months of chewing it before the bone and tendon had grown back, rolling my foot behind me on a little cart—and George, he got leave to sit around Kirk's house with us while I healed up."

"I've been in that house."

"Well, you couldn't have met Alice anyplace else. But George got bored, went back west so he could nail his high school girlfriend, but she kept him out there, got married, and what'd the girl do?"

"Probably dropped dead."

"Not your first rodeo, is it? Stroke at age thirty-four, just about kills our lad too, that messes George up but good. I've got my fellowship from UCSB, working on seed crops, so he comes out here in the summers, mixes one compound, spits in another, and this past July he and I cobble up this faster version of the Kuwaiti concoction, rich in omega-threes, gets pet odor out of furniture, and Kirk sends his little girl out here to try it on her to fix the kid's scoliosis. Ol' Kirk was scared spitless of her, I guess she'd gotten pretty rough with him—hard to picture."

Two blue-bottle flies had found their way onto her eyes, sipping away with their pseudotracheae. I waved them away.

"Then the other night ol' George drains the box of wine, passes out on the porch, wakes up with a kink in his neck, figures, 'Hey, it's all well and good for Kirk and his new pals, what good did our concoction ever do me?' Doses himself, fourteen times just to be sure. Good science, hey? No control subject at the dosage, does it all to *himself*. Kink in the neck. Dean'll take you out to the workshop in a second, you'll get a good look at George."

On cue, Dean bent under the doorframe to clump into the room.

"Hi, Dean," I said.

"Come look at this, Giller. See down there?"

I didn't budge, but Duffy pointed out the window as though I had.

"That animal lying there is named Hopper, you see her? Look at those wings. The pride of Pismo Beach colony."

"She's a him now," said Dean.

"You're entitled to your opinion."

"Why'd you treat the animal like that?" I asked.

"For the same reason that any field of medicine is pursued!" Turning, Duffy smiled slowly, gradually, as though he'd just figured out he was capable of it. "To answer the question, 'Exactly how much can this poor creature stand?' But I repeat, I don't answer to Alice on this. Not for ten seconds. And not even her dad talks to me like you've been doing."

His tone had changed like I had a spanking coming, and as the tiny hairs inside my ears detected the switch, I felt like I was already taller, though I was still sitting down, and my fingers curled into hard little animals, and the muscles in my neck turned hydraulic so I could head-butt the top off a guy's skull, and neither of them even noticed.

"That lion has a sister." Now with every word Duffy jabbed a finger down at the floorboards, like the soapbox hippie he was, every syllable *political* and *important*. "A *twin* sister, and her grafts have been much less debilitating. Dean'll take you down to her. Between the two of them, sir, you can consider yourself cured. Your problems, sir, are behind you."

"*His* name's Whistler," said Dean. "That other lion."

With hands the size of hubcaps he picked me up around the shoulders, which brought my forehead level with his nose. His armpits smelled of tangy human b.o. I bunched every iota of pink goop into the back of my neck, let it compress there while Dean went on talking.

"If we can," Dean told me quietly, "we'll—"

I launched my forehead through the bridge of his nose. His hands opened and I dropped to the floor, and he would've fallen flat on his back except the wall got in his way, and with a new hole in his face he wound up sitting down cross-eyed while the whites of his eyes filled with blood. I got up and faced the doctor, who stood with his hands spread on the wall, his back against the bright rectangle of window. My lips pulled back from my teeth like I was a saber-toothed tiger, though my main thing was still to stay inconspicuous. As I came closer he wheezed. I hadn't had any kind of fight since Pimples and Patrick Pig the day before, and my system wasn't engineered for such a long intermission.

"Think," Duffy finally stammered. "If your intent—"

I threw myself around his swirling pink-and-green middle and drove us out through the glass. I squinted against the violent sunlight at the oval of lawn stretching under us. We flipped once in the air, then I made sure my shoulder was against Duffy's sternum—in the name of medicine we'd see exactly how much impact he could stand. We'd come down in the middle of the lion. Some open-mouthed guy in a blue plaid shirt cast a shadow. The smell of grass wafted up.

After we hit I must've blacked out for one second, then I was peering at the yellowy dominoes of Duffy's spine. One of his shattered ribs was jammed against my elbow but I wiggled it loose and sat up with the sawdust reek of the lion dripping from my ears. Hopper's shaved hip rose to my right and her ragged shoulder on my left, but her middle had dissolved so it was like I'd pushed Duffy into a kiddie pool of yogurt. The doctor's eyes gazed up at me, though blood had burst from every opening in his face. I didn't even think that was gross. It was just science.

The sheep-faced guy stood framed against the white wall of the farmhouse. He held a blue syringe.

"I was trying to bring her temperature down," he said.

"This dumbass said there wasn't any cure." I staggered to my feet, shaking yogurty goop off my arms. "But that's not right, is it?"

He swallowed with his big Adam's apple. "There's no cure," he said.

I bunched up a yogurty fist. He dropped the syringe, and I was only a step from him when a wasp stung me familiarly on the side of the neck. I had to drop to one knee. I looked at the sheep guy but there were stars all around the periphery.

I saw Camouflage Mike bring a rifle down from his shoulder up on the driveway. A-ha, I said to myself: Good Old Tranquilizers (A Penzler Company).

I had to stay on one knee while Mike rolled his wheelbarrow across the lawn. At least I wasn't looking at Hopper and Duffy, I was sick to hell of those two. My shoulder-bone throbbed from its minor fall.

"You sure one's enough?" asked the syringe guy.

"You tell me, Tyrone."

Mike picked me up under the armpits, then Tyrone got my ankles and they floated me into the wheelbarrow. My arms and legs draped over its sides but otherwise I just melted into the bottom like it was a bathtub.

"Why not kill him?" Tyrone was suddenly ballsy.

Colleen, I thought, *Harv*. Luke Skywalker dangling from Cloud City. *Help*.

"What are we here for in the first place, baby?" Mike lifted the handles and I rolled across the lawn. "See what makes the fucker tick, right? Exploratory surgery."

"Jesus, but look at Doctor—"

"What would the doctor say if he was standing here, hey?"

"He'd say," Tyrone admitted, "'Get the heck back to it.'"

As we started up the slope my hands dragged across the grass. I tried to waggle my fingers, and they *did* waggle. Thirty more seconds and I'd be ripping some nuts off.

"And what else?" hissed Mike.

"He'd say, 'Call no one in authority until every invoice has been filed.'"

"Zigactly."

Mike pushed me onto the driveway. I saw his rifle propped against the bench on the porch between the broken screen door and ceramic cat.

"What about Hopper?" Tyrone asked.

"Thas one more chore for Dean," said Mike.

He rolled me toward the garage, and I tried baring my teeth. And did bare them. But then the wheelbarrow was set down.

"Just grab that gun," Mike said behind me. "Can't hurt to give him one more."

I WOKE UP in a fetal position with red bungee cords tight around my wrists. I was hyperventilating, so I slowed that down, took some deep breaths. Seemed that I was inside a long plastic case like delis use to display sausage rolls. Man, was anything better than a nice fresh sausage roll, if the sausage was nice and peppery, and the flakes of pastry melted like butter on your tongue? My mouth filled up with drool.

It's possible my head wasn't quite in the game.

I gulped back that spit, because maybe it held all the nitrites available to me. I pulled my knees toward my face, and saw my ankles were tied up too. The case was too shallow for me to even turn over, but I twisted my neck and saw cages and tanks around me, and a big blue tarp that was the ceiling. I took another deep breath, guessed that there was only about three cups of air left in there, and wondered if any other past visitor to Dickside Synthetics had been permitted as much pure enjoyment as I had.

Dear Josie & Ray,

You can ignore the letter that shows all the chunks I've had taken off me, because that was a downer. Instead let's look on the positive side with an inventory of my even-less-fortunate stablemates:

1. *In the terrarium across from me, a tabby cat with what looks like a salmon for his back half. His tail's splashing the greenish water while his poor wet paws cling to the sand. Panting like he just ran two hundred miles, he*

stares at some spot out ahead of him.

2.   *A bunch of foot-long squid zipping around the tank under him. Might not be anything weird about them but it's more likely they've switched brains with the architects of the Third Reich.*

3.   *Whistler. A lioness/lion pacing in a square cage, lapping her/his water, sniffing the air, acting like any lion does in a zoo when it's not passed-out asleep. I've watched her/him two minutes, and three times the half-dozen black wings she/he has sticking out of either shoulder sprang up all at once and flapped without any synchronization but with enough lift to pull Whistler three feet in the air before dumping her/him onto a trash can of dog food. Whistler has the same black balls as another lion, Hopper, but not the udder, thank god, and without that udder it seems Whistler is thriving.*

4.   *Some kind of big green snake, twisted back and forth all over itself. Maybe it's six snakes.*

5.   *A large caramel-brown sea lion, twisting and turning in the tank of water beside the squid's, and the tank must be a good size, kids, because half the time he disappears back into the murk. If there's something called* Bacon of the Sea *he's getting plenty.*

6.   *A black-and-white calf and a black chimp, both seemingly intact, in a cage right against my deli case. I have to twist my head almost backwards to see them, but their shaved hips are clear enough. The calf lies on its side next to a scattering of hay, its head sometimes up and sometimes down, and the monkey scampers up and down its carpeted Wal-Mart cat tree, throwing poop at the calf and sometimes swinging off to stand and pat the calf's head or sit abjectly on its hip while it sleeps. But then the calf springs to its feet like it's been electrocuted, and the chimp darts for its tree but isn't quick enough. The calf whacks him with the top of its little head so the monkey flies six feet and clangs its teeth against the bars. The calf shrieks like an air-raid siren. The air feels thin in here.*

Hope it cheers you up to never receive this horrible
letter written inside my head,
Dad.

Mike ran up, gumboots flapping against his shins, and put his hand between the bars into the calf's cage. It licked red powder out of his palm then slid onto its front knees. Mike whistled, wagging his sharp little beard, and the monkey came out from behind its tree to creep toward him.

"Hey, man!" I yelled, thumping my bound feet against the top of the deli case. "What the hell?"

"Shut up, zombie dipshit," he said. "Wait your turn."

"You too big a pussy to just chop my head off, is that it?"

I was a strategic genius. I was goading him into opening the case. He crouched in front of me, rapped a knuckle against the plexiglass.

"Can't get out, hey?" His tattooed forearm read IT'S CLOBBERIN' TIME! "We found Dean upstairs, ya see, and Dean was like the little brother, and we're so *happy* right now that we're moving up your schedule, good, right? What's not good is that Tyrone's not much of a surgeon. Doc gave him a chance a couple times but, God, it got gross. Hold on."

He moved to the left to crouch beside the cat-salmon, its paws thrashing the sand while its tail dragged it further into the water.

"See the Cat from Atlantis? Isn't he pretty, hey?"

"How long until I fight the lion?"

"Whistler? She's a *griffin*."

"A griffin's half-lion and half-eagle."

"Yeah, body mass was incompatible for that."

"Let me go home," I said.

Which didn't sound tough at all.

"This is all going to be big, man, you're on the fucking cusp—think of the military applications for the shit! Baboons flying around with machine guns! We'd kick Congo's ass! And look who's here! Ol' Roger!"

The sea lion pressed his whiskers against the glass then darted off into the murk.

"That's going to be *you*—your back end, anyway." Mike straightened up and twisted his hips to crack some vertebrae. "Then you'll be able to sit out on the rocks and call to sailors, you lucky dipshit. Suck some Filipino cock."

"Prep me, nurse. I can't wait."

"Har, har."

"Zombies don't float, either. Watch and learn."

He walked off behind the tanks. I could hear him muttering.

"Really?" another man shouted. Distorted somehow. "Let me—"

Then quiet.

Mike reappeared carrying a slab of ham and threw it between the bars to Whistler, but instead of gobbling it down she put a paw on it and looked over at me. Her wings shivered. Mike knelt in front of me.

"How long since you had bacon, zombie?"

"A zombie eat brains, and I don't eat brains," I said. "Bring me some bacon."

"Or to quit being a zombie maybe you *ought* to eat some brains, you ever think of that? Paradoxical reasoning like that might've got you out of this, but instead you get to be the first zombie mermaid to suck a Filipino cock."

"Yum," I said.

"Think I'm kidding? Roger's got more compound in him than any animal here, he pisses the stuff, and you know how a piece of a zombie falls off, zombie snaps it back on like Lego, right? Your arms've got more scars than Frankenstein, man, so you know what I'm saying. The FBI figured that out for us, Christ knows how."

"LRA detainees."

"Amen to that!" Mike stroked his little beard. "The doc figured out it worked for other species, too, so Penzler wrote him a blank check, then Doc got the idea that if *two* species fell apart you could put them back together wrong and it would *still* work, so Penzler wrote him an even *blanker* check."

"What in hell for?"

"Make his daughter happy."

"She said the horse didn't come out right."

"Shit, you're not wrong. You think that's ham the griffin's eating?"

Though the lion wasn't eating her meat. She'd laid down beside it.

"Get your jaw nice and loose," Mike grinned, and ambled off behind the tanks.

The Cat from Atlantis stretched on the sand, its shimmering tail raising dust. The snake slept. The chimp dangled from his tree by one hand, his dart-shaped penis gripped in the other. My nearest ally. The tarp flapped over us, sounding like distant helicopters.

It'd been a mistake to do this last stretch on my own. If I'd had the brains to bring Amber she'd be breaking Mike's head open with her good right arm; Franny would say, "Buck up, G, you're in sunny California and you're not even dead, and what're the odds you'd still be alive dressed like that? And this feels like a really special time in our lives, et cetera," even though those two were young girls who were dead now.

Colleen would've watched, wrinkle-cheeked, and waited for me to get on with it.

Lydia? My Lydia would tear my prison to pieces, lift me on her mighty shoulders and carry me off to the burst of white light she'd been inhabiting, six long months for me but still just a heartbeat for her. She could crush my fingers in hers as I kissed her brown neck and we told each other how lucky we'd been and ever would be.

Josie and Ray? There was no way I could spin that. I'd tell them run, get out of here on your mosquito-bitten legs, hold tight to your pretty lives.

"Right, right, right," Mike was saying. "Here's your big chance!"

I heard a rumble, something rolling across cement, then Mike pushed in some kind of aquarium on a cart, a round shape inside it—maybe a puffer fish. He plugged a dangling cord into a power bar and the tank immediately filled with bubbles and light.

"Fine, good!" Mike stomped out of view. "So socialize!"

The tank contained a man's head. It bobbed toward the surface then descended, smiling at me from behind the clear plastic mask it wore over its mouth and nose. A hose connected it to a tank strapped to the leg of the cart. Smiling. I'd seen roughly the same thing at Carver's, sure, but I retched a little anyway.

"Hey, hey, you know why I'm happy? This is Sprite!" the head grinned. "Get a sugar high right through my pores! Warm as spit."

A plastic G.I. Joe walkie-talkie lay on a towel in front of the tank, its talk button taped down. He was familiar as hell. Not the voice but the rest of the package.

"So," rasped the walkie-talkie, "maybe you're the shy type?"

Holy god. My feet shook involuntarily. *It's George Reid.*

All forehead and beard, my floating head of the Hoover High corridor. The George of Duffy's story. Twenty-five years he'd worked hand and glove with Penzler, then during his absence he'd mysteriously sent his class to Dockside? Where a pipe had coincidentally burst?

"Okay," he said, "I've been in here since the weekend—how'd the World Series turn out? I hear every molecular detail of the workings of Penzler Industries, but I don't hear shit about the World Series!"

"Last Monday the Red Sox tied it two all."

"Speak up!"

I repeated myself.

"Screw the Red Sox!" he yelled. "Fuck them, did St. Louis take it?"

He started to cough and bubbles filled the tank. The chimp watched him and hopped up and down at the bars, then ran a lap around the cage and mounted the calf from behind.

The Sprite became less turbid. George Reid got his breath back. He gazed at me without the trouble of having to blink.

"That was a bad start," he said. "What's your name, kid?"

"Peter Giller!" I yelled.

"You shit me. The substitute?"

"Yes!"

"How the hell'd you get here?"

How much story did he want?

"You splashed us with that pink crap on purpose. You just wanted to see what'd happen, that was why?"

"Yes, wasn't that great? Arm's-length study of your progress!" He bumped against the front of the tank. "Jones is keeping an eye on all of you, how's that going?"

"He chased us out of Hoover, now everybody's dead but me."

"Ah. Shit. That'll compromise the findings. I heard the FBI might sniff around, nosy customers. He must've had to disperse you."

"But why'd you do it to us?"

"You don't fool me, Peter Giller." He bobbed up six inches. "I had those kids for three years. They're vicious fuckers."

"Franny Halliday is a vicious fucker?" I yelled. "Harv—"

I couldn't get his name out.

"Jordie, Todd, Devon," he said. "That's who I'm talking about."

"Jordie, Todd, Devon didn't go *on* the field trip!"

"Not likely, they went. I'm changing what *needed* changing." A stream of bubbles came out his ear, and he settled in the back corner. "We set up geothermal science fair displays at the retirement home. And what? They pull the fire alarm. Deserve what they're getting."

"Sure. Sounds completely fair."

"Peter Giller, wait. Why'd you tell me you got splashed with pink crap?"

"Because that's what, I don't know—*infected* us! Pipe #9 broke open, and all the guys who—"

"What Pipe #9?" George smiled through the oxygen mask. "It was hot dogs."

"What?"

"You got served a free lunch, am I right? You must have, or you wouldn't be here. Peter Giller, there is *no such thing* as a free lunch. *And* they splashed you with crap? That's too crazy! That was emulsifier for Pink Pearl erasers or something."

I stared at the fish-cat. My pan of thought had been spilled on the floor.

"You never knew it was the hot dogs?" George went on smiling. "The concoction is this sawdust kind of stuff, right? Unless they're on a feeding tube you've got to make a subject sit and eat it, that's what I did myself—but sawdust in a hot dog, who'd notice? They're phone books and anuses at the best of times, but so delicious, right?"

"They said guys with beards set up the pipes. It had to be that pink stuff."

"That might've been Duffy, sure, last spring they had him in Velouria for new garbage bags—fifty percent less groundwater pollution, he's entirely eco-friendly."

"I ate the veggie dog," I said.

"Veggie, anus, they were one and the same. Get us as wide a sample as possible—they even gobbled that shit up at the company picnic!" He sat flush with the glass so his eyes magnified until he looked like Japanese animation. "We share a passion for education, Peter Giller, so glean one lesson from this," the walkie-talkie rasped. "Never eat a government wiener."

"Tell me how to get out of this box."

"*Je ne sais pas.* I don't like to ponder arms and legs."

So what next? I banged my fists and feet against the deli case, the back of my head too, then I made a high-pitched whine from behind my back teeth. Not sure what inspired that but it got the lion and the calf to their feet. What other resources did I have?

"Hey, shut up, shut up!" George yelled. "You bother everybody!"

My eyes watered to go with the juice trickling out my ears. The monkey was throwing anything he could get his hands on, going apeshit—I saw where the term had come from. Whistler's wings kept flinging her into the air in bursts, her butt banging against the barred ceiling. Roger the sea lion pressed his face to the glass and, Jesus, he had fangs to gnaw your head off.

"Quit it, dipshit!"

Mike ran in with his hands over his ears, circling the deli case and then behind me so I couldn't see what he was doing. A *clack* behind me and suddenly I had air again, then I got pulled up by the shoulders. The chimp screamed at us.

"Now," Mike choked, "I got ten CCs to—"

But I didn't wait for a shot, I kept rolling backwards and the case toppled so I landed on my ass in the wheelbarrow. Guess it'd been there all along. Mike drove his elbow down into my eye, a syringe flashing in his free hand, but I brought both feet up and kicked him in the back of the head. The syringe fell in the wheelbarrow and blood trickled out his ear. And you know what? I was *still* making that aggravating noise.

He grabbed my hair and punched me in the face again and again, and that was great because it meant I was really in a fight. I could have stretched out, enjoying the sparks behind my eyes and the pain in my front teeth, but eventually I had to make my way home so I could tell Josie and Ray that officially I was an insoluble problem, that if they wanted Dad around he'd just keep smashing furniture until his arms dropped off and they'd have to bury him in shoeboxes. It was my duty to do that.

So I opened my eyes as the next fist came down, grabbed it between my two tied hands and wrenched Mike's arm so a splintered bone broke out of the skin above his wrist, like a wiener breaking through a bun. Compound fracture, that's called—that'd happened to Scotty Barnes, some poor kid who was dead thanks to assholes who figured we deserved what'd happened to us only because it *had* happened to us.

Mike's face went blue as he gaped at his arm, and at that point all I could do was kill him. That was the corner he'd painted himself into when he'd said that I'd be a mermaid.

I rolled out of the wheelbarrow and quit my keening, but the animals were still shitting themselves. Now I had the mobility to reach down and unhook the bungee cords from my ankles. Mike staggered back, stumbling over Styrofoam coolers into the mound of green netting beside the lion cage, then he reached his good hand into his shorts pocket and brought out a tiny black gun. I kicked him in the belly, and he shot the leg I was standing on but that didn't even make me fall down. Must've been his gun for shooting girl scouts.

"Hey!" George bubbled at us. "Hey!"

Mike vomited a mouthful of what looked like lasagna onto his shorts. I kicked him in the elbow and the gun flew up and plopped into George's tank of Sprite. Came to rest with its barrel against his ear.

"Here," I said. "Take these off me."

Mike leaned back against the lion's cage, cradling his broken arm in his lap.

"I can't, I *can't*," he said.

"If you were a zombie you'd be doing fine right now, know that?"

"I *know*."

"Unhook the cords and I'll go away."

Without looking up he put his good hand on the bungees, and with one twist they let go. I shook feeling into my arms. I flexed my steel-crushing fingers and looked at him. He sniffed hard up his nose. Looked like the broken arm might kill him.

"Go away now," he said. "That was our deal."

Whistler shoved her muzzle between the bars and sank her teeth into Mike's neck—he must've been oozing bacon! He just slumped against her blood-frothy jaws, his eyes very wide. She held him like that, sighing out her flat black nostrils.

"Peter Giller! Jesus Christ, Peter Giller." George panted behind his mask—he'd have had his head between his knees if he'd had a body. "Peter Giller, Jesus Christ."

"What?"

"Take me with you!" He floated sideways and the pistol sank to the gravel. "See, there *is* a cure! Nobody knows but Kirk and me, and if you—"

I pulled the tape off the talk button. He floated backwards, mouth still flapping.

Now did the animals want me to blow them all to smithereens? I didn't have the brains to engineer that. I kicked in Whistler's lock so her door swung open, but she was too occupied with the tendons in Mike's neck to look up. I staggered down the aisle toward the exit and gave the calf-and-chimp's door an almighty kick too. The calf still looked stoned but the chimp shot out, vaulting along on his front paws and screaming. The aisle ended in a white metal door, swinging open as Tyrone stepped out, dressed in a hairnet and green surgical gown. He was pulling on latex gloves.

He asked, "Is something—?"

The chimp climbed the gown and drove his dirty monkey fangs through Tyrone's top lip—the tableau might've looked charming if it hadn't been for Tyrone's flailing hands and the spurting blood. They crashed into a rack of extension cords.

So as usual that left me to mop up. The room Tyrone had come out of was full of steel tables and fridges and freezers. Drains in the floor. And a sewing machine.

I circled the room, scrutinizing each shelf, my every finger a weapon to crush wisdom teeth to powder. At knee level I saw jars labeled FORMALIN, jars of Vaseline crowded on a table, and behind glass doors up at eye level sat copper canisters inscribed TEA and COFFEE and SUGAR, though they also had masking tape stuck across each that read DESERT STORM, D.S. 2 and D.S. 3, respectively. I took down number three. Inside were brownish-pink iron filings that smelled like a fresh-cut Christmas tree.

I put it under my arm. It wasn't the cure, as Duffy had said, just the opposite, but since I'd met that first lion I'd been running a train of thought about one particular thing.

Another door took me into a musty garage crowded with lawnmowers and tomato cages, and the next door onto the dusty driveway beside Mike's Jeep. Keys dangled in the ignition. Swallows chased each other from the garage's eaves to away up over the house.

ONE OF THE keys on the ring might've unlocked the black steel gates but I crashed through them at eighty miles an hour, crumpling the Jeep's hood like wrapping paper, then as I got to the road, I jumped out and let it roll across into the ditch. I walked D.S. 3 down to my turquoise Fiesta, dug the keys out of the exhaust pipe and drove back toward the house. I still had to perform certain tasks for my employer back in Preston. Only static on the radio but to me it sounded good. Maybe it *was* better to be alone at this late date in my dissolution because that left no one to complain.

I hustled back into the room full of cages. No sign of Tyrone or the chimp, though a trail of blood zigzagged behind a stack of pallets. The calf was gone. Whistler was still pressed against the bars of her cage, paws wrapped around Mike's neck while she patiently gnawed the skin off the top of his head. I picked up one of the Styrofoam coolers and turned to see George Reid staring at me through the bubbles, the hairs of his beard swaying like kelp, letting me make my own mind up.

So I showed him my best school-picture grin and walked out, still tasting the blood between my back teeth from those punches I'd taken. I wasn't going to unplug him, not after all the wondrous things he'd done for me.

I filled the cooler with operating-room ice, then carried it into the cool farmhouse and up the dark stairs. I stepped over Dean's sprawled legs. If Natalia had raised her green eyes then I *would* have kissed her, definitely, but she was cold as key lime pie.

I cupped her bottom jaw in my hands, the skin soft as daffodils, and steadily lifted her head away from the rest of her—I couldn't think of the contents of that bathtub as *her body* exactly. I heard a slurp like a plunger in a toilet as the head came away, trailing a foot and a half of spine. A previously undiscovered jellyfish. Maybe it'd inspire Kirk Penzler to tell me anything about D.S. 3 that I hadn't heard.

I lowered Natalia into the cooler. A lot had happened in the time we'd been apart and I couldn't expect Alice to just take my word for any of it.

Wednesday, November 2.

"GO NORTH AT Schafer," I said again and again. "Dirt road behind the dairy."

Otherwise I'd forget. Carver had said "C-A-M-P," that meant one specific place, and if I didn't keep reminding myself I'd forget where it was. I muttered while the country turned black outside the car, green light across my hands from the staticky radio. I kept catching myself licking the steering wheel. As the sun had risen pink over Utah I'd known the dairy's exact name, I'd written it down, but now I was trying to remember if there was really a dairy at all. Drool on my hands. The left-hand wiper had flown away into the night, and in the thick of the snowstorm the Fiesta felt like a one-window igloo sliding sideways down Interstate 70. I kept the heat off so I wouldn't have to put fresh ice in Natalia's cooler.

I thought about Colleen a little bit, and the shirt she'd worn in the sauna, and that tattoo around her thigh, and Deb in her muumuu. I hated them both.

"Dirt road behind the dairy," I instructed the gas gauge.

Farmhouses went by in the dark, whole towns, and every cluster of lights seemed like fishing boats out on the Gulf of Mexico, where I'd never been, but I told myself I was a fishing boat too. The signs all said KANSAS. I couldn't go north yet—no Nebraska until everything was done. A big tall sign like a red coffee pot, SAPP BROS. FOOD & FUEL, winked at the edge of the highway.

The wind howled between my shaky hands and the gas pumps. Lydia hovered over my shoulder. Alice floated right between my eyes, mouth open to say something.

This Sapp Bros. location also had the $6.99 Hotbar. I heaped up my third plate of bacon, stumbled over the edge of the carpet then sat and tried to draw my secret escape map on the takeout menu.

"Crap," I said to the next table. "Do you guys have a pen that works?"

"Sure," said the curly-headed woman, digging in her purse.

The guy wore a Donald Duck sweatshirt.

"Is that the Atkins Diet?" he asked.

"Yeah," I said slowly. "I have never felt better."

"Oh, it's a *red* pen," the woman said. "Hope that's okay."

I sat working on the map, tongue poking out of the side of my mouth.

"Do you guys know Dundy County?"

"Nebraska?" asked the woman.

"Is there a road that takes you from Palmerston into Schafer, or do you have to go up into Athens then down?"

"Don't know." The man tilted the salt shaker. "The only Dundy County route we've taken was 34, I guess, through Benkelman on the way to North Platte."

"They've got maps up behind the counter," the woman suggested.

"Are you guys truckers?"

"Yessir," she said.

"All the time together?"

He nodded, still salting his eggs.

"Is that really great, just the two of you?" I asked. "It sounds really great to me."

They looked at each other, poker-faced, then he swung his gaze back to me.

"She farts."

"It's a survival mechanism," she said.

Then with her spoon she put a dollop of sour cream on his forehead. He tickled her down her back and when he got to the bottom she let out a whoop. I would've traded places with either of them.

I ate bacon by the fistful, seven, eight pieces at a time. More nitrite than man. I studied what I'd drawn: two intersecting lines with the word "Athens" at the top. Was it a map of Greece? I glanced at the couple at the next table as she watched him eat his eggs. They both seemed familiar, and I had an idea they might be truckers.

"Hey there," I said, nodding.

They looked up at me.

"Crap," the guy said as he swallowed. "Jeez."

"Your *ear*." Her hand went up to her own.

I felt a tingling up either side of my head.

"Excuse me."

I put down my napkin and slipped up from the table. A lot of people stopped their conversations as I walked to the bathroom, and one woman—though stouter than that mom in Lincoln Airport—covered her daughter's eyes with a sari.

The men's room was thick with the spicy smell pee gets when guys drink too much coffee. Clean-shaven truckers stood at the urinals. I leaned between the sinks and in the mirror saw my left ear flapping against the side of my neck, attached just at the lobe. I waggled my head and watched it sway—a dangly earring above my collar. I gave my right ear a little tug to see if *it* was okay, at least, and it came off in my hand with a sound like biting into an apple. I looked at it there in my hand, its ragged edge wet under the fluourescents.

"This is such bullshit," I announced.

I looked into the mirror again to check my left ear but it was gone too, so at that point I had *no* ears. My hair stuck up all over but otherwise my head looked slick as a seal's, aerodynamic.

"Whoosh," I said into the mirror.

The guy beside me at the counter coughed and spat up, calling over his shoulder to his buddy, and I saw that my left ear had fallen into my own white sink. I'd had a good long run by the standard of any zombie, but I'd finally come to that stage where no amount of bacon or stapling will help. The two guys ran out of the bathroom while I wrapped my ears in a brown paper towel and dropped them past the chrome trash can's swinging lid.

The snow pelted down in chunks like calcium nitrate. I backed the turquoise Fiesta onto the highway and pointed it east, my fingers light on the wheel—I'd been living off anger for the longest time but I didn't feel the least bit angry anymore. That was the sad part.

Thursday, November 3.

I'D REMEMBERED THE name Hutchens Road, but I didn't remember McCauley until I saw it forking away to the left under the bare trees. The sky looked like cigarette ash. Everything looked different under all that new snow.

I thought the house would be a half-mile down the road but I came to it after fifty feet. I got out and stood beside the Fiesta, looking at the silent house and fingering the car key in my pocket like I was hoping to take a girl out for the first time and was nervous about meeting her father. If Alice was already dead I'd talk to Kirk Penzler without an intermediary.

I lifted the cooler off the back seat, pushed the Penzlers' gate open and crunched up the path. In the snow everything was silent—dogs barked somewhere behind the house but they might as well have been in another state. I hadn't slept since the plane to San Luis Obispo. I hadn't slept in a *bed* since my nap at the Lamplighter. I couldn't feel my legs though I saw them moving under me.

Flakes of snow blew off the branches and I caught one on my tongue.

It's funny to be dying at the hands of your own body. As everything slowly quits there must be some gland that purrs away so you say, "Well, all right, I guess this is okay." If a goon in a black gas mask had wrapped his hands around my throat I'd never have quit kicking and shoving thumbs into his eyes, but since my body had decided to disintegrate of its own volition I could only smile knowingly like it was a child falling asleep. My kids would be all right, sure. That blond girl waiting inside the house would be all right, and Colleen would be fine wherever she was. None of them really needed me. Good, said my body. Rest a minute.

I sat on Penzler's front step with my arms wrapped around my knees.

How long had I been there? My brain was evaporating, just like somebody had told me it would. We each fall apart in our own time and in our own way. I brushed the snow from my behind, picked the cooler up by its wire handle and pushed the bell. A tinny clang beyond the door.

While I waited, I pushed snow off the wrought-iron railing with my fingertip. I remembered: *Cam Vincent.* He was the one who'd said that a zombie would never notice its brain rotting but he'd been wrong, the stupid fucker.

The chipped white door opened an inch, and hot air blew out through the gap.

"Hold on," called a man's cheerful voice.

After a second it creaked back the rest of the way. I saw a square hallway of dark wood and a bearded man in a wheelchair holding the edge of door. He had charcoal hair and a broad belly, tightly packed into his plaid golf shirt.

"Peter," he smiled. "Come on in. I'm Kirk Penzler."

I stepped in and he shut the door before he offered his hand. I switched the cooler to my left hand so I could shake.

"Ah!" He beamed up at my face, rolling my fingers in his. "No pinkie!"

"No, sir."

"Call me Kirk, Pete, that's a lot better."

He spun the chair past a grandfather clock and rolled up a plywood ramp into a narrower hallway hung with sepia portraits. Women with hats like eggs.

"And no ears either now!" he said to the air ahead of him. "Streamlined!"

"Just lost them last night," I murmured to the back of his head.

"Well, Alice is a little different now too. You'll see."

The air turned to bacon and burnt plastic, and I stepped once more onto the yellow linoleum of his kitchen. The lino had been ripped up from in front of the fridge and replaced with a sheet of plywood, and instead of a hole out to the backyard there was a bare stud wall. The fridge was new, too, a beige one. The burnt cupboards had been ripped out so now there was room for a round table beneath the big window. Alice sat holding a coffee cup and staring down at a plate of bacon. In the gray light from outside, her face was the color of newsprint. She wore a green sweater, and her hair looked green too.

"Alice, sweetheart!" Penzler barked. "Get Pete here a coffee, the kid's wiped out."

She looked up at me. Her eyes were big and green, like her sister's. Or was this Natalia sitting here and it was Alice's head I'd been carrying around?

"Have a seat there, Pete, *I'll* get us coffee," said Penzler. "Alice, honey, I want you to eat up and get all of that into you. Listen up, Alice, all right?"

He rolled across the plywood and lifted two mugs out of the drying rack in the sink, then spun to the coffeepot. He held each mug in his lap as he poured.

Alice folded her hands neatly under her chin. I pulled out a plastic chair and sat across from her.

"How was…your trip?" she asked, like she'd been dragged out of the ocean.

"It was fine."

She folded a strip of bacon in half and shoved it in her mouth.

"Are you growing a beard?" she asked.

"There you are, sir!" Penzler rolled up and set a BOURBON STREET DIXIELAND mug in front of me. "Get that in you, you'll feel all right. You'll feel all right. So you got all the way out to California, did you? Where's Nattie now, is that her there?"

I'd put the cooler beside the table leg.

"Alice, just pop that outside the back door, would you? House is probably too hot for it. There now."

Alice stiffly pushed her chair back and shuffled around the table. I put my gray hand against the hip of her jeans but she just picked up the cooler and shuffled out toward the piano room. Outside the window, the blue stables lay under their tarp of snow, a DOCKSIDE refrigerator truck backed in at the far end.

"She hasn't been in much of a mood since you were here last—not that you should take that *personally*," grinned Penzler. "Her new boyfriend rides away, her heart breaks, that what you're thinking? No, I'll get her to show you." He blew on his coffee, took a sip. "And you should see Shamanski these days! But did you notice a couple of the boys put a bullet through Alice? Right through here." He prodded the side of his belly. "Tore up her liver, kidney, her gallbladder, and right away she went septic. People don't get better from that. I served in the Persian Gulf so I know they don't. Lingering death, that was the prognosis for my girl. My formula, my compound, you know all about that—it was for Nattie in the first place, did either of them tell you that much?"

"Maybe they—didn't Natalia have a bad back?" I asked, getting up. "I'm going to see if Alice needs—"

"She's all right!"

He pressed my wrist hard against the table, so I sat back down.

"Well, of course you know my little compound," he said. "Drink up now, while it's hot! Show me that hand again—funny how it healed, that little gap should've closed up. I'll need a closer look later on."

I sat with my cup between my hands and gave Penzler a hard sideways look. I figured without my ears I must've looked intimidating as hell, but he just raised an eyebrow like he didn't quite recognize a song on the radio.

"I want a cure," I said. "Then I'm leaving for home."

"Uh-huh," said Penzler. "Here's the thing. Alice has healed up real well—I'll get her to show you. The compound's real reliable for that sort of thing—the military's bought into the production, isn't that something?"

"Yeah," I said. "Josh, um…Josh Q. Carver."

"Oh!" Coffee sloshed onto his thumb, and he sucked it. "Must've been after you ran away from Jones that you figured that out, is that right? You're a keen little bugger—and you had *help* getting away from Jones, didn't you? We've looked into that."

I'd remembered *Josh Q. Carver*? Funny how the brain works, I won't quit saying that. I pushed back from the table again.

"Alice must've fallen," I said.

"No, no, sit tight!" Penzler patted my hand. "She's just slow these days. See, I didn't want her getting all *enraged* like you people were doing—that's just, I don't know, *untidy*. So I monkeyed with the numbers a little before her injections. So she's not angry like you, Pete, more like down in the dumps."

I'd been wiggling my toes inside my shoes, but it seemed like the ones in the left shoe weren't wiggling.

"I don't think anything I've said has *penetrated*, has it?" asked Penzler. "God gave you ears to listen with, man!"

He rolled away from the table, opened the door of the new fridge. Alice shuffled back in, a scattering of snowflakes in her hair. She sat down and I took her hand and she let me squeeze it there in the middle of the table. If there was anything to wring out of Penzler I was going to need her.

"Hee hee!" Penzler said. "I just realized what I said, hassling you about ears, I didn't even clue in! Ah, Christ." He rolled back far enough to eyeball me around the door. "You want salami, pal?"

"Yes, please."

He started slicing it on a cutting board beside the sink. Alice squeezed my hand back, her fingertips in my palm.

"You never told me Nat was in that thing," she whispered. "I *saw* her."

"I meant to say."

She wiped her eyes on her sleeve. I recognized her sister's upper lip. Five days before we'd been horny teenagers.

"Sweetheart," said Penzler, rolling forward. "You read that e-mail from California before I did, we knew by simple process of elimination what he'd be coming back with." He set a plate on the table. "Oh, holding *hands* now! A regular Hallmark card, you two." He opened a box of saltines from the bottom cupboard and arranged them carefully on a daisy-patterned plate. "Hallmark. So what are your intentions here, Pete? And how long before you degenerate completely, two, three days?"

"Two weeks at least," I said, though it'd probably be two hours.

"Alice, you've got years more than that. No reason to think otherwise, hey? Long years, I guarantee it, my dear."

"Yeah," she murmured. "That's great."

"But I want grandchildren. I need to raise a few more children in my last years, kids, because I did *so* well the first time around. Every thought I think is to keep my girls healthy, keep my family with me. Can you produce grandchildren, Peter?"

"I've got a friend named Colleen Avery, and last week you ran over her husband."

"I don't drive, Pete, but I sympathize. Traffic accidents break families apart."

"Sure. Natalia said about your wife in Columbus."

"Did she? I guess you know it all, then, you've got the world on a string."

Then I was lonely for the smell of Josie's sweaty socks on the coffee table and the way Ray balled up his fist to punch me in the ass. Penzler made a big show of looking at his watch.

"If you're wondering why we're still unchaperoned," he said, "the fellas have just run into town to get the isolation truck. Decided yesterday I'd better get it scrubbed for the great Peter Giller. We've been tracking you since you came out of Kansas, the folks at Pan-American have been so helpful—listen, didn't it ever cross your mind to rent that car under another name? That too complicated for the zombie Che Guevara?"

"I don't eat brains," I said. "And zombies only eat brains."

I looked into the bottom of my coffee cup. No weird powders. Penzler still had his eye on me. What the hell was he waiting for?

"Giller, you dumb bugger," Penzler said. "Look at your sleeve."

I still had both hands on the table, present and accounted for, but my right wrist was four inches further out of its sleeve. My left hand shot up to check the shoulder but just found some empty shirt.

"*Shit*, baby!" Alice yelled.

My heart thumped behind my sternum. I felt down in my shirtsleeve for the shoulder, stumbling to my feet, the ceiling spinning over me like a fairground octopus.

"Pete, calm down," said Penzler. "You're making a goddamn mess."

THE ROOM WAS long and twenty feet tall, cold as a snowbank, and from the blue paint and stone floor I figured that I was out in Penzler's stable. I was upright, and naked, as far as I could tell. Steel bands held me to a wall, each one cinched tight around me with a metal belt so that I was able to wiggle about a quarter-inch.

"Good," I said with my leather tongue.

Beakers and laptops on desks and tables, long tubes flashing like Christmas lights. Shapes like fish tanks with towels thrown over them. I smelled sawdust, pungent as molasses, and hay, too, and livestock poop, and that chalk smell, delicious, of calcium nitrate fertilizer—a full dozen bags stacked against the opposite wall, showing grapes and watermelons forever spilling from their cornucopia.

I could see my bare feet. Four white toes lay spilled on the floor, their exposed bones squinting up like worms. My right foot just had the big toe, then I remembered about my right shoulder. All I saw at the end of my collarbone was the edge of a hole like an open can of tomato sauce. Nobody'd bothered to nail my arm back on.

Alice, then the guy in the motel, then Carver, then the red-bearded guy, now Penzler—since leaving Hoover I'd been tied up and held captive *five times*. But I didn't mind. It's like a holiday when you're tied up as tight as that, because you can't make decisions anymore—good, my body. You can rest a minute.

I shut my eyes and inhaled sawdust. I felt no pain, nothing, maybe thanks to the cold. But being tied up also reminded me of the heinous shit that my kids might be getting subjected to while I wasn't lifting a finger.

Here was a better tombstone:

—PETER KINGSTON GILLER—

WOUND UP IN TEN THOUSAND PIECES

&

NOT ONE OF THEM

QUIT

So I leaned out from the wall to peer around the room. I could only see one exit, a rolling steel door in the middle of the far wall, and if the bands cut into my chest and I twisted my neck like a corkscrew I could just make out Alice on a gurney in the corner. She had a blanket up her chin and her bare arm hooked to an IV. Her chin looked like it had sunk into her neck.

"Hey, Alice!" I called. "Alice!"

I couldn't see whether her eyes were open or closed, but she didn't twitch. It looked like she was attached to bags of blood.

I stared across at the calcium nitrate. Hadn't someone taught me to blow shit up using that stuff?

"Hey, buddy?" Alice called, echoing just like in a gymnasium.

"I'm here," I said.

I craned my neck again but she still looked comatose under that blanket.

"Didn't know if you were asleep," she called.

I watched her head shift on the pillow.

"What's he doing to you?" I asked.

"Oh, it's the third transfusion this week. Wants to dilute his compound."

"Is it working?"

"Not a bit! But he *had* to give it to me," she said. "Except for that other guy, there's nobody left."

"To experiment on."

"Yeah."

"There's still *me*."

"Yeah, for now," said Alice. "Sorry."

I let her voice float around me like a cloud of pollen.

"I'm real sorry about the way I treated you, when you were here before. Felt like I roughed you up. But it seemed necessary. I wanted my sister back here."

"Don't worry about it. Too bad you got shot."

"Yeah," she called.

I shut my eyes. I leaned my cheek against the top band.

"Every time I go in your kitchen," I smiled, "my right arm comes off."

"My sister never got cured," she said after a while.

"No."

"Did you talk to her?"

I cast my so-called mind back. The edge of a bathtub.

"She said you were great," I called. "Glad that you sent me."

Alice didn't answer, so after a while I opened my eyes and lifted my head. She was curled on her side, her transfusion arm still up over the blanket. She must've been sobbing from the way her body jerked. I jabbed my teeth with my tongue, but they felt solid as marble. It's a different disease that makes your teeth fall out.

"You there?" she called.

I didn't lift my head.

"Sure."

"My dad's invented lots of stuff."

"Okay."

"Tires and raincoats and tons of stuff. And Nat had scoliosis really bad ever since we were kids, she could hardly move around. You know scoliosis?"

"I don't remember."

"Your spine curves sideways. And Dad was pretty messed about it because he said his brother had had it. So after Mom died he brought that goop out of cold storage to cure Nat. He couldn't just sit around, right, can you blame him? Do you have kids?"

"Two," I yelled. "You didn't know that?"

"Maybe you understand him then," said Alice. "She could walk around, doing really good, but then she'd lose her temper, ripped the doors off our bedrooms. Dad got mad at her."

"Even though it was his fault."

"She picked him up over her head and chucked him down the stairs. Broke his back. I had to fight her off after that, terrible, then his staff took him to the hospital and when he came home in his wheel-chair he made them take her to California."

"Because he'd made her a magic pony."

Her laugh sounded like a jar of gravel. "'Cause he was scared shit-less!"

The garage door went up with a clatter and Penzler rolled into the lab. He wore orange coveralls and a black scarf bundled around his neck. He pushed himself over to Alice—she'd rolled onto her back again. They murmured to each other while he felt her tubes. Then he rolled over to me while I stared at the calcium nitrate.

"I hooked that arm of yours to the electrodes," he announced, "and it jumped like a monkey!"

"I don't know why you bother with me," I said slowly. "I've wrecked your operation a thousand different ways."

"That's true," he said. "But I said to Josh Carver, and I'll say to you, that for a project with this *sweep* the world ought to be the laboratory. *Has* to be the laboratory." He shrugged so emphatically he hopped in his chair. "But here's a smaller lab, and I'm going to take some beguiling tissue samples before you quit ticking, how's that sound?"

I was too drowsy to answer, but I kept my eyes on him.

"Alice," he called, "did you want pasta? José said pasta."

"We're having a proper service for Nat," she called back. "At the church."

"Oh, of course!"

Penzler winked up at me like we'd really fooled her. Stapling some-body to a wall had to be the only way he'd ever made a friend.

"José, he lifted you up there for me," he smiled. "The others'll be another half-hour so he's getting lunch ready."

"Are you going to adopt me?" I asked.

"Oh, no, no. I'm just curious to know what-all you can retain."

"José," I said.

"That's the spirit!"

I had to put my cheek back down on the metal. Sleep was dumping all over me. I was lying beside a woman, in a motel. We had all of our clothes on.

"Lazybones," I heard him say.

PENZLER WAS TAPPING away at a computer on the desk in front of me. My right foot still had its single heroic toe.

"Oh, Pete!" Penzler grinned. "Wide awake! See here on the monitor? Let me magnify this. There, see the banana-shaped structures, the purple ones? These are the *spindle cells*, they run between the higher and lower portions of the brain, connecting abstract thinking with base instincts, you get the idea. I hope. You listening, Pete?"

His purple shapes really did look like bananas.

"They connect the top and bottom."

"Of what, Pete?"

"Of the brain."

"Correct, good—you could even say the presence of spindle cells separates man from animals. You *could* say that, except primates and cetaceans have them as well. You cool with all this?"

Any of my students would've agreed he was torturing me to death.

"But in every *Homo zumbi* I've examined—and, granted, that's only seven—in every one, the spindle cells have been the first part of the brain to have degenerated."

"How…how do you rebuild these, the spindle cells?"

"Rebuild them? Very pertinent question, you smart bugger. If I knew that I could unhook my daughter from the drip and send her to Tuscany to meet Guidos. But no, Duffy didn't have the slightest idea, I don't—nobody knows. Duffy had sideline projects anyway—I don't want to ride you about him, I was disappointed in his work anyway. I might sound like a heartless bugger if you're really listening, but from day one it's all been for my daughters. You can appreciate that."

"Are you going to rebuild a spindle cell in, um, the next couple minutes?"

"Cute. You're a cute bugger," he said.

He rolled back from the desk and darted through the clutter of furniture to Alice's gurney, where he switched bags and tubes and pulled the blanket back up to her chin. She must've been asleep. I wished I had a stuffed animal to lay my head on.

Then he was back, talking to me while texting somebody else.

"Now, the military will need to know how to rebuild spindles, of course, since they won the bid for all applications, and since you're still able to form a sentence at *this* late date I imagine you'll be an excellent specimen for us to observe the dissolution from spindle cells on down. It'll float in a nutrient bath while that happens, of course, and the rest of your nervous system will be wired to a—"

"I'll be like George Reid."

"George, yes, crafty buggers, the both of you." He rubbed his thighs. "Interestingly, Subject Two for the third version was a boyfriend of Alice's who died in a pit behind the barn six days after eating his own feet, and though the rest of his brain looked like vanilla pudding, the little old medulla oblongata was still sitting up like—"

"Medulla oblongata," I said.

"This file is Brad, Alice's old beau."

"Why'd you give the Kuwaiti stuff to him?"

"Because Natalia was in so much pain, and because Brad was, well, hanging around. I gave him fifteen hundred dollars. It had already worked on Natalia, it'd worked poorly, but I wanted a control. That's good science. See, like a little mouse crouched under there? In an unaffected person it's grayish brown like the rest of the brain, but on Brad it's almost orange, hey? So far the medulla oblongata's been that orange color in every subject. My best theory is that the resources which would usually preserve the *entire brain* were shunted into Brad's medulla oblongata to keep it intact come hell or high water. Isn't it a useful little article? I could easily synthesize a tree frog around Brad's hardy little stem now, a tree frog that would lift weights and watch NASCAR. Another singularity was that his penis became this—"

"So my medulla oblongata," I said, "is pumped full of these preservatives."

"Presumably. And for Subjects Three through Five I did everything conceivable to get the contents of the *previous* subject's medulla into them—injections, unguents, Jesus, I inserted suppositories!"

He looked to me for some joyous reaction.

"Did they *eat* the medulla oblongata?" I asked.

"Not *per se*—gee, talking like a zombie *now*, aren't you? At any rate, it never took, they kept rotting. So now Subject Six is just stewing. But I mean, what if a subject has some condition that the product can only improve—dyslexia, hip dysplacia? It's untapped. Might be the best thing that ever happened to them." He scratched holy hell out of his armpit. "One last thing—you'll like this. The human body weighs twenty-one grams less in the instant after death than it did before, that's been measured a thousand times over. So it's been argued for the last hundred years by certain learned buggers that man's immortal *soul* must therefore weigh twenty-one grams, right? But how much weight do you estimate *Homo zumbi* lose when the last electrical spark has flickered out of your brain, how much?"

"Fifty-six pounds," I said. "We take one last dump."

"No, you lose no weight at all." He grinned, showing teeth that could've cracked walnuts. "Which means, Pete, that you've *already* lost the twenty-one grams."

"Or maybe mine are locked up tight inside my medulla oblongata. Hiding from these damn zombies wandering the countryside."

"Still lucid." He lifted a stopwatch from the table. "Quick, what's your name?"

"Peter Giller."

"How many children?"

I could picture them so clearly: a boy and a girl. And one was older than the other, definitely.

"Two children," I said.

"Their names?"

My image of the two of them blurred like a rainy windshield. I turned my eyes backwards into my head, glimpsed them watching me, holding hands, wearing new running shoes with Velcro straps.

"Roy," I announced.

"You have no child named Roy."

"Susan," I said.

"No!"

He set the stopwatch down and started typing. It really was a milestone. I couldn't even picture them.

"So you did all this for one of your kids?" I asked.

"Oh, yes! A father gives his children everything of himself," he said. "That's just how the world was meant to be."

"This one time," I said, "I agree with you completely."

"Ah, *okay*," he said, studying his phone. "José says they'll be here in ten minutes to cart you off to the bunker for time without end. Won't that be nice? I already sent our old VHS tapes. Watch *Weekend at Bernie's*. And the boys'll be here with significant numbers and armaments to cart even *your* ass away, it's going to be impressive."

"Gaaaah!" said the fish tank at his elbow. Mechanical, female, ear-splitting, like a talking doll hooked to a truck battery.

"What was that?" Alice called.

Penzler rolled his chair back.

"Gah!" The covering towel jumped an inch.

"It's the stupid capuchin monkey," he called. "Stay over there, Alice!"

But she was already sitting up on the gurney, unsnapping tubes from her arm. She just wore jeans and a black bra.

"Gaaar," the fish tank said. "Ga-har?"

"Stay where you are!" Penzler called to Alice. "The enzymes fired it up sooner than I'd wanted!" He rolled between the tables to intercept her. "Not yet, understand?"

Alice ran around her father's desk just as Penzler swooped in from the other side, but she reached over him and got her fingers on the corner of the towel.

"Don't!" her father yelled.

She pulled the towel onto the floor, and in the tank we saw Natalia's head held upright on sparking metal rods. The right side of her face hung gray and slack but the left was turning itself inside out by winking and spitting and gritting its teeth. Blood ran out the corners of its eyes. Penzler gripped the arms of his chair.

"I'm going to bring her back," he said calmly.

Muscles twitched in Alice's back.

"That's not Nat," she murmured.

The head lurched its jaw back and forth, gagging, the eye still winking, until it shifted on the rods and thumped sideways against the glass.

"It might be someday," Penzler said.

Alice lifted her sister's head clear, the rods beneath it sparking, and brought it down with a crunch on her father's upturned face. Then she lifted it away. Penzler spat blood, one eye already swollen, and Alice smashed her dead sister down onto him again. That time Natalia's skull broke apart and a lot of stuff like mushroom soup sloshed out onto both of them.

"Gah!" Penzler yelled, his mouth full of shit.

As the wheelchair rolled backwards Alice jumped barefoot onto his lap. The chair tipped and she drove his head into the stone floor as they fell, then she leapt to her feet, fists ready like her dad might leap up with a switchblade. Her breath sounded like a screen door creaking.

Gravity pulled her father's knees toward his face until he did a backward somersault out across the floor. He lay face down in the contents of his head.

Alice wasn't angry, Penzler had said, just down in the dumps.

SHE LIFTED THE rotten pumpkin that was Natalia's head and lowered it back into its tank, threw the towel over it.

She said, "Why couldn't." Then she just folded her arms.

"Get me down, please," I whispered.

My tongue felt wobbly so I didn't want to overuse it.

She smoothed the towel down the sides of the tank, tugging either end until they were even, then ambled over with her hands in her pockets like I was her last choice for square-dance partner. Lifting a slot screwdriver from the table, she pried the belt back from my lowest band. It let go with a clang.

"Who's in the other room?" I whispered.

"Dad said he'd been batting for the other team, so I guess some gay guy."

When the last band released I fell naked right on top of her. Got a smear of Penzler's blood on me as I wrapped my one arm around her neck.

Then something was different in the air, a smell or a vibration, and we both lay there blinking at each other.

Helicopter.

"Get the hell off," she said into my good left shoulder.

I rolled naked onto the stone floor. She stood up her dad's wheelchair, set the brakes, then wrapped her arms around me like she was giving the Heimlich and dragged me up into the seat. It was still warm from Penzler's ass.

"I don't have a temper like," she said.

She pushed me between the tables and apparatus. The incoming noise set the specimen dishes rattling.

"They know we're in here?" I asked.

We rolled under the garage door into a musty hallway with straw on the floor. Another metal door stood closed right in front of us—otherwise we could turn left into what must've been the dark stables. Alice punched numbers on a keypad on the wall. I felt a spark shoot through my left shoulder. The door clattered up, and I got a whiff of something vinegary like hot dog relish.

"Which way will they come in?" I asked.

"Through the stable." She grabbed my handles.

Once we got past the forklift, we rolled into a lab exactly the same as the first—monitors, beakers, fish tanks, even a poor sucker strapped to the wall. His head hung forward, and at first glance I thought he had a severe birth defect, his features were sideways or something, but as we bumped over a wad of extension cords I realized the top of his head was missing. His gray brain presented itself like a jellied salad at a wedding reception. Whatever Penzler had intended, this guy was dead.

But then he lifted his head and peered down at us. Gary the ninja.

"You guys come to watch my dissipation," he said.

"He's only been here three days." Alice started snapping back his bands with her screwdriver. "Dad gave him too strong a dose, wanted to see how his brain would melt."

"Yippee," crooned Gary.

The sound of the helicopter was overwhelmed by a noise like a bulldozer on the other side of the wall—tanks or something.

"*You* can fight them, Giller," said Gary. "You killed every person I ever met."

My neck kept flexing like I was ready to head-butt the hell out of some people.

"You killed a lot of sixteen-year-olds outside Lincoln," I said.

"That was maybe a mistake," Gary murmured. "Those forensics were too much like Penzler Corporate Headquarters—made Jones bring me in for the talk, you know?"

Something yellow and bubbly ran out of the corner of his mouth, then down the bands to Alice's wrist and along her elbow as she pulled back the third belt from the top. He had a lot of white electrodes stapled to his chest, their wires trailing away to what looked like a chrome dishwasher. Now the tank outside was grinding its gears.

"Any weapons here?" I whispered.

Alice shook her head.

"Diesel fuel?"

"Drums in the corner," she said.

"Matches?"

"In those drawers."

"Blasting caps."

"Blasting caps by the tractor. The shelf with the—"

"Run get them, please. Oh, and fertilizer."

"That's Nebraska talking. I'm taking you guys and getting out of here, that's it."

"But if these guys—"

"And there isn't any cure," she said. "Sorry."

She gave a heave on the belt under Gary's chin and the whole band snapped, clanging back against the wall, but instead of catching the guy she turned to stare at me with her hair stuck to her shoulders by Gary's vomit. Meantime his knees buckled under him and he slid down the wall until he was sitting on his heels. He had a purple crust around his head where Penzler had cut his skull away. Me, my gums were tingling like mad. Not good.

"Tell the goons you're Alice Penzler and see what happens."

"They'll incapacitate me, that's standing orders. But I've got a get-away car."

"They won't let us *drive* anywhere!"

"Okay, shit. The roof, the roof, the roof."

Bent low like there were snipers in the rafters, she loped out the door. Gary crouched against the wall, his bare scrotum brushing the floor. He swallowed hard—the sawdust smell coming off him was strong as varnish.

"First Carver told me he wanted that HQ blown up. I did that." He shifted his square toes. "Then I had to collect a subject. Jones brought you in. 'Awesome,' I said. I got greedy, I know that, working for two bosses. But I'm getting old, man. I only have a checking account."

He leaned his chin on his bony knee. A shudder went through my left shoulder, then sparks ran up my ribs into that armpit—my one arm was coming off and no fleet of getaway cars could change that. My tongue turned to a square of masking tape.

"What," I asked slowly, "are you saving up for?"

"Aw, nothing. No kids. That was *your* house in Hoover, right, on Hawthorne South? I liked that place. Was it a Coronado, that old furnace?"

I fingered the cauterized absence of my right shoulder, expecting cigar ash to float away. I couldn't picture my house in Hoover, much less its basement.

"You might as well go with her," he said. "I'm not going anywhere." He glared at his chrome dishwasher as it churned away beside him—the goddamn thing had a little A/C adapter where it plugged into the wall. "Penzler said this'd keep me alive. Guess he filled me full of more shit than usual so he could see, really *see*."

He reached up to run an index finger across the gray coil of his brain. I retched up a mouthful of coffee. He squished the finger in up to the second knuckle.

"Shit," he said. "Now I feel hot all over."

The helicopter *whupping* sounded farther away. The apes were probably digging bunkers around the stables and laying in artillery because Gary and I were famous for doing backflips and ripping heads off.

I lurched up out of the wheelchair, still stiff as rebar, did a half-spin and flopped down next to him. He had his eyes closed, his right hand still clutched protectively around that A/C cord. He shifted over to bump his left shoulder against my armless right one, then shifted away again, eyes still closed.

"What's your name besides Gary?"

"It's Chinese," he said. "Cheuk Ho. Means 'Honored One.'"

"But who calls you Cheuk Ho?"

"Huh. No. Nobody does."

He looked at me sideways. His teeth looked so pointy.

"Guess you know what to do," he said. "You got those kids to think about."

"What?"

"Use that," he said.

He looked at the big slot screwdriver lying between our feet.

"Okay," I said, though I couldn't have said what I was agreeing to.

So I stared at my beautiful right toe. Why hadn't I killed him yet? I knew what he'd done at Penzler HQ and PBF. My hands weren't exactly clean either, but I could argue that I'd only put my hand up someone's nose when they had me against a wall. Maybe ol' Cheuk Ho had thought his back had been against a wall too.

"That stuff gives me the runs," he said.

A bag of fertilizer sat in front of us.

"Me too. Let me ask one thing—tell me what you'd do differently, okay? Like in your whole life."

"Easy. Screwed more girls. Gravy on everything." He nodded solemnly. "Wait with me another second. I'll make it worth your while. Okay."

His eyes rolled away from me, and he tried to wipe yellow crud from his chin onto his shoulder. He still protected that cord in his right hand, though I couldn't imagine who was going to hop in and unplug it.

"Oops," he said. "That doesn't look correct."

My right knee had been up against my chest, but it'd flopped on the floor like a capital G, soft as an uncooked bratwurst.

"Dudn't," I said, though I meant *Doesn't*.

I didn't feel as calm about the end then as I had in the front yard. Because Alice and I had *nearly* made it out—it's easier to relax when you're confident every option has been exhausted.

"You still get to have legs," I murmured.

"Nah. I'm done."

When my wife had been dying I'd sat beside the bed and stared at her face—there hadn't been much left of her but at least the stuff they were putting in her arm relaxed her so she quit rolling her eyes back into her head. Night after night I watched where the shadows under each of her cheekbones came across to meet the wings of her nose in a perfect curve, and how the etched bag under each eye mirrored those curves, like nature had sculpted her in utero knowing how perfect her face would look when those last nights finally came. How perfect death could seem.

I lifted my hand to my cheekbone.

"You know what to do," said Gary.

He nudged the screwdriver with his foot. I took a deep breath while my lungs were still on my side.

"Dif I was you," I said, "hangin' from ceilings, I'd keep sayin' 'Honored One' all the dime."

Gary gazed at the far wall without blinking.

"Funny you say that." The corner of his mouth attempted a smile. "Because."

His head fell forward between his knees, then his whole body slumped against mine, like Keister used to do as he fell asleep.

He'd pulled his A/C adapter out of the wall.

Dust drifted down from the rafters and computers swayed on their tables. The wall behind us shook, *Thud*. Then *Thud* again—Penzler's apes were making their own entrance, too scared of *shuriken* to use the regular doors.

No sign of Alice.

I looked down at the wet hemispheres of Gary's brain against my right shoulder. His bright orange medulla oblongata was hidden below them, and according to that fucker Penzler it was full of A-1 Zombie Preservative, though I'd never been a zombie, right? There's one thing zombies do that I'd never done.

I reached across and picked up the screwdriver, my whole arm shaking like hell. Another minute and my nameless kids would never see me again unless it was as a head in a jar in a sideshow their sweethearts had dragged them to, spoiling their evening quicker than diarrhea.

Thud, said the wall. Gary's empty steel bands swung out a foot.

I shut his eyes with the palm of my hand. Then I slid the sharp head of the screwdriver down into the fatty white stuff between his brain and the back of his skull, then dragged the screwdriver all the way around the perimeter like I was going to lift a cake out of its pan.

The screwdriver came out again, slick with purple goo, and as I looked at it my arm started to bend back on itself like Plasticine. Stick with the job at hand. I'd have to lever those top halves out but didn't want to spoil the medulla oblongata in the process—I figured it'd be near the back so I slid the screwdriver in just behind his right eye and jogged the handle until the suction around his brain let go, hissing like a soda bottle. I pushed the handle down flat and that right hemisphere lifted up as neat as a hatchback, but I realized I didn't have another hand to pull it out.

So I shuffled away and let Gary flop onto his side, then one more tilt of the screwdriver and that hemisphere toppled out. It was still connected to him with half-a-dozen gristly bits but the screwdriver tore those away, forever depriving Gary of his artistic nature.

Then I could see the medulla oblongata at the bottom of his head, a bright orange thumb hitching a ride. I reached down and tugged at it but the thing was too wet and wired in, so I stabbed at either end with the screwdriver then reached in again and Gary's warm medulla oblongata slipped into my hand like it'd been waiting to walk me down the aisle.

I bit it in half with my incisors—had the texture of a baked potato. I chewed fast, willing my jawbone to stay attached and do its work well, and found that Gary's medulla oblongata tasted like a rubber balloon filled with French's yellow mustard. Funny how the brain tastes, no doubt about it.

"Funny how the brain tastes," I said to the lab.

I swallowed, then swallowed again for good measure, and goosebumps rose all over my body and the cold of that stone floor seared my ass like it was a hot plate. I was *freezing* fucking cold, but instead of punching through the wall and biting on an electrical wire all I could think to do was wrap my one arm around my intact knee and wait to vomit. The sparks had quit shooting out of my shoulder.

Penzler's goo had rotted our brains away except for the brave medulla oblongata where, according to Penzler himself, the brain's preservative resources had concentrated. There was something in that, hadn't he said so? That an engorged medulla oblongata could even rebuild the all-important spindle cell, solidify our vanilla pudding, make us normal, and he'd tried everything to make his victims human again—*suppositories*, he'd said—short of actually feeding them a medulla oblongata. Like Duffy hadn't thought to put Natalia in the fridge. Russians' pencils! Hadn't Camouflage Mike said that eating brains might paradoxically help me quit being a zombie?

And now I only wanted to eat the tiger-tiger ice cream they sold at the U-Stop in Knudsen.

I picked up the screwdriver in my solid, solid left hand and twirled it between my fingers. I straightened my right leg in front of me and it had a solid shin bone again, that remaining big toe once more triumphant.

So I figured I was cured.

I CRADLED THE other half of Gary's medulla oblongata in my palm and decided I'd give it to Alice as an early Christmas present, wherever she might have gone. That left three more people who'd need a bite, and Gary's medulla oblongata couldn't go that far. But I knew where to find more.

Boom, said the wall, and the top bolts that had held the bands in place slid out of the cement and clattered to the floor.

"Give it one more!" a guy shouted. "Everybody in place!"

I could go home to *Josie* and *Ray*.

I crawled four feet across the floor and up into the wheelchair. I dropped the chunk of brain into the side pocket, and even with one hand for steering I managed to navigate toward the hallway. My ass was freezing and pure human adrenaline made my eyelids flutter like castanets.

With a crash I felt in my molars, the wall above Gary collapsed and buried him. I didn't wait to see whether a battalion swarmed in through the cloud of dust, I rolled as straight as I could into the first lab. Maybe I'd stay ahead of the apes for five seconds. *Thud*, said a wall ahead of me.

I banged into a hard drive and knocked over a bucket of something, but I got around to Natalia's tank before the next thud. I peered under the table and there was my Styrofoam cooler from San Luis Obispo.

I pulled the towel off, sat up tall and reached for her hair—I only had one hand now and I'd need a handle. The inside of her head might've looked and smelled like compost but that didn't mean the medulla oblongata wasn't in there.

I heard something from the hallway, the slow clatter of hooves on the stone floor.

"Shh, shh," Alice said.

With one hand clutching his bridle and the other stroking his velvet nose, she led tall, beautiful Shamanski through the lab. I saw a dozen pairs of black wings sprouting from each shoulder, and he shook his gray mane and brought the wings forward then back, ten feet out on either side like some ship in full sail.

She said, "How'd you get in—"

Eyes wide, she stared behind me. I looked too. Three guys in black Kevlar were watching us through a fifteen-foot hole in the wall.

"Acknowledge—Mr. P a casualty in Lab G," a gas mask buzzed. "Roger."

The tops of the desks exploded, filling the room with sparks and shards of glass. Purple blossomed across Shamanski's chest and with a ripping sound out his nose he dropped to his knees, black wings flapping hard, that air pressure sucking the breath out of my lungs. Alice's shoulder sent out a jet of dark blood and she dropped in front of me. I put my left arm in the sleeve of a perforated lab coat, then crawled back to the wheelchair and dropped that orange lump of cure in the breast pocket. Bullets clanged off the chair as Alice scrambled to her horse. I looked back at the hole in the wall and saw a half-dozen guys, standing now for a better angle.

"Hrh!"

Alice, behind me. She lifted a desk over her head, and bullets knocked holes out of the thing as she sent it flying toward the hole. The apes' arms bent to cover their heads then they disappeared under the desk. Through the hole, the white farmhouse beckoned. Alice scooped me up in one arm while Shamanski scrambled to his feet.

She threw me on his back. I reached across and lifted the cooler from the table, shoved it against my bare belly. Then I wrapped my arm around his neck—my intangible right arm tried to hold on too. *Thoom*, said the wall ahead of us. *Thoom, thoom.*

Alice put a hand on my thigh then jumped on behind me, her bare arms wrapped around my middle. I saw three holes from bullets through her forearms but they didn't look any worse than cigarette burns. What good work we fathers did, with our clouded judgement.

"Ow," she said.

She pressed her legs against the back of mine. Shamanski jangled his bridle.

Thoom again. A steel square came through the wall, knocking a hundred pounds of concrete onto the floor.

"Okay, *up*," Alice called.

Shamanski walked in a half-circle until the wide smouldering room stretched in front of him, then he bounded forward six steps like he was going to jump a fence, and I squeezed like hell with my arm and legs. I took a mouthful of his mane between my teeth. Then all together the dozen wings against my knees went forward then concussively back, exactly as though he had one massive wing on either side, and that backward thrust flung us four feet into the air. I squinted down at the battering ram as it broke another hole the size of a garage door through the wall, then the wings were flapping hysterically and my left hand tried to dig into Shamanski's throat to keep us from sliding off his back. We circled up, and instead of a horse it felt like I was riding the arm of a couch through a tornado as his wings pulled the air out of my chest then used that same air to batter me over the head.

"Ow, damn it!" Alice yelled in my ear.

She had a new bullet hole through her kneecap. He dove, tucking his wings in close, and we shot over the upturned desk then the light changed as we rocketed up again and, through my squint, I could see we were rising above the lab and the stables. The Penzler men, scrambling on the ground, shrank to the size of black mice running over toy tanks. Their helicopter lay on its side, blanketed with broken boards. We flew over the farmhouse as a corner of its roof burst apart in a cloud of shingles—they must've shot at us with artillery.

Then we were flying over Hutchens Road with only a black van driving beneath us and snowy fields stretching out on either side. From up there, tangles of bare trees looked like barbed wire.

Dressed in nothing but a lab coat, a thousand feet in the air, the smell of snow driving up my nose—before we got anywhere I'd lose that big toe. I was warm where Alice and Shamanski pressed on either side of me, sure, though his giant square vertebrae didn't exactly feel like a sponge bath for bare testicles, and the wind pulled tears and snot down my face. Gray clouds in every direction. Stephen Hawking could not have explained Shamanski.

I was cured and we were on a flying horse.

"Want to go west?" Alice yelled in my earhole.

I nodded, teeth chattering. "Can you find Interstate 80?"

"There's Preston down there," she said. "Lean right a bit! See, there's 91a going to the highway."

The leveled Penzler HQ looked like a black map of Australia. She squeezed me tighter around the ribs.

Then there was no road under us and I lost sight of the black van.

Every time his wings beat it felt like I was getting smacked with aluminium bats, and they beat a couple of times every second. But Alice was kissing the back of my neck, and we were already beyond Preston, maybe over Indiana, and I'd keep that cooler tucked against my belly until my eyes fell on Josie and little Ray.

The hole in Alice's knee had already healed over—just a coin-sized tear in her jeans. I sucked back my snot and swallowed it.

"How fast does he go?" I yelled.

"Dad figured eighty miles an hour! And we were both on a nitrite drip," she yelled. "Won't need anything for a day or so!"

Jesus, there were a lot of baseball diamonds in Indiana. Must've been one for every person.

It started to get dark and the lump in my pocket banged against my chest. I loosened my grip on Shamanski's massive throat so I could lean back, her collarbones hard against me. I could've let go and her zombie legs would have held us on that horse even if he'd flown upside down.

"North at Schafer," I said through chattering teeth. "Dirt road behind the dairy."

"Go to sleep!"

Friday, November 4.

NEBRASKA FROM THE air is not rife with landmarks, though crossing the Missouri in the morning it was easy enough to recognize the One National towering like a pencil case over Omaha. Then we spent hours following the braided valley of the Platte, west, west and further west, above three hundred brown miles of either round or rectangular fields. The snow hadn't stuck beyond Iowa.

I was hungry as hell but if a *horse* could stay in the air I would too. An orange smear appeared on the outside of my pocket. Gary's chunk of medulla oblongata was leaking but I still had that stuff in the cooler.

We saw helicopters and planes off in the distance, but nothing came close. It looked like I'd taken sandpaper to the insides of my thighs. When the North Platte River met the South Platte River, just before the town of North Platte's rail yard like an eight-mile ear of corn, Alice and I leaned hard to the left to hopefully point us southwest. The sky was so blue.

"That's Palmerston!" I yelled. "The yellow church? Ten more miles!"

Alice nodded, knocking her chin against my shoulder. She'd peed onto Illinois. I was numb by then except for the searing pain across my perineum.

Below us the trees sidled closer together and my pulse beat hard up in my throat. I draped myself over Shamanski's neck and stared down at every inch of woody landscape though the tears streamed out of my eyes and away up my forehead. We were low enough to make out individual mailboxes beside the road and kids dropping their footballs to point up at us. The dairy's long silver roof.

"Is that it over there?" asked Alice.

Off to the right—a turquoise smear in the shape of a frying pan.

"That is Lake Picu!" I yelled back.

Deb had known the camp's owners since before I was born. Shamanski turned without us even steering him. He flew lower and lower. I could see the cabins framed against the lake, and a twist of smoke rose from the cookhouse chimney. The ground everywhere was red and orange leaves. There'd be no people at Camp Lake Picu who weren't my people.

I saw the roof of a red Corolla tucked between the trees behind the boat shed. We circled over the dirt parking lot, casting a long shadow that became wider and blacker as we descended. A small figure ran out from under the trees—Ray, in his blue windbreaker, a green water pistol falling out of his hand. Then Josie in her Wahoo Warriors hoodie and what must've been a new orange scarf, running beside her brother but almost staggering, too, her mouth a perfect *o*, eyes pasted to us.

The sides of our shadow flickered like clapping hands.

Deb came out from under the trees in a pink sweater, sunlight glinting off her sunglasses, her arms wrapped around herself. She seemed to be laughing, doubled over.

"Dad!" The boy skipped, showing gapped teeth.

Beneath Shamanski's wings the dead leaves danced up in spirals.

"YOU FELL OFF the horse," said Ray.

He leaned over me, crouching, his hands against my grimy bare chest. I was flat on my back on the ground, covered with a scratchy wool blanket. My feet were so cold! He felt heavier than he should have, my ribs too vulnerable. I focused my eyes and looked through black branches at the blue sky I'd just dropped out of.

"Ray," I murmured. "God, it's nice to see you."

Then Josie knelt from above my head, pressing her warm hands to the sides of my face. With her features upside down she looked so much older than I'd remembered, tanned and paler simultaneously, and I knew that in distant years when she came home from college, slightly transformed, I'd look and say, "Déjà vu." You look like that time I rode the horse out of the sky.

She gazed down at me. Her hands pulsed with warmth.

"Was I gone years?"

Ray stood up, all business now, and slid his fingers into his pants pockets.

"She said a week and one day. That coat makes it look like you've got one arm!"

"Yeah, we'll talk about that. You guys look very different too."

"You don't have any ears," said Josie.

"That's from the accident!" announced Ray.

"A series of accidents," I said. "Guys, I'm better now so I came straight back."

I propped myself up, Camp Lake Picu pebbles digging into my one elbow. I saw the cooler on the ground beside me, and Deb's car, and all the cabins, and the smoking chimney and piles of leaves, but no other people.

"I guess you guys are totally real," I muttered.

"They're putting the horse in the boathouse," said Ray.

"Shamanski," Josie corrected.

"Yeah, so nobody can see him."

"Let's go see him," I said.

But my hips and the small of my back were so stiff I could barely sit. I spat something orange onto the dirt between my legs. Ray squeezed his arms around my knee.

"You're dying?" he asked.

Man, my head was spinning.

"No," I said. "Don't look in that cooler, you with me? Don't look in there."

"Okay," said Josie.

"Why not?" said Ray.

They tugged my arm and I got up and started under the trees for the boathouse, though I felt like I was on stilts. The lake looked like gray shingles. I rubbed the back of Ray's head and then Josie's, like my fingers would evaporate if they ever weren't touching my kids' hair. The boathouse door stood open, a black square, but I was having trouble walking a straight line to get there—I kept watching for one of the women to step outside into the sun, but no sign.

"Are you here for a long time?" asked Josie, an arm draped over my wrist.

"Just until we go see Grandma in Pawnee. But we'll stick together."

Ray squinted at me so hard that I had to steer him away from a tree.

"There's something gross in your pocket." He pointed.

Oh, I could've said, *that's part of a ninja's brain*, but if I had, it would've constituted Ray's dinner conversation for the next ten years.

"I told Grandma you weren't going to find us, but it's okay to be wrong." Josie let her hair hang over her face, then flashed a smile as though I wouldn't see it. "You look so weird with one arm. Are you going to a doctor?"

"No," I said.

Though it was tough to walk straight with the toes gone, too. Neither of them had mentioned those.

"You smell a bit like the bathroom garbage," my daughter informed me.

"You heard from Grandma Jackie?" I asked. "Did Evadare call?"

Ray knotted invisible eyebrows. "Nobody's supposed to know we're here!"

"Okay, okay, that's good. I'll call them in a minute."

We ambled onto the boathouse path, brown grass between the cobblestones, and even as I led my kids toward the weather-beaten walls I realized that the place was too quiet to be sheltering two women and a strange horse. It meant Penzler, though I'd seen him violently killed.

"Hello?" I called.

"Right here," said Deb.

So I led the kids in, touching one on the back of the head and then the other. The floorboards were sandy, the place still had its sweet, old mouldy smell, and a couple of the canoes had been moved against the wall to make room for Shamanski, who stood with his head down to better stare at a bucket of water.

Deb sprang up from a hay bale, wrapped herself around my ribcage and squeezed, then swung her face up beside mine and didn't do anything for a second. Then she kissed the point of my chin, since she couldn't kiss the side of either ear like she used to.

"I can't believe it," she said. "Peter. And one arm."

Something purple trickled out of Shamanski's eye and a dark seam ran up the back of his leg like it was going to split open. He shuffled forward a step, a shiver running through his wings, and I finally spotted Alice asleep in a wicker basket chair beneath the rack of canoe paddles. Her head had dropped back, her chin in the air and her scabbed-up arms stuck straight out on either side like a robot whose spring had run down. She had a big square scab on her temple, too, and the bullet hole through the knee of her jeans.

I didn't look across at her or at the kids hanging off my arm and think that I was about to lose them and had to run away again, even though there was an outside chance that SWAT teams were on the way. I thought, *Things get better now, and plenty of things still to do.*

"I'd thought you could carry her up to the cookhouse," said Deb, fidgeting with her glasses, "but—"

"Can we feed him the hay?" asked Josie.

"We tried, honey!" said Deb. "There's twenty bales from archery up in the shed, and he wouldn't even sniff them!"

"We should get a pan of bacon started for her," I said.

"No!" Alice sat up, wild-eyed. "Give the horse the bacon!"

"Oh, and this is for you," I said, digging into my pocket.

"I GUESS IT's weird I came without Lydia," I said to the oncologist.

"It's not unheard of." She clicked her four-color pen then put it back in her shirt pocket, beside a pen with a plastic fox for a lid. "What can I do for you?"

So I went into the speech I'd been practicing at red lights and in the classroom while I wiped the whiteboards, unsuccessfully trying to stay scientific, without my voice catching, glue on my larynx: could I donate blood, bone marrow, a kidney? What about our friends? We had a hundred friends who said they'd help if they could, and I'd read two dozen papers on these stem cells that can—

"Nothing like that." The oncologist pulled her braid onto her shoulder then shrugged it off. "And I'd say if there were. All I can tell any patient's partner is to go home and take care of them the best you can."

"You think I'm *not* taking care of her, seriously? You need to tell me that?"

"Nothing like that—just sit down, Mr. Giller. All I meant is that you're already doing everything possible."

"Well, I'm tired of making tea, okay, that doesn't keep her—I mean, if I'm not willing to do something crucial for her, who is?"

"All right." She briskly cracked her knuckles, loud as a pistol shot in the mint-green room. "I don't want to sound like the textbook but I really do understand how powerless you feel. In my own situation, I— wait, do you have medical training? You're a teacher, yes?"

"I started a biochem master's. My mom has got a disease similar to Parkinson's and I wanted to research that, but then, you know. Kids coming, needed an income. Seemed like there were already plenty of people getting nowhere as it was—though nowadays there's ten times more cash for stem cells."

"Parkinson's?"

"Her specialist in Lincoln says it isn't Parkinson's exactly."

"Jesus, you've got it coming from all sides."

I stared at the faux-brass knob of her office door and willed my eyes to remain dry, because she was describing what I spent my waking hours actively *not* thinking about. What I thought while I was sleeping was beyond my control.

"All I mean to say," she went on, "was that I have a good idea of what's going on inside my patients' bodies, and even so I feel powerless a good percentage of the time, I still lose patients, so if you feel like your head is, I don't know, a boiling kettle, you're not alone."

"How many patients have you lost?"

"It wouldn't help you or Lydia to know that."

"I think she should be on oxygen," I said.

"It hasn't metastasised to her lungs. There's no sign of it there."

So that night I climbed into bed and like always I let Lydia jam her iceblock feet between my thighs, and as she slept she went right on dying. You spend your life trying to fix a thousand problems and you're about as successful as a hole in the ground. How often are you actually handed the solution to any one of them?

We'd never be old people who stood in their yard to endlessly contemplate the positioning of a sprinkler. I felt like I was minutes away from an empty bed, without her cold callused feet or her new musty smell that neither of us mentioned.

"Thought you were getting *out* of bed," she said through her sleep.

Monday, November 7.

THE SKY WAS yellow-gray from the sun rising somewhere over the state of Missouri, and on the dash my wife's square photo, veteran of a dozen battles now, shimmered with reflected light. Finally alone again, the four of us.

Dear Lydia,

Went into North Platte yesterday and traded your mom's car for this Aerostar van in case that helps in disguising us. Plus I can only drive an automatic. The kids are still asleep but as soon as I see a truck stop we'll go in for oatmeal and maple syrup. We made good time into Kansas, straight down 81 from Hebron, and the sugar canister was right where I'd buried it behind the cottonwood at the first rest-stop east of Salina on 70. I already phoned Pawnee to make sure that the people I'd hoped would be at Mom's house really were there. I'd tried to make it obvious that once I abandoned them at Zagat's they should hide themselves at Mom's, I tried to make it obvious even while I couldn't actually tell them I was leaving.

Except for the ones who deserved it, I'm sorry for the people that I bashed around. I imagine a lot of those guys didn't even like the job that put them in harm's way, and they probably had families too. Penzler supposedly started the whole debacle with his family's best interests in mind, so you see how cockeyed things get.

Nothing on the radio about artillery fire outside of Preston, Ohio, which smells to me like the FBI just tidying their tracks. No mention of interstate manhunts either.

I'll probably never pass through Hoover again, and so never get a chance to punch Harv's dad in the face. As lifelong regrets go I guess that's not the worst. There are all of those kids I took to the Dockside plastics factory that will never get home and see their moms and dads, but I tell myself that I did my best on their behalf. But losing Harv that way, that's hard to swallow. And his dad had so much more son than he deserved.

Alice is cured too. She stands on the beach and paints watercolors, and they aren't good. She bought Camp Lake Picu with the capital from one of her numbered Virgin Islands accounts or some such thing, and like buying a summer camp was not unusual. We need to put insulation in those places. I might take up oils myself, hokey as that sounds, and even if I suck the paint off my brushes, go crazy and cut my ear off like Vincent Van Gogh, it gives me a pleased shudder that without complicated medical intervention I would not *be able to stick that ear back on. It would just lie there in the dirt, attracting flies.*

Just remembered, no ears. That's a funny one to get used to.

The medulla oblongata we saved for Shamanski might not have been enough to bring the old boy back around. He lies on his side, panting, syrupy stuff leaking from his grafts, and Deb and Alice take turns reading him My Friend Flicka. *I haven't been able to navigate shoelaces one-handed yet and may just wear these gumboots indefinitely. In the mirror I can see J doing that crazy sleep-thing with her fist, and R is whistling through his nose with the shoulder-belt across his face.*

Hope you've enjoyed this missive from my recently reconstituted brain, my dear.

"OH, SO HERE you are!" Evadare said in the doorway. "When they first come I think, hey, nice if he would have called first, but now they're here a week already!"

I took her by the wrist. The house smelled of baking.

"Where's Colleen? Aren't they here?"

"They mope around!" said Evadare.

I didn't see anyone behind her in the house, though of course someone would be sitting behind the bead curtain.

"But they're healthy?" I asked. "They seem okay?"

"Clint said today he had a sore foot. Too much dancing. Let me see these little ones!"

I wore a black-and-gold Steelers knit cap, so she hadn't noticed my ears, and she must've figured I had my right arm twisted behind me, waving to the kids or something—they were on either side of a blue-jay whirligig, seeing who could get their wing going faster. The bird tilted toward Ray then fell off its stick.

"You win, Sunshine!" Josie lifted his hand like he was heavyweight champion.

"Come give my hugs!" Evadare called.

They thundered up the steps and wrapped around her calico thighs.

"Where's Colleen?" I asked.

"Oh, they go out for walk every hour. They must know everyone in the countryside by now! And they are always in the garden shed, cooking their bacon—the smell was making her sick, it really was! And she got pimples, all that bacon cooked in the house, and she never even ate some!"

I kept my hand in Ray's hair.

"She used to love bacon."

"Sure she did. I see it in her eyes when they cook it. What have you got here?"

I carried my grocery bag to the dining room table.

"We happened to be driving through Kansas," I said. "So we stopped at the Czech bakery—"

"Oh, in Wilson!" She clasped her hands to her chest. "You were in Wilson!"

"*Knedliky* and *kolaches*!" shouted Ray, hopping in on one foot. "And we got prune for you!"

She pressed his blond self to her hip. "Oh, I *like* the prune!"

I crossed the living room—Josie stood in the midst of the bead curtain.

"Hi, Gram-*my*," she said, with the overly sweet delivery she'd picked up from Lydia. When your listener never responds it's hard to know how to talk.

"Mom," I said, "hi. Thanks for looking after my cronies."

She seemed to straighten herself in the recliner. She wore a pink floral sweatshirt and a long black skirt, and her ankles didn't look as bloated as the rest of her. They looked like they had in the Lincoln

Sunken Garden, brushed by butterflies.

"Has she eaten lunch?" I called back to Evadare.

She had Ray on her knee beside the table, both of them munching away.

"There is spinach broth in the fridge, you can feed it to her."

Josie kissed Mom's cheek, then ran out so she wouldn't miss the *kolaches*. I wiped Mom's mouth and kissed the top of her head—the same floral conditioner as always. I stood back and imagined her feet settling to the floor, her thick hands gripping the arms of the chair, then my mom actually rising. Her eyes darted over me.

"Yeah, I had trouble with my arm. I'll tell you about it. Let me get your lunch. You're going to like lunch."

My heart beat loud and fast in my ears. I rustled back out through the curtain.

"What is in this Tupperware?" Evadare picked through the grocery bag. "Is it custard?"

"Can we have it now?" asked Ray. "I'll share!"

"It isn't custard," I said, because it was Natalia. "I'd better pop that in the fridge."

I took the container from Evadare and she commenced brushing pastry from the kids' laps. I heard the front door open, so I leapt around the corner and they were coming inside just as I'd left them, Colleen in her tracksuit, Megan in her cardigan, Clint in that jean jacket and scarf. The Averys had Clint's arms around their shoulders, his foot dangling over the floor like he'd broken his leg. They looked up at me, eyes wide and black with bright daylight through the screen door behind them.

"My ankle." Clint heaved in a breath. "It's going, it's fucked."

"Don't move." I held up my hand like a traffic cop. "I'll get spoons."

Colleen followed me into the panelled kitchen.

"I'm sorry again that I left you there," I said. "I don't think I can explain."

She forced her mouth into a frown, then put her face against my shoulder and wrapped herself around me. She was shorter than I'd remembered. I put my arm around her too and squeezed tight, her shoulder blades against my forearm. Her heart thudded against my ribs.

Megan appeared beside us, her hair in anemic braids.

"Is this it? Give me the spoon!"

"Tell him it'll taste like mustard."

"*Hurry up*," Clint said from the hall. "I don't care if it tastes like shit!"

"Don't say shit in front of these two!" called Evadare.

"Are these your kids, Mr. G?" called Clint. "They look like you."

"And we have to divvy it three ways," Megan muttered as she strode out to him.

"Should I tell them it's two ways?" I asked Colleen.

She gazed up at me. The curtains' shadow gave her face a spider-web texture.

"I could tell on the phone that you'd figured it out," she murmured. "When you said it wasn't the pink stuff after all."

"And you never ate a hot dog."

"No."

"Oh, god," Megan gasped from the hallway. "It's so gross!"

"Not even a veggie dog. Jeez," I said, "I'd really thought I was living clean."

"Eat it *all*," said her mother.

I put my chin on the top of her head.

"I called Doug's sister," she said. "They're having a funeral up in Fremont."

"Are you going?"

"Is it safe to?"

"I guess we'll—"

"Jesus, look at you." She lifted off my cap and I tried not to flinch as the bare sides of my head met open air. "You look like something shat you out."

"Thank you. Appreciate it."

"Lucky for you the Masonic Express dropped us right in the drive-way, or I'd have a foot up your ass."

"Anyone alive enough to mouth the words, 'I am lucky,' is lucky."

"Listen to you, with your brain."

I leaned back against the counter. "I need to feed my mom lunch."

"Need help?"

I shook my head. After a second she swallowed, brushed hair out of her eyes and looked grimly at the fridge.

"We heard about PBF," she said slowly. "It's still on the news here every day, not one survivor." She squeezed the back of her neck. "Did you know all about that before you went?"

"Oh."

"Tug the shit out of your earlobe, I won't mind."

"I saw it on a TV," I said, "in the motel. Couple of times I could've told you guys, I guess. But I didn't."

"I realize you didn't."

"Look!" called Megan from the hall.

In a single bound Clint arrived in the middle of the kitchen, then he leapt straight up, his head rattling the light fixture, his skinny knees to his chest, and grinning. Aw, that stupid kid's grin. The same expression slapped on her face, Megan shakily set the one-third portion of not-custard on the counter—her eyes totally not on what she was doing.

"Tasted so gross, hey?"

"Sure did!" Colleen faked a smile. She'd fooled just about everybody.

"That's one solid ankle," I said.

Clint leaned over Colleen's shoulder and kissed me on the cheek. Then he turned on his pointy heel and went out.

"Go eat Czech pastry," I told Colleen.

"On one condition." She flapped my empty sleeve. "I never eat cured pork again."

I poured Mom's spinach broth into the blender, and while it pureed I took the ziplock out of my pocket and poured in a teaspoon or two of powdered D.S. #3. Didn't want to overdo it on the first try. The world really is just one potential loss after another, so you have to gobble up your potential gains and let them warm your belly.

I poured the concoction into the feeding bag and carried it across to the study. I had a spring in my step like Wile E. Coyote, even if my empty sleeve and missing toes left me off-kilter. I wasn't bothered. I inhaled Josie and Ray's chatter like perfume in a Persian garden.

My mom was still sitting up straight, her eyes flickering over me as if my parts might flit off in a million directions. Shadows were deeper on that side of the house.

"Well, Mom," I said.

I hung the bag from the rack, pushed the air out of the free end of the rubber hose and pushed her blouse up an inch to get to the g-tube's opening. She sighed.

"I've been through a lot with this concoction, and there's only one way to look at it. It makes everything better. Absolutely everything."

Wet eyes still on me, she moved her jaw enough for her teeth to clack together.

"You have a doze," I said. "I'll check back on you."

THE TV WAS in the back bedroom, and while Evadare waved the remote like a wand, Ray climbed into Josie's lap. They were nearly the same size. Colleen and Megan dumped a barnyard puzzle onto the card table.

"The pigsty again, seriously?" Clint yanked on his scarf as if to hang himself. "I want to check out that bowling alley with the crazy hall of fame—I totally want to steal those pictures!"

"Take it slow." I dropped into the green lawn chair in the corner. "Let your joints settle in."

"Our other grandma says we don't have to go back," Josie was saying to Evadare.

"I want to see Hoover," said Clint. "I miss that pile of crap."

"So homeschooling for you," said Evadare. "I know a lot of spelling words, okay, Ray? 'Mete,' like a punishment, spell that."

"Homeschool moms have hairy armpits," said Josie.

"Or the bonnets on!" said Evadare. "I see them at the Parkside. There are two kinds of those moms."

"I want to do homeschool!" Ray said. "Bows and arrows!"

"But you won't be allowed to huck your shoe through the roof," said Josie.

Evadare had settled on watching infrared snowstorms swirl in from over the Atlantic.

"Aw, come on," said Megan. "Please? Can't we watch a show?"

"Why?" Evadare set the remote in Josie's outstretched paw. "You used to like the weather so much!"

"We're changed people!" Clint leapt to his feet, jostling the pole-lamp. "In fact I'm sick of this fucking puzzle! Let's just get out of here!"

"No, no, we cannot swear—"

"Can Grammy come and watch?" Ray suddenly asked, blond and blinking.

Evadare reached for her crocheting bag. "She sleeps after lunch."

"Don't make any plans for tomorrow, kids," I said.

"Why not?" said Josie.

"I figure we'll go horseback riding."

"*Really*?" said Ray.

"Maybe," I said.

They found one of their crap Japanese cartoons, and I may've dozed off.

"Holy crow," Megan said at one point. "My arms feel really...solid, I guess?"

I opened my eyes at the end of the cartoon as all of the rag-tag characters assembled in a perfectly flat green field, a soundtrack of wailing guitars playing over their impossibly wide smiles. The monkey-in-a-diaper character rolled at their feet and all of the spiky-haired characters laughed. Josie slid out from under nose-picking Ray and stepped gingerly to the carpet.

"Ow," she said.

"What's wrong?"

"Leg's asleep."

She hopped across the rug and flopped into my lap, tucking her brown head, with its silver penguin barrette, neatly under my chin.

The guitars wailed over the credits. Hundreds of names flashed across.

"I couldn't keep track of all that," I said. "Did it have a happy ending?"

"Sure. It's a kids' show."

Mouth hard like a penny, Evadare hit mute on the remote and the suddenness of the silence made Ray withdraw his finger. She brought her eyebrows down against the top of her glasses.

"Did you hear it? That's strange."

"Hear what?" I asked.

She tilted her head, gray eyes twitching as she listened to the house.

"It sounded like the bead curtain."

Nineteen months later

THE WIRELESS MICROPHONE tugged my lapel down an inch, but I was the only one who'd look closely enough to notice—I gave an audience other things to gawk at. The lights up on their aerial racks made the studio hot as an August baseball diamond, and the pancake makeup worked hard to mask the sweat beading at my hairline. On the stool beside mine, Mary Warner momentarily thrust her arms out in front of her, maybe straightening her suit jacket, then gave me a nod, clutched her stack of note cards and addressed the red light atop the camera. The shuffling studio guys were only silhouettes behind it—someone could look right at them and never guess the mounds of desiccated corpses in their minds' eyes.

I practiced my quick-and-easy smile while my face bent toward my buckled Berg loafers padded with orthotic toes.

"It's 8:07 on *Nebraska in the Morning*, and we're joined by Peter Giller, Rotary International's Nebraskan of the Year." She twitched just enough for her curls to shimmer. "And I'd venture to call him our *Newsmaker* of the Year, wouldn't you, Harold?"

The TV monitor at our feet cut from Mary to the portly weatherman, chortling on the other side of the sky-blue studio.

"He's certainly made an impact," he nodded. "On my family and so many others."

The producer cut back to the two-shot of Mary and me—from such a wide angle, my anatomical design choices weren't obvious, I just looked like a guy with longish hair and a wide-shouldered suit. Alice had flown a tailor in from Naples who specialized in transhumeral amputees, a bona fide Neapolitan, so according to Josie and Ray I now had a closetful of ice-cream suits. Mary jostled a pantyhosed leg.

"Thank you for making this time for us, Peter."

"Oh, it's a pleasure, Mary. I've enjoyed your work for a long time."

I especially enjoyed it that she'd arrived in Gage County after Harv and Franny had already sunk to the bottom of the Republican River.

"Well, thank *you*! So, two years ago you were a small-town science teacher out in Hoover, now our changing world has to scramble more than *ever* just to keep up with *your* changes."

She glanced from the camera to me, smiling just enough to produce a dimple. PI's mermaid logo suddenly hovered beside my head on the monitor. I'd negotiated with the producer to get that.

"Um," I said, "is that a question?"

"What exactly *was* your path from little old Hoover to heading research and development at Penzler Innovations out in Ohio? I understand the story has its dark side, and I've also heard of teachers becoming *principals*, but…"

How many times had I provided the summary? Maybe a hundred since the day the National Health Service had signed our contracts in England, the US Health Department a week after that, Center for Disease Control, Centers for Medicare Services and all the other federal departments, me in a boardroom summarizing Shamanski in my ice-cream suit for the *New York Times* and *The Economist*, or via e-mail for the *Des Moines Register* in my Hulk T-shirt and no bottoms. Below our faces on the monitor, the scrolling titles read NEXT HOUR: WHITE HOUSE: AFTER CONGO, WHAT?

"Well." I scratched the back of my head so, to the folks at home, I must've looked like a chimp. "I'd visited Penzler's Velouria facility, right here in Nebraska, in a teaching capacity, and made enough connections that I was in touch with Alice Penzler just prior to all the tragedies that befell her company, just a horrible, horrible string of events."

Mary pressed her hand to my kneecap. "Those explosions in Ohio. Just tragic."

"An incredible loss. An incalculable loss." Was I honestly trying to—what?—quantify the emotion of those days, for the umpteenth time? Impossible and stupid? Yet my mouth went on talking. "Alice's father, he passed away in that lab accident, dozens of staff lost their lives in a related incident, and as the CEO Alice needed to rebuild Penzler, not just for the sake of its investors but to be able to give something back to those families that had lost so much. It might sound a little, you know, pie in the sky," I smiled, "but Alice set out to make the world a better place, and I found myself in a position to contribute."

"You'd seen tragedy of your own." She glanced gravely at the camera. "Tell us about that."

I'd yet to create sufficient distance between the talking me and the me that had watched PBF burn. I looked across at Harold, his sausage hands folded in his lap, and imagined sinking my teeth into his cheek.

"Yes," I said, "a number of students from Hoover lost their lives on a field trip, a research trip, really, to brainstorm how they wanted the world of their future to look. But there was a fire—your viewers will remember, I'm sure, it was on a farm just outside Lincoln—and all of the steps I've taken since then have been to honor their memories. With my science background prior to my teaching career, I found myself in a position to contribute, through Alice and everyone else at Penzler."

"Most of us have seen the coverage on CNN, but can you tell us in *your own words* what you've contributed?"

"Well, to anyone not familiar with it, this might sound like a fairytale, but at Penzler R & D we've isolated a compound that, over the long-term, looks like it may be able to heal just about any wound, to halt any disease, but, as always, I must stress that Shamanski is only effective in very small doses administered over many months. I took the very unscientific step of administering it to myself at one point in development and, well, you see the results." I shrugged an armless shoulder. "Patients think that if it's some miracle drug they ought to take as much as they can as quickly as they can, but fortunately I'm here as the poster child for the side effects of that scenario. Whether the patient's a kid with muscular dystrophy or a wounded soldier back from the Congo, we've already sent hundreds of people back to work, back to school, back to productive lives with their families, but I have to tell each of them, 'You want to hold onto your arms and ears, you take it slow.'"

"Everything in moderation." Mary tilted her head at the camera. "Even miracles."

"In fact." I quickly licked my lips, which my mom had said was my bad habit on camera. "Harold and I were talking just a minute ago, and he told me—is this all right to mention?"

"You go right ahead," Harold nodded, the lights flashing off his glasses.

"Harold told me that for years his dad had been in care for Parkinson's, but he was involved with our second round of trials and now he's been back at home for, what is it, four months?"

"Three." He nodded again. "Baking up a storm."

"Is *that* where those little lemon pies keep coming from?" asked Mary.

"Yes, it is!"

"Well," she beamed at the camera, "we will break for these messages while my waistline tears a strip off Harold, how about that?"

I smiled too, then lifted my hand six inches in a vague farewell.

"Okay," a silhouette announced. "Two minutes."

I slid off the stool onto the floor, swirling with green floral patterns from the lights, and unclipped my microphone. It slid out of my fingers to bounce off the tile.

"Ow!" a man in headphones called. "Put that back on, sir!"

"We aren't done yet," Mary said without moving her lips as a boy with a shaved head brushed powder across her cheeks.

"Wasn't I on for just the three minutes or whatever they said?"

"Oh, it *was*, I'm sorry, I guess nobody mentioned—the biggest pig in Burroughs County refuses to come through the service bay, so we'll do her in the parking lot as a button and that gives you three more minutes, that all right?"

As I climbed back up I saw the tattoo on the makeup kid's shoulder: Uncle Sam, his face gray and rotten like that half-eaten apple under Ray's bed, above the tricolor caption I WANT BACON. My stomach gave a lurch and I had to grip the edge of the stool.

"Nice—nice ink," I said. "What's the connection there, zombies and bacon?"

"It's *disgusting*." Mary's lips bunched up into a bee. "He has to hide it when my kids are here."

"No connection." He smiled thinly as he surveyed my complexion, his gaze never once darting toward where my ears ought to have been. "My friends and I were pretty drunk and we were like, 'It'd be awesome if zombies ate bacon, like instead of brains?' They'd still shamble around for our entertainment, nobody gets hurt."

The headphone guy adjusted my microphone.

"Nobody except the biggest pig in Burroughs County," I said.

Mary lifted her bottom to straighten her skirt. "Her name's Hermione."

"Listen," Makeup went on quietly, eyebrows climbing his forehead, "my cousin's HIV-positive and she's real excited about this stuff—about your medicine."

"She ought to be. It's early days for us treating HIV and AIDS, but with timing and dosage it'll work. Where's she live?"

"Indy."

"There'll be a free clinic first week in July. Tell her to look after herself in the meantime, really."

"Cool," he said, collecting his tool kit.

"Peter," Mary murmured, her lips still hardly moving, "are you sceing anyone?"

"Not at the moment," I said, because that seemed less pathetic than *no*. Then to be polite I asked, "Are you?"

"Okay," said the silhouette. "In five."

I watched Mary take a deep breath, then realized I ought to face the camera. I didn't want to also be Ogler of the Year.

"Welcome back to *Nebraska in the Morning*, it's now 8:15. What have we got coming after 8:30, Harold?"

"Another taste of the weird and wacky," Harold said to his camera. "A man out in Ohio, unemployed since a workplace fire eighteen months ago, claims that this past weekend his arms simply dropped off!"

The picture cut to a freckled man in thick glasses, too close to the camera and his eyes open very wide.

"I looked down at the ping-pong table," he said, "and there they were."

"Well!" Mary said. "I guess he can give up on that job search once and for all!"

"Reminds me of that California story, a couple of weeks ago." Harold frowned. "The gentleman out in the strawberry field."

"Oh, Harold Sayers, our investigative journalist! You missed your calling!"

They cut from Harold grinding his teeth back to me.

"Well, right now we are so fortunate to have with us medical researcher and philanthropist Peter Giller! Good morning, Peter."

I craved one of Harold's dad's lemon pies, wanted them smeared in my armpits.

"Hello again," I said.

"Now, I saw your picture in the *Journal Star* yesterday and I told the kids I'd be talking to you, so little Joshua asked me—"

"Oh," said Harold, his fist, hilariously, to his brow. "Oh, Joshua."

"He gives us plenty to talk about, yeah," Mary smiled. "So he wanted to know, if you've lost an arm, why don't you wear a prosthetic? 'A fake one' is what he said."

"Oh, okay. It's amazing how seldom I get asked that, I guess most people…okay, one reason is that I've entirely lost the humerus—"

"But not your sense of humor!" yelled Harold.

I had taken this hour from my precious life to appear on *Nebraska in the Morning* because our funding gurus, the Buffett Foundation, had decreed that Shamanski would need a human face if the typical American was ever going to see it as more than voodoo. We'd had 825 prospective patients in Des Moines, yes, but we'd prepped for five thousand.

"—so I'd have very little control over a conventional prosthesis. The military's made amazing strides with artificial limbs tapping into the nervous system—robotics, really—but what's more important to me is keeping my eyes on the prize of improving Shamanski to the point that I'll actually be able to get my arm *back*, and to—"

"You," Mary stammered, "you mean to say you still *have* the arm?"

Anyone who hiccups while imagining a severed limb has never spent time as a zombie.

"No. Our vision is that one day Shamanski might induce the body to regrow entire appendages. That may be promising more than we can ultimately deliver, but if Penzler doesn't dream about it, who will?" The corporate bumper sticker.

Mary tilted her chin meaningfully. "Ever since the name was first bandied around, Peter, I've wanted to ask, 'Why Shamanski?'"

"Shamanski was a very close friend of both Alice and mine." *And without the key ingredient of a flying horse's cloned brain tissue*, I failed to tell the audience at home, *we'd still be creating full-blown zombies from town to town, state to state, it's ninety-one percent more effective a stabilizing agent than the nitrate booster we mixed in initially.* "He passed away just as this was getting started and we owe him a great deal."

"Okay, now, we only have two minutes left with you, Peter, before you need to be on your way." She gazed at my widowed shoulder— maybe her mind had already gone to the next segment. "One point we haven't touched on is that Rotary's guidelines for selecting their Nebraskan of the Year talk a lot about volunteerism and giving to the community. Can you expand on your role there?"

"Sure. First off, there are thousands of Nebraskans doing absolutely unflagging work for the public good, year in and year out, whether it's candy stripers in hospitals, Meals on Wheels bringing breakfasts into schools or volunteers working with wounded veterans—"

Her eyes darted toward the silhouettes—I was eating too much time.

"—and keeping in that spirit, since January we've been able to offer clinics in many larger centers on a pay-what-you-can basis, teaming up with GPs and state agencies to make sure people are getting the right dosages for their specific disorders, making sure they aren't getting too much too soon, and of course that they're receiving the proper variant of Shamanski, because the formula for rheumatoid arthritis, for example, is not going to be as effective in treating, say, breast cancer, but the reason we've—"

"Sorry, if I can just jump in, yeah? You have a cure for *cancer*?"

I might've been teetering atop the stool but my mind was level as a bowling alley.

"To the best of our knowledge, yes. It may be that remission is not entirely permanent, that years down the road we'll—"

"But how could it get approval so quickly?" Were her eyes misting up now? I immediately thought of her kids. She had a sick kid. "Doesn't the FDA need five years, ten years to decide if a drug's really safe?"

"It's certainly crossed my mind that we've been fast-tracked, and there's no doubt that Steve Balfa at the FDA has been a huge proponent from the first. He's taken the stance that the gains from freeing people of these diseases, whether or not they're terminal, just entirely outweigh the risks. Even in enabling us to bypass the traditionally huge markup of more-established pharmaceutical companies, they've really been squarely in our corner, and I haven't taken that for granted."

Actually, Alice's first hire had been an IT girl to blow through the half-assed security on Carver's laptop a week after I dug it out of that locker at Lincoln Airport, and though the full import of his client files weren't immediately clear to us, the names on his invoices were enough to convince the feds that we could do each other favors. The CIA had paid Carver to recruit international investors for the Congolese LRA, for instance, a bare month before the LRA started mangling American personnel. Curing cancer must've been preferable to reading Carver's e-mails in the *Washington Post*.

"Okay." Nodding, chin trembling, Mary produced a Kleenex and dabbed the corners of her eyes more quickly than viewers could've followed.

"But most importantly," I said as my ass fell asleep, "we get people started with the process, because frankly most of us are terribly intimidated by the medical system, too intimidated to take the necessary steps because of the sheer bureaucracy involved, so I started setting tents up in parks on a given Saturday, there's always a band, kids dance around, tables with juice, spanakopita, people just relax, they walk in and say, 'Hey, I've had this problem a long time' or 'I've just been diagnosed, is it true you can help me out?' They walk in under their own power or we'll bus them in on a shuttle. I see the phone number for more information across the screen there, we'll be in Omaha next weekend starting at 9:30 for—"

"Say, Peter," Harold called, "when I told *my* kids you'd be on, they said to thank you for wrapping things up so neatly in the Congo!"

"Now that's not fair, Mr. Sophistication," smiled Mary. "Your kids are way older than mine!"

"Um," I said, "Of course I'm overjoyed the guerrillas have been overpowered, our troops are on their way home and the Congolese finally face, uh, a peaceful future, but Penzler hasn't played any role in that."

Harold lowered his jowls accusingly.

"No?"

"What *could* we have done?"

"There was that footage, a week, maybe two weeks—"

"Peter, have you been back to Hoover recently?" Mary consulted a bent card. "There must be *crowds* there who'd love to congratulate you on this award."

On the monitor my mouth hung open as if my jaw once again had its own agenda.

"Hoover? No," I told her, "not recently. But I'll actually be there this afternoon to watch the high school graduation. Can't wait."

"Oh, *wonderful*—Hoover, break out another folding chair! Thanks so much for joining us, Peter."

"It's been my pleasure."

The Penzler Healing Communities number disappeared as the monitor cut me out of the shot. Beside the camera, someone lifted a whiteboard crammed with text.

"That's Peter Giller, our Rotary Nebraskan of the Year. A luncheon in his honor is being held Friday at the Embassy Suites Hotel right here in Lincoln, tickets are twenty-five dollars and are available first-come, first-served."

"Yum," smiled Harold. "If anybody asks, I am *always* game for a twenty-five dollar luncheon."

"That is a well-documented fact. And what do we have after the break?"

"Well, Mary, the Omaha woman who spent twenty-four hours down a manhole in January says she's ready to get back in the dating game!"

We sat with rictus smiles. The monitor scrolled CONGO: WHAT TURNED THE TIDE?

"Ninety seconds," announced the silhouette.

I slid down again and waited for the headphone guy to unclip me, but he was busy sniffing a clipboard. The former Miss Nebraska stayed up on her stool, hands clasped around one knee, an ankle caressing the air.

"Peter." Her voice cracked the slightest bit, but she gave me her dimpled smile so to Harold it might've looked like we were benignly discussing the Steelers' recent and resounding Super Bowl victory. "I need a really big favor," she whispered. "My, my pap smear came back as irregular. I know that could be *anything* but I have a *really* bad feeling, and I know I should just call your number but—"

"Okay, you won't have to do it on your own, remind yourself that, but first I need you to go in and hear the diagnosis, all right?" I put my hand around her wrist. "You're tough, yeah?"

"Yeah."

She bit her lip, chewing on that word *diagnosis* as we all will eventually, then straightened up and looked entirely stoic as the makeup guy materialized to dab her temples with a foam triangle. Cervical cancer, presumably, and she had young kids at home. But I was not as helpless in this situation as I'd once been. The headphone guy reclaimed my microphone, whistling through his teeth.

"Thank you for having me, guys," I said.

"Oh!" Mary Warner beamed duplicitously. "Thanks for coming on!"

I hopped over a nest of cables and hurried down a barely lit corridor, crowded with ladders, toward the green room. The floor producer hissed something but I wasn't listening to these assholes anymore. I could go for weeks at a time seeing Shamanski as merely the greatest thing to ever happen to the human race, my smile wide as time zones, but whenever a young mother with cancer walked through my peripheral, I felt the same brick jammed under my ribs, and I'd shake my one mighty fist at God and demand He switch this young mother with my Lydia so my Lydia could instead be diagnosed in an epoch when a cure existed. It'd never occurred to me that anybody who'd lost a loved one to some horrific infection must've been even *more* pissed once Alexander Fleming started handing out penicillin to everybody in the ward who'd managed to hang on for one more lung-shredding day. That was what Alice and I had created: a line across history, before the flood and after.

So I pivoted on the ball of my shoe, squeaking the lino, and jogged back toward the pink wash of studio lights.

"One of the state's biggest events," Mary Warner was saying adoringly to the camera, "the Comstock Rock Festival at the Second *Wind* Ranch, is *breezing* ahead into another four-day happening this July."

Skipping from beside the blinking camera, the floor producer flicked his little headset microphone up beside his temple.

"What can I do for you?" he whispered.

I shook my head, slid my wallet out of my inside pocket as I walked past him into the wash, and produced her passport photo, creased from one-handed mishandling. Had I said *Sorry to barge back in?* The monitor showed Harold, smiling and wiping his chin with a knuckle.

"Oh," said Mary. "Here's Mr. Giller again."

"Please put that phone number back onscreen," I said to the camera. "Thank you, that's Shamanski. People have to call this number. This picture's small but it's my wife Lydia, she died two years ago from a liver cancer that didn't respond to chemo. If she'd been diagnosed now, today—" The number flashed at the bottom of the screen, already seconds from expiring. "So if you're sick, call. Give yourself a chance to fight."

On the monitor my fingers tightened into focus but Lydia somehow stayed blurry.

"Thank you!" I barked, and smiled up at the lights, at the silhouettes around the camera, before skipping over the cables and back into the dark. In the canals of my ears I heard my heart pounding. The technicians all faced away and the air smelled of hot dust, like that shimmering bubble back at Dickside Synthetics.

"More good advice from our Nebraskan of the Year," Mary told the world.

A bald guy peered out of a glassed-in booth and showed me a thumbs-up.

Just inside the spray-painted exit door, my driver Mark stood in a charcoal pinstripe, displaying his glamorous scar that cut across both lips. Once he'd driven me in an ambulance to the Lamplighter Motel.

"We're boxed in, Boss, got to hold up a minute." His scars compacted into waxen lumps as he smiled ever so graciously, as if at the end of that minute I'd be meeting the Pope. "I know you've got that thing to get to, but there's a swine the size of an elephant across our bumper."

Did I slug him, then pull the fire ax out of the glass case and start taking pieces out of the pig until we could steer around her? No, because I'd renounced violence. Wasn't the way to move the human race forward.

"Her name's Hermione," I said.

"Huh. Well, guy said the forklift's nearly here."

FROM THE FAR wall, the gray Hoover Hooves mustang looked down on the rows of expectant chairs facing the stage. The gymnasium was a mass of navy blue streamers dangling from the walls, the bleachers, the rafters twenty feet up, and I imagined the stacks of requisitions Cam must've filled out to get a scissor-lift that'd go that high. Great-aunts with walkers and brace-faced siblings filled every fire exit while the purple-gowned graduates adjusted and readjusted their mortar boards—because what in their lives could've prepared them for squares of cardboard on their heads?—and smiled for the many dads' many cameras. A younger brother with long bangs and acne had a cartoon baboon with wings flying across his chest. WAR IS OVER, the shirt said. I kept my hand in my pants pocket and sidled between the groups. Everything smelled like lemony deodorant.

Life is a highway, blared the school-wide PA, *I'm going to ride it all night long, yeah yeah yeah yeah*—

Carnal knowledge of a highway? I smiled at a young dad with Coke-bottle glasses as he told someone that the hail hadn't bothered *his* winter wheat, you kidding? Not having the outsides of my ears—the *pinnae*—made it impossible to differentiate where sounds were coming from, so I looked over my shoulder a lot.

"Holy smuts!" said Cam Vincent, detaching himself from a photo-op with two girls in massive yellow sunglasses. "The prodigal sub returns!"

The feds had assured me that everything was clear between Hoover and me—families paid generous settlements, no blame attached to the school or to me personally—but I still had a recurring daydream wherein Cam held me against a locker while the affected parents popped steak knives into my belly. A dozen beloved kids had died but now it was eighteen months later and here came Mr. Vincent with a goofy grin and a beard so long and fluffy that he looked like one of the Steelers' defensive ends.

"Holy smuts," I agreed, "is that a Super Bowl MVP Brett Keisel tribute beard?"

"Oh, buddy." He put a hairy arm around me—he was taller than I'd remembered. "Nobody else gets it. Nobody does. You heard a couple of yours are valedictorians?"

"Seriously, Megan and Clint?"

I could narrow it down quickly because they were the only ones left. The graduates around us went on laughing and taking pictures of each other's butts but a lot of the adults were looking our way, and though I looked for venomous stares beneath the bald heads and ballcaps, I couldn't spot any. I was a miracle worker for the downtrodden. There in the old gym where that Asperger's kid had knocked himself unconscious with a basketball, I felt more self-conscious of my floppy hair and Italian three-button than I did of the missing arm and ears. Most of the chuckling grandpas were missing at least a finger or thumb. Threshing accidents.

The "Life is a Highway" backup singers competed with hundreds of voices to drown each other out.

"You heard George Reid never came back either?" Cam kept his arm tight around me. "Maybe he'll roll in too!"

That was a lovely image. His aquarium cart.

"Hadn't heard anything about him," I said.

"Yeah, so we had to hire Kirsten full-time—she and I are expecting in August!"

"Jeez," I said, "the full-time position must look different than I thought."

"You might've been a beautiful mother if you'd given it a chance. Say, you ever quit your worldwide tours long enough to put your feet up, drink some beer?"

"Sure. My mom and kids are at a place up north, a little lake."

A bob-haired Asian woman, clutching the strap of a white purse, took a seat on a folding chair right in front of the stage. Dreaper, the now-beardless math teacher, materialized to tap her shoulder and direct her to the chairs at the back. "Life is a Highway" concluded midriff, so I could suddenly hear every cowboy-boot heel clonking against the hardwood.

"There a school up there, up north?" asked Cam.

"Homeschooling. My mom. They build volcanoes."

He rolled his eyes, then lifted his beard amiably at someone behind me.

"It's not about the education, really," I said. "I want them near at hand."

"Oh, they came along?" His eyebrows went up, which his beard somehow exaggerated—the beard was ridiculous. "Steer 'em over here!"

"I didn't bring them."

"Oh, good, well, that makes sense. Guess I better get this thing started." He lifted his arm away. "There'll be a memorial for your elevens, you want to say something?"

"There's a memorial *this* year?"

"They would've been graduating."

"But there wasn't one last year?"

"There was one last year."

He stared at me dully, then turned, winked at a mom who'd been pulling hay out of her pant cuff, then made his way through the crowd, stroking his beard and squeezing every shoulder he passed. He made it look easy. I couldn't imagine the number of people he must've been ready to strangle when he heard about PBF, twelve of his eleventh-graders burned to death.

He climbed onstage and thudded his finger against the microphone.

"All right, grads, showtime. Alphabetical order like we practiced."

Every eye was off me by then. While the kids in robes bobbed from one seat to another across the front, I waited for the families to settle themselves on the rear folding chairs, then I took a seat two in from the back corner. The Asian woman, still clutching that purse strap with her white knuckles, dropped onto the chair beside me.

"Are you Peter Giller?" she asked quietly. "Okay if I sit here? I'm Helen Bradford, I'm Grace's mom. You remember Grace?"

She raised her thin eyebrows, against the expectation that no one in Hoover would recall Grace. Really, *Grace*?

So I imagined the heat and light in that pig-farm walk-in cooler—the last sensations Grace ever had of this world. How she must've wanted her mom then. Wanted her, wanted her, then the bright light, too much heat for a nervous system to even register.

Thanks to that line of thought I folded up, put my face in my hand and let go a sob that shuddered up from under my kidneys. Snot streamed out of my nose and down my shirt cuff, and my ribs heaved because I couldn't get air in. Helen Bradford's light hand moved up and down my back. But Cam was welcoming all the parents and hangers-on by then, making a joke about the basketball team that got laughs and applause, so I didn't imagine anyone was paying me much attention. Just another wigged-out parent afraid to watch his chicks fly. The grads woo-hooed.

"All right," Cam announced, "now the jazz choir's going to give us a treat."

They started harmonizing a four-part arrangement of "Hakuna Matata" from *The Lion King*, Josie's second-favorite movie, and I straightened up in my folding chair as though this were the song I'd relied on to get me through the darkest nights. The choir members were all homely, with chin-length hair so I couldn't tell girls from boys.

I found the handkerchief Mark had dutifully placed in my inside pocket. Helen lifted her hand away and we smiled at each other like we'd survived an earthquake together, then she worked her own dripping nose into a Kleenex.

"You still live here?" I asked shakily.

She shook her head, balling up the tissue. "I came from Los Angeles."

The choir filed from the stage and I recognized Kirsten née McAvoy sitting up beside Cam. Her hair was longer now and parted down the middle, and though that may sound dowdy she looked ten years younger.

"We had a tie for valedictorian this year," Cam said into the microphone. "And with Megan starting up the sock hops and Clint taking over tornado drills, well, that just seemed fair. So give a big hand to Megan Avery and Clint Denham!"

Two figures popped up from the field of mortarboards, then seemed to float across the stage. Everyone clapped, some kids getting to their feet. I thudded my hand against my thigh and stomped my feet.

Clint's hair burst from under his cap like palm fronds, and Megan's blond dreadlocks swayed around her shoulders. Had Hoover held a hair-growing contest? They stood hip to hip, each gripping an edge of the podium. Colleen had to be sitting proudly in the crowd somewhere, but none of the backs of heads looked familiar.

"Hi," said Megan, her voice sounding fuller, throatier. "Twelve of our classmates died together in an accident last year, I guess everyone here knows that. Last year's grad class was bigger than ours, and next year's will be too."

"Woo!" yelped the spiky-haired kid in front of me.

Represent, Amber would've said.

"We knew those guys really well," said Clint. "And if they were here they'd want us to celebrate. So we're going to celebrate."

Mrs. Bradford shifted toward me to give a sympathetic frown, and I made myself give her a bleary smile, then had to push past her and stride long-legged for the exit, looking to all the grandpas like every other ice cream–suited asshole out in the world who figured he had more important places to be. I swabbed my eyes with the hankie. I fantasized that D.S. 4's packaging said MAY INHIBIT GRIEVING, in which case I'd mainline it into my neck.

"Hunh," I heard myself saying.

Of course there were sobs behind me too, the victims' aunts and stepdads who still saw that gauze fall behind their eyes even though for months they'd been holding it together. I heard them now while Megan hollered, like Henry V, about partying, but I knew Alice expected me to have more decorum than the rest of the stricken. Snot would not advance civilization either.

"And we'll do that tonight," Clint promised, "and every night!"

Out in the hall, I let the gym door click shut behind me. A freckled woman in a sundress shuffled past, saying "*shuh-shuh*" robotically while pushing a limp child in a stroller. As I quietly emptied my nose into the hankie, the boy sat up unsteadily and the freckled woman leveled a glare over her shoulder before disappearing around the corner toward the staff room.

Then I blew my nose with great volume as the ruddy-faced, hairy headshots of the Class of '81 gazed from their mahogany frame.

"Sorry," I called.

Restrained applause from inside the gym. I still needed to congratulate Megan and Clint, so did I wait in the hallway for an hour?

My car was parked behind the metal shop but I had let Driver Mark wander up to the town library so he could skim through *Hunter-Gatherer* microfilm for hilariously gory harvesting accidents—his Chicago sister was an aficionado—and even though the car was an automatic and I had keys, I didn't feel like driving four blocks to get him.

Instead I pawed my wallet out of my jacket and shuffled down to the benignly rattling pop machine in which Pepsi was still only seventy-five cents. *This* was what had pulled me back to Hoover. The deep blue can thudded to the bottom and I pressed it against my hot face, focusing all mental energies on the searing cold so I could quit thinking about Grace.

"Oh, yes, sir. Peter Giller, is it?"

A man's voice, an older man, and thanks to my non-ears I figured he was ten feet behind me but when I straightened up he was so close in front that I could've slapped him. His hair was white stubble.

"Sure," I said. "I'm Peter."

"Affirmative! I believe we have things to say to each other, sir." But he dropped his pointed chin against his chest and jammed his hands into his pockets like he couldn't work up the nerve to ask the soda machine to dance. "Ahem."

The fluorescents cast his diffused shadow in three directions; his brown suit smelled like a car floor mat in August after a kid had spilled chocolate milk on it and not told anybody. Maybe in San Luis Obispo I'd smelled like that.

"Can I help you?" I asked, without the deferential tone I'd perfected at clinics.

He pointed a square-nailed finger at the Pepsi. An angry-looking eagle's head was tattooed on the back of his hand.

"I'll have one of those, sure. Thirsty as—don't know. Hm. Thirsty as a horse! Little time before you need to be somewhere?"

Well, hadn't I been wondering how to kill the next hour? I set the can beside my shoe and flopped my wallet open. He slid his feet from side to side like he had to pee, and where his jacket parted, his belly looked distended, his waistband stretched tight. Irritable bowel syndrome? I could help.

"I've only got nickels," I said. "How much you got? I'll donate them."

"Oh, that's okay." He rubbed his chin, worked his tongue around his mouth. "I was on the ground floor with this ruddy thing, and what'd

I get out of it? Guy can't buy me a Pepsi. It'll rot your pancreas, though, so I don't much care. I saw you on TV this morning, and when Harold Sayers trotted out your good works in the Congo, and the look on, well, on your truncated face was just...*this guy needs educating*, that's what I thought. You know him well, Harold Sayers?"

"Who?"

"Harold Sayers, TV weatherman? Strikes me as a good man. Now, me, I want everything above board, none of this—don't know what *your* life's been like in every respect, but I'm put out by men behind the curtain, aren't you? If not for you, these high school kids would be going to the Congo! This all ought to be a party for you, and the valedic-tor-ian ought to give you one of their arms, hey? Pop it up your sleeve, everybody cheers!"

"There are two valedictorians in there."

"So you'd have three arms, think of your tennis game *then*! You play? Never thought to ask."

"Heh," I said.

My buckled loafer knocked the Pepsi over, but I didn't think it wise to take my eyes off the old man while I bent down to retrieve it. By then Driver Mark ought to have stepped in with his brawny forearm.

"Excuse me, Peter."

Colleen at my elbow, her hair longer too, tucked behind her ears with wide silver-beige streaks through it. She took my wrist in her two small hands.

"Oh, thank god," I said to her.

"Come back in. They just finished the diplomas." She smiled, though in her eyes it was a wince. She wore low heels and a pinstripe skirt and blazer. "They're starting the slideshow for the kids, the 'In Memorium.'"

"Now, you're the wife, I remember." The old man smiled shyly at her, all dry lips, but then his cream-colored teeth came into view. "You're holding up well."

He was such an old tomcat, I'd expected to see a snapped-off fang. Colleen squeezed my wrist so hard like she might've been barefoot waterskiing.

"The *wife*?" she asked him. "Have we met?"

"Doug Avery was your husband!" He shook his head, overjoyed that she couldn't remember her own husband. "Doug Avery, correct? Dead up on Hawthorne Street, oh, flattened!"

She kicked the can too, and it rolled toward the trophy case.

"Have we?" Her voice cracked. "Have we met?"

"Yes, ma'am, and on that very fateful day!" He threw his shoulders back, barking up at the light fixtures. "Svendsen, Christopher, US Air Force lieutenant, retired, and friend to the common man!"

My hand on the small of her back, I felt her spine go straight as rebar. Restrained applause from inside the gym.

"Flattened?" she asked.

"Well, Mr. Svendsen," I said, "I've come a long way to see this slide-show."

I bumped the gym door with my hip and piloted Colleen through, toward hundreds of black silhouettes with blue light on their faces. The movie screen was down. In my parting glance Svendsen bent spryly at the knees to retrieve the can of Pepsi.

Through the half-light, Mrs. Bradford saw us coming and shifted over to leave us two free chairs. She patted Colleen's sinewy hand as we sat down, then gripped her white purse against her belly. On the screen, a blond girl with braces—*Kathy Ackerman*—sat astride a springy horse at a playground.

"Don't remember her on the trip," I murmured.

"She wasn't," Colleen said in my ear. "Drug overdose last summer."

Grace Bradford in a NBZAMBI MARCH T-shirt, flashing a peace sign.

"Oh," her mom said. "That's good."

Willow Cooke squinting on a golf course, Little Craig nowhere in sight. Then Lydia, Ryan, Eric, each sitting by a Christmas tree or astride a pony. I'd remembered them as all being much cooler. An emaciated-looking girl I didn't recognize—anorexia?

"Car accident two weeks ago," whispered Colleen.

No Franny Halliday? But Little Craig, both cheeks intact, in a karate *gi* on an oil-stained driveway. Ursula Leiber, Shawn Melloy with an electric guitar but no amp, Eric Millar. Amber grinning in an orange bikini on a muddy-looking beach—not appropriate, but probably how she'd have wanted to be remembered. Grandmas clucked their tongues. Jacob Rhenisch, coldsores and all, crouched over a red-eyed cocker spaniel.

"Ah!" somebody said: the image captured Jacob's abiding essence.

I steeled myself for Harvey Saunders to appear onscreen, probably in his blue Hoover Hooves uniform, basketball pinned between forearm and hip, all teeth and bright eyes like a Prairieland Dairy ad. I felt my eyes heat up despite myself, and I had to swallow whatever was in my throat.

But instead an IN MEMORIUM title flashed on the screen, the lights came back up and people shifted in their seats and coughed. No governmental authority could say officially whether Harv or Franny were dead because, thanks to me, no trace of them had ever been found. Cam and Dreaper monkeyed with the screen above their heads—the cord to roll it up had to be tugged with a ten-foot pole but neither of them could manage it. Colleen sat dry eyed beside me, her lips pressed together like the edges of two bricks.

"Appreciate your patience," Megan said into the onstage microphone. "Be right with you."

And *that* got Colleen going—she gave a half-swallowed snort and a drop of something ran off her nose onto her skirt. My nose must've been running too, because Mrs. Bradford handed us each a Kleenex as she rose from her folding chair.

"I see Amber's parents up there. They're not together so I should sit with them," she whispered. "Those girls made a wonderful team."

We nodded as she slid past. Colleen inhaled raggedly then blew her nose with a majestic resonance. She dabbed her eyes. How long had it been since I'd seen her?

"That old fucker was right." Her tongue seemed to be sticky. "Doug really was flattened and Jocko didn't know *what* to do."

"Old guy shouted like he'd seen the whole thing, didn't he?"

Though I couldn't remember any old guys out on our block that day—of course my memory was shaky. Maybe there'd been nbzambi witch doctors watering mums.

"One of my salvage guys got into the DMV for me," she went on, "but the yellow Mustangs and ones we talked about were all the wrong years, at least the ones registered in Hoover."

"That leaves the whole rest of Nebraska."

"Even in Burroughs County alone, eighteen yellow sports cars with spoilers but the wrong years, so they were all too big, but I've got guys keeping their eyes open, and weekends I still drive around the impounds. It's good you met Doug even for a minute, you know? He'd be doing just as much if it'd been me, I know that."

Up amongst the front seats, a tall, gangly brunette jumped and threw her mortarboard in the air, well ahead of schedule, so on stage

Clint raised his hands and made a face to discourage anybody else from joining in. I remembered the yellow car disappearing around the hedge, the woman's gardening gloves—but why fixate on that, when we had dead kids scattered on all sides?

An old couple glanced back at us, then quickly away.

"I'd seen people who were dead before," I said slowly. "But he was the first poor guy I ever saw killed right in front of me. Plain murdered."

"They've got it on the books as an *accident*, but after—"

"No," I said, "that's right."

"I'll find the guy." She smoothed the hem of her skirt. "And I'll smash his head."

"I will be right there with you."

Though if she ever did find him I'd likely be on the other side of the world.

"That old fucker was right," she murmured again.

Cam tapped the microphone though the screen still swayed above his head.

"All right, guys, a couple of announcements and then we're done! The grad committee has snacks prepared in the library if you'd like to mingle for a few minutes, be happy to see you there. So thank you all for coming, and even though it's already a hundred degrees outside, the mayor's asked me to remind you that Hoover's a great place to stay and raise a family. Okay, at this time, grads, you may move your tassel from the left side of your cap to the right, signifying graduation. Please rise, turn and face your relatives and friends. Ladies and gentlemen, we present to you the Hoover High School graduating class of 2015."

Boys produced air horns from beneath their robes and blared them into the ears of their venerated classmates, while others let loose cans of green and orange spray foam down the front of people's robes and arcing onto the rows of grandparents. A clutch of blond girls covered their ears and burst out the exit doors onto the football field.

"This concludes the ceremony," said Cam.

The relatives rose from their chairs like a time-lapse lawn growing.

"And I keep wondering," Colleen said as they filed past, "did Doug see it coming, did he try to get out of the way? Had he been scared? When I try to sleep it's still in front of me."

"It's not the same, I know that," I said. "My wife, Lydia, she knew for a long time she was going to die, and Doug, maybe he only had a second or two. Hopefully he never knew at all. But the last thing my wife told me was, 'I've been so lucky.' The pain she must've been in if the morphine wore off, I didn't see how that could be possible. 'Lucky.' Made me think maybe *everyone* thinks that in their, you know, the last thing. So don't keep thinking about the death, because he didn't. Really he thought about everything else." I tried to smile, which couldn't have looked good. "Okay. I'm right-handed, I'm a Libra, I had a love of my life but she passed away, none of that's going to change. I figured that out sitting in the car a couple of weeks ago. I realized that Lydia will keep going as long as I keep going, which was about the least depressing thought I'd had in a long time. No matter what else happens, that part never leaves."

Here we were, two years later, and finally it was Lydia's day to sit up with the sun on her face. Colleen rolled her eyes. "Thanks, Father Time, for that fucking insight."

She blew her nose again. Already the gym was mostly empty, so I realized I'd have to hustle to the library if I wanted to give Megan and Clint so much as a hello.

I hustled past Colleen's unjust looks toward the hallway, and held the door for a brown-haired woman who looked familiar, though anybody in Hoover ought to have looked familiar. No sign of Svendsen skulking beneath the Class of '81.

"Mr. Giller! You remember me?" the woman asked. "Kim!"

She held a mound of hair against her shoulder. She wasn't old but was too old for me to have taught.

"I was Harv Saunders' stepmom, it's so good to see you!"

She threw her arms around my neck and I confess I got my hand onto the small of her back and held her pretty tight, because she sure looked different without lipstick on her cheek. I glanced back into the gym for her husband.

"How—how are you?" I said into her temple.

"Oh, good!" She stepped back and looked at me, all bright eyed. "You must remember Dave."

"Your guy, right, the masseur?"

"Well, he's gone to parts unknown. I'm seeing Bill the optician now! Hey, Myrtle and I were saying just the other day how *sweet* it was of you to come to the house that time, just to see Harv! His sister, you met Myrtle—she said, 'I wish *I'd* had a teacher like that.'"

Yes, then like her brother she might've been torn apart by dogs.

"Myrtle was the one at Pizza Hut?" I asked.

"She *was*. She's at agricultural college now in Curtis—she loves sheep! Now, you weren't here last year or you'd be running to the snack table for their rolled-up bacon, amazing, and I have a client meeting in twenty-five minutes, we'd better move! Oh, gosh, I forgot you only had one arm now." She bunched her jacket up at the throat, looked up at me beseechingly. "I'm so sorry for your loss."

"I'm sorry for yours too. More than you can really know."

"Oh, Dave? Don't be, no, he's a piece of shit."

MRS. ABEL STOOD in a hairnet beneath the American flag. The hungry crowd bumped me on either side as I loaded my paper plate with pineapple segments, and all the time I smiled up at Mrs. A with zero effect while she surveyed the snack tables despotically.

"So I guess you want gum?" Grace's mom asked someone—I couldn't pinpoint if she was behind or beside me.

And what I'd thought were humdrum cantaloupe cubes were actually mango! Gary had been alive the last time I'd tasted bacon, and since then my gastronomic energy had turned entirely toward tropical fruit, to the detriment of the kids' birthday parties. Did they have the least idea how hard it was to get mangosteen in season in Nebraska? Someone squeezed my elbow.

"Are you free for dinner?" Kim asked, despite the bacon between her incisors.

"Uh, no, afraid not. I need to get back to my kids tonight."

"Oh, that's sweet—you've got kids of your own?"

Fuck you if you think I don't have kids. I turned and showed Mrs. Abel my twenty-eight fierce teeth, all wolfman, the thin veil protecting civilization, but Mrs. A didn't notice that either. My plate bent in my hand like a big taco. Kim swirled away into the square dance of small talk, but Megan and Clint, surrounded by celery-chewing admirers, had circulated nearer.

I led with my elbow to get within six feet of them, until I ran up against Colleen. She raised an eyebrow and stole a segment of my pineapple.

"Megan looks beautiful," I said gently.

"If you're so stressed, go ahead and pull your ear."

"Hilarious. Are you still pissed off?"

"I'm here for Megan, period. And for that matter I don't need you around to be pissed off." She tucked her toothpick into my breast pocket. "I quit the insurance so I could work full-time at the junkyard, know why?"

I shrugged, nearly tipping the plate—a hundred people were talking so I had to concentrate like hell on what she was saying.

"Because that's what the world is—salvage. Junk. Selling insurance demands that you care the least crap about the future. Anyway, forget that, I'm going to stand here smiling for Megan's sake, that's good parenting."

"Sure," I said.

We gazed at the valedictorians. A white-haired woman swayed in front of them, miming she was dragging on a joint. Clint guffawed good-naturedly. Kirsten née McAvoy stepped in and Megan hugged her tight, the purple gown enveloping them both.

Colleen started talking without looking at me, so I didn't catch on right away.

"And I'm right where you are," she said, "I understand you're broken up about her, you did cartwheels on the stupid TV, but don't take it out on your kids, you know? I bet your daughter looks more like her all the time, but even so you should hang out with your daughter instead of these kids, because what do these kids care?"

With the plate in my one hand, I realized I'd have to eat straight off it like a dog. She folded her arms and seemed to study my face. I was trying not to listen to her.

"When's the last time you saw the poor kid?"

"Yesterday," I said.

"I can't get used to how weird you look."

I pushed the paper plate against her chest and she grabbed it before it tipped, then I angled past the white-haired dope-smoker to extend my hand to Clint. We shook.

"Clint, buddy," I said. "So great to see you up there. I'm so proud of you guys."

He gave a tight-lipped smile and let my hand go. Kirsten took a step back, watching, so I shook Megan's hand too. It felt dry and tiny.

"Oh, hey, Mr. Giller, you came! That's so great."

"Sure," I nodded. "Wouldn't have missed it."

They defaulted to their toothiest smiles. They'd rehearsed watching the "In Memorium" slideshow a dozen times so it was all old news, which was how it ought to have been. Maybe they didn't even remember Velouria. It was time for them to start college and have sex with hundreds of people. They swayed their enormous sleeves back and forth.

"So," they asked, "everything good with you?"

I WALKED BACK down the hallway, past bored younger sisters pulling off each others' Band-Aids, toward the open doors to the parking lot—a square so bright I couldn't look right at it. I was done with Hoover. The dead kids had all graduated, so I could forget that everybody had been put through a meat grinder in order to further the military-industrial complex. I could exhale. I stepped out into the grasshoppery heat.

"Here now, Giller. Okay," Svendsen said.

It was too bright to even see him at first, but who else could it have been?

"Not entirely polite to leave a citizen waiting so long. But, oh well."

He took a swig from a can of Pepsi, pivoting on the ball of one foot there beside the yellow garbage can.

"Yes, sorry, Lieutenant." I scratched hard at the back of my neck. "You know, I think we might still have a couple of things to talk about."

"I'd better show you something," he said. "Any private place around here?"

He straightened his red tie and grinned at a pair of grandparents hunched in the dark doorway, squinting out at the shimmering cars.

"You know, secluded," he murmured, "where the children give each other their, I don't know. Their hummers. Don't you have a house around here?"

"Not any more, no." Asshole. "Got a car parked over here."

We crossed the sticky blacktop, Svendsen clenching and unclenching each hand like a wrestler coming out of his corner.

"The Federal government, see, allows its citizens to get away with anything if the Federal government feels that behavior is for the greater good, though history inevitably proves the Federal government wrong." He raised his chin high. "This your car? Must be, big enough!"

It was a special-edition Lexus hybrid with a cushy leather backseat as wide as a church pew, and Mark had even managed to park in the shade. I unlocked it with a beep and flash of tail lights.

"I do a lot of business in it," I explained. "Lobbyists."

"My, this *is* where the children come to get hummers!"

It would've been easy, standing behind him, to grip the back of his stubbled head and break his nose against the side of the car. But violence was no way to move the human race forward so I held the back door open for old Svendsen and he slid into the cognac-and-cigars atmosphere that the interior perpetually exhaled.

I sank in beside him, shut the door then opened the mini-bar that Penzler Innovations had installed between the front seats. I was sweating from my forehead so I pressed the button on the key to start the ignition, and the air-conditioning came on.

"Have a drink?" I asked.

"Any make of bourbon's okay."

He threw his head sideways and arched his spine so I thought he was commencing a fit, but he was only tugging something from his back pocket.

"I bought this iPhone, you ever hear of these? Hell, you probably invented it."

"That's true." I set a glass on the armrest and poured him four fingers of Maker's Mark. "Invented it for an elementary school project."

"Just let me find this little movie here. It's an ugly damn thing."

He glared at the phone, prodding the screen with his thumbs. A movie? Maybe Doug Avery. Svendsen had presented himself as such an authority on the subject, probably just footage of a blood-stained sidewalk. But maybe there'd be a shot of the yellow car. If it was useful I could always track Colleen down in the phone book.

"Once you find the thing we'll patch it through to here," I said. "Easier to watch."

I dug the USB cable from under the mini-bar and plugged the narrow end into the screen in the back of Mark's seat.

"Good, good," he said, "this thing's so damn small. Friend on active duty sent it to me. Here's the bastard."

I plugged the wide end of the cable into the phone. The play arrow appeared on the big screen, then a swirling circle telling us it was nearly ready. Active-duty video of Doug Avery?

"So this is classified?" I asked.

"I thought so!" He took an inaccurate slurp of whiskey and wiped his lips with the back of his hand. "But then, other goddamn day, I see some kid in the doughnut shop looking at it, so it must be on the internet too already! I don't know. Here it is."

His movie started: a flickering patch of golden dirt on the back of Mark's seat, and we heard wind whistle across a microphone. Then the camera swung up from the dirt to show black-bottomed clouds, then slowly came down again past tin roofs a hundred feet away. Buildings looked like black burnt frames. We heard flies.

"Here it is." Svendsen nodded encouragingly, jogging his knee up and down.

The picture had settled on a thin black arm, severed at the shoulder, lying in the dirt, a mottled black pig sniffing it. The arm's hand still gripped some kind of machine gun. A leafy branch shooed the pig away as voices spoke gravely in a language I couldn't understand. Offscreen kids laughed and shouted. The camera backed up a couple of steps and turned to the left, where thin dogs circled a pile of eight or ten more arms and legs. An object in blue cloth might've been a head.

This looked like Africa, the Africa that the word *Africa* suggested to the American mind—butchered people were that continent's expected output, sad but true.

Someone lifted an arm from the pile, turning it appraisingly, to show the clean purple lip where the limb had come away from the shoulder. Someone had dropped to pieces just like I had.

Our wildly imperfect D.S. 3 had been deployed to Africa.

I gripped the Maker's Mark between my knees so I could uncork it.

"Had enough?" Svendsen balanced the iPhone across his fingertips like a tray of martinis. "There's more good stuff."

I took two long swigs of the whiskey.

"The feds never got it," I said. "No, we said no way."

"You see for yourself they had it, do have it and will continue to have it. I've dipped a toe in many an organization, sir, and no one ever knows what everybody else knows."

The grave voices began to shout. Near the half-burnt buildings, women milled around in what might've been giant beach towels, but then the camera swung unsteadily into the clouds, then cutting left onto a wide-winged bird flapping lazily above the rooftops.

"Take hold of your *cajones*," said Svendsen.

Had too many legs to be an ordinary bird. Jesus, so what was it? The shouting became more distant and urgent, but the picture still hadn't budged and we heard what had to be the cameraman's breathing.

Women screamed, "*Ack-ack-aye-aye.*"

The flying creature moved closer with an up-and-down loping motion across the sky, and though the wings looked wide as a vulture's—no, the thing filled the screen: an open-mouthed baboon, head tilted accusingly, eyes so wide it must've seen the two of us there in Hoover. Raised something dark in its hands. We heard a mechanical bark, then the camera swayed back nauseatingly. It filmed nothing but gray sky. A black wing tip passed across the edge of the frame. The *ack-ack-aye-aye* never let up.

The gray sky froze and the white play arrow reappeared.

"Get it? The monkey must've shot the guy—great stuff."

Svendsen leaned forward to smile, like he'd caught me sleeping. Shit, maybe he had.

"This was Congo," I said. Not even a question.

"Democratic Republic of. How'd it come to pass, yeah? Some glimmers have come down to me of you handling yourself in Velouria and points east, sir, and I wonder some why you haven't been in handcuffs since then. You're familiar with a lot of deals on your behalf, clemency and such?"

"For handcuffs you need two wrists."

"They can cuff your ankles." He pawed at the phone again. "I've seen it on those trials on TV. Here's a—here's another quality segment."

Blue sky above blowing green jungle, and a baboon, sitting in profile on a huge fallen log, its brown wings drooping to the ground. Only the wind could be heard. The picture tightened on the thing's face as it lifted something to its mouth, tearing a strip away with a sidelong pull. It chewed placidly. The object had fingers—another baboon.

The screen went black. This was Duffy's lab, spilled out across the world.

"Isolated incidents," I said.

"My buddy scooped that camera up 'cause he was first on the ground in that village—they sent the baboons in ahead of him! The Rangers, the Green Berets!" Svendsen leaned back into his corner of the seat, studying me, massaging a kneecap through his brown trousers. "I saw our guys chasing a pack of those LRA into the woods. And one of our boys, he didn't have his helmet on."

Svendsen refilled the glass, running his tongue over his teeth.

"That might've compromised his head," I said.

"Well, yes, it did!" He flopped into the corner. "Son of a bitch had half his head compromised, just a pound of raw hamburger, but he had an Uzi in each hand and he was hopping over the logs." He gulped back half the glass. Belched succinctly. "Think your concoction might've done that too?"

Jesus, was D.S. 4 really that good? Alice couldn't have been handing it around—had to have trickled out during Duffy's day.

A shiver up my neck, *someone walking on your grave*, Mom called it. Our miraculous formula, used only for the betterment of humanity? No, thrown in my face like flat beer.

"Show me that video," I said.

"Got rid of it! Gave me nightmares. Kept dreaming a lot of boys standing for reveille, but no arms to salute with." He looked at me sideways, like a shark drifting by. "So. How'd you lose the ears?"

"Be surprised how seldom I get asked that."

"Know what I think? And I've got to tell you, it's relief like a week's shitting at once to be hashing all this out, *capiche*? I think with all your hellfire in Velouria you crushed so many toes, your bosses had to give the medicine up to save your bacon, yes?"

"That might be," I said.

I fished my phone out of the inside pocket. My bosses were only one person.

"Call Alice," I told the phone, then asked Svendsen, "Can you play Angry Birds for a minute?"

He pursed his lips and tapped a fingertip on his knee—there was one more topic we had to touch on, he and I.

"Hey there," said Alice.

The old guy glanced our way. It wasn't on speaker but might as well have been.

"Hi," I said. "You busy?"

"Yes and no," she said. "You're making a splash today. If you felt that strongly about not doing TV, you should've said so."

"I've just seen that maybe D.S. 4 hasn't only been used for medical applications."

"Oh, have you?" She muttered as if she wasn't quite listening, which was possible since she usually watched televised tennis when she was on the phone, even if Warren Buffett was on the other end and it was a rerun of a match from the seventies.

"I'm looking at some images here that—"

"Okay, you got me. Well done. I won't even ask what you're seeing since it could be anything with a mangy dog in the background, am I right?"

"It's not—"

"Well, you've risen to the occasion on the R & D, I'll give you that, rerouting the nitrate situation—"

"Ni*trite*," I corrected, purely out of habit.

"Exactly, but you aren't a money guy. Something's got to pay your salary, manufacturing, distribution—can cancer cure itself? No, pal, it needs finessing. We work it from both ends. So do I start with abstracts or specifics?"

Svendsen took a pocketknife out of his trousers and started whittling his thumbnail. His sour-milk smell was infiltrating my robust interior.

"Neither one," I told Alice. "I'm taking time off. See my kids for once. Lena and Glen can run the clinics. You don't need me."

"I actually planned for this. Know why I kept you out of the loop? I knew you couldn't swallow this scenario. You were a bloodthirsty nut when you were a zombie, true, but—"

"So I know exactly what the future should *not* look like."

Though what really nauseated me about flying baboons with machine guns was that pointy-bearded Mike had predicted the future with one-hundred percent accuracy. I watched graduates pile into cars to back out of their parking spots, stereos booming. Svendsen helped himself to bourbon with sixty percent accuracy. Mark would have to wipe the seats down.

"You still talking?" she asked. "Sorry, pal, I'm brushing my hair before this Uzbek embassy guy comes in."

"He came out to Preston?"

"Fuck, no, I'm in Washington. Before you go, you need to absorb this stuff and realize D.S. 4's done a world of good that'd never have happened if you'd had any say in it. Is it better to heal the wounded with unprecedented success, pal, or for nobody to be wounded in the first place? Oh, and Harvard's sending a team into Kuwait to look into the Bedouin origins of the compound and whatever else they can drum up, wanted to know ..."

I pictured her staring into space in her white *Flava* T-shirt, but, no, it was probably her ruffled blouse and the tall boots. Svendsen licked spillage off the back of his screaming eagle.

"Wanted to know what?"

"Sorry," she said, "I've got two other calls. Yeah, Harvard Middle Eastern Studies wanted to know if you could tag along but I said you'd be too busy homeschooling your kids at an undisclosed location. They thought I was kidding."

"Wanted me in what capacity?"

"Call me back sometime when your head's together. I've got to make open-pit coal miners indestructible. See you, pal."

I threw the phone into the front seat.

"That's right." Svendsen set his glass down, smiling vaguely, and I almost liked him. "We doing our best for the big boss but in fact the big boss had something else in mind all along, and poof, you're on the outs. Wash their hands of you."

"I said no military applications. Basic stuff!"

We both shook our heads at the calculated injustice of it all, though as I looked out at two guys in suspenders shake hands in the parking lot and a broad-hipped woman strap a baby into a carseat, it suddenly seemed that whatever had upset me was intangible and even unimportant. Violence wasn't the way to move the human race forward, and however they'd done it, the Congo war was over. Eventually those baboons would run out of ammunition.

"See, in the forces it was always clear as a bell." Svendsen sat back with his hands out on the armrests, like the Lincoln Memorial, no slapping his gums, no jitters. Bourbon was medicine. "Before every mission there'd be the briefing, spell it out for you like winding a watch. No briefing? Then you do your chin-ups, you wait around. But, by God, when I tried to freelance afterward—I've got a pension but I want airfare to Patagonia, right? See how they grow their soybeans? So I talk to a gentleman on the phone, seems like a good man, sounds like there might be a little wetwork in it for me, as they say. So I have a little to drink, feeling loquacious, friend to the common man, maybe I say too much about the nature of the work to this Douglas Avery. And I realize I've mucked up! You know what I had to go and do?"

I was watching him with my mouth open. My orphan shoulder tingled.

"You had to run him down," I said. I swallowed the trace of bourbon swirling behind my teeth. "That's, uh, sure, that's understandable."

This topic took precedence over baboons.

"Sure it is! Nobody'd told me to do it, not so much, but this guy was a liability! If I didn't do it, it'd be somebody else, so why not show the highers-up I'm willing, right? They never gave a briefing on it one way or the other!"

"Gosh."

"That's what working a job is like! Do one thing for the boss man, just like you, and all along the boss man wants another thing. A joke. So, how'd you lose the ears?"

He clacked his lips together, all bug-eyed intensity, then fell back and cradled his cheek in his hand, gazing at the floor.

"And you knew this Doug Avery's wife?" I asked. "You recognized her?"

"I don't know anyone in this town." He shut his eyes. "Not a welcoming place."

"But it must've dented the car up when you hit this guy, hey?"

"Oh!" He sat up like I'd finally called a briefing. "I had to get the hood hammered out! Told the garage I'd hit a *seagull*, they believed it. People are ignoramuses. Ignorami."

He smacked his stubbly lips, trying to look me in the eye, it seemed, but not getting higher than the armless shoulder.

"Sure," I said, "that's professional, take the customer's word for it. How big a car did you say?"

"That's the thing, just a—just a little Cobra! Parked right over …"

He waved a finger beside his ear.

"A Cobra." Had that even been on our list? "Let's take a peek, buddy. I can't quite picture how you did it."

He started to climb past my knees, though the door wasn't open yet, and his armpit in my face smelled of parmesan. I pulled the latch and slid out ahead of him. Asphalt heat climbed me like rising water. The parking lot was nearly empty, the kid in the WAR IS OVER shirt climbing into a pickup.

"Hey!" I called, pushing my hair back. "Where'd you get the shirt?"

He grinned. "My dad made it!"

"Here, here," Svendsen said behind me. "Down here by this dumpster."

We strolled, his back straight as a flagpole, and now that he was upright I could see his distended belly. We rounded a motorhome with Arizona plates and the next five spots were empty until the yellow Cobra parked in the corner.

Colleen studied the front bumper, one hand in her purse. She eyed us for three or four seconds as we ambled toward her.

"This yours, sir? Nice car," she called, her voice thin as glass. "Don't see a lot of these Mustang Cobras. What is it, a 2000?"

"She's a 2003," Svendsen drawled affably. "It's mostly the women who stop me about it, you know that? Must be the color—or might be it's my abs."

He couldn't have been anticipating problems. He kept moving toward her.

"Of course, '03." Sounded like her throat could barely let air out. She wandered around to the back. "Brake lights right there in the spoiler."

A chunk of gravel bounced away from under her silver dress shoe. Svendsen breathed on a handprint on his side window, then diligently rubbed it with his sleeve. This was a model of little yellow car I hadn't seen in all our searching—only looked six or eight feet long, and the rest of the car was an afterthought behind its mass of front bumper, like it had been designed specifically for running people over. I realized Colleen was staring at me, still with her hand in the imitation-crocodile purse. I flicked my hair off my forehead and gave her what I intended to be a meaningful nod—here I was to help her. Not from the other side of the world but the other end of the car. The corners of her mouth turned up in a smile, which disappeared just as quickly. The sun was an arc welder on the side of my face.

"You'll have to pardon our manners, Miss," I said. "We've had a little to drink."

"Oh." Svendsen resumed his flagpole posture. "Thought, thought you two knew each other."

"Enjoy the ceremony?" I asked, still trying to prove our ignorance of one other.

"I guess there's parties all over town now." She tapped a knuckle on the spoiler. "You gents know of any? Bet you're on your way someplace right now."

"No." Svendsen kept his gaze on her lower half. "This town's not too friendly."

Colleen looked at me stonily, then behind me, so I glanced back too and saw the parking lot was empty of people. She stepped forward and put a hand on Svendsen's shoulder, her eyes artificially bright like a model's in a catalogue.

"There's one in my neighborhood we can go to," she said softly. "You boys are ahead of me, though, I've just been eating Ritz crackers! But I've got some pot, do you want to smoke some pot? It's been *such* a busy day."

"Yeah?" Svendsen dropped a thick gob of spit between his shoes. "Lady, we're the same kind of people. We are."

Colleen turned on her silver shoe and led us between the pick-up trucks toward that patch of woods beyond the parking lot. A dirt path cut between the weeds then up into the trees, and she stopped at the edge of the pavement to beckon us on like an usher at a wedding. She still kept her hand in her purse. I wasn't thinking about whether I could get back to Picu in time for dinner or of Penzler's shareholders around the big oak table, I was back in that morning when our house had been on fire, the desruction of all that for the kids and me, Deb had come to pick me up because I'd been covered in blood, when we hadn't been in control of anything. Not like now.

Colleen stayed four steps behind us.

"Is she coming?" Svendsen asked out of the corner of his mouth.

I gave his thin shoulder a squeeze, and he went right on walking. The path ran up a slope and then across it, black bugs scattering from the undergrowth, and when I looked back toward the school all I saw was the trees. We'd come into another country.

I'd renounced violence; it was no way to move humanity forward.

We came to a campfire ring beside a trickle of water disappearing into a culvert. The circle of stones was littered with cigarette butts and twisted ends of joints, so Colleen had known what she was talking about.

"Here's a peaceful spot." He talked in a higher voice, nodding. "This is the kind of thing I like."

With his shoe he prodded the rotten orange cardboard of a Lucky Bucket case.

"Enjoy the view a minute," she said behind us. "I'll get us organized."

Between the tree trunks we could see new red-roofed duplexes at the edge of town, a blue slide curving down beside a backyard pool, then the green corn beyond that and a plume of dust where someone was driving through the fields fifteen miles away. It wasn't the same Nebraska we'd driven our ambulance through—now the world was fertile, openhearted.

"I do like this." Svendsen shoved his hands into his pockets and walked forward with a strange tin-man gait. He'd have made a memorable grandpa for somebody.

Then motion. My brain translated what I saw in my peripheral vision as Charlie Chaplin twirling a bamboo cane—that motion was so distinctive—but of course it was Colleen, wet-eyed, showing her yellow bottom teeth and swinging her telescoped baton.

"Ah." Svendsen put his hands on his hips. "It reminds—"

I set a leg behind his knees, pressed my hand against his chest. As he tensed I felt a sinewy strength, but all the same he tumbled back toward the cigarette butts, his two hands grasping air, gaze wide like he was a kid falling off the monkey bars. His eyes found mine but that one-third of a second wasn't long enough to explain why we were doing this thing to him, to point out the beauty of such a just act, and that was too bad. At the midpoint of his descending arc Colleen brought the steel down on his head.

Acknowledgements

THANKS TO NICOLE Handford for her patience, resourcefulness and rare ability, as well as for her valuable feedback and belief in the project. Thanks to editors Barbara Berson, Anna Comfort O'Keeffe, Derek Fairbridge and Chris Labonte, who soak overnight in enthusiasm, savvy and skill.

Thanks to all students and colleagues at UBC Okanagan Creative Studies, both the hyperactive and low-key; to the Scotts, Purton-Schwarzes and Alex-Longs; and especially to my resilient mother-in-law, Carol Handford. Thanks to Rob MacDonald for Rob Aiken, and to Sgt. Gary Yeung for himself.

Thanks to all of my Advents, Collises, Handfords, MacArthurs, Schroeders and Suttons.

PHOTO CREDIT: Nicole Handford

About the Author

ADAM LEWIS SCHROEDER is the author of three previous books: *Kingdom of Monkeys* (Raincoast Books, 2001), *Empress of Asia* (Raincoast Books, 2006) and *In the Fabled East* (Douglas & McIntyre, 2011), which was a finalist for the 2011 Commonwealth Writers' Prize for Best Book, Canada/Caribbean region, and chosen as one of Amazon.ca's best books of the year. Schroeder currently lives in Penticton, BC, with his wife and two children. You can read more about him at: adamlewisschroeder.com.